Alive and Kicking

Beryl Kingston was born and brought up in
Tooting. After taking her degree at London
University, she taught English and Drama at
various London schools as well as bringing
up her three children. She and her husband
now live in Sussex.

ALIVE AND KICKING

Beryl Kingston

ARROW

First published by Arrow in 1996

Copyright © Beryl Kingston 1995

Beryl Kingston has asserted her right under the Copyright,
Designs and Patents Act, 1988 to be identified as the author
of this work

First published in the United Kingdom in 1995 by

Century, 20 Vauxhall Bridge Road, London SW1V 2SA

Random House Australia (Pty) Limited
20 Alfred Street, Milsons Point, Sydney
New South Wales 2061, Australia

Random House New Zealand Limited
18 Poland Road, Glenfield
Auckland 10, New Zealand

Random House South Africa (Pty) Limited
PO Box 337, Bergvlei, South Africa

Random House UK Limited Reg. No. 954009

A CIP catalogue record for this book
is available from the British Library

Papers used by Random House UK Limited are natural,
recyclable products made from wood grown in sustainable
forests. The manufacturing processes conform to the
environmental regulations of the country of origin.

ISBN 0 099 48591 5

Typeset by Deltatype Ltd, Ellesmere Port, Cheshire
Printed and bound in Great Britain by BPC Paperbacks Ltd,
a member of The British Printing Company Ltd

To Louise, Steven, Charlotte,
James and Phoebe

who are the apples of my eye

CHAPTER ONE

The war against Germany was barely a month old and all over Great Britain patriotism burned like fever. London was crazed with it.

Newspaper headlines grew taller by the day, bragging of victory at the River Marne: citizens strutted and preened: shop windows erupted into an enthusiasm of ribbons and bunting and brand new Union Jacks. Some windows sported a picture of King George and Queen Mary, looking severe, and a hand-painted slogan, like '*Britons Never Shall Be Slaves*', or '*For King and Country*', or even more passionately '*God Bless Our Boys!*' Others gave space to the new recruiting posters, with their demanding, professional type, '*Do Your Duty! Enlist Now! Join Today!*' and their huge, noble faces – white whiskers drooping like the bags under their eyes – each one confident in the expectation that the young men of the capital would spring to the defence of their country in her hour of need. It looked and felt like a carnival – and on the third Saturday in September 1914, it sounded like one too.

It was just after five o'clock and the market in Lambeth Walk was at its busiest, the street almost impassable for stalls and shoppers, when there was a sound like a sudden clap of thunder. It was so loud that it made Rose Boniface jump. She'd been picking over the second-hand blouses at Mrs Tuffin's tot stall, looking for something decent to cut down for her younger sisters to wear to school. She'd already found a blue cotton for Mabel. Now she stopped, one hand on the white lawn of a lady's blouse that she was considering for Netta, and looked up at the sky.

'What on earth was that?' she said.

1

'Drums, you ask me dear,' Mrs Tuffin said, her eyes firmly on the merchandise. As befitted a lady of her trade, she was a decidedly blowsy woman with a plump pink face, plump pink arms, fat fingers, a bosom that billowed over the tight leather constriction of her belt, and hips like cushions bulging under her long black skirt. She wore one of her own blouses, a confection in bottle-green taffeta threaded with tartan ribbon and decorated by rows of small jet beads and, squashed on top of her bun of black hair, a large straw hat of indeterminate colour.

Standing before such an abundance of flesh and finery, Rose Boniface looked like a waif. At seventeen, she was no taller than she'd been at fourteen when she took over the care of her brothers and sisters and became the mother of the family – a mere five foot and skinny with it. Her neck was too slender under the soft twist of nut-brown hair pinned at her nape, her hands too small with thin supple fingers, her wrists so fragile you felt you could snap them by looking at them. Yet, despite a childhood marred by too much hard work, too many worries and too little food, there was a gentleness about her face that was quite remarkable. It was already womanly, oval-shaped and set off by a natural fringe of wispy curls. True, her cheeks were too thin, her skin had the town dweller's unhealthy pallor and there were poverty shadows under her eyes, but her forehead was high and broad, her nose retroussé, chin prettily rounded, mouth a perfect Cupid's bow and her eyes themselves were widely spaced, dark grey and fringed with thick brown lashes. In short, Rose Boniface had the makings of a beauty.

The sudden thunder-crack had progressed into rhythm. 'It's a parade,' our beauty said, eyes gleaming at the thought.

Mrs Tuffin could see her sale slipping away. 'Would you like me to put that by for yer?' she asked, tucking a straying lock of hair under her hat. 'It's a good bit a' cloth. You could come back for it tomorrow.'

Rose pulled her mind back to the business in hand. 'It's

gone under the arms,' she said, lifting up the sleeves. 'It'll need a lot a' working over. It ain't worth thruppence, Mrs Tuffin.' She wasn't bargaining – she was too open and honest to do that – she was simply pointing out the flaws in the purchase.

Normally, Mrs Tuffin would have argued until a better price had been agreed but she liked Rose and knew what an effort she made to keep her family well fed and respectable.

'Tell you what,' she suggested, picking up another white blouse. 'I'll throw this one in an' all, and you can use it for repairs. It's in pretty good nick at the back. See?'

'It's a bad colour,' Rose said. 'I'd rather have that old ecru one, Mrs Tuffin, if it's all the same to you. The one with the torn sleeves. That'ud make a nice contrast.'

Mrs Tuffin considered for a second, as the music drew near enough for them to discern a tune. 'All right,' she said, making her mind up. 'As it's you, Rose, you can have the three for a tanner. I can't say fairer than that, can I, gel?'

The sixpence was handed over and the blouses bundled into Rose's clean shopping-bag. Now there was no doubt that the rhythmic noise *was* a band and at the end of the Walk, what's more. People were heading towards it all along the street, agog for excitement. Rose trotted after them and arrived at the Black Prince Road just in time to see the tail-end passing under the railway bridge. It was a detachment of the Queen's, marching briskly and pre-ceded by a drum and fife band, drums in pounding unison, pipes squealing like pigs. What a lark!

To her surprise she saw her big brother Bertie, standing outside the pub on the other side of the road. She hadn't expected him home from work so soon, but there he was, tall and dependable and cheerful, nodding his head in time to the music. He looks just like Dad she thought lovingly, taking him in – flat cap, old jacket, muffler flying in the breeze – you can see what a worker he is. Dear Bertie.

'Whatcher Rose,' he said, as she crossed the road to join him. 'What price this for a lark, eh? If we was to run, we could catch up with 'em and see the whole thing from start to finish.'

So they ran, shopping forgotten, two of a great crowd hurtling off to enjoy the display. And were not disappointed, for seen from the front, the soldiers looked as grand as they sounded, their kit immaculate and their expressions determined. They were led by a resplendent recruiting officer, a sergeant major with a brick-red face and a chest like a pouter pigeon, and by the time they reached Kennington Cross, they had drawn a long, straggling crowd behind and beside them, like a magnet trailing iron filings – factory workers like Bertie, women out shopping like Rose, clerks with self-important expressions, grimy boys in rags, elderly gentlemen stepping out boldly in time to the music, and, down beside the well-polished boots and carefully wound puttees of the contingent, a flea-bitten collection of Kennington mongrels yapping themselves silly with uncontrollable patriotism.

The procession continued into Kennington Road and came to a halt outside the Town Hall, where it was greeted by a councillor, sweating under his ceremonial topper. The sergeant major took up a stand in the middle of the small green called Kennington Park, while his detachment stood in bright ranks on either side of him and drummed for attention. Within two minutes all trade and traffic had come to a standstill, as cars and carriages were ordered to stop at once, errand boys forgot their errands, eager faces appeared in every window on all five storeys of the houses round the green and the Saturday shoppers told one another there had never been anything to equal *this*, never in a hundred years.

The sergeant major surveyed the scene with satisfaction, fondled his moustache and silenced the drummers with a glance.

'This 'ere band,' he bellowed at his fascinated audience, 'will be playin' for the next two minutes. No more nor less! Two minutes. Then Councillor Thomas has got sommink to say to you, and *I* got sommink to say to you, and you won't none of you want ter miss a word of it, believe *me*. If you got friends what ain't here, do 'em a favour. Nip orf an' get 'em. Sharpish! 'Cause I tell you, they'll kick theirselves if they ain't here to hear this.' He paused to let his words sink in. 'Two minutes,' he warned, and shot another steely glance at his instrumentalists who instantly began to play their tune again, very loudly.

Young men scuttled off in every direction to do his bidding, more faces appeared at the windows, the crowd grew by the second and the band completed its two-minute entertainment with a drum crescendo, white gloves flying like birds. Then the councillor began his speech, which was blown into inaudibility by the evening breeze. But because he smiled a great deal and waved his arms about, his audience gave him a happy cheer when he seemed to have finished. Then the sergeant major took over again.

'Hever since our glorious vic'try at the Battle of the River Marne,' he bellowed, 'we got the 'Un on the run. Thirty miles from Paris they was when our lads got stuck into 'em. And what did they do then, lads? I'll tell you what they done. Beggared off out of it as fast as their little yellow legs'ud carry 'em. That's what they done. And for why? I'll tell you for why. For two reasons. Because your 'Un is a coward. And because the British Hexpeditionary Force is a fine body a' men, highly trained, perfessional soldiers, British an' proud of it.' He paused to give his audience time to cheer, which they did, with fervour. 'Nah then,' he continued. 'I come down here this evening, to give you the chance to join our victorious Army. Chance of a lifetime. Come Christmas, the German war machine'll be finished for good an' all. We nearly knocked the stuffing out a' them all-a-ready. So whatcher say boys? All you got to do is take the shillin'. Just think a' the benefits. Free grub, free uniform, free lodgin', *an*' seven bob a week on top of all that. You'll have the world at your feet my lads. The world at your feet an' any girl you want jest for the asking. There ain't a girl alive what don't love a soldier.' Appealing to the women in his audience. 'Ain't that right my darlin's? An' if you're a married man, sir – since you're asking – even better. Wife's allowance nine bob, wife an' child fourteen shillings, two an' a kick for every child on top a' that. You could live like lords. Like lords me lads. An' all you've got to do is cross the road to the recruiting office over there, an' take the shillin'. What could be simpler?'

What indeed, put like that? The recruiting office at the Town Hall was clearly labelled. The flags were flying. There was even an army sergeant standing by the door ready to welcome them in.

The sergeant major looked at the ranks of ardent young faces turned towards him and his world – at dark cloth caps and work-grimed clothes, at collarless shirts and frayed mufflers, at the trusting innocence of young men lifted by his oratory and, in their unaccustomed stillness, touched with glory by the setting sun.

'Well?' he demanded.

'He's right,' Bertie Boniface said to his sister. 'I ought to do it, our Rose.'

Rose tucked her hand into the crook of his arm and gave it a squeeze. Ever since this war had been declared, she'd known he would volunteer for it, sooner or later. She was so proud of him. 'A' course,' she agreed, smiling at him. 'You go our Bertie.'

A queue was forming outside the recruiting office and young men were running towards it from every side.

'Three cheers for our brave lads,' the sergeant major cried. 'Hip-pip-pip-pip! Hooray!'

Bertie ran at the second cheer.

I shall never forget this moment, Rose thought, watching him as he stood in the line. Our Bertie going for a soldier. And all them young fellers running to take the shilling and defend the country and everything. She was proud of them all. But specially Bertie, dear loving

6

Bertie, who'd fathered the family ever since mum died, and worked like a Trojan to look after them all. He's so good, she thought. Always has been. Wait till we tell them in Ritzy Street. Won't they be thrilled!

It took a long time to enlist. By the time Bertie came striding out of the recruiting office, it had grown quite dark. The band had long since marched away, the gas lights were being lit and the air was chill and smelt of soot and smoke.

'Come on,' he said, taking charge in his usual way. 'Pie and mash tonight. We've got somethink to celebrate.'

So they stopped off at the Cross for five portions and a large bottle of ginger beer. Then they took the short cut to Ritzy Street through Windmill Row, across the main road to Courtenay Street – where some lovely, new, yellow-brick houses were being built for the Duchy and there were gas lights to mark the way – left by the pub and north for home, Rose trotting to keep up with her brother's lengthy stride.

Unlike the roads in the Duchy estate, Ritzy Street was short, narrow and poorly lit. It had once led down to the Thames, to a landing-stage between the Doulton pottery works and the Gunhouse stairs, but now it was cut off from the riverside by the railway embankment and the wide sweep of the London and South Western railway line, which filled the area with the chuff and clutter of engines, day and night, and dropped sulphur stains and black smuts on to doorsteps and curtains and any washing the inhabitants were foolhardy enough to hang out. The houses were built in long, soot-blackened terraces and each house contained a basement kitchen and nine living-rooms, three on each floor. It wasn't the most comfortable place in which to live, but it had provided a home for the Bonifaces at a time when they stood in danger of the workhouse, and for that Rose was fond of it and felt at ease and happy there. When they first moved in to number 26, they'd occupied the second-floor back, which was the worst room in the house; now they had

7

graduated to the two front rooms on the first floor and she and Netta and Mabel had a bedroom of their own, divided from Collum and Bertie by a wall instead of a curtain.

Netta was leaning out of their bedroom window with her hands on the sill, watching out for them. The light from the gas lamp outside the front door edged her sharp features with gold, and made the long straggle of her hair gleam like dark water as it hung over the sill on either side of her gilded hands. But her voice was far from romantic.

'Where've you *been*?' she wanted to know. 'I been waiting *hours*. I'm famished!'

'Set the table,' Bertie called up to her. 'We got pie and mash. Where's the others?'

'Playing out,' Netta said in a tone that implied he was foolish even to ask. 'Where d'you think?' And she left the window to prepare the table.

Bertie put two fingers in his mouth and gave a long shrill whistle –once, twice, three times. It was his usual signal to call the kids home and, sure enough, after a second there was a scramble at the blocked-off end of the alley and one of Mabel's boots appeared at the top of the wall, followed by a black-stockinged leg and a flash of white pinafore. Then the rest of her body appeared and she sat on top of the wall, swinging her legs, ready to jump down. She was ten years old but, because she was simple-minded, she looked younger, short, stout and moon-faced, her clothes patched and grubby and her hair in perpetual tangles. But she was a cheerful creature and full of affection. ' 'Lo, our Bertie,' she called.

'Look at the state of you,' Rose scolded as her sister ran towards them. 'You been playing up the embankment again ain'tcher. Where's your ribbon?'

Mabel thought for a long time and then produced the answer, speaking slowly but with triumph as she always did when she'd managed to get something right. 'In me pocket.'

'Don't tell her off,' Bertie said mildly as the three of them climbed the stairs. 'Not tonight.'

'Why not tonight?' Mabel wanted to know, stomping up the stairs behind them. 'Why not tonight, our Rose?'

'Tell you when Col gets home,' Rose promised. 'Get your hands washed, there's a good girl. It's pie and mash and you like that don't you. Look sharp and then you'll get the beauty of it while it's hot.'

The gas was lit, the fire made up and Rose dished out the supper, while the others took it in turns to wash in the basin in the bedroom, splashing out just enough clean water from the ewer to cover the backs of their hands and emptying the dirty water away in the pail afterwards. And five minutes after his brother's whistle, as Netta was folding the towel and hanging it back on the rail, Collum came charging up the stairs, just as they all knew he would. He was nearly fourteen and although he was small for his age and as skinny as the rest of the family, he considered himself far too grown-up to come at a call. Five minutes was enough to mark the distance between obedience and independence and to set him apart from his younger sisters.

The meal began at once because they were all much too hungry to wait. For quite a while they ate without speaking, their five tousled heads bent low over their five enamel plates. Then, when they'd taken the edge off their hunger, Rose told them the thrilling news.

'Passed me A, they did,' Bertie said with justifiable pride. 'Think a' that. A. Fit for military service in the front line, the surgeon said.'

'Well a' course,' Rose approved, mopping her plate with a chunk of bread. 'What d'you expect, the size of you?'

'Military service in the front line,' Netta echoed, food temporarily forgotten, she was so awed by the importance of it. 'It don't half sound grand, our Bertie.'

'D'you have to wear a uniform?' Mabel asked.

' 'Course.'

'Won't he look a swell, our Rose.'

'I wish I could go for a soldier,' Netta said, gazing

earnestly at her brother across the rim of her beaker. Her pale face was peaked with yearning, the tangle of uncombed hair that framed it making it look thin and huge eyed.

'Well you couldn't, could you,' Col said disparagingly. Sometimes Netta said the silliest things.

Netta tossed her head at him, swinging her hair. 'I don't see why not,' she said, defiantly. 'I could fire a gun as well as anyone, and ride a horse – if someone'ud learn me – and carry the flag.' She waved her spoon like an imaginary flag, her dark eyes ardent. 'I'd make a jolly good soldier. I could cut my hair off, couldn't I, and wear trousers and boots and everything. Who'd know?'

'I would,' Col said flatly. 'Anyway, you can't because you're a girl.' The world of war and soldiery was entirely masculine. There was no place in it for women. It was a matter of pride and patriotism, strength, nobleness, valour, comradeship, courage under fire – all the things women couldn't understand. And all happening now, in his lifetime, that was the wonder of it. 'D'you think it'll go on long enough for me to join up an' all?' he asked Bertie.

'Shouldn't think so,' Bertie said. 'We got them on the run, the sergeant said. Be over by Christmas, he reckons.' Then, pitying Col's disappointed expression, 'Still you never know, do you.'

The plates and beakers were empty so Rose and Mabel began to clear the table. Then Netta lifted the kettle from its hob on the fire and poured hot water into the washing-up bowl on the living-room wash-stand so as to clean the dishes, while Col and Bertie pushed the table into its usual position under the window and set the chairs in a neat circle round the fender. There was a routine to everything they did and a place for everything too, for their rooms were small and cramped and contained too many people and too much furniture to allow for any untidiness. In this one, beside the wash-stand and the table and chairs, there was also Bertie's single bed, which had Col's truckle bed tucked underneath it and did duty as a settee during the day, and a dresser which held all their most prized possessions, jugs and dishes, cloths and crockery, a row of well-read books and Rose's precious Singer sewing-machine.

That machine had been the family's most expensive purchase. But they all agreed it had been well worth the money, for Rose's skill at making over old clothes and running up petticoats and pinafores from old sheets and pillow cases had saved them the price of it many times over.

Now she settled beside the table, spread out the three blouses she'd just bought and began to ponder while Mabel reverently laid the pin cushion, the tailor's chalk and the tape measure beside the blouses and threaded up two needles with white tacking-cotton.

In the pause between the end of the meal and the resumption of conversation, it was quiet and peaceful in their little room: Netta dried the dishes and Mabel put them away, working slowly but taking great pains to have everything in its right place; Bertie and Col took the boot box from the dresser and set to work to patch Mabel's boots; Rose cut away the worn cloth from all three blouses and began to unpick the side seams. This was the time of day she enjoyed most, the time when they were all back together again after work and school, at ease and happy in one another's company. The room was full of familiar domestic sounds – the occasional tap-tap-tap of Bertie's hammer, the clink of dishes, the shuffle of shifting coals, the purr and pop of the gas light, the steady clonking of mum's old painted clock on the mantelpiece. There were so many things in the room to remind them of their mother. The dresser had been hers and so had most of the treasures that crowded its shelves; she had made the rag rug on the hearth, the patchwork cushions on Bertie's bed and the embroidered sampler hanging in pride of place on the wall beside the fireplace.

It was a very ordinary sampler, worked in cross-stitch on a piece of rough canvas and signed and dated – '*Emily*

11

Jones her work aged 11 years June 1887'. It depicted a rose-spotted house with four windows, a central door and a thatched roof. There was blue smoke rising boskily above it from a decidedly crooked chimney. Three square rabbits sat on their haunches on either side of it, and beneath, in bold capital letters, was their mother's motto, the precept they all tried to follow – 'LIVE WITH DIGNITY'. And isn't that just what our Bertie's done today, Rose thought, looking at it. If she can see him now, she'll be so proud of him.

The last plate was dried and put in its place on the dresser, the wiping-up cloth was hung on its string to dry, the last nail was knocked into Mabel's boot, the mending-box tidied and put away. Bertie balanced his feet on the fender and hooked his packet of Woodbines from his inside pocket, ready for his evening smoke. He looked across at Col who was sitting on the other side of the hearth watching him with admiration, and, on a sudden impulse, held out the little battered packet towards his brother. 'Time for a fag?' he said.

It was carried off with such splendid nonchalance that no outsider watching them would have realised what an important moment it was. But Rose and Netta knew and drew in their breath in surprise and pleasure ready to enjoy what would happen next.

'Ta,' Col said, with equal aplomb. 'I don't mind if I do.' He'd been smoking out on the street with his friends for nearly a year now but never in the house. As he drew in the first bitter breath, he narrowed his eyes and smiled at Bertie with open affection – the two men of the house sharing a gasper for the first time. This *was* a day, and no mistake.

'You'll have to mend all the boots on your own when I'm gone,' Bertie warned.

'I don't mind,' Col said. 'I'm getting to be a dab hand with that old leather, ain't I gels?'

'Cack hand, more like,' Netta teased.

'Come over here and let me try this pattern on you,' Rose said.

12

Netta stood to attention while Rose chose a brown paper pattern from her pattern box and fitted it against her sister's chest, folding the paper into neat tucks and pinning it together until she was satisfied with it.

'I'll take the sleeves up,' she decided. 'We can lose a good four inches an' that'll make a nice new armhole. Then if I cut out four new side panels from the ecru, and new cuffs, bit a' lace round the collar, you'll look a treat.'

'What about mine?' Mabel wanted to know, breathing heavily at her sister's elbow. 'What about mine, our Rose?'

'Yours'll have a new yoke and a nice front panel. I shall cut out all this bit where the stains are, see. An' I shall put this pinky lace round the neck and the cuffs. I might even have enough left over for a hair-ribbon. How's that?'

'You're ever so clever, our Rose,' Mabel said, watching with admiration as Rose pinned the pattern to the back panel of the ecru blouse.

It was true, and they all knew it so well that Rose didn't need to respond. It was part of the background knowledge to their lives that they all took for granted – like the fact that they worked well as a family and were fond of each other, that their lives would get easier in two months time when Col was fourteen and out at work, that Bertie was always dependable and Netta sometimes tricky and that Mabel would always be simple-minded and that they would always have to look after her. It was on a par with all the other accepted truths that they didn't have to think about either, that husbands worked and wives kept house, that, except for Mabel, they would all marry and settle down in their turn and be happy like their mother and father before them, that London was the greatest city in the world, that the sun never set on the British Empire, that they were bound to win this war.

Col tossed his fag-end into the fire. 'Well, that's it,' he said, smoothing his hair with both hands. 'Time I was off or old man Porky'll get the 'ump.' He worked every Saturday evening at one of the fruit and vegetable stalls in

13

the market at Lambeth Walk and his employer was a stickler for punctuality.

'We'll be up presently,' Rose said. This family usually followed him to market at about ten o'clock of a Saturday evening, because that was when the remaining meat was sold off cheap – and the stale bread and buns and the 'specks' from the fruit and veg stalls. Sometimes they could get enough to keep them going till the middle of the week – especially if Netta was in one of her saucy moods.

'My brother the soldier,' Col said, standing in the doorway. 'I can't wait to tell Porky. When d'you reckon you'll have to go?'

'Not for ages yet, I don't expect,' Bertie said. 'There was hundreds joining.'

But he was wrong. The British war machine was geared for speed and his call-up papers arrived a mere seven weeks later – two weeks before Col was due to leave school and start work in the vinegar factory.

He came home from his last day at work, emptied his pay packet on the table and sorted the coins into five neat piles.

'Now there's two week's rent to tide you over,' he explained to Rose, putting the first pile into its jar on the mantelpiece. 'And there's the coal, and the boot club, and that's the housekeeping. You'll be all right till I get me pay.'

'What about you?' Rose said, touched by his care for them. 'You'll need a bit a' money.'

There was still fivepence left on the table. 'That'll do me,' he said cheerfully, putting it in his pocket. 'Now you *will* be all right wontcher. I done all the boots and the lavvy's all scrubbed. This'll keep you going won't it?'

'Who's going?' Mabel said, screwing up her face. All this talk of money bewildered her. 'Who's going?'

'You know who's going,' Netta said proudly. 'Our Bertie's going. For a soldier.'

CHAPTER TWO

Thirty-three thousand men enlisted for the army that September, most of them on the same weekend as Bertie Boniface. There were so many from London that special trains had to be commissioned to take them off to camp and the local councils turned their departure into a gala. Lambeth Council did their lads proud, sending the municipal band to Vauxhall station to give them a rousing send-off. When the Boniface family rushed into the station that morning, they found it hung about with so much bunting it looked like a fairground and the noise was deafening.

Mabel's eyes grew round with amazement at the sight of it.

'Is this all for you, our Bertie?' she said.

'Me and all the others.'

There were plenty of others. The platform was thronged with young men and their families, all talking at once and giving one another last-minute hugs and kisses for all the world as if they were in the privacy of their homes instead of being out in a public place. None of the Bonifaces had ever seen anything like *that* either. It was extraordinary and exciting and a bit embarrassing. When a courting couple who were standing right beside them kissed one another passionately – full on the lips – Col blushed furiously and didn't know where to look.

But Bertie said it was 'a right turn-up for the books' and slapped his brother on the shoulder to show he shouldn't mind.

The engine was already chuffing puffballs of white steam into the vaulted air so that the bunting jumped and bounced like leaves in a breeze. The band paused for breath and brayed into a march by Sousa. Col and Bertie grinned at one another. Netta and Mabel began to skip about in time to the music. Only Rose was quiet and still, waiting patiently beside them.

'Now you're not to worry about the rent,' Bertie said to her, as he climbed into the carriage. 'I'll send you a Postal Order the minute I get my pay. Being in the army'll make a lot of difference. You'll see.'

The guard was shrilling his whistle and flicking his green flag in and out of the steam clouds. Rose knew only too well what a difference it was going to make. She'd known it from the moment she woke that morning and now it was inescapable. But she swallowed her feelings and stood on tiptoe to kiss him goodbye.

'Look after yourself,' she said, trying to smile at him. 'Write soon.'

'Every day,' Bertie said as the engine began to haul him away. 'I promise.'

The little family huddled together on the crowded platform and watched until the train was out of sight. Its departure left an ugly gap in the station and an even worse one in their lives. Now all four of them were aware of how much they were going to miss their big brother. Everything had happened so quickly it didn't seem possible that Bertie was gone. But the crowds were drifting away, whispering and forlorn, the last shred of steam was melting in the high roof, the bandsmen were tidying their music and packing their instruments. Even the bunting had lost its vitality and hung like washing on a line, limp and disconsolate. As they stepped out into the chill daylight of the Kennington Road, Mabel began to cry.

Col got cross with her because he was perilously close to tears himself. 'You can stop *that*!' he ordered.

'I can cry if I like,' Mabel sniffed. 'Can't I, Rose.'

Rose gave permission by hugging Mabel's arm. It was spitting with rain as they turned left into Goding Street, walking briskly.

'We shall have a letter from him in a day or two,' Rose

said, 'you'll see, and he'll be home on leave 'fore we know where we are. It'll be all right.'

Things began to go wrong with Bertie's second letter home.

His first was a quick note to say he'd arrived. He was at a place called Roffey Park, he said, somewhere near Horsham, living under canvas, in a field *like a sea a mud on account of it's been raining for four days*. The grub was pretty good. No uniform yet. *'They keep you on the go from morning to night. Hope it stops raining soon. Roll on pay day that's what we all say.'*

But the rain continued and when pay day arrived it brought a disappointment and a problem. *'I only got a single man's pay,'* he wrote. *'I'm ever so sorry. I've sent you a P.O. for five shillings. They say you are not a dependant, being my sister. It looks as though they mean to cut up rough about paying for brothers and sisters. Can you manage the rent? I'll send you what I can but I can't manage five shillings every week on account of we have to buy soap and matches and a bit of grub. They don't let you argue with nothing in the army.'*

Rose wrote back at once to assure him that of course she could manage and he wasn't to worry, but it was a blow because they all knew they couldn't pay the rent without his allowance. That night, after supper, as the rain pattered against the window, the four of them sat round the fire and tried to work out what was to be done.

'We've got the rent for *this* Saturday,' Rose started off. 'And that's one thing.' Their landlady collected the rent every Saturday morning and they always paid on the dot. It was a point of honour with them.

'We shall be all right by Friday fortnight,' Col said. 'Once I get to work that'll make a difference, won't it our Rose?'

It would. But not difference enough, because he was only going to earn six shillings and ninepence a week.

'I could work Sat'days with ol' man Porky,' Netta offered.

17

But even that wouldn't be enough.

'We won't have to go an' move will we?' Mabel asked. The thought that they might have to leave their nice cosy rooms was making her lip tremble.

'No,' Rose said, patting her hand to placate her before she could work herself into a state. 'I shall have to get a little job to tide us over, that's all. I'll start looking tomorrow. We'll manage. We always have. You two'll have to get the shopping, do a bit a' cooking, that sort a' thing.' She was being deliberately cheerful because there was no good in looking on the dark side, but privately she knew it wasn't going to be easy. There were plenty of positions advertised in the evening papers but they all required references, and although she'd worked as a housemaid from time to time when they first moved to Ritzy Street and money was tight, she'd never stayed long enough in any one job to get a reference.

She spent the next two days out on the trail in the never-ending rain – offering her services as seamstress, parlour maid, charlady, maid-of-all-work, anything that was possible – but most of the jobs were filled before her arrival or turned out to be unavailable when her prospective employers discovered that she lacked that vital piece of paper.

At the end of the second day, she walked back to Ritzy Street, damp, footsore and rather depressed. The corner shop was still open and on an impulse she went in to buy a reel of red machine cotton. There was just enough red flannel left in the dresser to make Netta a petticoat, and a bit of sewing would cheer her up.

There was a display board inside the door. It was full of local advertisements – as usual – so Rose browsed through them as she was waiting to be served. The third one down was a plea for a servant at Monk House.

'An experienced parlourmaid required, age 16–25, to help with housework and serve at table: five other servants kept: generous terms: reference essential. Apply between 8.30 and 9.30 a.m. or write.'

18

'Has that been up long?' she asked the shopkeeper, nodding at the card.

'Come in this afternoon,' he told her. 'But you know Monk House. They've always got a card in. I never knew such a place for getting through domestics. You interested?'

Rose wasn't sure. She didn't really want to work at Monk House. It was too close to home – down at the end of Ritzy Street in a huge garden beside the railway embankment – and she knew too much about its formidable owner. She saw her in church every Sunday, sitting in the front pew as if she owned the building, and everybody had tales to tell about how badly she treated her servants. But there wasn't anything else on offer. And as they were always short of staff, they might be prepared to overlook the reference, even though they said it was essential. I'll go up tomorrow morning, she decided as she took her red cotton. It might do for the time being. If there's five other servants it shouldn't be too hard and it's only till the end of the war and I don't have to stay there if I don't want to.

Netta was horrified when she heard about it. 'Couldn't you find nothing else?' she scowled.

'Not in time to pay the rent,' Rose said.

'But that Miss Monk's horrible. Everyone says so.'

'We don't know she is,' Rose said reasonably. 'It's only talk. Admitted, she looks a bit fierce but she could be a really nice old lady.'

'She ain't,' Mabel said, slowly and earnestly. 'She throws things. Ruby says. She shook that Dolly till her teeth fell out. You can't go there, can she Col?'

Col was biting his nails.

'It won't be for long,' Rose said, trying to reassure them. 'It's only till the end a' the war.'

'If she so much as breathes at you,' Netta advised, 'you walk straight out and come straight back home. Don't you stand for no nonsense.'

Rose promised that she wouldn't come to any harm.

'I'm a big gel now,' she teased, stretching to her full five foot. 'Look at me muscles!'

But they were still anxious and Mabel was so concerned that she kept waking up to worry all night long. The next morning she actually offered to carry the slops downstairs *and* emptied them in the outside lavatory without a word of complaint. And when they parted at the front door, she flung her arms round Rose's neck to kiss her goodbye, as if they were parting for ever.

'Look after yourself, our Rose,' she pleaded. It was another dank misty morning and, in the half-light, the black brickwork behind them was oily with moisture. 'You will, won'tcher?'

'You just cut off to school with Netta,' Rose said firmly, stopping her short before she could get worked up, 'or you'll be late.'

They went obediently and Rose watched them as they walked away along the damp alley, hand in hand. What with Mabel's excessive concern and the chill in the air, she was beginning to feel anxious herself. It was making her shiver. Enough standing about, she scolded herself, frotting her hands together to warm them. Time to get down the road and open that gate. It can't be as bad as they say.

After the dim light and blackened walls of Ritzy Street, walking into the grounds of Monk House was like stepping into the country. Everything on the other side of the wall was green and gold and glistening. Even the gate was patched with green and orange lichen and the hedge was festooned with the wet, white nets of countless spiders' webs. Dead foliage lay thick and soft under Rose's feet and the path before her was edged with moss. It led between two banks of shrubs that were so overgrown that she had to push a way between them, before she could walk out on to the great green lawn of the back garden, where Miss Monk held the church fête every summer.

It was the first time Rose had seen it without stalls and

marquees and it looked enormous. A watery sun cast pale shadows on the wet grass and Monk House stood revealed in all its eighteenth-century charm, pretty as a postcard, and covered with white stucco.

There were three parts to the house: the main building, which was two storeys high and had five lancet windows overlooking the garden on each floor; a rounded tower at one end; and a single storey outhouse at the other, lined with the same curved windows as the rest of the house and covered in ivy. A wisteria climbed the tower in a convolution of knotted trunks and wintry grey branches. All the paintwork was grey too, a faded blue-grey like the smoke coiling from the chimneys. A gravel drive led to the back door and curved about the building, leaving semicircular flowerbeds to right and left, all newly dug over and emptied of everything but small shrubs. And in the middle of the lawn – to complete the picture – there was a great Lebanon cedar, spreading its branches so low that they touched the grass. It looked so charming that it reminded Rose of her mother's sampler. She wouldn't have been a bit surprised if six square rabbits hadn't come hopping out of the shrubs to take their places on either side of the house.

The garden path curved between the shrubs to the back door, where Rose rang the bell and waited patiently to be answered. Now that she was close to the walls she could hear a servant's bell jangling furiously and somebody shouting, 'All right! All right! I've only got one pair of hands!' But she didn't have long to wait before the door was opened by a slatternly woman in a cook's uniform.

'I've come about the . . .' Rose began.

The cook had no time for lengthy explanations. 'I daresay,' she said. 'And I daresay you won't like it much, neither. Still you'd better come in.'

The side door led straight into the kitchen which was a large, warm, biscuit-coloured room containing a cooking-range, two Welsh dressers full of pink, red and white china, more doors than Rose could count and an abundance of shelving where brass jelly moulds, meat dishes and saucepans were ranged in order of size. There was a kitchen table in the middle of the room where the cook had obviously been making pastry for an apple pie. The smell of stewed apple and cinnamon filled the air above the cooking-range and a pile of cores and peel lay browning at one end of the table.

'She's in the front parlour,' the cook said, sucking in her cheeks. 'She's none too happy this morning. You'd better go straight in. Follow me.'

That sounded ominous and made Rose prickly with apprehension. They progressed along a dark corridor into the light of a large hall – gentle stairs, floral wallpaper, brass umbrella stand, green jardinière growing a yucca plant, six doors leading in all directions.

'This is it,' the cook said abruptly. 'Front parlour.' She knocked on one of the doors, opened it and pushed Rose inside.

The front parlour was a small square room. After the light in the hall it seemed dark and rather oppressive, lit by the flicker of firelight and full of heavy colour, crimson, gold, forest green, peacock blue. For a few seconds Rose was overwhelmed by it. The wallpaper was a heavy flock in dark crimson, the mantelpiece marble, the fireplace surrounded by decorative tiles in gold, green and scarlet. There was a Turkey carpet on the floor, a chiffonnier crammed with china statuettes and piled with vases, and so many paintings on the walls that in 'some places there was barely a finger space between them.

But, naturally, it was the lady sitting by the fire who took Rose's full attention, because this was the first time she'd seen her face to face. She was ensconced in a wide leather armchair which was heaped with embroidered cushions and adorned with a crocheted antimacassar and, large though it was, she was so stout that she filled it to capacity. Although she was only in her mid-forties she looked older and her face was both petulant and powerful. It was as round as a clock beneath tightly waved, jet-

black hair and all her features seemed too small for it –
except her eyebrows, which were thick and dark and
incongruous, as if they'd been pencilled on to her
forehead with a very firm hand. She wore a magenta day
gown, tied about the waist with a pink sash and there was
a triple string of pearls about her neck and eight or nine
rings flashing on her plump hands which at that moment
were busy stroking the fur of a large golden-yellow chow
who was spread across her knees, panting with the heat
from the fire.

'And about time too!' she said, without looking up.
'I've been ringing that bell for twenty minutes, I hope you
realise. I thought you'd been struck deaf – or died.'

By now Rose was so nervous she didn't know what to
say. She looked at her potential employer's fingers as they
patted the yellow fur and kept quiet. Then she realised
that the lady was staring at her, brown eyes calculating, so
she cleared her throat and made the proper response.

'Ma'am.'

The shrewd eyes didn't blink. 'What's your name?'

'Rose, ma'am. I've come about the position . . .'

'Well you're about the right age. I'll say that for you.
Have you brought any references?'

Rose swallowed. 'No ma'am,' she admitted. 'I'm afraid
I haven't. But I *have* worked as a parlourmaid.'

'Hm,' the lady said. 'Well I suppose you'll do. I expect
my servants to be here from eight in the morning until
eight at night or six until six, depending. You understand
that? Ten o'clock when I have a dinner party.'

'Yes ma'am.'

'Nine shillings a week, uniform provided. No followers.
Half day Wednesday. Half day Sunday. I shall want you
here on Sunday mornings, every other Sunday. You
won't mind missing church?'

'No ma'am.'

'Good. I presume you can wait at table.'

'Yes ma'am.' She'd done it once or twice and was sure
she could remember.

'Very well then – Rose, was it? When could you start?'
'Tomorrow?'

'What's wrong with today?' the lady said. 'You can start today can't you? The uniforms are in the kitchen. Mrs Biggs will show you. Get properly dressed and then you can clear the breakfast things.'

And that was that.

It was an exhausting first day because, as Rose soon discovered, she and Mrs Biggs were the only servants in the house. There was so much work to do that she could barely keep pace, dishes to clear and wash up and put away, three rooms to sweep and dust – and very difficult *that* was with so many knick-knacks to attend to – coal to bring up from the cellar, Miss Monk's bell to answer – and it was astonishing how often she needed attention – and, on top of everything else, a meal to help Mrs Biggs prepare. She was accustomed to sweeping stairs, polishing furniture and answering bells but, until that morning, her cooking had been limited to using a frying-pan over the fire in her little room at home. Being required to work with a large kitchen range, a cupboard full of ingredients and a variety of pots and pans was very confusing. She did her best, asking when she wasn't sure and trying to follow instructions, but she was really quite relieved when six o'clock came and Mrs Biggs told her to go into the scullery to wash her face and hands, tidy herself up and put on her best uniform ready to serve the meal.

'How many will there be?' she asked as she splashed cold water on her hot face.

'Only Madam,' Mrs Biggs called back. 'Nothink to it.'

'Do I look all right?' Rose asked, smoothing down her uniform. The frilly apron was too big for her and there didn't seem to be any pins to fasten it to her bodice. 'I'll take it home tonight and alter it.'

'Safety pins are in the vase on the mantelpiece,' Mrs Biggs said. 'I should have told you. She always gets big sizes. You should've seen mine when I first put it on. There's the bell. This'll be it. Tell her I'm ready to serve.'

It took a surprisingly long time for Miss Monk to eat her evening meal and she had Rose running backwards and forwards from kitchen to dining-room through all three courses. But at last the new parlourmaid was told to clear the table and her long working day was almost over.

'By rights there should be seven staff here, you know,' Mrs Biggs complained as Rose pushed the trolley into the kitchen stacked with dirty dishes. 'We should have a scullery maid to do all this.'

Rose put the dishes into the sink and took a damp cloth to clean the trolley.

'It's not good enough,' Mrs Biggs went on. 'I've been on me feet since seven this morning. She don't think a' that. Was there any a' the pie left over?'

'Yes,' Rose said, 'about half of it.'

'Good. Then we'll have that between us.'

Rose was shocked. 'What, take it, you mean?' That sounded risky. What would happen if Miss Monk found out?

'Waste not, want not,' Mrs Biggs said, sucking in her cheeks. 'It'll be no good by tomorrow. She don't like leftovers.'

'Won't she want to know where it's gone?'

'She'll know I've ate it,' Mrs Biggs said easily. 'She has to provide me keep, see, on account of I live in – and on account of I was here in her father's time – and on account of she'll never get another housekeeper to put up with her.'

So Rose went home with four slices of cold beef, a quarter of an apple pie and half a jug of cold custard, and very good eating they made. Even Netta modified her opinion of Monk House on a full stomach. But she was anxious to know how her sister had got on.

Rose decided to tell them a white lie. It wasn't honest – but she couldn't upset them by telling the truth.

'It ain't bad,' she said. 'I can manage.'

'But what about Miss Monk,' Netta wanted to know.

'She's all right,' Rose said, pushing away the image of

that dominating face. 'Bit eccentric, that's all.'

'She ain't hit you or nothink?' Mabel asked, still slightly anxious.

'No. 'Course not.' Rose said stoutly. 'I told you. She's all right.' But it hurt her to be untruthful, even in a good cause, and she felt so ashamed of herself that she couldn't look at Mum's sampler.

Mabel was happily reassured. 'Can I scrape out the jug, our Rose?' she asked.

Their lives changed day by day. On Thursday of that week, two more servants were taken on at Monk House, a second parlourmaid called Daisy, who told them she wasn't going to stay if Miss Monk roared at her, and a bootboy cum general dog's-body who said his name was Ebenezer but he'd rather be called John. Mrs Biggs said she didn't mind what he was called so long as he took his share of the work and handed him the coal scuttle to fill to prove it.

The following week Col started work at Beaufoy's Vinegar factory and even though he had to wait six impatient days before he got his first pay packet, he was pleased to be out in the adult world. Because Rose was working such long hours, Netta and Mabel had to take over all the daily shopping and do their best to cook supper when their sister wasn't home. Mabel burnt her fingers on the frying-pan – to nobody's surprise – and cut her thumb peeling potatoes. And Netta scorched her new red petticoat when she was doing the ironing and knocked all the spills into the fire when she reached up to light the gas. But at least they were better off now that they had two wage earners in the family. They didn't have to worry about the rent and they could afford a joint of meat for Sunday, which was a great treat.

Like most of the other tenants in the street, they had no stove in which to cook a joint, but the local baker rented out his ovens on a Sunday morning and that was better than cooking it yourself. All you had to do was carry your baking-dish down to the shop early in the morning – with the meat all nicely larded and the potatoes packed around it – and collect it, done to a turn, at one o'clock. Ritzy Street was full of women scuttling home, each with a steaming baking-dish covered with a cloth to keep in the heat. As they told one another on the run, 'There's nothing like a nice bit a' roast.' Even though they had to pay fourpence for the use of the oven, it was well worth it.

Rose's only sadness was that Bertie wasn't there to share their good fortune. But at least she could write and tell him how well they were managing.

'*Col has settled in lovely at Beaufoy's,*' she wrote. '*Really got the hang of it. He comes home smelling of vinegar just like you used to do. Netta and Mabel are being very good helping round the house. Mabel cooked the chops last night and didn't burn them or nothing. You needn't worry about us no more. We're all managing lovely. It's easier at Miss Monk's now she's got some more servants and I can work there till the war's over. Do you think it will be finished by Christmas like they say? Won't we have a lot to tell each other Christmas time. I can't wait.*'

But two days later Bertie wrote back to say that nobody was getting any leave until they'd done their training and *that* wouldn't be for another seven weeks. So he wouldn't be with them for Christmas, he was sorry to say. '*Still chin up,*' he finished. '*Keep smiling, from your ever loving brother Bertie.*'

They'd all assumed he would be allowed home for the holiday, so his letter was another disappointment and a very miserable one. Netta was furious and declared it wasn't fair. Col bit his nails. Rose, who'd missed his support most keenly, felt as if the ground had been cut from under her feet. And Mabel had one of her tantrums, spinning off into a torrent of tears and screams and kicking the furniture and the walls and any leg that hadn't jumped out of reach.

'It ain't fair!' she screamed. 'It ain't. It ain't. It ain't. We *always* have Christmas with Bertie. They got to let him home. They got to! It ain't fair!'

'Come on, our Mabel. We can't help it,' Col tried to reason. 'There's a war on.'

'War?' she yelled. 'What war? They ought to stop it for Christmas. It ain't fair. I hate that old war!' And she wept louder than ever and banged her head against the door.

It was the worst tantrum she'd had for a very long time and it was very difficult for them to handle because, until then, it had always been Bertie who had calmed Mabel down. It took them more than half an hour to make her stop screaming and by then they'd all been kicked, Rose had been bitten and they were all exhausted. But at least they'd fought her back from abuse to whimpering.

She sat on the floor with her back against the wall and wept like a two-year-old. 'I want to see Bertie, Rose. I want to see our Bertie.'

'We'll make up a parcel and send him,' Rose said, as she wiped the tears from her sister's hot cheeks. 'That'll be nice, won't it, even if we can't see him. I'll knit him a pair of mittens and you can help me. It says in the paper that's what they want.'

'We'll send him a nice long letter an' all,' Netta weighed in. 'You can do a drawing, can'tcher Mabel. We can do it Christmas afternoon when we've washed the dishes.'

But, as it turned out, only Col and Netta and Mabel were at home that Christmas afternoon, because Rose's services were required at Monk House until late on Christmas night. Miss Monk had made up her mind to it and you didn't argue with Miss Monk.

CHAPTER THREE

Miss Augusta Monk had ordered an expensive dress especially for Christmas Day. Now she was suffering into her corset so that she could wear it, pulling in her breath and her stomach, her face puce with determination.

'You're not trying girl,' she said crossly to Rose, who was acting as lady's maid that Christmas morning as well as assistant cook and parlourmaid. 'You can pull it a lot tighter than that.'

Rose had been hard at it since six o'clock – lighting fires in all the main rooms, sweeping and dusting, setting the table, even filling the bran tub and hiding presents in the bran for Miss Monk's two brothers, their wives and three children. Now she was beginning to tire but she obeyed orders and tugged at the corset strings as hard as she could. It didn't do any good. The lady's flesh was too copious to be squeezed back any further.

'They don't make these damn things strong enough, that's the trouble,' Miss Monk declared, scowling down at the corset. She was panting from her exertions. 'Oh well. Perhaps I can get it on this time.'

Her new Christmas dress was a handsome garment, made of figured velvet in a rich peacock green that matched the cluster of peacock feathers she intended to pin into her hair. But it was still too tight. Even when the buttons were left undone it bulged at every seam.

She skinned it over her head and hurled it at the nearest chair. 'God damn it all!' she yelled. 'That stupid woman's taken the measurements wrong. I knew this would happen. She would keep arguing. Now what am I going to do? All that money gone to waste. Total waste and now I've got nothing to wear. Damn stupid woman.' She

29

stamped about the room, frowning so horribly that her eyebrows were drawn together in a black V.

Rose was so alarmed by her anger that she felt compelled to do something about it. Greatly daring, she picked up the dress and examined the seams. 'I could let it out for you, ma'am, if you'd like me to,' she offered.

The prowling and scowling stopped in mid-complaint. '*How* could you? You're not a seamstress, are you?' And then, seeing that it was a possible solution, 'How long would it take?'

'Ten minutes,' Rose hoped. 'If there's a cotton to match.'

'Look in my workbox,' the lady instructed. 'She should have left it there. That's what I told her to do.'

Cotton and scissors were found and the seams unpicked.

'What a time you're taking!' Miss Monk said fiercely, poised above the work. 'How much longer are you going to be? They'll be here in ten minutes, you know that don't you. They're never late. Oh come along girl, for heaven's sake. If you can't work any quicker than this, I shall put it on and you'll just have to sew me into it.'

The very idea made Rose quail but the lady had already snatched the dress from her hands and was pulling it over her head. 'Now look sharp!' she said.

It was an unfortunate choice of words for a girl with a needle in her hand.

It's all very well her shouting at me to be quick, Rose thought. You can't be quick with a job like this. What if I stick a pin in her, or sew the dress to her corset? The very idea was making her nervous.

But she managed without mishap and Miss Monk was impressed, despite her bad temper. The girl was skilful even if she *was* slow. Now that it was on at last, the dress looked quite excellent. 'Yes,' she said. 'That's not bad. That's not bad at all.'

Rose put the sewing things neatly back into the work-box, relieved that the job was done. Miss Monk's bad temper had upset her. It wasn't seemly to be so angry on Christmas Day, especially now, with a war on and lots of families kept apart because of it, and especially over something as trivial as a dress. After all, it wasn't as if Miss Monk was short of pretty dresses. She had an entire wardrobe full of them.

'You can go back to the kitchen now,' Miss Monk said, fixing her feathers and admiring her reflection in the long mirror. 'Tell Mrs Biggs to bring up the sherry glasses. They'll be here directly.'

They were here already. Rose heard the first car scrunching onto the drive as she walked down the back stairs. She only just had time to run into the kitchen, give Mrs Biggs her orders and put on her parlourmaid's apron before someone was ringing the bell.

It was a gentleman with his wife beside him and they made their entry without speaking, so she didn't know which of Miss Monk's two brothers he was. He didn't look a bit like his sister. Where she was short, stout and florid, he was tall and etiolated, with a long thin body, long bony hands, long flat feet and the merest fringe of sparse grey hair edging the pale dome of a long bald skull. His eyes were so small and insignificant and his mouth so small and smudgy that his face was dominated by bones, his nose and jaw too long and too obtrusive. In his dark overcoat and with a slight forward stoop to his head and shoulders, he made Rose think of a rolled umbrella with a carved ivory handle that she'd seen once in a shop window. But he was quiet and courteous and seemed a gentleman. He put down the parcels he was carrying while his wife took off her coat and walked across to the hat-stand to check her appearance in the mirror.

'How do I look, Edmund?' she asked, patting her hair. She spoke with a drawl that made her sound rather affected.

So it's Mr Edmund, Rose thought, taking his coat, hat and gloves. And she's the arty wife Mrs Biggs told me about.

'You look very well, my dear,' Mr Edmund said in a voice too flat to be convincing.

Privately Rose thought the arty wife looked rather gawky in a coffee-coloured lace dress that did nothing for her pale complexion. She should wear pink, she thought, with pleats down the front or an embroidered panel and a nice long string of beads in toning colours instead of those discoloured pearls. And a hair band in pink and gold and russet colours. That would be nice. And . . .

'Are you ready, my love?' Mr Edmund said, picking up the parcels.

The two of them plunged into the front parlour, arms outstretched as if they were diving.

'Merry Christmas darling!' the lady cried. 'How lovely you look! What a darling dress!'

'And you too Louella dear,' Miss Monk said, smiling knives. 'I always think you look so nice in that dress. You wore it last Christmas, didn't you. Yes, I thought so. Yes. Very nice. If a thing suits you, why go to the expense of something new?'

How catty! Rose thought, watching the arty wife's discomfiture and wondering how she would answer. But then a second car scuffled to a halt outside and she had to go off to open the door again.

Mr Cedric Monk was very obviously Miss Monk's brother. He was short and stout and had the same sharp brown eyes and the same black hair, greying at the temples. His wife, who was wearing an evening cloak of dark blue velvet, was even shorter than he was and similarly rotund. Her hair was a curious reddish colour, and dressed in an old-fashioned style, smoothed until it reached her ear lobes and then curled into tight, fat ringlets that bounced like springs as she bounded into the hall. She was carrying a basket full of brightly wrapped parcels and she was cross and anxious.

'I told you we should have driven faster,' she complained. 'Now they're here before us. If you'd put your foot down a bit we could have been the first. But not you.'

Her husband answered her in a foreign language. '*Pas devant*, Winifred my dear,' he warned, looking at Rose.

Rose busied herself hanging up the coats and hats so that he would think she wasn't listening. Some people were funny about servants hearing what they were saying.

Mrs Cedric Monk tugged at her dress which had got twisted out of shape during her journey. It was a bright creation in shades of blue, green and rust but, as Rose could see from the corner of her eye, it was a bit too tight about the hips and the lady was having quite a struggle with it.

Behind her, three plump children ambled into the hall, two small boys in velvet jackets who wore macassar oil on their hair and spoke with very plummy accents, and a girl about the same age as Mabel, who wore a white silk dress and a petulant expression and pinched her brothers when her parents weren't looking.

But they all put on bright smiles when they walked into the parlour to greet Miss Monk, calling out, 'Merry Christmas, darling Augusta!' and 'Augusta, my sweetheart!' and 'Merry Christmas Aunty dear!', just as the first arrivals had done, and kissing her obediently when she proferred her cheek.

'We will have our sherry now, Rose,' she said. 'Dinner in half an hour, tell Mrs Biggs.'

'You should see all the parcels they've brought,' Rose said when she'd delivered her message. 'There's a great heap under the Christmas tree. I do think Christmas is lovely.'

'You can have it,' Mrs Biggs said curtly, basting the turkey for the last time. 'Just means a load of work to me.'

'Don't you like to see people happy?' the second parlourmaid said.

'Happy!' Mrs Biggs snorted. 'That lot! They don't know the meaning a' the word. Can't see eye to eye for more 'n a minute at a time. We shall have doors banging presently, you see if we don't. I wonder they don't have them off their hinges sometimes. You just look sharp

33

Daisy Mullins and put those hot plates on the trolley. We got enough to do without thinking about who's happy.'

'She ain't right, is she?' Daisy asked as she and Rose pushed the loaded dinner-trolley along the corridor towards the dining-room.

'No,' Rose said positively. 'She's in a bit of a bad mood that's all. They're ever so happy. Why shouldn't they be? They got everything they could possibly want. You wait till you see the table and the tree.' Daisy had been kept busy in the kitchen while the dining-room was being prepared. 'It's a sight for sore eyes.'

She was right about that at least. The room was dazzling, the scarlet and yellow roses on its wallpaper echoed by the red and gold paper lanterns that glimmered overhead, suspended on long red strings from the central rose of the ceiling to each holly-hung corner of the room. The Christmas tree was so heavily decorated that they could hardly see the pine needles for baubles and the blaze of red candles. There were red candles on the table too, their yellow flames flickering in the draught from the opened door, the fire leapt and crackled, the crystal wine glasses sparkled, the crystal lustres on the mantelpiece gleamed with the rainbow colours of a myriad reflected lights. It was just what Christmas ought to be.

And the food! Rose had never seen such a feast in all her life – the turkey steaming, succulently brown, the ham criss-crossed with cloves, carrots gleaming with butter, sprouts green as grass and sprinkled with roasted almonds, roast potatoes browned and tempting, bread sauce, cranberry sauce, three different stuffings each in its own little dish, red wine glamorous in cut-glass decanters, white wine mysterious in green bottles with foreign labels, and in the centre of the table – as if all that food weren't sufficient – an epergne made of pink glass and piled high with fruit and nuts. It was enough to make your mouth water just to look at it. And when Mr Cedric carved the first slice from the turkey, the aroma that rose from it made both parlourmaids ache with hunger. How could anybody be anything less than happy when they had food like that to eat?

'Oh my!' Daisy said, when the meal had been served and she and Rose been given leave to retire, 'I hope Mrs Biggs has got our grub ready. I'm starving!'

It was a nice leg of pork and waiting on the kitchen table.

'Eat hearty,' Mrs Biggs said to them as she carved into it. 'Help yourself to apple sauce. We got a lot of work ahead of us afore we're done. And you never know what'll happen in this house. They'll be quarrelling presently. You mark my words.'

She was a good prophet. Along the corridor in the red and gold of the dining-room, Cedric Monk was already beginning to annoy his sister.

'So they were wrong, you see,' he said in his calculating tone. He poured himself another glass of hock and leant back in his chair to gaze through the glass at Augusta.

'Who were?' Augusta asked sharply, a forkful of ham and turkey halfway to her mouth. With food on her plate, she had little inclination to talk but thought of a quarrel gave zest to the meal. Whatever he was going to argue about, she'd be more than a match for him.

'The pundits, sister dear,' Cedric went on. 'All those clever men who were so sure this war would be over by Christmas. A fat lot they knew! Well here we are you see, Christmas Day, Christmas dinner, and no sign of an end to it. More hock for you, Winifred?' And he looked at his wife in a pointed way, to remind her that she had a part to play in this too.

'I can't understand it,' Winifred said, backing him up at once and nodding her agreement to another glass of wine. 'All those men joining up. You'd have thought they'd have the Germans well on the run by now. Especially after the way they've been fighting at that place with the funny name. But they do say they're running short of munitions.'

Cedric opened his mouth to push the conversation into

its next and more important stage, but before he could say a word, he was forestalled by his sister-in-law, Louella, who had seen a chance to brag and took it at once. Damn woman.

'Ypres,' she said, in her drawling voice. 'It's rather a pretty place, actually, Winifred. We saw it two years ago, didn't we Edmund, on our way to Brussels. We only drove through, of course, but I think I can say we saw most of it, the Cloth Hall, the Cathedral, things like that. We were quite impressed. You should go there, my dear. When this war is over.' And she gave Winifred her most superior smile, knowing that her sister-in-law had never been out of the country.

'I don't hold with foreign travel,' Winifred said. 'As well you know.'

'Travel broadens the mind, my dear,' Louella said, looking at Winifred's sweating forehead and smiling again.

'My mind's quite broad enough, thank you.'

Edmund felt he had to intervene to keep the peace. 'According to the papers,' he observed, 'the town was rather badly damaged in the recent battle.'

'Yes,' Louella said. 'I read that too. It's just as well we saw it when we did, isn't it Edmund.'

'It seems such a pity,' Edmund went on.

Augusta shrugged her shoulders. 'That's war for you,' she said, heaping her fork again. 'You can't make an omelette without breaking eggs.'

Edmund gave her a disparaging look but decided to say nothing further. Augusta was difficult enough to handle at Christmas time without being provoked – as he knew, from bitter experience.

'Be that as it may,' Cedric said, attacking a potato, 'the war continues and will continue for some considerable time. Anyone with half an eye can see that now. Which being so, I have a proposition to put.'

These words alerted everyone round the table, even the three children who had been eating steadily and silently since the meal began. Augusta narrowed her eyes and Louella stopped eating. Here we go again, Edmund thought, depressed by the inevitability of it all.

'I've been thinking of investing in munitions,' Cedric announced. 'There are some good openings. In fact if I could lay my hands on a little capital . . .'

'How much?' Augusta asked bluntly.

'A few hundred pounds,' Cedric said, trying to sound casual and failing.

Augusta turned her head away from him. 'Well you can't have it from me, if that's what you're thinking.'

'You could spare a few hundred, surely,' Cedric fought on. 'For the war effort if nothing else. Think what an investment it would be.'

'There's a crying need for munitions,' Winifred said, weighing in. 'It's our patriotic duty, Augusta. And besides, it would be such a good investment.'

'Then you invest it,' Augusta retorted. 'I'm not stopping you.'

The recognition that he'd lost his appeal almost before it had begun turned Cedric sour. 'You stop me at every turn,' he said. 'It's all you ever do. A few hundred pounds, that's all I want, for God's sake, from capital that should have been mine.'

'But it isn't yours, is it,' his sister pointed out, wiping her chin with her table napkin.

'It should be,' he said, anger rising. 'It should be. And well you know it.'

The three children were listening avidly, their attention swivelling between their father and their aunt as if they were watching a tennis match.

'Leave it, Cedric,' Edmund tried to warn. 'Season of goodwill and all that.'

He was ignored. 'I've got a moral right to that money,' Cedric said to Augusta, and now his voice was as heated as his face. 'I was the one who should have inherited, in case you've forgotten – the first-born, the elder son. If it hadn't been for you smarming round Dadda when the poor old man was half out of his mind, you wouldn't have got a penny. If there was any natural justice in the world, I'd be the one at the head of this table every Christmas, not you.'

'Allow me to point out,' Louella said acidly, 'if it hadn't been for *your* father smarming round Granddad when *he* was dying, *my* father would have inherited and *I*'d be the one with the money now. If you're going to talk about natural justice, that's where you should be starting.'

'You're just digging up old bones,' Augusta said, enjoying their anger. 'There's nothing you can do about it. It's over and done with. I tell you that every time. You'll just have to learn to accept it. That's all there is to it.'

'God damn it! It's not over and done with,' Cedric shouted. 'And I will *not* accept it. Why should I? You've no right to withhold any money from me at all. It should have been mine in the first place. The whole thing's been immoral from start to finish. You wheedled it out of the old man.'

'It's not my fault I was the favourite,' Augusta said, smugly. 'He wanted to give it to me. What was I supposed to do? Refuse it and upset him when he was dying?'

'Wanted to give it to you, my eye!' Cedric roared, red in the face and breathing heavily. 'You wheedled it out of him. Tricked him, poor old man. In and out of that bedroom every minute of the day, putting on the act, pretending to love him.' He mimicked her voice. ' "Darling Dadda! I'm the one who loves you. You will leave me the money won't you." We all know how you went on.'

'You're just jealous,' Augusta replied. 'That's your trouble. You're riddled with it. You can't stand it because he loved me best. It wasn't enough for you that you were Mummy's pet. You wanted to be his too.'

'I can't stand unfairness,' Cedric said. 'That's what sticks in my craw. Unfairness. You snuggling up to him behind our backs to get what you wanted.'

'You could have "snuggled up to him" too if you'd wanted,' Augusta sneered. 'There was nothing to stop you.' But as soon as the words were out of her mouth, she realised she'd made a mistake and lost her advantage.

'*I* was out in the fields,' Cedric said triumphantly, 'hard at work, earning his bloody money for him. Earning his bloody money for you! I didn't have the time. Or the opportunity.'

'He's always been a worker,' Winifred weighed in again. '*He* doesn't lounge around in an armchair all day eating chocolates. Which is more than can be said for some people.'

Augusta bristled. 'I nursed my father all through his last illness, in case you've forgotten,' she said. 'I was on my feet every minute of the day and night. Up and down stairs waiting on him. I never left him for a moment.'

'No,' Cedric said, heavily sarcastic. 'We know you didn't. And this is the consequence.'

'Oh, you'd have liked him neglected. Is that it?'

'That's not what I meant and you know it.'

His anger had lost him his advantage, as it always did. 'You wanted him to suffer all on his own all those months,' Augusta said, settling to the attack. 'I always knew you were heartless, Cedric, but this is the worst . . .'

'Nine weeks,' Winifred pointed out. 'It wasn't months.'

'Nine weeks *is* months.'

'Shall we ring for the pudding?' Edmund suggested, trying to change the subject. 'If we've all finished, that is.'

But their bitterness had been unplugged and couldn't be diverted.

'You were always the same, even as a little boy,' Augusta cried. 'Always unkind. Always making trouble.'

'And you were a saint, I suppose,' Cedric sneered.

'Look how you made me ill. You were always making me ill.'

'Ill my eye! You were always making me *sick*.'

'Oh that's it. Mock! I should. You enjoy tormenting me. I'm only a woman.'

39

'Woman? Woman? What's that got to do with it? You twist everything I say.'

'You were always Mummy's pet. Mummy's darling boy. That's what made you cruel. You've been cruel all your life.'

'You should know about cruelty, Gussie. I've never met anyone as cruel as you.'

'I don't know how you can sit there and say such things,' Augusta cried. 'After all the trouble I've taken to give you a good Christmas. It's just black ingratitude.'

They were shrieking at one another, neither of them listening to anything but their own grievances.

'Twisted, that's all you are . . .'

'Cruel! And spiteful. Just because you didn't get your own way.'

'A wicked, wicked woman. Smarming round Dad-da . . .'

'You didn't get your own way,' Augusta screamed, thumping the table. 'That's what all this is about. That's what it's always about.'

Cedric rose to his feet in rage, looming at her across the table. 'I'll get it one of these days,' he threatened. 'You mark my words! I'll have justice. I shall fight you every inch of the way. You can play as many games as you like, it won't matter. I shall fight you and I shall win.'

'How dare you talk to me like that!' Augusta yelled. 'Can't you see you're making me ill. Oh! Oh!' She clutched at her throat, swaying from side to side. 'Oh! The pain! I'm in agony.'

Messages flashed from eye to eye – Edmund signalling alarm, Louella appalled but amused, Winifred pleading with her husband not to say any more. The children were transfixed by the drama of it all. And Augusta rose, gasping and groaning, took three tottering paces towards the fire and fell in a roaring swoon.

'Quick!' Winifred yelled. But no speed could have prevented this collapse. Her sister-in-law was already flat on her back on the hearthrug with her eyes tightly shut, her fists clenched and her toes pointing at the ceiling. Her neck and jowls were speckled purple and she was breathing heavily and noisily.

'My God!' Louella said, alerted at last. 'She's having a fit.'

Edmund left the table, at once, and went to kneel beside his sister, loosening the collar of her dress. Louella rang for the servants. The three children stood on their chairs to get a better view.

'*Is* she having a fit?' Ethel asked with a ten-year-old's dispassion.

'She's ever such a funny colour,' Hereward observed, equally interested.

'Sort of mauve,' Percy said with satisfaction.

Their mother paid no attention to them at all. She didn't even rebuke them for standing on the chairs. She was too badly frightened. What if Augusta were to die! It didn't bear thinking about. There would be a scandal and it would all come out that she'd collapsed in the middle of a row. 'Get a doctor!' she shouted at her husband. 'Quickly Cedric! Don't just stand there.'

'Lift her into a chair,' Louella suggested, as Cedric sped off to the hall.

'No!' Winifred cried, her face distraught. 'Don't. Not if it's a fit. We might injure her.'

'We can't just leave her on the ground.'

But she was still on the ground when Rose arrived to answer the bell.

'I'm afraid your mistress has had rather a nasty turn,' Edmund said. 'Would you get her bed ready for her, please?'

Cedric blundered back into the room wiping his forehead with his handkerchief.

'Well?' Winifred demanded. 'Is he coming?'

'As soon as he can, he said.'

'And what does that mean?'

'It *is* Christmas Day.'

'What of it?' Winifred said, wildly. 'She's his patient,

for heaven's sake. She could be dead. Augusta dear, do wake up.' She looked anxiously at Edmund, who was still kneeling on the hearthrug.

'Should we try cold water, do you think?' he wondered.

'There are smelling-salts in the chiffonnier,' Rose told them. 'Would they help?'

'Fetch them,' Cedric ordered.

The little blue bottle was retrieved from the cupboard, unstoppered and waved from side to side underneath Augusta's flaring nostrils. It took effect almost immediately. The lady coughed, sneezed and opened her eyes.

'Stop that!' she said. 'Do you want to choke me?' She waved the bottle away with both plump hands, her eyes watering. Then she looked up at Cedric and her expression changed from petty annoyance to passionate reproach. 'How *could* you!' she shrilled. 'My own brother! My own *brother* to speak to me like that. You could have killed me. Oh dear, I feel so *ill*.'

'I think we ought to try and get you into bed, my dear,' Winifred said. 'Do you feel well enough to stand?'

'Stand?' Augusta was appalled at the very idea. 'In *my* state?'

It took Cedric, Edmund and both the parlourmaids to manoeuvre Augusta up the stairs, carrying her awkwardly between them as she sagged in their hands and groaned about how ill she felt. By the time they had hauled her up into her bedroom and up onto the bed they were all panting and dishevelled.

'We've sent for the doctor,' Edmund said, patting her hand. 'He'll be here presently. We'll go down and wait for him, shall we?' And he and Cedric made a quick exit leaving the two parlourmaids to cope as best they could.

Between them, they coaxed Miss Monk out of her finery, cutting the few stitches that had caught her corset, eased her into a nightdress, helped her onto her commode and off again, and finally struggled her into bed.

'I feel so ill,' she groaned, as they tucked in the sheets. 'I thought I was dying. I've always had a weak heart, but I never thought I'd go and collapse like this. Oh dear, oh dear!' Then she stopped and cocked her head, listening intently. There were people on the stairs speaking urgently, their voices low. 'What's that? Is it the doctor? Go and see.'

It was Dr Felgate, his grey hair sleek above the green velvet jacket he'd been wearing when he was summoned, his expression disagreeable. Mrs Biggs had put on a clean starched apron in his honour and was escorting him upstairs, swishing at every step.

Despite his ill humour at being called out in the middle of his Christmas dinner, he resumed his bedside manner as soon as he entered the bedroom, taking command at once.

'I shall require a jug of warm water and a clean towel,' he said to Mrs Biggs. 'Open the curtains if you please. I need light for my examination. Now then, my dear lady, what have you been up to?'

To Rose's amazement, Miss Monk bridled at him as though she was sixteen and he was her suitor. 'Oh Doctor,' she said, assuming a good little girl's voice and batting her limited eyelashes at him. 'I can't think how it happened. It's too silly for words. One minute I was standing by the fire talking to my brother and the next I was falling down.'

'Any fever?' the doctor said, laying a professional hand on her brow as the two maidservants ducked out of the room.

'She looks awful,' Daisy said when they were out on the landing. 'Here, you don't think it's catching, do you?'

Rose was already in the linen cupboard. 'Cop hold a' this,' she instructed, handing out the clean towel. 'I'll just go and get the hot water and then we'll stay in here and see what he says.'

So they lurked in the cupboard while the doctor murmured in the bedroom. Presently they heard feet on the landing and Mr Cedric's voice muttering to his wife. Then there was a discreet knock on the bedroom door.

More voices. The doctor saying, 'no cause for alarm . . . a nasty fall . . . rapid pulse . . . shock. I will call in again on Monday.'

And Mr Cedric's voice, much clearer now, 'May we see her, Doctor?'

There was some more muttered conversation until Miss Monk cried out. 'No! No! I don't want to see anybody. I couldn't bear it. Tell them to go home.'

'Now what'll happen?' Daisy whispered.

'Wait an' see I suppose,' Rose whispered back.

They didn't have long to wait. Not long after the doctor's departure, Mr Cedric rang from the parlour to order tea and to give instructions that his family's luggage should be put in the boot of the car.

'We must get back,' Mrs Cedric explained to Mrs Biggs, as she stood waiting in the hall to see them out. 'The farm animals you know.'

Half an hour later, Mr and Mrs Edmund came downstairs, followed at an embarrassed distance by John-Ebenezer, who was carrying their luggage and being careful not to look at them. Despite the fact that he was behind them and that Rose was waiting for them in the hall, Mrs Louella was protesting.

'Is this wise Edmund?' she hissed, stopping in her descent. She stood so awkwardly that her body seemed out of alignment, as if her legs weren't connected to her hips.

'Wise and politic,' her husband said, flashing a warning glance in the direction of the hall. 'Leave well alone. Sleeping dogs and all that. There's nothing we can do. If we stay we shall get embroiled in another argument and I've really had enough for one day.' His face was warning her that she shouldn't say any more.

Rose was as discreet as she could be, handing them their coats and hats, opening the door, simply saying, 'Good afternoon sir. Good afternoon madam.' And John-Eb scuttled down the stairs after them and ran out to the car as if he wished he was invisible. They were both relieved when they were back in the kitchen again.

Daisy had made them a cup of tea. And very welcome it was.

'Pop up and see if she wants some an' all,' Mrs Biggs said to Rose, when they had emptied their cups.

Miss Monk was lying propped up on her pillows with her chow sprawled across her lap. She was stroking his fur and staring absently at the fire.

'Beg pardon, ma'am,' Rose said politely. 'Mrs Biggs was wondering. Would you like any tea?'

'Tea?' Miss Monk said, as if it was the last thing in the world she could possibly want.

'She was wondering,' Rose felt she ought to explain. It seemed pointless to be offering it when the poor lady had just had a fit.

'A little pot of Earl Grey,' Miss Monk decided. 'That would be sustaining, I think. A little pot of Earl Grey and a slice of cake. Some petticoat tails. Two mince pies maybe. I've got to keep my strength up.'

She kept it up amazingly, gobbling every morsel that was set before her. Rose didn't know whether to be glad at her rapid recovery or horrified at her greed.

Mrs Biggs said she wasn't surprised. 'What did I tell you?' she asked, making her cynical grimace. 'She'd have to be good and ill to be put off her food. Never knew such an appetite. *And* she'll want supper. You see if I'm not right.'

She's very heartless, Rose thought. She's talking as if she thinks Miss Monk's been putting it on. And yet she *had* eaten that tea. And she *had* got better very quickly.

It was a long confusing day. By the time Rose walked wearily into Ritzy Street late that night, she no longer knew what she thought about her employer or her illness. But the minute she was home, inside their lovely, familiar, uncomplicated living-room, she forgot all about Monk House and everybody in it. The fire was blazing, the walls were hung with Mabel's home-made paper chains and the presents were laid out on the table.

Her sisters fell on her and kissed her passionately. 'Now

45

we can have *our* Christmas,' Netta said. 'And about time too. Come to the fire. Your hands are like ice.'

Because she'd been out at work all day, they insisted that she had to open her presents first. Such thoughtful loving gifts they were, handed over with kisses and the hopeful expectation that they would please her; a pair of hair combs from Col – 'I got them from Tony up The Cut, real tortoiseshell he says, all the go' – a made-over blouse from Netta – 'I done it all mesself' – and an embroidered needle-case, full of needles, from Mabel – 'I was ever so careful our Rose. I used me thimble. I only got blood on it the once, see. That little spot there. You can't hardly see that, can you?'

Rose looked from one honest, loving face to the other. 'You *are* dears,' she said. 'They're lovely presents.' If only Bertie could have been home with them, it would have been a perfect moment.

46

CHAPTER FOUR

Edmund and Louella Monk had been married for eighteen years and had known one another since they were toddlers, for as well as being husband and wife they were also first cousins. It was one of the things that had drawn them together in the first place, that and their decision to become artists. Edmund had been cruelly teased about his choice of profession and mocked as an idler, a cissy, a ne'er-do-well. It was Louella who had blazed to his defence, citing artists from Ancient Greece to the present day, her long horsy face bright with passion. After that it was plain to both of them that they were made for one another.

'We are like all the great lovers,' Louella said dramatically. 'Romeo and Juliet. Dante and Beatrice. Antony and Cleopatra. Alone against the world! But what of it? With a love like ours we're a match for anyone.'

Unfortunately their parents didn't share her opinion. When they announced their engagement there was such heavy disapproval that Edmund was of two minds whether or not it was wise to proceed. Their fathers said it was a folly and would never work, their mothers that it was unhealthy and that they would breed idiot children. All four forbade it and the rows went on painfully and interminably for nearly three months. But Louella never wavered. She was so strong in her determination and so prone to tears if Edmund raised the slightest doubts of his own, that in the end he allowed himself to be convinced. They slipped off quietly one afternoon and were secretly married in the nearest register office.

'It will all come right in the end,' Louella promised, as they walked out of the building after the ceremony.

'You'll see. They'll come round in time. The great thing is that we love one another. And we do, don't we?'

But the family rift had continued and was healed only when the two principal antagonists were dead – Louella's mother after a slow decline, Edmund's when a sudden chill turned to pneumonia.

After such a start, Edmund rarely quarrelled with his wife. Their life together had to be as calm as he could make it and under perfect control, so that everyone could see they were making a success of it. As the years passed they gradually evolved a workable pattern, using mockery instead of argument, knowing that if it failed it could usually be laughed away. Their spat at Monk House was the nearest they had come to an outright quarrel in years and it had upset them very much, he because it had been necessary to take a firm line, she because she felt she had been defeated. They were quiet in the car going home and, once there, they went their separate ways – as they always did when they were in difficulties – he to his study, where he had a gas fire and plenty of books to comfort him, she to the corner of the drawing-room that she called her studio. There she coaxed the fire alight, donned her painter's smock, tied a silk scarf round her hair, set up her easel and began to paint and plot.

Running out of Monk House like that meant that the next two days were going to be rather uncomfortable. There was very little food in the larder besides bread and cheese or bacon and eggs, and they had given the cook, the general and the companion three days' holiday, so they would have to fend for themselves. But at least they were on their own and away from Augusta's venom. By Sunday evening Louella had evolved a plan of campaign.

First she had to smooth away any trace of their little difficulty. 'I'm sorry I made a fuss at Augusta's,' she said to Edmund over their supper of toasted cheese.

'Water under the bridge,' he told her mildly. Soothed by his books he had almost forgotten it.

So that was all right. 'I've been putting my mind to this

situation,' she went on. 'I think we could make capital out of it. Cedric has really blotted his copy-book this time. I don't think she'll forgive him in a hurry. Nor should she after all the awful things he said. Now, she's had two days to get over it a bit. I think we ought to go out tomorrow morning and buy some flowers and visit her.'

That was too alarming for Edmund. 'I think we should leave well alone,' he said. 'It'll only drag everything up again if we go visiting and the doctor said she wasn't to be disturbed. We walked out on her too, don't forget. That will have put the odd blot or two on our copy-book, don't you think?'

'No, it won't,' Louella said, sipping her tea. 'Not the way I'm going to handle it.'

Edmund made a wry expression. 'I can't see why you have to handle it at all,' he said, using his faintly mocking tone to show her that he wasn't to be taken seriously. 'Some people might say we've handled it quite enough. Which is not a criticism, you understand, just a statement of fact.'

Louella picked up her knife and used it to wave his words aside. 'I'm going to handle it,' she announced, making eyes at him to show that she understood his tone and that she wasn't going to quarrel, 'because it's high time she passed over some of her unearned cash to you, my love. Cedric isn't going to get any of it – not just now at any rate because she'll alter her will again – and you're the next in line. We must strike while the iron is hot.'

'She won't oblige. You know how she is about money.'

'She will if I have anything to do with it,' Louella said, her smile determined. 'You deserve a studio of your own, my love. Nothing less will do. And I mean to see that you get it.'

'I can live without a studio,' Edmund demurred, still using the same self-deprecating tone, 'I'd rather have a quiet life. Anyway, it's only money, Lou. Nasty sordid stuff.'

She teased back. 'You can revivify it with the power of

art. Art conquers all. Isn't that what you're always saying?'

Edmund smiled wryly. 'That's going it a bit,' he said. 'I'm not an artist, you know. I'm just a hack. A hack teaching hacks, if the truth be told. None of us are worth the name of artist.'

'*That* is because you don't have the right support,' Louella said, energetically. 'If you had a studio you *would* be an artist.'

'Ah,' Edmund said. 'So that's what it takes.' And he picked up his book again.

'So we'll visit her?' Louella asked.

'No,' Edmund said, opening the book. 'Not us. Not this time. That's too risky. We'll send Miss Spencer. She'll be back tomorrow, won't she? Very well then, send her with a message of some sort and if Augusta is in a better mood, we'll make our visit later. You can take her flowers then if you like, when we know she'll appreciate them.'

'Excellent!' Louella said. 'Yes, of course, that's exactly right. You have a good brain, Edmund my love, a very good brain.' Their equilibrium was restored. They were agreed. They knew what to do.

After the ease and happiness of her two-day holiday at home, Rose Boniface had no desire to go back to Monk House on Monday morning. She didn't tell the others what she was feeling, naturally, and she was deliberately cheerful as she set off to work, waving goodbye to the girls and smiling as much as she could. But knowing that she would soon have to face Miss Monk's unpredictable temper and Mrs Biggs' acid tongue was making her quail.

In the event, she needn't have worried, for Mrs Biggs wasn't in the kitchen when she arrived. There was no one there except John-Ebenezer who was languidly polishing a pair of shoes.

Rose took off her hat and coat and went to hang them in the outhouse. 'Where's Mrs Biggs?' she asked.

'Up in the bedroom with the old gel,' John-Eb told her, spitting on the shoe. 'Getting instructions.'

'Is she better?'

'Well, she's still in bed,' John-Eb said. 'Been there ever since. But if you ask me, I don't reckon there's much up with her. You should have seen the food she's been putting away. Great piles of it. I never seen such an appetite in all me born days.'

'You sound just like Mrs Biggs,' Rose rebuked, annoyed at him for being such a parrot. 'She was ever so ill on Christmas Day. Unconscious.'

'Wait till you see her now,' John-Eb grinned. 'I'll betcher when you go up she'll be sitting up in bed, large as life, gobbling up chocolates. You see if I'm not right. Fit as a flea, you ask me.'

Somebody was knocking on the back door so there wasn't time for any more conversation.

It was a girl wearing a beige felt hat trimmed with blue and white ribbon, a neat blue suit and a blank expression.

'Can I help you?' Rose asked. And when the girl didn't answer, 'Was it about a job?'

It didn't seem likely. Now that she looked at her closely, the girl didn't look like a servant. She had an oddly withdrawn face – snub nose, rounded forehead, pale cheeks, no chin to speak of, round eyes obscured behind a pair of steel-rimmed spectacles. But her hair was too carefully combed, her face too clean and her clothes much too good. Her suit was made of casement cloth, neat and serviceable but definitely not the sort of thing even a parlourmaid would run to. And neither was her blouse, which was a pin-tucked beige lawn, nor her hat and gloves come to that.

'Oh, no, no, nothing like that,' the girl confirmed, looking straight at Rose with round brown eyes, her plain face coming alive as she spoke. 'I'm Mrs Monk's companion. Mrs Edmund Monk. She left a scarf behind at Christmas. She sent me here to see if I could find it.'

All was clear. 'I see,' Rose said. 'Well, if that's the case, if you'd like to come upstairs with me, I'll show you where to look.'

The girl walked meekly into the kitchen, keeping her head down and taking small steps as though she was trying to withdraw her body into itself.

How shy she is, Rose thought, as they climbed the back stairs to the room Mr and Mrs Edmund had used. I'll bet she wouldn't say boo to a goose. It must be hard for her if she's supposed to be Mrs Monk's companion.

But this was a girl full of surprises. When they'd made a quick – and useless – search through all the empty furniture in the bedroom, she gave Rose a grin that was positively devilish.

'I'm not surprised,' she said. 'I didn't think we'd find it.'

'We'll look in the dining-room,' Rose offered. 'She could have left it there.'

'I shouldn't bother,' the girl said. 'It was a ruse. I saw it in her chest of drawers this morning, when I was laying out her clean clothes.'

'Then why . . . ?'

'So that I could spy out the lie of the land, I should imagine. See how Miss Monk is and if she's got over her temper.'

'How peculiar!' Rose said. 'Why didn't they just telephone and *ask* if they wanted to know how she was?'

The girl grinned again. 'Don't ask me. Mine not to wonder why. Mine but to do as I'm told.'

Now that they were talking so intimately, Rose was warmed by how frank and funny this girl could be. There was a playground sharpness about her, a sense of fun and daring and danger, a glint in the round eyes behind those steel spectacles.

They walked out onto the landing and headed for the main stairs, passing Miss Monk's bedroom door on their way.

'Do you want to go in and see her?' Rose asked.

'I suppose I'd better.'

'I'll knock,' Rose said.

Miss Monk was sitting up in the bed, slumped against a pile of pillows, gazing bleakly at the grey sky beyond the window. There were newspapers littered over the bedclothes, a half-eaten box of chocolates on the bedside cabinet and a tray full of dirty breakfast things at the foot of the bed. The chow was asleep across her knees, snoring audibly, and Miss Monk lay perfectly still, breathing slowly, as if she was asleep too. She looked unkempt and sullen, her hair uncombed, her skin pasty and her face sagging as though her features had fallen in upon themselves. There was a good fire blazing in the grate – Rose could feel the heat of it from where she stood – and the room smelt of stale sheets and unwashed dog.

'Good morning ma'am,' Rose said cheerfully.

The lady didn't even glance at her. 'What do you want?' she said. 'I didn't ring for you.'

'Mrs Edmund's companion has come to see you,' Rose told her. 'Shall I show her in?'

Miss Monk's expression changed at once. She sat up, smoothed her hair, straightened her nightgown. 'Well of course,' she ordered. 'You silly girl. She'll be anxious, naturally.' The tone of her voice had changed too. She looked and sounded quite perky.

Well, well, well, Rose thought, as she walked to the door to let the companion in. What a transformation! I wouldn't have believed *that* if I hadn't seen it with my own eyes.

'Come in! Come in!' Miss Monk urged. 'Miss . . . um . . .'

'Spencer,' the young woman said, moving delicately into the room. 'Muriel Spencer. How are you Miss Monk?'

'I've been terribly ill,' Miss Monk said, assuming a suffering expression. 'The doctor had to come in on Christmas Day, so you can see how ill I was. They don't come out on Christmas Day, you know, unless it's serious.'

Miss Spencer was politely sympathetic. 'I'm so sorry to hear that. Are you any better today?'

'Well the doctor's coming in to see me this morning,' Miss Monk confided. 'We shall know more then, I daresay. He thought it would be wise. He was most concerned about me, you see, knowing how I'd collapsed. I don't know what time he's coming. It could be any minute if I'm the first on his list – which I ought to be. What's the time, Rose?'

'Half past eight, ma'am.'

'Ah! Then it'll be a while yet. Still, while you're here, Rose, you'd better clear the tray and straighten up this bed. Mind what you're doing, girl. I don't want anything spilt.'

Her sudden switch from self-pity to ferocity made Rose nervous and nervousness made her clumsy. Struggling to balance the cup and saucer on a plate smeared with grease, she pushed the saucer just a fraction too far and knocked the milk jug on its side. Milk flooded the tray and spilt over onto the counterpane.

Instant pandemonium. Miss Monk drew up her legs under the coverlet so that the tray tipped sideways and the tea was spilt too and roared at Rose that she was a fool and a simpleton. The chow began to lick the tray. Rose scooped the whole thing up and carried it dripping to the dressing-table.

'Not there!' Miss Monk yelled. 'You'll spoil the wood. Put it on the floor! Get this mess cleared up. Look at the state of this bed. Ring for Mrs Biggs!'

Miss Spencer had found a towel and was mopping the coverlet. Rose rang the bell, found another and joined her. Between them they stripped the cover from the bed before the tea could stain the blankets, but Rose was taut with nerves and still clumsy and Miss Monk was still yelling.

'I'm surrounded by imbeciles!' she shouted as Mrs Biggs arrived. 'Look at the state of this bed. Oh get out! Get out, the pair of you!'

Mrs Biggs took it all calmly. 'Clean linen,' she said to Rose. 'An' take the tray outside.'

Both girls ran, only too glad to obey.

'Is she always like this?' Muriel Spencer asked, when the clean sheets had been handed through the door and they were on their way downstairs with the tray.

'Worse sometimes,' Rose said, recovering now that they were out of range. 'I could've got the sack.'

'Heavens!'

'What are you gonna do now?' Rose asked, when she had given the tray to the scullery maid.

'Wait till the doctor's been.'

'It could be a long wait.'

'I don't mind.'

'I shall have to light the fires in the parlour and the dining-room, now,' Rose said. 'In case she's allowed up. You could wait there with me, if you'd like. The kitchen's a bit . . . Well you know how it is, this time a' day.'

'Thank you,' Muriel said, her entire face lifted by her smile. 'I'd like that very much.'

The parlour struck cold and it took quite a while for the fire to catch. But a quick flick with the duster made it look presentable so Rose moved on to the dining-room. And got a shock at the state it was in. Plainly no one had been in to clean it since Christmas Day. The grate was full of grey ash and shards, the candles were still on the table, deformed by trailing wax, the bran tub lay on its side dribbling sawdust onto the carpet, the Christmas tree was shedding needles and several of the paper decorations had fallen loose and now lay incongruously across the chairs. And there was dust everywhere.

'My stars!' Rose said. 'Fancy leaving it like this. That ain't like Mrs Biggs.'

'I'll give you a hand,' Muriel offered. 'Might as well make myself useful while I'm here.'

That was a surprise. Rose had expected Muriel to sit on a chair and watch, given her status as a lady's companion. But her new friend took off her hat and coat, rolled up her sleeves and set to work without another word.

It took them more than an hour to put the room to

rights, but for once Rose hardly noticed the work, because she and Muriel had so much to talk about. They discovered that they were almost exactly the same age, born in June 1897 and their birthdays a mere three weeks apart, which delighted them both. Then to add amazement to coincidence they found out that they had started work for the Monk family in the same month. 'Born under the same star,' Muriel said, happily. Then they found that they were both 'orphans'. Muriel had never known her father and her mother had died when she was three.

'So you ain't got no brothers and sisters,' Rose said with sympathy.

'No. Not so far as I know. Sometimes I imagine I've got a big family somewhere out there and they find out about me and search me out and find me. It's a sort of game. Working out what it would be like to have a family.'

So naturally Rose told her all about *her* family and how Col was working in the vinegar factory and how Mabel was simple-minded – 'but ever so loving' – and how Netta had a will of her own but was 'ever so good with the housework' and how Bertie had joined up.

'It must be lovely to have brothers and sisters,' Muriel said. 'I wish it was me.' Her envy was so open and so warm with admiration that Rose felt suddenly fond of her.

'You'd love our Bertie,' she said. 'He's been like a father to the littl'uns since Mum died.'

'What about your Dad?'

'He died before Mum,' Rose said. 'Got crushed by a brewer's dray.' But that was too painful for her to talk about.

There was a pause in their conversation while they started to dust the ornaments on the mantelpiece. Muriel could see that they'd touched on a nerve and didn't want to upset her new friend by saying anything else until she'd recovered a little.

'You've done this before,' Rose said, appreciating how gently Muriel handled Miss Monk's precious pair of Doulton vases.

'I was three years as a housemaid,' Muriel said, dusting the lustres. 'In a big house in Hampstead. I've learnt all the tricks. Then the warden at the orphanage said I'd do better for myself as a companion and they gave me elocution lessons and sent me to the Monks.'

'And is it better?' Rose wanted to know.

'Well I don't have to scrub floors and that's one good thing,' Muriel said, 'but the food's not so good – she's very tight with the housekeeping – and I miss the company. There were five of us at Hampstead all of an age so we had some sport below stairs. With the Monks it's only me and Cook and old Betsy. It's a bit lonely sometimes.'

There was no self-pity in her voice or on her face. She was simply stating an accepted fact. 'Tell you what,' Rose said impulsively. 'Me an' Netta go to the pictures of a Friday. How d'you like to come with us?'

The delight on Muriel's face gave her answer before she could put it into words. 'I'd love to. Not this Friday though. I'll have to give them notice I won't be there.'

'Don't you get your evenings off then?'

'Not always. She expects me to be available. In case she wants me to read to her.'

'That's not fair,' Rose said with some warmth. 'You ought to have your evenings off.'

'I get Wednesday afternoons.'

'Do you? So do I . . .'

With excruciatingly bad timing, the doctor's car crunched into the drive. 'Drat!' Rose said, tidying herself up to admit him.

The lady of the house had heard the car too and was making her own preparations. By the time Rose ushered the doctor into the bedroom, the chocolate box had been hidden in the bedside cabinet and the lady lay back elegantly against her pillows, wearing a suffering expression, her eyes closed, pale and patient, as though she was asleep. Rose took one look at her and decided to listen outside the door.

Dr Felgate pronounced himself pleased with his

57

patient's progress and suggested that she might get up for an hour or two in the afternoon, provided she kept clear of draughts and didn't overdo things.

She promised to take great care of herself. 'It doesn't do to run risks with your health, does it Doctor?' Her voice was soft, sweet and rather faint. Nobody listening to it would have imagined that this was the same woman who had been shrieking at her servants just a few hours ago.

'There you are,' Rose said to Muriel, when Dr Felgate had washed his hands and departed and she was back in the dining-room. 'You can tell them she's recovered.'

'Yes,' Muriel said. 'Well we knew that, didn't we. After all that business with the tray.'

Rose grinned at her. 'Yes. I think we did.'

'I'd better go then,' Muriel said, picking up her coat and hat. But she looked and sounded reluctant about it.

'Meet me at the side gate Wednesday.'

'What time?'

'Can you make two o'clock?'

'I'll be there,' Muriel promised.

Mrs Louella Monk went straight to the telephone after Muriel had given her report and ordered the florist to make up a large bunch of mixed chrysanthemums. Then she donned her best hat and coat and set off to catch the bus, walking with determination, head forward and feet splayed.

By the time she arrived at Monk House, her cousin was sitting by the parlour fire with her slippered feet on the fender, consuming a huge high tea.

Louella swept into the room, her arms full of flowers and her mouth full of apologies. 'Darling!' she cried. 'I'm *so* relieved you're better. We've been worried out of our wits about you. Edmund sends his love. He's at the college today, otherwise he would have come with me. They work him *so* hard.'

Augusta wasn't particularly pleased to see her sister-in-law and made no bones about it. 'Oh, it's you,' she said. 'What do you want?'

'We didn't know what to do when you collapsed,' Louella said, wearing her earnest expression. 'We were beside ourselves with worry. We wanted to telephone, but Edmund said we shouldn't upset you. The doctor said you weren't to be disturbed, you see. As if Cedric hadn't disturbed you enough! How you must have suffered.'

Augusta admitted that she had. Terribly.

'He's heartless!' Louella said, warm with indignation. 'Going on at you like that. And all so unnecessary.'

'He's after my money,' Augusta confided, as if the information was news to them both. 'That's what it is.'

'Disgraceful!' Louella commiserated. 'I don't know how he can be so unkind. The things he said to you! Well, Edmund and I were shocked. Absolutely shocked! There's no other word for it. Edmund was *so* worried about you. Well, he said to me at the time, "I wonder at Cedric. I really do. Does he *want* to make her ill?" He'd hardly got the words out of his mouth when you collapsed.'

'Cedric doesn't care,' Augusta said, warming to her theme. 'He was always hard, even as a child. Would you like some tea? I'll get Rose to bring another cup.'

Tea was taken and flowers given and the two women settled to the most agreeable occupation of reducing Cedric's reputation to well-chewed threads. And when he'd been dealt with to their entire satisfaction, they started on Winifred, who, in their opinion, not only ate too much but was as money-grabbing as her husband.

By the time Louella decided she really ought to go home and attend to Edmund's dinner, they were declaring how fond they were of each other.

'I've half a mind to make a new will and leave everything to you and Edmund,' Augusta declared, half joking. 'That would just serve him right.'

Louella put her hand on her sister-in-law's arm and smiled compassionately. 'We wouldn't want you to go to any inconvenience on *our* behalf,' she said.

'It wouldn't inconvenience me at all,' Augusta said.

Seeing how completely Augusta had taken the bait, Louella was all sweet reason. 'Perhaps it might be better to wait till you're quite well again and see how you feel then.'

But now Augusta wouldn't be deterred. 'No,' she said. 'I've made up my mind. Bring a chair out into the hall. I'm going to phone Mr Tilling here and now. Cedric's too big for his boots. He needs teaching a lesson. It's no good making that face, Louella. You're too kind hearted. He needn't think he can treat me like that and get away with it. I shall change my will and cut him out of it altogether. It's nothing more than he deserves.'

Louella was already carrying the chair out of the room. 'Well if you really think you must,' she said. 'But I didn't come here to worry you, you know.'

All in all it was a most successful visit.

comprehensible. And at that point the tea-trolley would be
wheeled into the room and Mr Tilling would take tea and
instructions.

When their business was nearly concluded, Mr Tilling
would take his leave, return to the office to assure Miss
Monk that he could see himself out and to add that the
new will would be ready for signature the following

CHAPTER FIVE

Mr Charles Tilling, of the firm of Fordham, Tilling and
Fordham, was an enthusiastic solicitor, although he did
his best to curb his enthusiasm when he was interviewing a
client. He was small and dark and wiry, with a small dark
face, small dark eyes, an excrescence of wiry black hair
and legs that were so excessively small and wiry that they
looked as though they were made of corkscrews. He
invariably wore a black jacket and pin-striped trousers
because he felt it gave him a certain dignity. And so it did,
when he posed before a mirror. But when he leapt eagerly
up the stairs to Miss Monk's drawing-room to earn his
next fee, there was nothing dignified about him at all. He
looked like a spider rushing up his web towards a fly,
mandibles at the ready.

He had been Miss Monk's solicitor for the last eight
years, ever since she inherited her father's house and all
his capital, and during that time she had changed her will
on no fewer than six separate occasions, always in the
privacy of her drawing-room and always to the considerable advantage of the firm of Fordham, Tilling and
Fordham. The junior Mr Fordham said he hadn't got time
for her, but Mr Tilling enjoyed his visits, pocketed his nice
fat fee and dined out on tales of her eccentricity.

Over the years, their meetings had acquired a routine.
Miss Monk would spend the first quarter of an hour
castigating the greed of whichever brother was out of
favour. Mr Tilling would commiserate at some length,
wondering how such perfidious creatures could possibly
live with their consciences. Then Miss Monk would ask if
she was being too sensitive and the solicitor would assure
her that her feelings were not only understandable but

commendable. And at that point the tea-trolley would be wheeled into the room and Mr Tilling would take tea and instructions.

When their business was nearly concluded, Mr Tilling would take his leave, pausing at the door to assure Miss Monk that he could see himself out and to add that the new will would be ready for signature the following afternoon. Then he would wait, balanced on his cork-screw legs, his wiry head held to one side, eyebrows lifted.

And Miss Monk would give him his final and most important instruction. As she did now.

'I think it would be a good idea – while you're about it – to send a letter to Mr Cedric Monk and just let him know what I've decided.'

'I will attend to it.'

'You're such a comfort to me,' Miss Monk said, batting her eyelashes at him. 'I don't know what I'd do without you.' It was an exaggeration, and she knew it, but there was an element of truth in it just the same. She spent so much of her time feeling aggrieved and unhappy that any source of comfort was welcome and this man, with his sharp, attentive face and his unfailing assurance that she had every right to feel aggrieved, made her feel important and cared for.

'Not at all,' Mr Tilling said, giving her his professional smile. That stinking dog of hers had woken up and was waddling towards him, making snuffling noises.

'I feel so honoured, you know,' Miss Monk went on, still flirting, 'that *you* should be the one to attend to my affairs. Being the senior partner in the firm, I mean. It's very good of you.'

The chow had reached his trousers and was nipping at the turn-ups, growling throatily. 'Good dog,' Mr Tilling said, trying to ease the cloth away from its teeth. They were his best trousers and if they had to be invisibly mended he would be very annoyed. But she would pay for it. The cost would be added to her bill.

'I tell all my friends how good you are,' Miss Monk said.

Down in the kitchen where the servants were busy preparing her usual three-course dinner, Mrs Biggs was giving vent to a rather less flattering opinion of the gentleman.

'He's a dratted nuisance, that's all he is,' she said, using her rolling-pin with vigour. 'He'll be in and out of here like a yo-yo, you mark my words. It'll be "Scones for tea tomorrow, if you please Mrs Biggs and make sure Rose has a clean cap an' apron." As if we haven't got enough to do.'

'Daisy,' Rose corrected, stirring the soup.

'Whatcher mean Daisy?'

'Daisy'll have to wear the clean cap and apron. It's my afternoon off tomorrow.'

'Well thanks very much,' Daisy said.

'She'll have that changed,' Mrs Biggs warned dourly.

'Can't be done,' Rose said firmly. 'I've made arrangements.'

'What's this then?' John-Eb teased, struggling up from the cellar with a pail full of coal. 'You got yourself a feller?'

'No I ain't,' Rose told him, putting down her wooden spoon. 'I'm going to the pictures with Mrs Edmund's companion, if you must know.'

'Oh-er!' John-Eb mocked. 'We *are* going up in the world.'

'There's her bell,' Mrs Biggs said. 'Your turn Daisy. "Scones fer tea tomorrow." See if I'm not right. Are you making that fire up today or what, John-Ebenezer? You don't get paid for standing around.'

I don't care what she eats tomorrow, Rose thought, adding salt to the soup, just so long as I don't have to be here to attend to it. This would be the first time she'd been out with anyone other than her family since Mum took ill and died and she'd had to leave school to look after the littl'uns. That was three and a half years ago and suddenly seemed a long time. Now and at last she was going out just for a lark and she couldn't wait for it.

The next day was dark and miserable and it was raining again but not even a downpour could dampen her high spirits. She did her work at speed, singing softly to herself. Even when Mrs Biggs kept her behind for an extra quarter of an hour to set the tea-trolley, she was still cheerful and went skipping off to the side-gate as soon as she'd finished, clutching her umbrella low over her head, ready for anything.

She could see Muriel waiting for her inside the entrance to the corner shop.

'Muriel!' she called, running towards her. 'Coo-ee! Sorry I'm late. Mrs Biggs kept me.'

Muriel looked at her, but she didn't smile and she didn't say 'Hello'. She was standing awkwardly, her spine stiff and her shoulders hunched, and her face was devoid of expression, the way it had been when she was waiting on the doorstep.

But Rose was too happy to pay attention to details like that.

'How about a Charlie Chaplin?' she said, cheerfully. 'There's a new one out called *The Tramp*. Daisy saw it Saturday. She says it's ever so good. We could go up West and see it. That'ud be a treat.'

It was too. A real treat. For this was Charlie Chaplin at the top of his form, hooking them into his zany world with the first flick of his cane. They laughed and cried and admired and thoroughly enjoyed themselves. By the time they emerged from the fusty darkness of the cinema into the chill of the early evening, Muriel was quite her joking self again, reliving the best bits and imitating Chaplin's grimaces so comically that it made Rose laugh to see her. And the weather had changed for the better too.

The rain had stopped – at last – and the air was clear and cold. Clouds drifted above the darkening rooftops, indigo and grey like smoke. And in the rain-washed air the scents and smells of the city rose in a pungent mixture – engine oil cloying, horse manure pervasive, the musty stink of dirty clothes as a street sweeper toiled past, heady perfume drifting back from the open door of a cab as a rich woman climbed in adjusting her furs, the warmth of leather and polish from carriage and harness, the spice of cigarettes, the tinny tang of burning gaslight . . . and, above all the others, the sweet waft of violets from an assembly of flower sellers who were sitting with their backs against the dome of the public toilets, their baskets lit by the four globes of the gas lights.

While the two girls had been in the cinema, the few street lamps that were allowed under the new regulations had been lit and, although all the shops had put up their shutters and withdrawn into darkness, the centre of the road was hung with yellow globes of light like a string of gigantic beads. As horses hauled their burdens past, their rumps shone briefly, muscles rippling, and the cars that roared and clattered in every direction glittered like fireflies as they darted in and out of the light.

'I *do* like London at night,' Rose said, taking Muriel's arm as they set off to catch their tram. 'It's so full of life. Everything on the move and all the lights and everything.'

She was surprised when her new friend made a grimace and began to apologise to her. 'I'm sorry I was offish, back in Ritzy Street. I shouldn't've been. It wasn't nice.'

It took a few seconds for Rose to realise what she was talking about. 'Oh that!' she said. 'I didn't mind. It was raining cats and dogs. Enough to put anyone off.'

'It wasn't that,' Muriel said. Now that she'd started this apology she felt she had to make a clean breast of it. 'I thought you'd changed your mind about coming, you see. I thought you didn't want to go out with me. I wouldn't have blamed you. I know what it's like. People are always changing their minds.'

'Not me,' Rose said stoutly. 'If I say I'm going somewhere, I go. We could go out every Wednesday if you like.'

Muriel said she would like. Very much indeed.

'We can't come up West every time,' Rose warned. 'That'ud be a bit pricey. But we could go to the local pictures. Or up The Cut.'

'What's that?'

'A market,' Rose told her. 'It's a lark. You'd love it. We go there every Saturday evening. Either The Cut or Lambeth Walk. We have some sport. Lambeth Walk's a riot, with all the lights and everything, and the fruit all piled up and the stall holders calling out at you. All sorts of characters in a market, there are.'

It was a tempting offer, as Rose could see.

'Could you get time off?' she asked.

'Well, yes I could. But won't your family mind? I mean, I wouldn't want to butt in.'

'No,' Rose said. ' 'Course they won't mind.' Warm with impulsive generosity, she didn't have the slightest doubt about it. 'They'd love you to come.'

But she was wrong. Netta minded – very much. And being Netta she didn't hide her feelings.

'You done what?' she said, her long face dark with annoyance. She'd been putting on her hat ready for their outing when Rose made her announcement. Now she paused, hat-pin in hand, fierce and disapproving.

'I asked her to come with us,' Rose said. 'We're gonna meet outside the pub.'

Netta sniffed. 'Whatcher want to go and do that for?'

'She's all on her own, Netta. She's an orphan.'

'And we're not, I suppose?'

'Not in the same way.'

'Oh I can see what it is,' Netta said. 'We're not good enough for you no more now you got a classy friend.'

'Oh come on, Netta! She ain't a classy friend. Don't talk tripe!'

Netta bristled. 'Oh! Tripe is it?'

'Don't be daft, our Netta,' Col said. 'Why shouldn't she come with us?'

' 'Cause she's posh,' Netta said crossly. And she took

66

off her hat and hung it on the hook. 'Well that's it then. If *she's* coming, you can count me out.'

'That's childish,' Rose said. She was confused because Netta was making her feel that she'd done something hurtful and until that moment she'd seen it as a kindness. 'I thought you'd welcome her.'

Netta was truculent. She sat by the fire and turned her face away. 'Well you thought wrong.'

Col got to his feet, tossed his fag-end into the fire and sloped off towards the door. 'If she's in one of *them* moods, I'm off out,' he announced. 'See you later our Rose. Ta-ta, our kid.'

Rose tried persuasion. 'Come on, Netta,' she coaxed. 'Come with us. You'll like her.'

The answer was adamant. 'No.'

There's no point going on with this, Rose thought. You can't shift Netta when she's in a mood. 'Come on then, Mabel,' she said. 'You and me'll go. We'll have to look sharp or we shall miss the best cuts. I'd like to get some of them nice sausages like the ones we had last week. I could just fancy a plate of bangers and mash.'

So it was just Mabel and Rose who escorted Muriel round the market. And although the Walk was as lively as ever, despite the fact that it was raining, and although they got a string of sausages for supper, along with six slippery slices of liver and four ragged lamb chops all piled on top of a shoulder of mutton, all for one and ninepence, Rose's pleasure was diminished by Netta's absence.

But Muriel was so happy her face shone. She walked from stall to stall enjoying everything from the clutter of orange-boxes and discarded wrappings at her feet to the cries of the barrow boys deafening her ears. 'Tuppence a pahn' pears!' 'Eels! They're luv'ley!' 'What am I bid fer this lovely bit a' shmutter? Half a dollar? Can't say fairer than that, can I darlin'?'

Every stall was a magical world, like a stage set, curtained by awning, lit by naphtha flares and displaying its wares on a shelf that sloped towards her. The under-lit face of the stall-holder loomed in the darkness behind it like some mysterious backcloth and the crowds pushed and jostled for a better view, some faces eager for a bargain, some anxious that they wouldn't be able to afford it, whatever it was. And what an abundance of goods on display – cups and saucers piled on top of one another, painted trays and cheap tin kettles, cottons and bobbins in every colour, cards full of buttons in every size and shape, strings of bright beads chinking together, long poles glittering with bracelets and bangles, dresses and blouses so tightly packed on their rails you couldn't distinguish one from another, shellfish in wooden tubs, live eels all a-wriggle, their black skins shimmering with a fluorescence of blue and green, fruit of every description, red apples so highly polished she could see the reflection of the flares in their burnished skin, oranges in golden pyramids on green cloth like artificial grass, bananas suspended from the awnings like clumsy gloves. Magical.

Mabel was loitering by the beads and bangles, trailing them with her fingers and making them rattle.

'Ain't they pretty,' she said to her new friend.

'Which one do you like best?' Muriel asked.

'Them red ones.'

They were the gaudiest on the pole.

'There you are then,' Muriel said, lifting them clear. 'Present for you.'

Mabel was so thrilled she clapped her hands like a baby. And Rose was touched. 'That's ever so good of you,' she said. 'She loves beads.'

'Quite right!' Muriel said, paying the stall holder. 'So do I.' Then she hung the beads round Mabel's neck and gave her a hug.

When the shopping had all been done, she kissed Rose and Mabel goodbye, shyly but with real affection. 'It was ever so good of you to let me come with you,' she said. 'I've had a lovely time.'

'Thanks for the beads,' Rose said. 'See you next Wednesday. Same time, same place?'

'Same time, same place,' Muriel affirmed and made a joke, grinning at them. 'You never know, it might have stopped raining by then.'

And Netta might be in a better frame of mind, Rose thought.

But Netta was short tempered all the next week and the rain seemed set in for eternity. It blocked the drains in Ritzy Street, deepening Netta's ill humour; it turned streams to raging torrents and flooded country lanes all over Kent and Sussex; it reduced the newly dug trenches on the plains of Flanders to a nightmare of mud and slime; and on the plains of East Anglia it clogged the ditches that should have been draining the meadows on which Cedric Monk grazed his beef cattle.

On the morning that Mr Tilling's letter arrived, Cedric was out with a team of ditchers, trying to repair the damage. Winifred put the envelope behind the clock on the mantelpiece and hoped that, whatever it was, it wouldn't annoy him too much.

It was a vain hope. He didn't get back that day until well after sunset and by then he was bone-weary and bad-tempered. The letter reduced him to bellowing.

'God damn it all! Damn silly woman. Look at this, Winifred. I'm cut out of her will again, if you ever heard anything so bloody silly. I thought we'd got that all settled after the last time. But no, you see, she's off on her old tricks again. I'm nòt a fit person to inherit, so she says. It's all being left to Edmund and Louella.'

'Then Louella's behind it,' Winifred said, nodding sagely. 'I've never trusted her, Cedric. Not that one. She's too cunning by half. And she's always been after the money.'

'Augusta can't be spoken to, that's her trouble.' Cedric snorted. 'Bloody hell, Winifred, I only asked for what's rightfully mine. To help the war effort. You'd have thought she'd have been pleased. A chance to help our brave boys out in France. You'd have thought she'd have jumped at it. There isn't an ounce of patriotism in her. Not one ounce. Our boys can die out there for want of some decent ammunition. *She* doesn't care. She doesn't care for anyone. Except that bloody awful dog. And now we've got to go through all this nonsense again. Well I shall have something to say to *her*. She needn't think she can insult me like this and get away with it.'

He charged into the parlour, Winifred at his heels, and banged the bureau open. 'I'll make her wish she'd never been born. I'll make 'em *both* wish they'd never been born.' He seized a pen and wrote with such fury that his nib spiked holes in the paper.

I have received your communication for which I will not thank you. Gratitude is inappropriate in the circumstances. My conduct is never anything if not appropriate.

As to the contents of your despicable missive, I would have thought some element of patriotism would be in order at this parlous stage in our national history, when men are being urged to fight to the uttermost for King and Country. Apparently you do not share this opinion, the more shame to you. It is a grief to me to think that I have a sister with no regard to the exigencies of the national war effort. It is also patently obvious to me, as it has been since our father's lamentable demise, that you have the most limited understanding of the laws of natural justice. You had no right to any of father's money. By the laws of primogeniture I should have inherited and well you know it. How am I supposed to run this farm without capital? You tell me that.

It is decadent to be sitting at home doing nothing at a time of national emergency, wallowing in luxury, eating chocolates all day with that damn silly dog. It can't go on. I won't have it. God damn it, what sort of a man do you think I am? I shall oppose you to the end and you need not think you can leave any of my money to Edmund or to Louella either. I shall fight that too. Does it mean nothing to you that I am your elder brother?'

When Augusta received his letter she went puce with

the pleasure of justified anger. Mr Tilling was summoned at once.

'Not very pleasant, my dear lady,' he agreed when he'd read the letter. 'Would you require me to compose a suitable reply?'

'Yes, I would,' Augusta said, her double chin shaking with vehemence. 'And in the strongest terms if you please. He can't be allowed to speak to me like that and get away with it. I never heard anything so scandalous. Didn't I tell you he was a horrid man?'

She lived on her anger for the rest of the day, stomping up and down in the parlour, striding through the garden in a fury, stabbing at the shrubs with her stick, trampling the young daffodils, pausing only to rekindle her fury by another reading of the letter. Her energy was as prodigious as her appetite.

When Rose finally got home that evening she declared she was sick and tired of Miss Monk. 'It's a horrid thing to say,' she confided to Netta, 'but there she is in the middle of an awful quarrel with her brother and she's enjoying it.'

'They're up to something in Chelsea, too,' Muriel said when the two friends met on Wednesday afternoon. 'Mr Edmund's had architects in. I think she's going to build a studio. There's lots of plans all over the place.'

There were so many, in fact, that Louella had to cajole the cook into lending her a long wicker basket so that she could carry them over to Monk House. But she wasn't so foolish as to show them to Augusta right away. There was sympathy to express first.

'So unkind,' she agreed when she'd been shown the correspondence. 'But then Cedric always *was* a horrid little boy. Look how beastly he was with that cat, drowning all her kittens poor thing. I've never forgotten.'

Augusta had drowned plenty of kittens in her time, but she professed a suitable horror. 'There's a nasty streak in him,' she agreed. 'A very nasty streak.'

'Let's talk about something pleasant,' Louella suggested. 'I can't have you upset by Cedric. That's playing into his hands. Come into the dining-room. I've got something to show you.'

'What?' Augusta said, suspiciously.

'Some plans,' Louella told her. And she picked up her basket and led the way.

'What do you think?' she said when she'd spread the plans on the dining-room table. 'Aren't they grand?'

Their professional assurance gave the game away. Augusta realised at once that Louella was going to ask her to pay for this building work and in the same instant she knew what her response was going to be. She would give Louella two hundred pounds which wouldn't break the bank but would be impressive enough to put Cedric in his place.

'Tell me about them,' she said coolly.

Her tone disconcerted Louella but she pressed on. 'They're plans for an artist's studio for my dear Edmund,' she said. 'We're going to build it in the attic.'

Augusta looked at the plans and then at her cousin, her face shrewd.

'I can't make up my mind, do you see,' Louella said, beginning to gabble. 'Should we plump for the single studio with north-east light, like this? Or convert the entire attic while we're about it and have something really grand, like this? I've been thinking about it all night. I should so value your opinion. You know far more about these things than we do. You always were the clever one, even when we were children. What do you think?'

'What is it all going to cost?' Augusta asked, going to the heart of the matter.

Louella wasn't sure whether to be relieved or alarmed. When Augusta was in one of her cold moods it was very difficult to know how to respond. Perhaps she'd better plump for caution. 'Not a great deal if we use only half the attic space and add another room later. A full studio would be a lot cheaper in the long run. You see how difficult it is.'

Augusta saw exactly how difficult it was and was

exhilarated by the knowledge. 'Well my dear,' she said. 'You will have to make your mind up, won't you.'

'I was rather hoping you'd help me,' Louella confessed.

'Yes,' Augusta said, watching her squirm. 'I daresay you were.'

'You will help us, won't you,' Louella said. It was the wrong moment and she knew it. But Augusta was in such a peculiar mood she was afraid that if she didn't make her appeal now she might lose the chance altogether. 'I told Edmund you would. He's *such* a good brother – *he* wouldn't upset you like that rotten Cedric – and *such* a wonderful artist. We owe it to him, don't you think? Yes of course you do. So you will help us, won't you.'

'Help you?' Again that awful shrewd look.

'Yes, yes,' Louella rushed on, swooping back to the table, as if the plans would give her support. 'With half the cost. I mean if you could see your way to helping us with half the cost it would make all the difference. To Edmund's career. He's such a good brother . . .'

Augusta pinned her with another look, enjoying the sense of power. 'What's the estimate?'

'Five hundred pounds,' Louella said quickly and when Augusta recoiled visibly, 'Oh I know it sounds a lot . . .'

'Far too much,' Augusta said. 'I couldn't afford five hundred pounds.'

'No, no, of course not darling. That's the total. I thought you might help us with half of it, that's all. Two hundred and fifty. For dear old Edmund who's never said an unkind word about you in his life. Not one, the dear boy. Isn't he worth it? And just think what it'll do to Cedric. It'll show *him* a thing or two and no mistake. He'll be absolutely green with envy.'

True, Augusta thought. And I've made you beg for it until you're pretty green about the gills as well. 'Two hundred,' she said. 'And not a penny more. I'm not made of money.'

'You're all heart!' Louella said, pouncing at her cousin to kiss her with relief. 'You'll never regret it.'

Augusta regretted it the moment her visitor left the house, as she so often did when she'd handed over any large sum of money. Pecuniary triumph is very short lived. Now she felt she'd been too quick. She should have played Louella along for a lot longer. Enjoyed herself more. 'They're only after my money,' she sighed to Chu-Chin. 'It's always the same with that lot. Money, money, money.'

Her sense of dissatisfaction grew and began to rankle. Even composing an abusive letter to Cedric didn't ease her at all. In the morning she shouted at Daisy; in the afternoon she roared at John-Eb and threatened him with the sack; and finally, when Mrs Biggs' *charlotte russe* arrived on the dinner table, leaning like the tower of Pisa, her discontent erupted into temper and she swept the offending pudding off the dish and onto the carpet.

'Can't you do anything right?' she shouted at Rose.

Rose had had a bad day too. She'd had a letter from Bertie that morning saying he didn't think he'd get any leave until the end of February. She'd coped with Daisy's tears and John-Eb's misery and Mrs Biggs' temper. She burnt her finger on a hot meat dish. She'd cleaned up after Chu-Chin when he'd messed on the drawing-room carpet. Now her finger throbbed and her feet ached and she felt hurt to be blamed for something she hadn't done.

I wish I didn't have to work here, she thought, as she cleaned up the *charlotte russe*. I wish this rotten war was over. I wish our Bertie was back.

CHAPTER SIX

Spring began on the day Bertie finally came home to Ritzy Street. It was actually early in March, but a faint sun shone, the air was warm and above the grey roofs and the rows of chimney pots the sky was a lovely clear blue.

Everything had been prepared for ages. The rooms were polished from floor to picture rail, the fire laid, his bed made up ready. Oh, they couldn't wait to see him again.

Col went off to the vinegar factory whistling as though it were just another ordinary day, but Rose was so excited she left her shopping-basket behind and had to come back for it, and Mabel and Netta played truant because, as Netta said, 'Let's face it, our Rose, there ain't much point sending our Mabel to school at the best a' times and I shall never be able to pay attention on a day like this, never in a thousand years.'

There wasn't much point in staying at home either, for they were so impatient that they couldn't settle to anything. They spent the entire afternoon leaning out of the living-room window watching for him and chatting to their neighbours in the street. Even their landlady, Mrs MacLaren, who usually kept herself to herself, caught the general excitement and began to twitch at her half nets, hoping to see him.

But, of course, being Bertie, he arrived home exactly when he'd said he would, at six o'clock in the evening when everybody was at home and waiting for him.

It was wonderful to see him again, so tall and handsome in his soldier's uniform, hung about with bulky luggage, all straps and belts and great black boots, his legs bound in khaki puttees, a kit-bag on his back, a rifle over his shoulder.

Mabel flung herself at him bodily so that he had to lift her up and swing her about, big though she was. Col thumped him between the shoulder blades. Netta kissed him rapturously, declaring it was just as if he'd never been away. And Rose kissed him too, but she was surprised by how much he had changed. He looked taller and was certainly a lot less skinny, his face wind-tanned, his cheeks filled out, his mouth firm under the winged curves of a new soft moustache. And his bearing was different too. He stood and walked like a soldier, holding his head high, straight-spined in the stiff khaki of his new uniform and the stiff pride of his new and valued occupation.

But his behaviour hadn't changed in the least. He took charge of them at once, just as he'd always done.

'Right then,' he said when they'd finished their tea. 'Where we off to tonight? How d'you fancy a trip up the Halls?'

The days passed in a blur of excitement and pleasure. The sun woke them every morning and they went out every evening, as if they were all having a holiday.

When Wednesday came round, Bertie told Rose he thought it would be a lark for the two of them to go for a picnic, 'seeing it's your afternoon off.'

At that point, Rose remembered Muriel and was ashamed to realise that she'd been so happy she'd forgotten all about her until that moment. 'I promised to go out with my friend,' she said. 'You know – Muriel – the one I wrote to you about . . . Wednesday's our afternoon out.'

'Let her come and all then,' Bertie said at once. 'The more the merrier.'

'She's a bit shy,' Rose warned.

'Not with me she won't be.'

And rather to Rose's surprise, she wasn't. Bertie had her laughing within two minutes and telling jokes within five. In fact, the picnic was a great success, even though it was really too cold for eating out of doors and the sky over Wimbledon Common threatened rain all afternoon. But there was so much to talk about. Rose told them how Miss Monk collapsed and how impossible she was. Muriel told them how the builders had been arriving to give their estimates and imitated Mrs Monk telling them what she wanted, her tone getting steadily more acid – 'I trust you won't put *greasy fingers* on my Anaglypta. You will remember that my aspidistra is *a delicate plant*. You'll be so kind as to spare my stair carpet from any further depredations, *if* you please.' And Bertie responded by telling tall tales about his life in camp.

'Grub?' he joked. 'You never tasted nothink like it, I'm telling you. All cooked up in the same dixie it was, tea in the morning, stew at night.'

Both girls made a grimace. 'Ugh!'

'Couldn't tell the difference most of the time,' Bertie went on. 'We had tea with lumps of meat in it and stew with tea leaves. And if you think tea was bad, you should have seen the biscuits.'

'I don't think I'd want to,' Rose told him. 'It's a wonder you wasn't poisoned.'

'No,' he laughed back at her. 'It's good for you. Toughens you up. Toughest battalion in the army we are. Toughest and best.' He was glowing with pride. 'We got all sorts in our battalion. There's fellers from Whiteley's and Harrods – you should've seen *them* on parade – all left feet they was – and a platoon from over the river, dockers mostly. Toughest and best.'

'Are you all moving on together?' Muriel wanted to know.

'That's right,' Bertie grinned. 'All them months under canvas, waiting for the camp to be built and then the minute they got the last tile on the roof, it's "Oi, you lot, you're off ter Mansfield." '

Speaking of Mansfield reminded Rose of how soon this leave would be over. 'I wish you wasn't going so far away.'

Bertie decided to ignore that. 'What say we go up the Canters again on Friday evening?' he suggested and grinned at Muriel. 'You'll come with us, won'tcher?' he said.

She smiled at him. 'If I can get time off. I'd love to.'

'Tell them it's for the war effort.'

'I don't think that they'd believe me. But I might be able to persuade them. I've got two evenings owing.'

'So you'll come?'

'Yes. Thank you.'

That's torn it, Rose thought. I ought to have warned him about our Netta. She'll get the hump good and proper if we bring Mu along. I'll have to see if I can talk her round. I'll tell her tomorrow when we wake up and it's quiet. Break it to her gently.

But Netta was at home when they got in, sitting by the fire with her feet on the fender, and Bertie was in such an ebullient mood he broke the news to her at once, without being aware that he was breaking anything.

' 'Lo our Netta,' he said, ruffling her hair. 'We're all going up the Canters Friday. Whatcher think?'

Rose's heart sank at her sister's answer. 'Who's we all?' Netta wanted to know, her face suspiciously sharp.

'All of *us* and your friend Muriel.'

Now we're for it, Rose thought. We shall have a scene. But Netta was grinning.

'Yeh! Why not?' she said, and seeing Rose's expression, 'Can't say no to our Bertie can we? Not on his first leave.'

'Ta,' Rose said and smiled at her sister, conveying in one short word and one swift expression all that was needed – such is the loving shorthand of family conversation – relief at a quarrel ended, gratitude for Netta's sudden magnanimity, love in great measure. 'Ta, our Netta.'

So Muriel joined them on Friday evening at the Canterbury Music Hall and sat in the stalls between Bertie and Netta. It wasn't long before she found she had a lot in common with Netta Boniface. They laughed at the same jokes and sang the same choruses. After the show, when they all bought a penn'orth of chips, Muriel ate them greasy-fingered along with everybody else as they strolled to the tramstop. And there, after a moment's awkward hesitation, Bertie suddenly announced that he was going to see her home.

'Can't have her travelling on her own,' he joked. 'Not with all them rough soldiers about.'

Netta was intrigued but Rose had half expected it and headed the rest of her family off to the tramstop before any of them could say anything.

They were more than halfway home before Mabel noticed that he was missing.

'Where's our Bertie?' she wanted to know, her round face puckered. 'Where's our Bertie?'

'Gone a' courting,' Netta told her and laughed at her when she didn't understand, poking her in the ribs and making her giggle.

'That's putting it a bit strong,' Col said.

'I'll betcher!' Netta said.

'Would you mind?' Rose asked her.

Netta considered. 'No,' she said at last. 'Not really. Not if it come to it. I still think she's a bit posh but she's all right. Nice and cheerful.'

She wasn't just cheerful. She was rapturously happy. To be escorted home by this handsome young man and talked to all the way was making her feel delirious.

'It's funny,' Bertie said as their tram rattled over the points. 'I feel as if I've known you for weeks.' They were sitting so close together they were almost touching. 'Rose has been telling me all about you, see. I knew it was you the minute I seen you.'

'She talks about you all the time.'

'That's our Rose.'

'She's been ever such a good friend to me,' Muriel said. 'I mean, inviting me everywhere.'

'And why not?' he exclaimed. 'You're a good friend to her. Cuts both ways.'

They had reached their stop.

'Come out again with us tomorrow,' he said, as they walked past Chelsea's impressive terraces.

The suggestion was wonderful but it made her feel nervous. 'I don't think she'd let me.'

'Why not?'

'I'm supposed to read to her of an evening.'

'She don't possess you body and soul,' Bertie said. 'You tell her.'

It surprised the entire Boniface family when Muriel got permission to be out of the house every evening – except Tuesday – and all day on Saturday, which was the last precious day before Bertie had to return to camp.

'How *did* you do it?' Rose asked.

'I just asked,' Muriel said. 'They've got another lot of builders in, you see, measuring up, and they're all arguing and she's in such a state, I don't think she realised what I was asking.' It was making her giggle to think of it.

'Never mind how you did it,' Bertie said. 'Just make the most of it. That's what I say.'

So they did and great fun it was. And on that final Saturday Col took time off work and they all went to the station to see their soldier off.

'See you soon!' he yelled, being deliberately cheerful as the train bore him away. 'Ta-ta!'

It was midsummer before he was allowed home on leave again. And all through the spring and summer the news from France got worse and worse.

In April a terrible battle began near Ypres. The newspapers said the front was a hundred and twenty-five miles long and wrote about attacks and counter-attacks and 'valiant hand-to-hand fighting' but, at the end of it all, the army didn't seem to have advanced at all and the casualties were frightening. The French losses alone were sixty-nine thousand men killed and one hundred and sixty-four thousand wounded, and the British casualty lists were so appalling that nobody at home could be unaware of how savage this war had become.

Miss Monk opened her gardens for a bring-and-buy sale to raise funds for the wounded. The local hospital sent a contingent of their walking wounded to give support and the vicar made a speech in which he praised their courage and Miss Monk's public-spiritedness and said she was one of the pillars of their society.

At which Mrs Biggs sucked in her cheeks as if she were going to spit. 'Pillar my eye!' she said. 'Pile driver more like.'

But pillar or pile driver, the sale made a lot of money and the wounded soldiers seemed to have enjoyed it. Which had to be a good thing.

In May the papers were full of the latest atrocity story. A German submarine had torpedoed the great Cunard liner *Lusitania* and over a thousand men, women and children had been drowned.

'I think it's awful,' Muriel said when she and Rose met for their Wednesday outing. 'All those children killed. The Germans are terrible people.'

'Bertie'll sort them out once he gets over there,' Rose said, as they walked into the noise and bustle of the Kennington Road.

'I'm sure he will,' Muriel said. 'But sometimes I wish he wasn't going.' Then she stopped and blushed. 'Not that it's anything to do with me. What I mean is, I wouldn't want him to get hurt.'

'He'll look after himself,' Rose hoped, speaking more confidently than she felt. The thought of her brother being hurt was too dreadful to contemplate and Miss Monk's sale had made her very aware of how many men were wounded.

'I think he's the nicest man I've ever met,' Muriel divulged. 'He's so kind. And so fond of you all. He writes about you all the time.'

So they're writing to one another, Rose thought, and she gave her friend a guarded look that was half question and half approval.

'Yes,' Muriel said answering the look. 'He writes twice a week.'

'And you write back?'

81

'Of course.'

Rose decided to tease her a bit. 'Next thing you'll be telling me you've gone and fallen in love with him.'

'I think I might have,' Muriel confessed, biting her lip. 'I liked him the minute I saw him.'

'Only might have?' Rose said, still teasing.

'Would you mind if I had?'

Rose threw her arms around her friend's neck and hugged her hard. 'No,' she said. 'I wouldn't mind a bit. I think it'ud be lovely. You *would* have a family then, wouldn't you. Has he said anything?'

'Oh no,' Muriel said, quickly. 'Nothing like that. Not yet. It's only me thinking . . . I mean, there's nothing . . . I just feel it might be . . .'

But when Bertie came home for his next leave at the end of June, it was obvious that this *was* a courtship and that he was smitten.

By dint of working non-stop for three weeks before his arrival, Muriel managed to get every evening off except the sacrosanct Tuesday. Although they still went out as a family, Bertie escorted her home at the end of every evening. It didn't escape Rose's notice that he got back to Ritzy Street later and later as the week progressed, and that Muriel grew prettier by the day.

On the first evening he kissed her goodnight, holding her tentatively by the shoulders and brushing his lips against hers for a few daring seconds. On the second she put her arms round his neck and they kissed one another properly. By the last night of his leave they stayed on the Chelsea Embankment for nearly two hours. And between kisses he told her he thought he loved her.

'I think I love you too,' she said. She was perfectly sure about it now but she let her declaration echo his because she didn't want to sound forward.

'I wish I wasn't going back,' he said when he'd kissed her again.

'So do I.'

'I wish I could have this leave all over again.'

'There'll be others.'

But the next one turned out to be his embarkation leave.

'We won't waste a single minute of it,' Rose said, to cheer them all up. 'We'll save up for it and plan it all out and make it extra special.'

But even Rose, clear sighted as she was, couldn't have foreseen how very special it would turn out to be.

CHAPTER SEVEN

Bertie's embarkation leave was surprising right from the start. He'd written to say that he would be home about midday on Saturday but on Friday evening, just as Rose and her sisters were preparing the tea, there was the sound of army boots on the stairs and there he was.

Netta and Mabel rushed at him, shrieking with delight, to throw their arms round his neck and kiss him. And Rose, waiting her turn in her patient way, smiled at him through the blur of flailing arms and legs and found herself gazing into the eyes of a strange young man. A very handsome young man, with a soldier's cap on the back of his head, a shock of thick brown hair tumbling over his forehead and a wide, full-lipped mouth which was just beginning to spread in a smile as he caught her glance. Oh, a tender, beautiful mouth. A mouth made for kissing. Heavens! What a thing to be thinking and him a perfect stranger. But she thought it just the same – aware that her heart was beating much too fast and that she was staring at him as though she was mesmerised.

Then he and Bertie stepped out of the shadows on the landing and into the light of the room, and she saw that his eyes were brown and his lips were the colour of raspberries and, before she could stop herself, she realised she was thinking really immodest thoughts – imagining what it would be like to be kissed by a mouth like that. And that made her blush with confusion so that she had to turn aside and pretend to be busy with the bread and marge.

'This is Jack Jeary,' Bertie was saying. 'We been together since day one. He lives round here, don'tcher Jack. Me an' him, we're mates.'

'That's right,' Jack said. He had a gruff voice, which was rather a surprise seeing how handsome he was and, when he shook hands with them, very formally, one after the other, his hands were rough too. 'How do.'

'I said he could come back with me for an hour or two,' Bertie explained, 'Cause he says he's at a bit of a loose end. Which I don't believe, knowing him.'

They grinned at one another and Jack Jeary said, 'It's true. Straight up!' with the boldest expression on his face.

'Anyway,' Bertie said to Rose, 'I told him you'd give him a bit of tea. Is that all right?'

There was a trace of anxiety in his voice so Rose reassured him at once. 'Yes. Course.' But it was a problem and she'd have to think quickly to solve it. There was enough bacon but she'd bought only two slices of liver each. He can have one of mine, she decided, and Netta and Mabel can have three slices between them and then I can manage. 'Come in. Make yourself at home.'

It was the happiest meal. Col came rushing home when the liver was frying. He'd been to the off-licence and had an armful of bottles which he plonked down on the table so that he could thump his brother's arms and grab Jack Jeary's proffered hand in a rough greeting. 'I bought these fer tomorrow,' he said looking at the bottles. 'That's a bit a' luck, eh?'

'Shift your great feet,' Netta scolded them happily. 'How am I supposed to fry these onions with you all over the place?'

What with the awkwardness of all their equipment, the unyielding bulk of their uniforms and the length of their legs, the two soldiers seemed to fill the room. Netta and Mabel had to dodge between them as they tried to set the cloth and Rose was acutely aware of them. When they were huddled round the table ready to eat, they were wedged knee to knee. It set Mabel off into a fit of the giggles but Rose was disturbed by it and suddenly unsure of herself.

It was as if there'd been a light somewhere inside her

and some one had lit it and turned it right up until it was blazing. She saw everything so clearly and she was aware of her brother's friend all the time, keenly aware, even when she wasn't looking at him. She noticed everything, the way his hair fell across his forehead when he bent towards his plate, the way he broke the bread in half with strong rough fingers, the way he showed his front teeth when he laughed – such sharp teeth, milk-white and uneven – the way his eyes widened when he looked across the table and caught her glance.

'What say we all go out for a night on the town?' he suggested suddenly. 'My treat. What about the Gattis?'

'Thought you was meeting your mates,' Bertie said.

'Changed my mind,' Jack winked at him.

'You're a fine one, Jack Jeary.'

'You know me,' Jack said easily. 'What about the Gattis then?'

'It's a bug-hutch,' Bertie said.

'No it ain't. You ever been?'

'Once or twice.'

'Well then. You have some sport up the Gattis. They pelt the turns sommink rotten.'

Mabel was thrilled to hear that. 'Can we pelt them, Mr Soldier?' she asked.

' 'Oo said you was coming?' Col teased.

'Course she's coming, Jack said. 'I told you. My treat.'

'What about Muriel?' Bertie wanted to know. 'Is she coming over tonight? Did you say?'

But she wasn't, naturally, because she wasn't expecting him back till the next day.

'Pick her up on the way,' Jack Jeary suggested.

'They won't let her off,' Bertie said.

'Yes they will,' Jack Jeary replied. 'Leave it to me.'

So they all went to Chelsea first and the Bonifaces waited at the end of the road while Jack and Bertie strode off to knock at the door. It was a great surprise when they came back a few minutes later with Muriel smiling between them.

'How on earth did you manage that?' Rose asked.

'It was Jack's doing,' Bertie said, looking at his friend with admiration. 'He charmed the old lady.'

'Nothink to it,' Jack grinned. 'Putty in me hands she was.'

'He could charm the birds off the trees,' Bertie said.

Looking at him, Rose could well believe it.

'And a good job he can,' Muriel laughed. 'I'm very grateful to him.'

So they all went to the Gattis together and sat up in the tuppence ha'pennies in the balcony and joined in all the choruses and cheered when the magician was duly pelted – with bits of bread roll, orange peel, apple cores and some marvellously squashy tomatoes.

'He weren't half in a mess,' Mabel said delightedly as the stage was swept ready for the next turn.

'They give him the bird good and proper,' Jack encouraged her. 'Didn't I tell you it'ud be good?'

'Will they pelt another one, Mr Soldier?' Mabel wanted to know.

'Bound to, kid,' he told her. 'You watch.'

After the show they strolled off together through the darkened streets, Mabel, Netta and Col chattering and laughing, Bertie and Muriel happily arm in arm. And Rose found herself walking several paces behind the others, beside the handsome Jack. Being so close to him and without the noise and bustle of the rest of her family, she was suddenly tongue-tied.

But he was perfectly at ease. 'We don't wanna play gooseberry, do we,' he said. 'Not when they're sweet on each other.'

She was touched by his tact. 'No,' she said. 'We don't.'

'He's a good chap, your brother. One of the best. I got a lot a' time for him.'

'Yes. He is.'

'There's our tram,' he said. 'We shall have to scoot.' And as if it were a natural thing to do, he put a hand under her elbow and scurried her across the tramlines.

To be touched like that took her breath away. She was so close to his body she could feel the warmth of it. She was aware of the rough smell of his uniform, the scent of the cigarettes he'd been smoking all evening, she could even smell his sweat – salty and sharp and different. Then they were in the middle of the road and the contact was broken.

'You cut off to Chelsea then,' Jack said to Bertie. 'I'll look after this lot.'

'Saucy sevenpenny worth,' Netta cheeked him. 'We ain't kids. We can get home by ourselves, thank you very much.'

'I'm looking after our Mabel,' Jack said, winking at Rose as they climbed aboard. 'Ain't I sunshine?'

'Yes,' Mabel said, delighted to be looked after.

'Rather you than me,' Col teased, following his sister. 'You don't know what you've took on, mate, I'm telling you.'

But Jack seemed to be equal to anything. He sat between Mabel and Rose all the way home and flirted with them both.

'See you tomorrow,' he said when they reached their front door.

And Mabel said, 'Yes, *please!*'

It took Rose a long time to get to sleep that night and when she finally did, she dreamt that Jack was kissing her and telling her he loved her and woke with her heart pounding, feeling confused and extraordinarily happy.

Am I falling in love, she wondered. Is that what it is? Can you fall in love as quickly as this? She remembered Muriel saying, 'I liked him the minute I saw him.' And wondered how she would feel when she saw Jack Jeary again. And how she would get through a day's work without making mistakes.

He was back on the doorstep at eight o'clock the next evening, full of plans for another evening out. It disappointed Rose that he didn't offer to take her out on her own. But then Bertie didn't take Muriel out on her own either and they'd known one another a great deal longer.

They went to the pictures on their second evening and to the halls again on their third. And this time, when they parted at the front door, Col and Netta went leaping up the stairs, singing one of the choruses and dragging Mabel with them, so that Jack and Rose were left on the doorstep together.

'You don't have to go in just yet, do you,' he said, as she turned to follow them.

She didn't.

'Let's take a turn round the block.'

She laughed at that. 'It's a dead end,' she explained looking towards the brick wall at the end of the alley. 'It don't go nowhere down there.'

'It goes to where you live up here,' he said, flirting with her. 'That ain't nowhere. Not in my book.'

He offered her his arm, and she took it and held it, smiling at him. 'There's only one way we can go in this street,' she warned. 'Really.'

'Suits me,' he grinned. 'There's only one way I want to go.'

The words were spoken lightly but there was an intimacy about them that made her catch her breath. He was marvellously handsome in the gaslight, hair darkened, jaw line gilded, brown eyes gleaming like water.

'You've bowled me over,' he told her as they walked off together. 'You know that, don'tcher.'

'I didn't do it deliberate,' she felt she ought to excuse herself.

'No,' he said, making eyes at her. (Now *that* is deliberate, she thought.) 'I know *that*. That's the beauty of it. You just done it, that's all. Couldn't help yerself.'

'Is that bad?' she teased, making eyes back and wondering – Am I flirting? Is that it? It was an easy game to play, although there was danger in it as well as delight.

'Depends on you,' he said. They had turned the corner

away from the prying eyes of Ritzy Street and were heading towards Tyers Street.

'Does it?'

'You're the prettiest girl I've ever seen,' he said. 'What would you do if I was to kiss yer?'

She was bewitched, tremulous and breathless at such a question. It was as if he was reading her mind.

'If I'm speaking out of turn,' he said, putting his left hand over the fingers that held his arm, 'just say and I'll pipe down. Am I speaking out of turn?'

'No,' she said. 'I'm not *quite* sure, mind, but I don't *think* you are.'

'I'd never do nothink to upset you,' he said. 'If you say, "Buzz off Jack Jeary, I don't want nothink to do with the likes of you," I'll buzz like a bee. Straight off.'

'That'ud be sommink worth seeing,' she laughed at him.

He pretended to misunderstand her, daring her with his eyes. 'Is that it then? Have I got me marching orders?'

'Not yet,' she said.

'I can stick around then?'

'For a little while.'

'How long?'

'Ten minutes. How's that?'

'Nowhere near enough.'

She was in control of the situation now, knowing what to say. Somehow, as they'd flirted he'd passed on the message that nothing would be attempted or spoken without her permission. They walked on in silence for several happy yards and he went on holding her fingers.

Soon they would be in Kennington Lane and the enveloping darkness would be left behind. He stopped and turned them both so that they were standing face to face.

'When I first seen you, that afternoon,' he said, 'I thought you looked like an angel but now . . .'

'Now?' she prompted, flirting again.

'Now, you look like a right little devil.'

'That's your influence.'

'Well I should hope so, seeing there's only me around.'

They were so close together she could see the reflection of the street lamp in the dark pupils of his eyes, and feel his breath lifting the wispy curls on her forehead. Was he going to kiss her now? He'd as good as promised and she wanted him to. So much.

Her hand was still resting lightly on his arm and as she wondered he picked it up very gently, lifted it to his lips and kissed her fingers. It was the merest touch and yet it made her lips tingle and her scalp prickle with pleasure as though her hair were standing on end.

'You're gorgeous,' he said softly. The words were little more than a breath, and that lovely mouth of his was so close that if she leant forward – just a little . . . She swayed towards him, breathless and wide-eyed. And then they were kissing.

It was everything she'd dreamt it would be, tender passionate, prolonged. Oh everything and more. The rest of the world was lost. London didn't exist. There was no Great Britain, no Germany, no France, no such thing as war. Only this languorous, magical sensation going on and on and getting more and more pleasurable. 'Gorgeous! Gorgeous!'

She had no idea how long they stayed in one another's arms that first evening. Time is relative when you are bewitched. But at last they were back in Ritzy Street again and finally had to part.

'See you tomorrow,' he said. And winked at her.

Afterwards, when she was lying in bed re-living the evening, she realised that he hadn't said he loved her. But he didn't need to, did he? Not after all that kissing.

In the days that followed she lived like a creature under a spell, dreaming of love. She spent the day aching to see him again and missed him the moment they parted. It was as if there was no one and nothing else in the world.

I'd do anything for him, she thought. He's so handsome and I love him so much. But she couldn't think of anything particular she could do. Not until he started making plans for their last evening together.

They'd been to the local flea pit and were all walking home. 'Tell you what,' Jack said. 'What say we go up West on our last evening and make a real night of it. Up the Alhambra. We could take a box and have supper and everything, the full works.'

Rapturous agreement. What a lark! What style! What a way to end their leave!

'But what shall we wear?' Muriel worried to Rose when their three young men had popped into the off-licence. 'You have to be a bit dressy in the West End.'

'I could run something up for you, if you'd like,' Rose offered. 'A new blouse, maybe.'

'Could you?' Muriel said. 'That would be lovely. I'd pay for the material and the cottons and everything.'

'I might even try me hand at a dress,' Rose said, feeling daring. 'There's lots of paper patterns about and the new styles are ever so pretty. I reckon I could do it, don't you? Don't say nothing to Bertie and Jack though. I'd like to surprise them.'

She surprised herself by the ease with which the two new garments were made. It took her every spare and secret moment for the next two days but the resulting dress and blouse were stunning.

She chose a heavy cotton in hyacinth blue for the dress and a rose pink for Muriel's blouse and she bought sufficient material in both colours for off-cuts to be used as trimming. Muriel's pink blouse was soon made, with a triple collar and long cuffs all bound with blue. Then she turned her attention to the dress. She cut the skirt full and to the new fashionable mid-calf length, adding a deep band of rose pink at the hem to finish it off. It took time to sew but presented no problems. However, the bodice was complicated, with long straight sleeves, a low V neck and a shawl collar edged with a frill. And that needed thought and care.

Apart from Bertie, the entire family and several of the

neighbours were in on the secret, popping into her bedroom when Bertie was out so that they could pull back the covering sheet on her tailor's dummy and check on the progress of the work.

Mrs Cartwright, from three doors up, declared it was the prettiest dress ever. 'Can't wait to see it on and that's a fact.'

But in the event it didn't get worn.

On that special Friday evening, the family were ready and waiting long before Jack and Muriel arrived. But there was no sign of Rose.

'I can't make it out,' Netta worried. 'She's always home on the stroke of six of a Friday and here it is twenty past. I've half a mind to go down an' see what's keeping her.'

'You do that,' Bertie instructed. 'We don't want to miss the first half. Tell her to look sharp.'

But there was no looking sharp in Monk House that evening. Miss Monk had arranged an impromptu dinner party for Edmund and Louella and, when she told her staff about it that afternoon, she was insistent that both her parlourmaids should be there to serve at table.

When Netta came knocking at the back door, it was seven o'clock and Rose was still in her uniform and hard at work.

'Tell them to go on,' she said. 'And don't make that face. I can't help it. Tell Bertie I'll catch up with you later. I can make me own way there.'

Jack had other ideas about that. 'You lot go on,' he said. 'I'll wait here. She can't travel up West on her own. I'm not having that.'

So they left him sitting in Bertie's chair by the fire. Which was where Rose found him when she finally got home.

She was tired and disappointed. There was a burn on her right hand and her feet ached. But the minute she saw him, rising from the chair to catch her in his arms and kiss her, she felt better at once.

'Come on,' he said. 'If we look lively we shall just be in time for the supper.'

There was no time to wash and change into her new dress. She scrubbed her hands and took a damp flannel to her face and then they were off, running to the tramstop, hand in hand. And they *were* in time for supper so the evening wasn't spoilt and the second half was spectacular.

But it was the end of their leave, however wonderful it was, and Saturday morning came round much too quickly. The entire family went to Waterloo station to see them off, taking Muriel with them. Col joked that seeing Bertie off at the station was getting to be a habit.

But this parting was no joke. The impossible seconds before the two men had to climb aboard were fraught with unspoken worries, tremulous with pride, anguished by a dragging sense of imminent loss.

Chatter was too trivial for a moment like this. None of them knew what to say. Rose brushed invisible dust from her brother's tunic. 'Don't you go getting yourself killed,' she admonished, pretending to scold so as to make light of her feelings.

'You know me,' he said. But his face was strained.

'I'll look after him for you,' Jack Jeary promised.

'You!' Bertie tried to joke. 'You couldn't look after yourself.'

'Don't you believe it,' Jack said, looking straight at Rose. 'I can look after the both of us.' And the expression on his face was a promise.

It wasn't possible to keep up the pretence. 'Oh please do!' she begged, turning to touch his arm. 'I couldn't bear it if anything happened to you.' How can I say goodbye to you, Jack Jeary, she grieved, knowing we might never see one another again?

He put his arms round her – right there in the open air with everyone looking – and kissed her lovingly. 'I'll be back,' he promised into her hair when the kiss was done and they stood with their arms still wrapped around each other.

Netta and Mabel and Collum took this without comment. They merely looked away while it went on and

94

busied themselves by kissing Bertie goodbye. But Bertie was looking at Muriel and had put out a hand to pull her towards him.

'Write to me,' he said, as they moved towards one another.

Her face was very pale. 'I will, I promise. Every day.'

Public though it was, he couldn't part from her without one last embrace. He scooped her into his arms, quite violently, and kissed her long and hard.

Tears fell from her eyes as the kiss went on. They ran down her cheeks into the corners of his kissing mouth but they didn't stop him. 'I love you,' she said as they drew apart.

There was no more time. The guard was shrilling his infernal whistle, the engine was puffing up unnecessary steam, doors were opening and banging shut in a terrible bullying way. All along the platform, soldiers tore themselves from the clinging arms of their loved ones and climbed bulkily aboard. They were going. Framed in the windows and already more like pictures than living men. Going. Growing smaller and smaller as the train pulled them away. Blurred by distance and tears. Going.

CHAPTER EIGHT

The brigade left for France in the early hours of the morning of November 16th, 1915. It was bitterly cold and as they crunched along the frozen lane to Tidworth station, it began to snow, white flakes curtaining the darkness all around them.

'Sod this for a game a' soldiers,' Jack grumbled, humping his kit into a more comfortable position between his shoulder blades, but he was grinning as he grumbled and the grin made Bertie feel more cheerful.

Now that they were actually on their way to the front they were both nervous although neither of them admitted it. After twelve months' training, they were so accustomed to army routine that they didn't talk about what was happening to them. They simply went where they were told, carried along by orders – even now when they were off to war.

There was a brass band on the platform, shivering and stamping their feet, but ready to play them off with 'Auld Lang Syne' and that kept their spirits up too. Nevertheless, it was hard to be leaving England – valiant though their mission was – and especially for Bertie, now that he knew he'd met the girl he wanted to marry.

Not that he said anything about *that* to Jack. Emotions were private matters and he didn't want to look soppy. Those impassioned kisses at the station had caused him enough embarrassment on the journey back to camp, without adding to it. Still, at least going on like that had given the game away, so there wasn't any need to talk about it. At the moment, they had a twelve-hour journey to Folkestone to contend with and then a sea crossing, to say nothing of what was in store for them in France.

Kidding was really the only possible means of communication in circumstances like that.

It was snowing in Boulogne when they arrived and still snowing when they finally came to a halt at a village called Steenebecque, where they were billeted in farm sheds and bedded on straw. They couldn't keep warm on that first night no matter how much straw they packed about them and no matter how hard they tried. They lay awake, tossing and turning and listening to the distant roar of the guns. And that chilled them even further because they knew the front was no more than twenty miles away.

'How long d'you think it'll be before we're there?' Bertie wondered into the musty darkness. It was okay to worry at night and in a whisper.

'Don't ask me,' Jack whispered back. 'I'm just a poor bloody infantryman.'

But there didn't seem to be any rush to get them into the front line, as Bertie was happy to report in his first letter home – when he finally had the leisure to write it. By then they'd been marched on to Cambrin to join the 2nd Division, 99th Brigade for a twelve-day instruction in trench warfare so the fighting felt a great deal closer. But Bertie kept both his letters cheerful.

'It is snowing like billy-oh here,' he wrote to Rose. 'We had a good crossing. The sea was calm. Jack and me thought we was in for a storm so that was a relief. We been here three days now. Not going up the line just yet, so they say. Grub is quite good. First three nights we slept in a barn now we are in billets. It used to be a girls' school. There are baths in the basement so we keep pretty clean. We are both well. Jack sends his love. They have some pretty cards here, they call them silks, they are all embroidery. I will get you one if you like. Hope you will write back soon. Letters mean a lot when you are out here.'

Then he licked his pencil trying to think of something else to say.

'Tell her about that bloke with the bayonet,' Jack suggested.

'Why don't *you*?' Bertie retorted.

But Jack only shrugged.

The gesture made Bertie feel annoyed. 'I'd've thought after all that carry-on at the station, you'd've written every day,' he said.

'What carry-on?' Jack said, grinning.

'*You* know,' Bertie said, embarrassed to have to talk about it. 'All that kissing.'

'You know me,' Jack said. 'I kiss all the girls.'

'This one's my kid sister.'

'I know mate. And very nice too. I'll write to her one of these days. It's just I ain't much of a one for writing letters. Perhaps I'll get her one of them silks. She'd like that.'

'She'd like a letter better.'

'A letter better!' Jack laughed, turning criticism aside with a joke. 'You're a poet and you don't know it.'

Bertie didn't insist because he could see Jack wasn't going to write. But it upset him, after the way he'd kissed Rose goodbye. Not writing after that wasn't nice. I hope he ain't leading her up the garden path, he thought. And then felt ashamed of such suspicions because Jack was a good mate.

But the next day the mail arrived from England and he discovered another reason for his mate's reluctance to put pen to paper. There were four letters for Rifleman Boniface, one each from Rose, Col, Netta and Muriel, and Rose had written a postscript to Jack.

'There y'are,' Bertie said tossing the letter across. 'That's for you. That bit on the bottom.'

Jack was sitting on an upturned biscuit tin, drinking a mug of tea. He looked at the letter for a long time, creasing his forehead into folds like corrugated iron. 'I can't quite make it out,' he confessed at last. 'Read it to me, would you?'

'Whatcher mean, you can't make it out?' Bertie said, bristling at the implied insult to his sister's calligraphy. 'She's got lovely writing our Rose. Anyone could read it.

You got a sauce, Jack Jeary, saying you can't make it out.'

Jack gave the letter back to his friend. He looked shamefaced and it was a quite a long time before he could bring himself to answer. 'To tell the truth,' he said, 'I can't – sort of – read it. What I mean is – I can't make out the words.'

'What, none of 'em?'

'Well some. Some a' the little words. I can read me name.'

'Can't you write neither?'

It was plainly a bitter confession. 'No,' Jack said, looking down at his blunt fingers. ' 'Fraid not. Never got the hang of it. You won't say nothink to your sister, will you. She'd think I was a right Charlie.'

Now everything was clear. 'She wouldn't think none the worse of you,' Bertie consoled. 'Not our Rose.'

'Well I'd rather she didn't know.'

'All right,' Bertie reassured him. 'I'll read this for you, shall I?'

'Ta,' Jack said. 'I'll get her a silk. You could put a little message for me, couldn'tcher?'

So a silk was bought and the message sent *'Kind regards from Jack.'*.

Rose was very disappointed by it. After being kissed goodbye so publicly, she'd been hoping for a love letter, so the postcard – beautiful though it was with its embroidered roses and forget-me-nots and its pretty pink legend, *'A Kiss from France'* – was a let-down. But she tried to be sensible. He'd never told her he loved her. It was early days yet. I'll write him a nice long letter to thank him, she decided. I can send it with Bertie's and perhaps he'll write to me properly next time. I expect they keep them too busy for much letter writing.

But it was only another postcard the next time and the third message was a postscript on the end of Bertie's letter, explaining that Jack had asked him to drop her a few lines because he wasn't much of a one for writing.

'He never writes me a letter,' she said to Muriel. 'You'd

think he would, wouldn't you, after all the time we spent together and – well – everything.'

'I think they have to be careful what they write,' Muriel said. 'It all gets read by the censor. He can't very well say what he'd like to, can he? Not with somebody looking over his shoulder. Perhaps it puts him off.'

'Bertie writes to you,' Rose pointed out. 'He ain't put off.'

That was true. He was writing at length now and declaring his love more strongly with every letter. But this wasn't the time to tell Rose. This was the time for a gentle white lie. 'But he's very careful,' she said. 'Like they all have to be, I suppose. There are so many things they're not allowed to say.'

'I wish they weren't in France,' Rose sighed. 'I know that's unpatriotic but it's a fact. If they were still in England, they could come home on leave and we could see them again and they could tell us what they really thought. It's awful to be parted now.'

'Let's send them something lovely for Christmas,' Muriel suggested.

'It was going to be over by *last* Christmas,' Rose observed sadly. 'We all thought Bertie'd be out there, fight for a few months and come home covered in glory. And now look where we are.'

'I wonder where *they* are,' Muriel said. 'They can't tell us that either. *"B.E.F. Somewhere in France."* It could be anywhere.'

'I wonder whether they're thinking about us,' Rose said.

But their two soldiers were in the front line for the first time and they were too overwhelmed to be able to think about anything at all.

The route march to the trenches had been long and exhausting; beside the weight of their packs they'd also been carrying ammunition. Although the paths were frozen dry they were so badly rutted it was hard for the soldiers to keep their footing. Bertie slipped and fell

100

within minutes of setting out and had to be hauled to his feet again by two of his mates because he was too heavily laden to struggle up on his own. By mid-afternoon they were all chafed and footsore. And at that point the guns began to fire from somewhere behind them, thudding – surprisingly gently – one after the other, like somebody beating a mat against a wall.

Looking up, Bertie saw that the grey sky ahead of them was hung with puffballs of white smoke and, as he watched, another one appeared suddenly, as if by magic.

'That must be the front,' he said to Jack.

They both stopped trudging for an instant to look at it. It wasn't like any sort of battlefield they'd ever imagined – just a wide expanse of frozen grassland broken by a ragged line of dark earthworks. No sign of any soldiers or guns or tanks. In fact, surprisingly peaceful.

'Keep moving!' the corporal shouted at them.

They struggled on, bent almost double under the weight they were carrying and they were both thinking the same thing. If that's all it is, perhaps it won't be so bad after all. But after a few hundred yards the smells began, strong, rank, sickly smells that filled their nostrils and made them retch.

'Good God! What is it?' Jack hissed.

'Rotting meat,' Bertie hissed back.

But then they passed a stunted clump of trees and saw what it was. A mule team had received a direct hit and all four animals lay where they'd died, their bodies torn apart, green with decomposition and stinking. As the brigade passed, about a dozen large brown rats slithered from the belly of the nearest mule and scurried off in every direction. They were the biggest and most bloated that Bertie had ever seen.

'Christ!' he said, and he was thinking, so that's what happens to you out here. You get blown to bits and the rats eat you.

The smells got worse, the nearer they got to the support

trenches. Besides decomposing flesh they could recognise human shit, horse manure, ammonia, cordite.

'That's war,' the corporal said, trudging beside them. 'That's the stink of war, lads. You'll get used to it.'

There were a lot of other things to get used to in those first stinking days. They spent the first three in the support trenches, where they rebuilt a parapet, bailed out foul water from the pits under the duck boards, kept their rifles clean, learnt to distinguish between the sound of shells, sling bombs, grenades and trench mortars, kept their heads down when the wizz-bangs went over, and lived on biscuits and stew, all taste ruined by the pervasive smell. On the fourth day they were sent to the firing line, three men to a bay the full length of a trench that wound like a snake.

Even here there was a sort of routine. The front was fairly quiet when they arrived. The Germans fired Minniewerfers for half an hour or so during the afternoon and there was some answering fire from the British trenches, but that was all.

'Nothing much happens by day,' their sergeant told them. 'Use your periscope and you can see them coming. It's night time you got to be on the *qui vive*.'

That night Bertie and Jack and a boy called Muffin took it in turns to keep watch, one man on guard, standing on the firestep, one cleaning the trench, one snatching an hour's sleep huddled against the sandbags. It was eerie out there in the darkness. From time to time a Verey light would meander up into the night sky and the shell-pocked landscape of no man's land would be lit up like a stage set. They watched as long shadows extended from the broken trunks of the dead trees and then receded like some unnatural tide as the light dropped back to earth. Now and then there was a bang somewhere along the line, once a rattle of rifle fire, and towards dawn there was another flurry of snow.

Breakfast was a slice of cold ham and a mug of tea three quarters full. By then all three of them were feeling cold and hungry. But at least they were alive, they hadn't been under fire and, as Muffin said, 'we only got two more days and we'll be back in the support trench.'

'Your turn to put the periscope up, Muffin,' Jack said. 'Go and have a look-see.'

Muffin put down his mug. 'You don't half bully me,' he laughed and walked out of the bay and along the trench to the bend where they'd got the best sighting the previous afternoon.

What happened next was so sudden that it was over before Jack and Bertie could take it in. There was a blinding flash of light, a terrible roar. Earth and débris shot up into the air as they were blown backwards against the side of the trench, gasping for breath. Then it was over and there was a horrible silence broken by the patter of debris falling back to earth. Bertie realised that he was shaking, Jack that he'd shit himself. And they couldn't see Muffin at all.

'Muffin!' Bertie yelled, finding the strength to run. 'Muff! Where are you?'

He was lying on his side at the bottom of the trench, covered in blood and twitching in the most terrifying way. They knelt beside him, turning him gently. And saw that the side of his head had been blown away and that there. was a gaping hole in his chest full of torn flesh and bits of bone. His limbs might be twitching but the one eye left in his shattered face was already glazed in death.

'Jesus!' Jack said.

Somebody was yelling for stretcher bearers. There were feet alongside them in the trench. The corporal was shouting orders. 'Who's on guard?'

There were things to be done, orders to obey. 'Me, Corp,' Bertie said.

'Then get bloody guarding!'

So this is war, Bertie thought, looking away from the carnage in the trench, as he pressed his shaking belly against the sandbags. One minute you're alive and laughing, the next you're dead. Dear sweet Jesus!

Sickness rose in this throat and he remembered inconsequential things – how Mum gave him peppermint when he was sick as a boy, Dad trudging off to work, Col mending boots, Rose, calm-eyed at her sewing-machine. If only he could be back in Ritzy Street, safe and warm by the fire, with her and the kids. Or back at the vinegar factory. Anywhere but here in this God-forsaken place.

Oh Sis, he thought, if only you knew. But he couldn't tell her. He could never tell anybody. Not about this. It was too obscene.

CHAPTER NINE

'They're going to introduce conscription,' Edmund said. He put down his copy of the *Evening News* on the hall table and took off his coat and hat, moving delicately, his long body stooped and weary. He was late home that evening because one of his classes had run over time and he was afraid Louella might scold. Offering her a tit-bit of news about the war was a way to deflect any possible ill temper.

Louella was checking her reflection in the hall mirror. 'Quite right too,' she said firmly. 'I'm sick of all these mimsy-pimsy young men. They've had their chance. They could have volunteered if they'd wanted to. Now they'll have to do their duty whether they like it or not.'

Edmund was upset by her callous tone. 'Would you say the same if they were to conscript me?' he wondered, adjusting his tie and making his self-deprecating face.

Her answer was casual and crushing. 'Don't be silly, Edmund. You're too old.' She turned away from her image, her tone changing. 'Come and see the studio.'

The eagerness in her voice could mean triumph or disaster. 'Not more problems,' Edmund dreaded as he followed her up the stairs.

'No, my dear,' Louella reassured him. 'I think we can safely say we've finished with problems. They can conscript Mr Hurlingham as soon as they like. And all his dreadful workmen. They might be a bit more useful in the trenches.'

'You mean it's finished?'

She led him up the third flight of stairs and the fourth. And there it was, their studio, cream walls, north-facing window, William Morris carpet splendidly green and yellow, artistically draped William Morris curtains, two easels set up, two canvases stretching, brushes and paints lined up on the table. Finished. There were even three of her oil paintings strategically hung to face the door. And not a sign of a workman anywhere. Not even so much as a dirty rag.

'Good gracious!' he said.

'They finished the last bit of painting this morning,' Louella said, well pleased by his reaction. 'I've been working flat out all day to get it ready for you. Well? What do you think?'

He kissed her with relief and gratitude. 'I think it's splendid,' he said.

'Now,' she said, actually kissing him back, 'you will be a proper artist.'

In the warmth of her approval and the unexpected pleasure of her kiss, he almost thought he might. 'The light is quite excellent,' he said, walking towards their new tall windows.

'Not an extravagance?'

'No my dear. Take back all I said.'

'The view is quite breathtaking,' Louella said, strolling across the studio towards it. 'I've been watching the sunset. In fact, I think you will find that window quite an inspiration.' Then her tone changed abruptly from a purr to a snarl. 'What's *he* doing here?' she said.

'Who?' Edmund said, looking down.

'Cedric. That's who. Isn't that his car?'

It was – and Winifred blundering from the passenger seat.

'They're up to something,' Louella said and went downstairs to pre-empt it, whatever it was.

Winifred was red-nosed with the cold and gushing with embarrassment and curiosity. 'Louella my dear, we were just passing – Cedric's been to Smithfields, haven't you Cedric? – and we thought we couldn't go home without calling in to see how you are.'

'We are well,' Louella said, narrowing her eyes. 'As you see. Allow me to take your coat.'

Winifred struggled out of her coat and disentangled her hat from her elaborate curls. 'And what *is* going on in your attic?' she said. 'Is it a new window or what?'

Damn woman, Louella thought. Now I shall have to show her and she'll make capital out of it as sure as eggs are eggs. But she smiled her sweetest smile and led the way upstairs. 'Come and see,' she said gaily.

They were both very annoyed. Cedric said it was 'very fine' and then drew in his mouth so tightly it was little more than a red line of jealous disapproval. And Winifred's mouth positively fell open.

'My word!' she said. 'That must have cost a pretty penny.'

Her reaction was gratifying to Louella's *amour propre*. 'These things don't come cheap,' she said, waving an artistic hand so that her bracelets gave a pleasing chink. 'You get what you pay for, I always say.'

Or what you can make Augusta pay for, Winifred thought furiously, because don't tell me you can afford it on a lecturer's pay.

But Louella wasn't telling her anything. She was busy playing the hostess.

'I mustn't keep you up here in the cold,' she said in her charming way. 'That wouldn't do at all, would it Edmund. Let's go back downstairs, shall we? Would you like some tea?'

After their unwanted guests had consumed an unnecessary quantity of fruit cake, spilt tea all over her Brussels lace cloth and departed, Louella turned to her husband and snorted with rage.

'Your damned brother,' she said. 'I'm sorry Edmund. I know a lady shouldn't swear. But really! "*Driving past*." Who do they think they're kidding? They came to make mischief.'

'Not out of brotherly love?' Edmund quizzed, one eyebrow raised.

'They don't know the meaning of the word.'

'Then out of brotherly jealousy, perhaps. They were green with envy. You've got to admit that.'

'Serve them right,' Louella said. 'But they'll make trouble. You see if I'm not right.'

But you knew that, Edmund thought. You've known it all along. We've both known it all along. If we cajole Augusta into giving us money and we spend it ostentatiously, Cedric is bound to find out. But he kept his opinions to himself. 'Time for our drink,' he suggested. 'What gastronomic delights do you have in store for me tonight?'

Louella wasn't interested in food. 'Mutton chop, I think,' she said vaguely. 'With onion sauce.'

I shall have indigestion, Edmund thought, pouring a Dubonnet with poker-faced resignation. If only there were some way he could tell her to avoid mutton chops without provoking a sulking fit. He remembered the lovely simplicity of the Pre-Raphaelite paintings he'd been studying that afternoon and grieved that life was so complicated and so messy.

Louella was recovering, soothed by the warmth of her aperitif.

'I think I shall paint for an hour or two after dinner,' she decided. 'The view from the window is quite inspirational. What do you think?'

Edmund told her it was a good idea, thinking she could paint while he suffered the pangs of ill-digested mutton.

'I shan't let them upset me,' Louella said. She took a cigarette from the silver box on the dresser and tapped it briskly on the lid, feeling controlled and sophisticated. 'The important thing is to paint. You ought to try a landscape, you know Edmund.'

'Not my style,' Edmund demurred. He was honest about his lack of talent and knew that a landscape would be beyond him. If he had a choice he would have preferred to paint a portrait. That was what he'd always done best. A quiet portrait of a quiet face with hidden depths. Somebody like Miss Spencer, for example. She would be a challenge. He'd been watching her ever since she started work and had been intrigued by how guarded

108

she was. Sometimes, when he knew she wasn't looking, he found himself examining the planes of her face, fascinated by the green tones in her skin and the unexpected colour of her eyes, which had an amber translucence like pale ale, and by the woven mesh of shades that would have to be attempted in order to catch the curious quality of her hair. And then there was her lack of expression. For most of the time her face was so guarded and withdrawn it looked two-dimensional – which was a challenge in itself. But now and then, when he made a joke or when Louella was at her most outrageous, that little flat face would change, the cheeks rounding out, the eyes glinting, the contours suddenly and miraculously altered into a sort of laughing devilment. Now if he could catch *that*, he really could consider himself a painter.

Louella's drawl cut into his thoughts. 'I think the time has come for us to exhibit,' she said.

'Us?' Edmund queried, eyebrows leaping in alarm.

'Why not?' she said. 'Your work is quite good enough for exhibition. Just think if we were both to be hung in the same season. What a success that would be!'

'Success?' Edmund said drily. 'It would be a miracle.'

She took a nice long puff from her cigarette. 'You're such a tease,' she said.

Out in the damp streets beyond Louella's inspirational window the traffic splashed and rattled towards Kennington. Cedric, grappling with an intractable gear-stick and the onset of a headache, grumbled as the rain streaked his windscreen.

'I can't see a damned thing, Winifred,' he complained. 'Why don't they light the damn streets properly?'

'I shall have something to say to that sister of yours,' Winifred growled. '*You* get cut out of her will for asking for money for munitions and she's shelling out a fortune for a silly studio.' She was working herself up, ready to fight, steaming with righteous indignation. 'She's gone too far this time. Much, much too far.'

By the time they burst into Augusta's parlour they had talked themselves into a temper. Their entry was so furious that they set the room a-tremble. The gas lights popped and flickered in the draught. The lustres rattled. The lampshade bounced its silken fringe. The very flames of the fire leapt sideways as if they were trying to escape the wrath to come.

Their onrush of fury steeled Augusta. 'Why Cedric dear,' she said, ice-cold with disapproval. 'How nice to see you.'

'I shan't stand on ceremony,' Cedric said, standing on the hearthrug. 'We've just been to Chelsea.'

'Fancy,' Augusta said. 'How nice for you. It's more than I have.'

The implication of what she'd just said stopped Cedric in his tracks. 'Do you mean to say you've given them all that money and they haven't even invited you round to see what they've done with it?'

'Exactly.'

Brother and sister were both changing direction but Winifred didn't notice. She was still riding her fury and was too angry to understand what had just been said. 'I think it's a disgrace,' she cried, sitting herself in the armchair. 'It was *not* nice for us. It was *very* unpleasant. It was an experience I would not wish to repeat. You refused to consider our request for a small sub for *munitions* and you've just shelled out hundreds for an artist's studio. Where's your patriotism? Where's your sense of fair play? Where's your family loyalty?'

'Be that as it may,' Cedric said, turning his backside to the fire so that he could warn his wife with a scowl as well as lift his coat to warm his buttocks. 'What we actually came for, was to ask you out to dinner. *Wasn't it Winifred.*'

But she was still in full flow. '*Cedric* asked you for money to help the war effort. But *that* wasn't good enough. Oh no! We can't help the *war effort* when Edmund and Louella need a studio. This is all her doing.

110

Here's our poor soldiers dying for want of ammunition and you're prepared to waste money on an artist's studio.'

Then she noticed that Cedric was swaying like a cockerel in mid-crow, stretching up onto his toes and dropping back again, up and down, up and down. The see-saw motion looked threatening. He'd always been so determined, even as a young man, shouting her down to get his own way. Now, middle-aged and overweight, he made her think of a steamroller gathering power ready to squash her flat. 'What?' she said.

'Out to dinner,' he urged her. 'That's what we came for, isn't it. To invite Augusta out to dinner.'

She recovered her loyalty at last. 'Yes, yes,' she agreed. 'That's right.'

'Louella's upset her,' he explained. 'Let's go somewhere really nice, eh Augusta? And you can tell us all about it. I'll bet she's been putting you through the mill to get that money. She has, hasn't she?'

'She was insistent,' Augusta said. 'Where are you taking me? The "Blue Moon" can still manage a good steak.'

That evening they managed three and Augusta ate hers with gusto while her brother told her what he thought of Louella.

'Greed,' he said. 'That's what it all boils down to. She's always been after your money, my darling. Well you know that as well as I do. Remember how she nagged poor Daddy to buy her that awful silk dress. On and on and on.'

Augusta remembered the dress. 'She looked a freak in it,' she said. 'But then she never was much to look at.'

'We've got the looks, old thing.' The restaurant was full of hothouse flowers and there were pink candles glowing on the table between them. He'd ordered two bottles of wine and she'd already drunk one dry. It was the perfect setting for flattery.

Augusta smiled and bridled at him in the candlelight. She always felt beautiful by candlelight. 'Yes, we have, haven't we.'

111

'No wonder all the men fell in love with you.'

'I could have had my pick you know,' she confided. 'I've never been short of suitors. And they're always so attentive. But gentlemen, naturally. I seem to attract the better class. Mr Tilling, my solicitor . . .'

'That's better,' Cedric said, leaning across the table to pat her hand.

The caress pleased her. 'What is?'

'To see you smile. You've got a lovely smile, you know.'

Augusta smiled again.

'It's wretched of Louella to put you through the mill like that.'

'Her and her stupid studio,' Winifred said, playing up gamely now she knew what was expected of her.

'She said it was for Edmund,' Augusta said, gulping more wine.

'Well it's not his paintings on the wall,' Winifred told her. 'That's all I can say. It's full of her awful daubs.'

Augusta closed her eyes and shuddered. 'That's what I was afraid of. Poor Edmund.'

Cedric and Winifred were in full command now, sure of their ground. A third bottle of wine was ordered, a lavish sweet chosen, an after-dinner brandy decided upon. For the next hour, Louella's character was analysed and demolished, Augusta's applauded and supported. By the time the meal was over she had been wined and dined into a condition that was almost mellow.

'It *has* been nice to see you again,' she told them as Cedric drove her home. 'Don't leave it so long next time.'

'Actually,' Cedric said, 'I shall be up again next week. I've got to visit the factory. To see if I can raise some funds.'

'You got involved with it then?' Augusta said.

'Oh yes,' Cedric lied. 'Got to help the war effort you know. Can't let our brave boys go to war without shells and bullets. That wouldn't do at all.'

'You're a good man, Ceddy,' his sister said, her voice

112

slurred with wine and sentimental affection. 'We've had our ups and downs over the years but you're a good man.'

'I do my best,' Cedric said modestly, noting how woozy she was. 'And of course, this is very dear to my heart, looking after the troops.' He turned towards her briefly, gave her his most affectionate smile and waited hopefully.

'I tell you what,' Augusta decided. They'd been so kind to her all evening and Louella had really been foul. 'How would it be if I gave you some money for this factory?'

'It would be an act of patriotism, my dear. Nothing less.'

'Well it's only fair,' Augusta said, warmed by his praise. 'After all, I've wasted enough on that stupid studio, thanks to Louella.'

Cedric waited again, willing his wife to stay silent.

'How much would be appropriate?' Augusta asked.

This would have to be handled very delicately. 'Well it's up to you my dear. It's your money. A hundred is what most investors put in. I started off with one hundred and fifty. It was lavish, I'll admit, but in such a good cause . . .'

'Two hundred,' Augusta suggested, delighted to be topping his offer. 'How would that be?'

'It would be generous in the extreme.'

'You shall have a cheque,' Augusta said, warm with wine and goodwill. 'A gift for my brother. You don't have to mention my name to the company. I'd rather you didn't, you understand.' They had arrived at her front door. 'Come in for a few minutes and I'll write it for you now. And tomorrow I shall change my will and restore the *status quo*.'

So the next morning Mr Tilling was pleased to accept his customary summons, his new instructions and a large fee, and ten days after that Mr Cedric Monk became one of the shareholders in the new TNT factory of Brummer, Maud and Company in North Woolwich. And just after Christmas – when Bertie and Jack were in the firing line for the third time – he took his seat on the board.

The management were debating possible means of increasing production given the growing demand for their explosive. Some were of the opinion that they ought to move into bigger premises. Others were doubtful, arguing that they would have to re-apply for planning permission for any new factory and that they would lose all the advantages of the present site.

Their new board member knew at once how they could achieve their aims without moving at all.

'Work round the clock,' he said. 'Three eight-hour shifts, the way we farmers do at calving time.'

'We should have to increase the workforce,' the chairman pointed out.

'That shouldn't present a difficulty,' the treasurer told them. 'We pay good wages. It would mean a concomitant increase in profits.'

'We'll print off some of our recruiting leaflets,' the chairman decided. 'See what sort of a response we get. This could well be the answer, Mr Monk. I'm much obliged to you.'

CHAPTER TEN

'That's what I want to do,' Netta Boniface said, fishing a crumpled leaflet from the pocket of her pinafore and smoothing it out on the newly cleared oilcloth on their table. Her fourteenth birthday was a mere ten days away so she would be starting work at half term. 'See?'

Her brother and sisters crowded round the table to look at the leaflet. '*Brummer Maud & Co. North Woolwich,*' it read. '*Munitions workers wanted. Shift work. Training given. Uniform provided. Good wages.*' 'I thought you was gonna work with our Rose,' Collum said.

'Well I ain't,' Netta said, her face so fierce she looked quite frightening. 'If you think I'm gonna be a skivvy you've got another think coming. And I ain't working in no shop, neither. No *thank* you. Standing around all day, terrible wages, forever on your feet, at everyone's beck and call, having to be nice to all them lah-di-dah women. No *thank* you.'

'I never said you had to,' Collum protested, taking an involuntary step backwards. 'You don't half jump down a person's throat.'

'Tell us about it,' Rose said, smoothing things over.

'They make TNT fer the shells,' Netta explained. 'An' they pay two pounds two and six a week.'

Mabel was flabbergasted by such riches. 'They never!'

'Men two pounds two and six, top whack,' Netta said. 'It says here. Look. Women one pound seventeen.'

Even Col was impressed. 'Blimey!' he said. He'd only just risen to one pound ten and he thought *that* was good. 'You *will* be in the money!'

But Rose felt she ought to sound a warning, if only a little one. 'It could be dangerous Netta,' she said. 'People get hurt making munitions. There was that girl in the papers only last week, lost an eye.'

Netta tossed her hair. 'I don't care,' she said. 'That's what I want to do. It'll be a lark. Pearl's sister's been there since September and she says it's good. They give you a uniform and everything. Oh come on, our Rose! I can't be a soldier and drive a motorbike and go to France. I can't even join the WAACs till I'm eighteen. This is the next best thing. I don't mind a bit of danger. You can't help danger, can you, not with a war on. Think what the army has to put up with out in France. We can't none of us just sit back and do nothing. Not with all that going on. It wouldn't be right. Besides, someone's got to do it.'

'*Live with Dignity*,' Rose said, looking at Mum's sampler.

'Live with dignity,' Netta agreed, glad to be understood.

'You're a good girl our Netta,' Rose told her. 'You're right. Someone *has* got to do it. I just wish it wasn't explosives.'

'I shall make tons and tons of the stuff,' Netta said cheerfully. 'For Bertie and Jack, personal.'

Being reminded of Jack Jeary saddened Rose, because he still hadn't written to her. She turned away from her brother and sisters and occupied herself with the washing-up so as to hide her feelings. Bertie wrote to Muriel twice a week – as she knew because Mu had shown her some of the letters – but all she ever got was a postcard with a printed message on it and just his name and a couple of kisses. What was she supposed to make of *that*? He's either lost interest, she thought sadly, as she swilled their dirty dishes through the soapy water, or I never meant much to him in the first place.

Somebody was knocking at the door. 'Coo-ee! It's only me. I'm not disturbing your tea, am I?' It was Mrs Cartwright from three doors up, pink-faced and panting from her climb up the stairs, shoes down-trodden, fuzzy fair hair standing on end. 'You got a minute Rose?'

116

'Yes,' Rose said, smiling at her neighbour. 'Come on in.' She emptied the slops in the pail and dried her hands.

'It ain't sugar this time,' Nancy Cartwright said. With four children and a husband away at sea for months at a time, she was perpetually short of cash. 'I ain't on the scrounge. My Albert's been home a week. It's just I was wondering.'

'Sit yourself down,' Rose said. 'What was you wondering?'

Mrs Cartwright eased herself onto a chair, smoothed her skirt, grimaced through a difficult thought, screwed up her eyes. Finally, she said, 'You know that frock you made.'

'And never wore,' Netta said, bristling at the memory of it. 'That was ol' Miss Monk's doing. Rotten ol' bat.'

'Yes well,' Nancy Cartwright said. 'That's what I come about. I got a suggestion to make. Well a favour really. Say no, if you don't like it.'

Rose smiled at her and waited.

'It's my Marigold,' Nancy said. 'Wants to get married to that Charlie of hers. He's got a place on Albert's next ship, you see. We're ever so pleased. So they want to get married before he goes.'

'Coo!' Mabel breathed, fired by the romance of it. 'Fancy a wedding in our street. I love weddings.'

'When'll it be?' Netta asked.

'Too soon for my liking,' Nancy said, grimacing again. 'I don't like being rushed. Slow but sure, me. But you can't stand in their way, can you? Not with a war on. They're calling the banns on Sunday week.'

'So what's the favour?' Rose prompted.

'Well it's the frock,' Nancy said. 'Say if you don't agree. It's only an idea, seeing you ain't worn it, sort of thing. Only what we was thinking was, it'ud make a lovely wedding dress. You wouldn't think a' selling it would you?'

Rose hadn't thought about the dress at all. After her disappointment at not wearing it, she'd put it to the back of the wardrobe, still wrapped in its dust sheet and left it there. Now she made rapid calculations. 'It cost rather a lot,' she said. 'The material was nearly seven and six what with cottons and buttons and everything.'

'Say nine bob,' Nancy Cartwright offered. 'Would you let us have it for nine bob?'

Rose would have let it go for eight. 'You sure?' she asked.

'Quite sure,' Nancy nodded. 'That'ud be a real bargain.'

So it was agreed, to general and happy approval, and while Nancy was scrabbling in her purse for two half-crowns and two florins, Rose offered up another, private bargain. This time to God. If I sell the dress, she prayed, You'll let Bertie and Jack come home safe, won't You. It's the best thing I've ever made and I've never worn it, not even once. So it's a lot to give up.

It felt like the answer to her prayer when Bertie sent a letter ten days later to say that he and Jack would be home on leave at the end of April, just in time for the wedding and to see Netta in her uniform. *'I'll bet she'll be bossing them all around after a couple of days, knowing our Netta.'*

But in fact Netta found life in a munitions factory much harder than she expected. As a beginner, she wasn't paid as much as she'd hoped – although she *was* promised a rise after six months – and the rules she had to obey seemed endless and unnecessary. From her first day she stood out against authority – to the delight of her new friends on the factory floor.

'Whatcher mean, we ain't to wear nothink metal?' she said to the foreman, when he read her the list of regulations.

'Hooks an' eyes,' he explained. 'Metal rings on your corsets.'

'Do me a favour,' she mocked. 'Do I look as if I wear corsets?'

He decided to ignore that. 'Hairpins,' he said.

'How am I supposed to keep me hair up without pins?' Netta protested. 'That's daft.'

'Stick it under yer 'at,' the foreman said. 'That's what it's for.'

'Oh Bli'*me*!' Netta said. But she was actually rather impressed by her uniform and came home bragging about it.

'We got all regulation overalls,' she said. 'And a special hat, like a sort of mop cap with a brim. Very *a la*. They even give us shoes. All in pale blue like a uniform. You oughter see us.'

'I'll bet you're a sight for sore eyes, our Netta,' Mabel admired.

'With me hat on, I look like a soldier,' Netta said. 'You oughter see our factory, Mabel. We have to put this TNT stuff into great vats. You never seen nothing so big. You could put a house into them. Half a terrace.'

She made new friends, grew skilled at her new job and learnt how to swear – although she was careful not to bring her bad language home. She bought an extravagant hat for Marigold Cartwright's wedding and new boots and shoes for all the family. Now and then she had bouts of inexplicable sickness, which upset her a bit, and by the beginning of April her fringe had become decidedly tawny and her face had taken on the unmistakable yellow tinge of most girls who worked in munitions. But that was something to be proud of.

'Well you're a canary girl now, and no mistake,' her new friends told her. 'You're really one of us.'

'Wait till Bertie sees you,' Rose said. 'He'll be that proud.'

'Roll on the end of the month,' Netta said.

'Everything's happening this April,' Muriel said. 'It's all go at Chelsea. Mr and Mrs E are painting every evening. They're going to have their pictures hung in the summer exhibition. At least that's what *she* reckons.'

'You don't?' Rose asked.

'They might take one of his,' Muriel said. 'But I can't see anybody choosing hers. They're all the same. *Scenes from my Studio Window*, she calls them. They're awful.

All wishy-washy colours and sort of flat-looking and she does them in two seconds flat. The paint's daubed on. Not like his.'

'What are his like?' Rose was intrigued. There was a new warmth in Muriel's voice that she'd never heard before when she was speaking about her employers.

'They're portraits of his students,' Muriel said. 'I think they're good. He takes real pains with them. In fact . . .' Then she paused. And blushed.

Rose was even more intrigued. 'In fact what, Mu?'

'He wants me to sit for him,' Muriel confessed. And seeing the shocked expression on Rose's face, 'Oh, not like that. It's all right. I'd be fully dressed. And she'd be there all the time. He just wants me to sit in the studio of an evening while they're both painting and see what sort of a picture I'd make. What do you think?'

'Would it take long?'

'Hours and hours I expect. That's what's putting me off. I told you, he's very careful. It takes him weeks to do a portrait.'

'What will *you* do all that time?' Rose wanted to know. 'You can't just sit there. You'd be bored to tears.'

'I could do some sewing, if I had any.'

That gave Rose an idea. 'Tell you what,' she suggested. 'Let's make two new blouses for when Bertie and Jack come home. I'm in the money since I sold my frock. We could do them between us. I'll cut them out and sew the seams and you can do the hand-finishing while you're sitting.'

It was an admirable solution. And in more ways than they knew. It gave Muriel something to occupy her and something that made her think of Bertie. And it enraptured the painter.

Having a sitter actually at work before him was a novel experience for Edmund Monk. After the carefully posed figures he'd worked with at the Art School, this quiet young woman was a revelation. Her dark hair *was* a challenge, just as he'd known it would be, and so was the rhythm of her fingers, but it was the expression on her face that inspired him. It was almost as if she were dreaming, she looked so absorbed. But a good dream, he thought, roughing in the line of her cheeks, a satisfying dream. It rounded every contour, lifting her cheeks and lighting her eyes and spreading her chin into quite a presentable shape. (Her worst feature, without a doubt, that disappearing chin. Her best was that delicious neck. So young, slender, vulnerable.) But it was the faint flush of colour that suffused her complexion in the evening light that pleased him most, delicate as faint cloud, an apricot behind gauze, warming and enriching the eau-de-Nil highlights of that pale complexion, echoing the streaks of amber in her brown eyes. Quite delightful. Of course, she's got a lover, he thought, mixing colour thoughtfully. That's who she's dreaming about. And why not? She's young and beautiful in her own individual way. If I could only catch it . . .

Spring rushed in upon them as April passed. The evenings lengthened and lightened, the river Thames was suddenly blue and green, and all over London front gardens were warmed with yellow blossom as forsythia erupted into clusters of golden stars, daffodils bounced and bobbed, laburnum shook its butter-coloured curls. In the garden at Monk House wallflowers scented the air and the first rosebuds made a tentative appearance. Soon it would be Easter and the season of resurrection, new life and hope.

There was a terrible battle going on in France, so the papers said, but it was in a fortress called Verdun and was between the French and the Germans, so it didn't worry the Bonifaces unduly. Bertie would soon be home and out of it and that was what mattered. As the end of the month grew nearer, everything they did, said and thought was geared to those ten precious days. Not a letter was written that didn't end 'See you the end of April.'

But when the end of April finally arrived so did a letter from Bertie to explain that all leave had been cancelled and that he wouldn't be home *'just yet awhile on account of something is afoot out here and we have to be ready.'*

Their disappointment was dreadful. Mabel wept for hours and kicked the wall until a great patch was marked and scuffed by her boot polish. Col and Netta swore. Muriel shed private tears and was pale-faced for days. Even Rose found it hard to be sensible because her disappointment was twice as bad as anyone's else's.

'They're bound to send them home soon,' she hoped. 'They can't go on for ever without any leave. That wouldn't be fair.' She still hadn't had a letter from Jack and she'd waited so long and so patiently, living for the moment when he'd come home and see her and she'd know how things stood between them. 'They *must* have some leave.'

'When?' Mabel sniffed, her moon face streaked with tears. 'When our Rose?'

There was no way any of them could answer that. They simply had to wait, write cheerful letters and hope.

The pictures for the Chelsea summer exhibition were chosen and to Louella's considerable annoyance hers were passed over and Edmund's old-fashioned portrait of Miss Spencer got hung. She congratulated her husband with as much sincerity as she could feign although the words stuck in her craw. If the selection committee had so little taste, there was nothing she could do about it. Then she cheered herself up by writing to Winifred to tell her the good news because she knew how much it would annoy her.

Winifred wrote back almost at once with some good news of her own. *'Cedric is going rather well himself,'* she said. *'There is such a shortage of food, farmers are going to be paid a subsidy from the government. Did you know that? He says it is the first time he has ever felt valued for what he does. The munitions factory is doing rather well too. His first dividend was bigger than we expected. He is considering the purchase of a twenty-acre plot adjoining our farm. Isn't that good?'*

122

Louella was not pleased to be upstaged. 'Your sister-in-law is such a bore,' she drawled to Edmund. The two of them were sitting at breakfast and she'd read the letter while she sipped her tea. Such nasty tea these days. No better than sweepings. 'All she ever talks about is money and "doing well". She didn't have a word to say about your success. Not one word.'

'Art is an eclectic taste my dear,' Edmund said. 'Do you have any more marmalade?'

'No,' Louella said, crossly. 'We don't. There's a war on.'

'It looks as if it's hotting up,' Edmund said. He'd been reading *The Times* when the letter arrived. Now he returned to it, giving it a little shake to release his exasperation about the marmalade. 'The French are putting pressure on General Haig to open up a summer campaign. I should say we shall see some sort of offensive before long. Let's hope they get it right this time.'

But in July, the generals made their most costly mistake of the war. They opened the campaign that was later to be called the Battle of the Somme. Right from the start the casualty figures were so dreadful it was hard to comprehend them.

Muriel and the Bonifaces were worried sick, crying at night and snappy by day.

'This is why they didn't get their leave,' Muriel understood. 'I hope to God they're all right.'

'What's the good of saying that?' Rose said irritably. 'How would we know? They can't write an' tell us, can they? Not in the middle of a battle. Anything could be happening to them and we wouldn't know.'

'They'll be all right,' Col consoled, with more confidence than he felt. 'They can look after theirselves. They ain't babies.'

'I should've known something was up,' Netta said, brushing her ginger fringe with her fingers, 'the amount of TNT we been making. At least they'll have plenty of ammunition this time round.'

But thought of all the ammunition that was being used just made Rose and Muriel more and more desperate as the news got worse.

By the beginning of August, over a hundred and fifty-eight thousand British troops had been killed. And there were still no letters to tell them how their two soldiers were. From time to time standard issue postcards arrived from one or the other to say that they were fit and well and adding as a postscript, *'Please write. Letters keep us going.'* From time to time the news was so awful that they were afraid when the postboy came up the road. From time to time there seemed to be a hope that the campaign was coming to an end. But the battle went on and on, in an endless terrible slaughter.

August was hot and airless. Life in the local factories grew more difficult day after sweating day. Rose did what she could to keep their two rooms comfortable – covering the milk jug and standing it in a bowl of water, scattering old tea leaves on the floor to keep down the dust, buying all their food little and often, even though it meant queuing for hours. Margarine was rancid more often than not, the national loaf turned green within twenty-four hours of being bought, and what little meat there was went off before they had a chance to eat it. The drains stank and the outside lavvy was crawling with cockroaches – despite a daily dusting with Keatings. And on top of everything else, there was a plague of flies and bluebottles. Rose hung up two new fly-papers every morning and when she got home from work they were black with dead insects, but still more came buzzing in through the open windows to settle on the frying-pan and crawl across the table and fly aimlessly round and round above the gas mantles.

Nevertheless, no matter how uncomfortable they were, and no matter how irritable they got, Rose wouldn't allow any of her family to complain.

'Think of it this way,' she told them. 'It might be hot and smelly but at least we're all still alive and so is Bertie.

That's what matters.' She had a superstitious feeling that if they didn't make a fuss they could somehow keep their two soldiers out of harm's way.

So they endured through August, irritable and sweating and each privately willing the battle to end. It must stop soon, they thought, surely to God. It can't go on like this for ever.

But the battle *did* go on. September began. Mabel returned to school, trailing along the road as slowly as she could, sucking her thumb. The heat gradually subsided. Now it was possible to sit by the open window of an evening and breathe in cool air. Which was how Netta and Mabel saw the messenger.

Netta was on the night shift that week and didn't have to go into work until eight o'clock, so she and Mabel had prepared the tea and were sitting by the window, waiting for Rose and Col to come home and eat it.

As they watched, the wheel of a bicycle turned the corner. 'Who's that?' Mabel asked, cheerfully curious.

Then the rider appeared and Netta realised that it was a girl and that she was wearing a uniform.

'Oh God!' she said. 'It's a telegram.'

'Here's our Rose,' Mabel said, still cheerful.

Rose had seen the telegram girl too and was running towards the house. To Netta, watching in the room above, everything seemed to be happening in silent slow motion, like something at the pictures. The girl got off her bike and propped it against the wall. Rose reached her. There was a flutter of yellow paper – an ominously small yellow paper – passing between them. Rose opened it, read it, searched in her pocket for a sixpence, gave it to the girl. Then the bike was being wheeled away and they could hear Rose's feet on the stairs, Rose's voice groaning. 'Oh God! Oh God!' And then they were in one another's arms and weeping.

What could they say to one another? What good were words? Or prayers? Or anything? Mabel was screaming and pounding the wall with her forehead and for the first time in their lives, they let her scream, because there was nothing they could do to console her. Bertie was dead. Their dear, loving Bertie, who'd worked so hard and looked after them so well and gone to war so bravely. There was the terrible message on the telegram, shaking in Rose's hand, the message they'd been dreading ever since this endless battle began. *'We regret to inform you . . . Rifleman Herbert Boniface . . . killed in action . . .'* What did the war matter now? What did anything matter? There was nothing for them but grief.

CHAPTER ELEVEN

Collum Boniface came home while his sisters were still weeping. Because their grief was so extreme he managed to keep his own more or less under control – at least for the first few fraught hours. He would weep later, at night, when he was by himself. For the moment, he was the man of the family and had to be responsible for the others. When he'd absorbed the first terrible shock of the news, he was the one who remembered Muriel.

Mention of her name provoked renewed weeping. 'Oh poor Mu,' Rose sobbed. 'How are we going to tell her? Poor, poor Mu!'

'I'll go,' Col said, rubbing his sister's back to comfort her. 'You stay here and look after one another, eh? I'll tell her.'

Having something to do made his grief bearable. To catch a tram, walk to the house, knock at the door, ask the parlourmaid if he could see Miss Spencer. But when Muriel came into the parlour, the thought of what he had to tell her cracked his control so that his face crumpled towards tears and he had to swallow several times before he could speak.

'Mu!' he said.

She knew what he was going to say. 'It's Bertie.' And when he nodded miserably. 'Tell me quickly. Wounded or dead?'

'Dead.' God, what an awful word! Never to be seen or heard again. Gone for ever. Beyond help, talk, love, everything. Dead. How could you accept a thing like that? How could you even understand it?

Muriel put her hands over her face but she didn't cry. For a long time she simply stood in front of him, rocking slightly backwards and forwards as if she were being buffeted by gusts of wind. Then she began to groan – low, involuntary, terrible sounds dragged from her as if she were in the extremes of pain.

The noise she was making was so awful that Col didn't know what to do. He clenched his fists in indecision, shifted from foot to foot waiting for her to stop. But the groaning went on.

'Would you like to come back to Ritzy Street with me?' he asked at last. 'Be with the others?'

She opened her eyes and looked at him wildly. 'I'm sorry,' she said, struggling to speak normally. 'I can't . . . Excuse me.' And she ran from the room.

Left on his own, Collum felt awkward and angry, his fury swelling with the pain of his loss. Those bloody Germans! he raged. Doing this to our Bertie. If I were there now I'd kill the bastards. Give me a machine gun, that's all, and I'll mow them down in their hundreds. I'll be revenged on the whole bloody pack of them. They don't deserve to live.

His grief and anger were so extreme he couldn't go straight back to Ritzy Street. Having to sit still on the top deck of a tram was impossible. He fidgeted where he sat, wanting to prowl and swear and cry for vengeance. Eventually he got off the tram two stops before he should have done and walked off at a furious pace through the darkening streets. The shop assistants were putting up their shutters ready for night, alternate gas lamps were lit and glimmering, the trams rattled along the middle of the road one after the other, jerking over the points. It was all friendly and peaceful and familiar, and Col's heart stabbed with anguish because Bertie would never see any of it again.

He became aware that he was passing a shop that was still lit and open, bright in the darkness on either side of it. Almost idly, he glanced back to see what it was. And it was an Army Recruiting Office. It was providential. Straightening his spine and his face, he pulled himself up to his full five foot eight and marched through the door.

When he finally got home, his three sisters were sitting side by side on his bed, drinking tea. Their faces were swollen-eyed and blotchy with weeping but they had recovered enough to be talking.

'Well that's it,' he said, standing before them, bold with pride and anger. 'I've took the shilling.'

Mabel was thrilled, flinging herself at him to kiss him and hug him and tell him he was 'ever so ever so brave'. But Rose and Netta were appalled.

'Oh Col! You can't have,' Rose said, lifting her hands in protest. 'You're too young.'

'Not no more I'm not,' Col said. 'According to the sergeant, I'm eighteen. It says here.' He fished his papers out of his pocket to prove it.

'But they'll find out,' Rose said.

'They know,' he told her. 'When I first went in I told 'em I was sixteen and the sergeant said, "Just take a walk round the block, eh son, and see how old you are when you get back." And when I got back I was eighteen. Says here. All signed, sealed and delivered. Oh come on, our Rose, I thought you'd be pleased. I can't stay at home an' do nothing. Not now. Not after this.'

'You're a fine brave man,' Rose said, kissing him. 'It's just . . .'

'They ain't going to kill me,' he comforted. 'Don't you worry. I'm going to have a machine gun and kill them.'

But not yet, Rose prayed, stroking his dark hair. Not just yet. It's bad enough that Bertie's dead without thinking of you out there. You mustn't go yet.

The next three days crawled by, weighed down by grief. Col went to work as usual and, on the following evening, so did Netta, vowing to 'make so much TNT them Jerries'll wish they'd never been born.' But Rose and Mabel stayed at home to grieve. After her first hysterical outburst, Mabel had sunk into a state of puzzled confusion. She did as she was told but she didn't seem to understand what was happening around her, and Rose was too stunned to respond to her, or to anything else.

They made beds, emptied slops, swept the rooms, washed such dishes as were dirty, working automatically and without registering what they were doing. When Netta got home in the early morning they cooked her what breakfast she could eat and put her to bed. When Col came back in the early evening they made his tea and polished his boots. Neighbours called in on them from time to time with tit-bits to cheer them and while they were glad of the company and comfort they couldn't eat the food. It was as if their normal lives had stopped, as if they would never function properly again.

On the afternoon of the fourth day, when Netta was back on evening shift, there was a rap at their door that was so sudden and sharp that it made them all jump. Rose went to open it, her face pale with grief and alarm.

A posy of wilting flowers was being held out towards her – mostly sweet peas and daisies – and behind them the jaunty cap and handsome face of Jack Jeary. It upset her that she felt no emotion towards him at all.

But Mabel jumped up at once, her round face beaming. 'It's our soldier,' she cried, trotting towards him to pat his arm and stroke his hair. 'How's our Bertie, Mr Soldier? He ain't dead is he?'

The question was more than Jack could bear. He shook himself free of her clinging hands and held out the flowers to Rose, awkwardly as if he didn't know what to do with them. 'They're for you,' he said. 'I had to come. You don't mind do you?'

'Oh Jack,' Rose said wearily. There was only one thing she wanted to know. 'Was you with him when . . . ?'

He could tell them the truth about that at least. 'Not far off.'

'So you saw what happened,' Rose said. Did she want to know? Could she bear it? Could she bear not knowing?

He stood before her, weary in his stained uniform, remembering. The terror of waiting to go over the bags, the endless, mind-numbing noise of the bombardment, the raw taste of rum in his mouth as the whistle blew. And then the run over no man's land, feeling as if his heart was beating in his throat, the high-pitched screams of men caught in machine-gun fire, the stabbing red of explosions – Bertie lying in a pool of mud and blood, flat on his back. *'Give us a fag, Jack.'* Bertie groaning in pain, apologising for the noise he was making. Bertie putting his left hand into the space where his right arm should have been. *'Has it gone, Jack?'* Bertie's blood spurting from his terrible wounds like red fountains as his face drained grey. How could he possibly tell them all that?

Netta had been sitting in the chimney corner, too miserable to get up or to acknowledge him. But now she spoke. *'Did* you see what happened to him?' she asked and her question was more urgent.

'He never knew nothing about it,' he lied to spare them. 'He didn't suffer. He was killed outright.'

'Oh thank God!' Rose breathed. 'I've been lying here at nights thinking about him. Thinking how awful it must've been. It's the not-knowing. That's the worst part.'

'Well you can stop worryin' now, can't you?' he urged her. 'He never knew nothing about it.' Then he turned their attention to practical things, knowing he couldn't lie like that for very much longer. 'I suppose you ain't got such a thing as a cup a' tea, have you? I'm that dry I couldn't spit on a sixpence.'

They made him tea and sat him at the table to drink it while Mabel put the flowers in a vase. They invited him to supper and he walked down to the Cut with them to buy what they needed. And he stayed with them and shared the meal and let them talk about their brother until Netta had to leave for work. Then he and Rose escorted her to the tramstop and waved her on her way to New Cross.

'Come for a walk?' he suggested when Netta was gone. 'It's a nice evening.'

The sky was stained by sunset, orange and mauve above the darkening rooftops. But Rose didn't care what sort of evening it was. She trailed off towards the Vauxhall Gardens where the drinking-fountain was a grey ghost in the twilight and the black trees were shrill with roosting starlings, calling in the branches like lost spirits.

She asked him how long his leave was.

'Forty-eight hours,' he told her. 'Compassionate. Took a bit of wangling.'

It hardly seemed any time at all to Rose. 'That means you'll be gone tomorrow.'

' 'Fraid so,' he said. 'But I'll be back soon as ever I can.'

She was too listless to respond. It was as if all her emotions had been switched off. She sighed, turning her face away from him. 'This war's so dreadful. And now Col's joined up.'

'It'll soon be over,' he said. He didn't really think so, but he felt he had to console her, somehow or other. Her listlessness was dreadful. 'It'll be all right.'

She wasn't consoled. 'Will it?' she said and her voice was bleak.

He took her in his arms and kissed the top of her head. 'Yes,' he promised. 'It will.'

But nothing was all right that autumn. It was seven days before Muriel came to Ritzy Street to see them and then she was in floods of tears all evening and couldn't be comforted, no matter what they said to her. Rose was so alarmed by the state she was in that from then on she made sure that they visited one another at least twice a week. But nursing one another through their grief took a very long time and it wasn't helped by the fact that the terrible Battle of the Somme still dragged on and on and the casualty lists grew longer and longer. By the time the campaign finally ended, the British casualties alone numbered more than four hundred thousand men and, as far as Rose and Muriel could see, it hadn't affected the course of the war at all. Bertie had died along with all those others and nothing had been decided.

Col went to camp at the end of September, much sooner than Bertie had done and in a mood of hideous cheerfulness. But he'd always been a cocky little boy, tough and self-confident like all street arabs, and had always accepted that men endured whatever life flung at them and did what they could to protect their womenfolk.

His first letter home was full of how *'grand'* everything was and how well he was getting on and what a *'fine bunch of lads'* his fellow recruits were. In fact his training was hard and brutal and there were men in the camp who told him at first hand all about the obscenities of trench warfare. But he kept the horrors to himself and remained resolutely optimistic in all his letters home. At the beginning of December he was given embarkation leave and by the middle of the month he was in France and *'bringing up supplies'*.

'You are not to worry,' he wrote to Rose. *'I can look after myself even if they do send me up the line. They are a grand bunch of lads out here. Best in the world. Fritz don't stand a chance. Keep your pecker up. Your loving brother, Col.'*

But she did worry. They all worried. And although they admired his spirit they knew he was shielding them from the truth.

That winter of 1916 was the worst they had ever known in their lives. It was dark, cold, heavy with grief and impossibly cheerless. So many women were in mourning that the very streets looked black and, to make matters worse, food was in very short supply. The three Bonifaces spent most of their spare time standing in food queues and they all lost weight, like everybody else in their neighbourhood. Only Miss Monk remained fat and well-fed – on meat sent up by her brother in Suffolk and food delivered to her back door by well-paid tradesmen.

In the New Year, both Germany and Great Britain decided that they needed new leadership after the bloodbath of the Somme. The man Great Britain chose was a maverick called David Lloyd George, who set about his tasks immediately. On the home front he announced that there was to be a scheme of voluntary rationing. Each citizen was to restrict himself to four pounds of bread, two and a half pounds of meat and three quarters of a pound of sugar a week.

'Where's he think we're gonna find three quarters of a pound of sugar, stupid man?' Netta scoffed. Now that she was earning such good money at the factory they could afford to buy what little there was. But sugar had virtually disappeared from the shops.

'They say the price of bread's going up again,' Nancy Cartwright said, as she and Rose and Mabel set off for Lambeth Walk one Friday evening in January. Netta was on the afternoon shift and wouldn't be home until after eight o'clock. 'Scandalous, you ask me. Makes you wonder what'll happen next. I'm beginning to think them suffragettes was right. We ought to have the vote and put some of them stupid buggers out of office.'

'I'd vote to stop the war,' Rose said. 'Then all our men could come home and not get killed.'

'Amen to that,' Nancy said. 'The number of ships gone down you'd never believe. High time they stopped that an' all. How's your poor friend Muriel?'

'About the same,' Rose told her. 'Very quiet. She's meeting us tonight, so you'll see.'

'Poor gel,' Nancy sympathised. 'She wants taking out of herself. Is that her, look, waiting by the pub?'

It was and she was still very subdued, following them silently from stall to stall, holding on to Rose's arm.

'I'd like to get a nice little chop for our Netta tonight,' Rose said, heading for the nearest butcher's stall.

'Well you don't wanna buy none of this,' Nancy exclaimed, examining the goods on display. 'Rotten load of old cag-mag, this is.' As she spoke they were all startled by the sudden roar of a distant explosion.

'What in the world was that?' the butcher exclaimed, looking up at the sky. There was a cloud of smoke rising in the east, a glimmer of flame above the chimney tops. 'Good God Almighty, look at that. Summink's gone up.'

'That's Rotherhithe way,' a woman exclaimed, staring at the smoke.

'No it ain't,' the butcher replied. 'It's further over than that. Greenwich or Woolwich, you ask me. I'll bet it's the Woolwich Arsenal.'

Netta's in Woolwich, Rose was thinking. Oh please God don't let her be anywhere near it. Wasn't Bertie enough?

Netta had worked through a long, tiring shift at Brummer, Maud and Company that afternoon. She'd been on her feet since two o'clock, funnelling the treated TNT into barrels ready to be taken away for delivery. As the clock ticked round towards seven, her back ached and she felt decidedly sick from breathing in the fumes, which were particularly strong that afternoon.

'I could do with a mug of tea,' she said to the foreman. 'It's long past six.'

'Wouldn't hurt just to wet our lips, sort of thing,' Netta's friend Mavis urged. 'Netta'd go for it, wouldn't you Netta?'

'Yeh, rightoh,' the foreman said, watching his machine. The stink of the explosive was filling his nostrils too. 'Cut off and get it. Only look slippy. If the boss comes in and you're off out we shall be for it.' He and his gang had an arrangement that their tea would come from the local café, where it was made hot and strong. 'Don't ferget the Nestlé's milk.'

Thank God for that, Netta thought. It would be a relief to be out in the air and away from all those choking fumes, if only for ten minutes. She took the tea jug, wrapped herself in her coat, heaped her knitted muffler round her neck and set off along the Albert Road at a trot.

But just as the café was within sight, there was a noise like some gigantic animal roaring. Before she had a chance to think or even turn to see what was happening, she was pushed off her feet by something punching her violently in the small of the back.

For several seconds she was in the air, as if she were flying, her hands spread out before her like starfish. Then she landed against a wall with a thud that knocked the air from her lungs and for an endless time she lay where she'd fallen, too stunned and shocked to move. The air around her was furnace hot; there were people screaming and feet running; she could hear an odd pattering tinkling sound, thuds and crashes; but nothing seemed real. She knew that her heart was beating in her throat, that she was struggling for breath, that she ought to get up and run away but she was pinned to the ground as if someone had dropped a boulder on her chest.

With a dreadful effort, she opened her eyes and looked up. There was dust everywhere, clouds and clouds of it, rolling like fog and people were running through it in all directions, their legs like black shears, their feet trampling on shards of white glass and broken bits of wood and brick. But the sky was worse than the street. The sky was a nightmare, full of roaring flames and writhing black smoke and appalling things falling – a steel girder, turning as it fell, part of a chair, old rags, a shower of bricks and dust, something round and dark, like a misshapen ball, hurtling towards her. Something round and dark with something sticky stuck to one side of it and gobbets of treacly stuff falling from it as it fell. Something round and dark with two eyes glinting in the half-light. And panic rose in her throat, as she realised what it was. A head. Oh my dear, good God, a human head!

She sprang to her feet, screaming in terror and horror. She had to get out of this. Now. This minute. She had to go home. Still screaming and with her hands stretched before her, she ran full tilt towards the river. If she could get to the ferry she would be all right. If she could cross the river. She had to cross the river.

The ferry had been taking on passengers when the explosion blew them off their feet. Now, stunned and bloodstained, they were picking themselves up, as well as they could. One woman had blood pouring from both arms where she'd been lacerated by flying glass, another was still on the ground crawling towards the ferry, two old men were bent over a third who was holding his leg. There was a knot of men and women gathered on the pier, covered in dust and dirt but otherwise unharmed and uncertain whether to go on or back. When they saw Netta hurtling towards them, they made way for her at once, their faces anxious.

'What's happened?' they wanted to know. 'Where was it?'

But she was beyond speech and could only weep that she wanted to go home.

'I'll take you across gel,' the ferryman said, climbing out onto the jetty. 'Don't you worry. And some of them and all.' Indicating the other casualties, who were staggering towards him. 'They can bring the ambulances down to the water's edge over the other side. Pick her up and carry her mate. She'll be better on the other side.'

It took a long time to ease the wounded aboard, as the sky roared with fire behind them and the stink of explosives clogged the air. Netta wept and rocked and couldn't be comforted. She was still weeping as the ferry crossed the Thames, and took her on the first stage of her journey.

Afterwards she had no idea how she got back to Ritzy Street. She had a vague memory of changing trams at New Cross, of a woman who helped her up the step onto the second tram, of sitting beside a little boy and trying not to cry for fear of upsetting him. But at last, at last she was in Kennington Lane and running home to Ritzy Street.

Her lungs straining, she fell forward into the street. 'Rose!' she screamed. 'Rose! Help me! Please! Please!'

Rose and Muriel had been fraught with anxiety ever since the explosion. They'd come straight home from the market so as to be in the right place in case they were wanted. Now they ran to the window together, relieved to

137

hear her voice but terrified by the sound of it. The sight of her gave them a shock like a blow to the stomach. They plummeted down the stairs, two at a time, and were beside her before she'd stopped calling.

She was totally hysterical, weeping and raging. 'A head!' she cried. 'All the glass . . . there was a chair . . . a great girder falling out the sky . . . falling out the sky . . . and a head there was . . . dropping bits of blood . . . a human head. I can't bear it . . . falling straight at me, our Rose . . . all bits of blood . . . everywhere. Straight at me.'

Rose and Muriel were more concerned with the blood on her sister's clothes. 'You're all right,' Rose tried to soothe. 'You're with us now our Netta. We got you.'

They led her into the house, eased her up the stairs, sat her by the fire, put a kettle on the hob for some hot water.

'You'll need a hot water bottle,' Muriel said. 'Her forehead's clammy. Have you got one Rose?'

They stripped off her coat, noting without comment how badly shredded it was. They put her feet in a bowl of warm water and mustard. They eased away her blood-stained uniform.

'Nasty,' Muriel whispered to Rose as the long abrasions were revealed.

'We'll have to clean this all out, Netta,' Rose warned, 'or it'll turn septic.' But Netta was too hysterical to care what they did. She wept and babbled as Rose took cotton wool to her torn skin and did her best to clean away the dirt and grit. She didn't notice that Mabel had been sent to the corner shop for iodine and lint and that Muriel was tearing up old sheets for bandages. She howled when Mabel came back and Rose poured the iodine into her wounds but she didn't resist and she didn't complain.

Muriel made tea and put a mug of it into her hands. Mabel dried her feet and put on a clean pair of stockings. Rose filled a hot water bottle for her and found cushions to ease her back. They were so absorbed in their concern

138

for her that for the first time since they'd heard about Bertie's death they forgot their grief.

But it took them nearly an hour to soothe her from hysteria and more than two before she could tell them what had happened. By then her voice was hoarse from the fumes she'd inhaled and she was finding it more and more difficult to breathe. They were horrified by what they heard.

'I can't go back there, our Rose,' Netta finished, weeping again. 'I can't never go back.'

Having seen the column of smoke and the height of the flames in the sky, Rose couldn't help thinking there wouldn't be much to go back to but she didn't say so because that would have been too distressing for Netta to cope with.

'You don't have to go back,' she reassured. 'First we got to get you well again. You've took a nasty knock on that back of yours. It'll take a bit of time to heal. We'll think about what you can do next when you're well again.'

Netta was gasping for breath. 'But what about the money?' she worried. 'How're we gonna manage without the money?'

Rose had already decided not to worry about money. 'Save your breath,' she said. 'We'll think about *that* later too. We're all right for the moment.'

'I shall have to go back come the finish,' Netta panted, tearful and fatalistic. 'How else am I supposed to earn me money? Besides, there's the war effort.'

'Damn the war,' Rose said. 'We've got to protect ourselves from the war. All of us, every way we can.' This sudden burst of useful activity had put her in touch with her own power for good. 'For a start, you ain't going back to munitions, Netta, and that's flat. Look at the state you're in. Next time you'll be killed. Enough's enough.'

'We'll find some other job for you,' Muriel comforted. 'You'll see, Netta. There's plenty going. Rose is right.'

'That'll pay as well?' Netta asked, clutching the hot water bottle to her stomach. 'How're you gonna find one that'll pay as well?'

Rose looked idly round the room, trying to gather her thoughts. There must be something Netta could do. Something that would earn good money and not put her in danger. 'Trams perhaps, nursing, in a shop?'

But Netta wasn't listening. She didn't notice that Mabel was stroking her hands nor when Muriel put a hand on her forehead.

'You're still too clammy, you know,' Muriel said. 'I'll get you a blanket. You must keep warm.'

Rose watched as her friend walked into the bedroom and returned with a blanket over her arm. Behind the bedroom door, shadowy in the unlit room, she could see behind her mother's old tailor's dummy. It was still wearing that half-finished blouse, the one she'd been making when she heard about poor Bertie. I ought to sell that, she thought vaguely. I shall never wear it. And in that instant she knew what they were going to do.

'We'll make dresses and sell them in the market,' she said. 'There's a lot of women earning good money nowadays. I'll bet they'd sell like hot cakes. There you are Netta, you could work at home. I could cut them out and you could sew them up and we could finish them off between us of an evening.'

'What a wonderful idea,' Muriel said. 'You *could* do that, couldn't you Netta. I'd help, if you'd like me to. I used to sit and sew when Mr E was painting that portrait, if you remember. I've got stacks of time. She's always out with her friends. It's quite boring being a companion sometimes. It would be something to do.'

'Where would we sell them?' Netta wanted to know, ever practical.

Rose knew the answer to that. The entire plan was in her mind complete in every detail, where she'd buy the cloth, how it would have to be costed, even the pattern of the first dress they would make. 'On Mrs Tuffin's tot stall,' she said. 'If we offered her a percentage, I bet she'd let us have a corner. Half a rail maybe. Sale or return, the way she does with the blouses.'

It looked more possible the more she thought about it. Netta calmed a little and began to take an interest.

'D'you think we could, our Rose?'

'Nothing venture, nothing gain,' Rose said. 'I'll ask her. What's the time?' And, seeing that it was still early evening, 'I'll go now. This minute.'

CHAPTER TWELVE

If Mrs Tuffin was surprised by Rose Boniface's suggestion that evening, she was too good a business woman to show it. She looked across the stall at the eager young face before her and pursed her lips as she calculated.

'What sort of percentage was you thinking of?' she asked, standing four square between her two naphtha lamps, the feathers in her black straw hat gleaming green and purple.

'Five,' Rose told her. And as always with Rose Boniface that was a decision, not a starting-point from which to barter.

'It ain't much,' Mrs Tuffin said, considering it. 'Not unless you're going for quantity. How many frocks was you thinking of making first off?'

'Three or four. We could deliver them a week Saturday.'

'Make it four for Friday night,' Mrs Tuffin suggested, 'and you're on. I do a good trade Friday night. Pay day you see.'

Rose had been prepared to argue her case for some time, so Mrs Tuffin's rapid agreement felt like a triumph. She ran back to Ritzy Street to cheer the others with her good news.

'I'll go and buy the material after work tomorrow,' she told them, 'then I can cut out the first one tomorrow evening and we'll get sewing on Sunday. Whatcher think?'

Mabel was all beams at the idea but Netta was coughing so much she couldn't speak.

'Don't try to talk,' Rose advised, full of pity for her. 'Tell me in the morning. You'll feel better then.'

But Netta was worse the following morning and by then the papers were full of news about the explosion. The landlady Mrs MacLaren brought her copy straight upstairs for the Bonifaces to see.

'I thought it only right and proper to show you,' she explained, 'seeing your Netta was involved, so to speak.'

The factory had been completely destroyed and sixty-nine people had been killed. Ninety-four were seriously injured, nine hundred houses had been damaged and the fire was still raging. It was even more dreadful than they'd thought, but although Netta was still shocked, Rose let her read the paper, thinking it would be better for her to face the worst and get it over with.

Although she was still finding it hard to breathe, she was unnaturally calm about the news. 'I knew it yesterday,' she sighed. 'No one in the factory could've lived through an explosion like that. There was people injured all over the place. It's a wonder I wasn't killed and all.'

'I shall have to go to work presently,' Rose said, 'but Mabel'll stay with you. You'll be all right won't you?' Having taken charge of their lives she was full of her own energy, despite the horror of the explosion – perhaps even because of it – the lethargy of grief finally lifted. 'Once we really get going with these dresses, you'll feel ever so much better,' she promised Netta, 'you'll see. Look after her, Mabel.'

Mabel was stolidly washing the breakfast things. 'I'll see to her,' she said. 'I'll see to her, our Rose.'

'If you need any help you can pop down to Nancy Cartwright's,' Rose said, putting on her coat.

But naturally, Ritzy Street being what it was, the neighbours popped in and out. And just after ten o'clock Muriel Spencer arrived with a jar of Brand's Essence, 'to tempt the invalid', a woolly jacket 'because your old coat's no good now', and a bar of scented soap 'because I thought it would be nice'.

'Mrs Monk's gone out for the day,' she explained, 'and when I told Mr Edmund what had happened, he said I could come and see you straight away. I can stay as long as I like. He doesn't mind. So here I am. If you don't want me around, just say.'

Her company was the best cure they could have found. She was such a good listener and Netta needed to talk.

'They was my friends,' she grieved, when she'd told the story for the third time. 'They been my friends since I first got there. And now they're dead – Mavis and Mrs Porter and Phyllis. All the lot of them. Sixty-nine was the entire shift. It ain't fair, is it Mu? I should've been dead too, if I hadn't gone for the tea. We always said we was like soldiers but I never thought none of us 'ud get killed. Mavis was only eighteen. It ain't fair.' And she coughed until she was red in the face.

'Life isn't fair,' Muriel said. 'I used to think it ought to be but it never is. If it was fair we'd all be rich and beautiful and nobody would ever die.'

'I ain't got over Bertie yet,' Netta said sadly. And coughed again.

'Nor have I,' Muriel confessed.

It was time for confidences. 'You loved him ever so much, didn't you.'

'Yes. I did,' Muriel sighed. 'We were going to get married. He was always writing about it, where we were going to live and the children we'd have and how happy we were going to be. I thought he was the best man I'd ever met in my life.'

'He was,' Netta said. 'I still can't believe he's dead, you know. I find myself thinking, I'll write and tell our Bertie. After all these months. *I'll write and tell our Bertie.* Daft innit.'

'I don't think it's daft,' Muriel said. 'I think of him every single day. It sort of keeps him alive. That and reading his letters.'

'You got all bits of glass in your hair,' Mabel said to Netta, looking down at it as she passed them on her way to the dresser. 'Shall we wash it?' She enjoyed the ritual of hair washing.

So they boiled up enough water and swished up a lather of soft soap to wash her mop of hair, and were amazed at the debris that came out of it.

'Look at all that glass,' Muriel said, emptying the basin and brushing the little shards into the pail. 'Just as well your hair's thick, or you'd've been cut to ribbons.'

They removed her soiled dressings, examined her wounds and bandaged her up again. Then they sat round the fire to make toast and cocoa for their dinner and she ate it as well as she could for coughing.

'I'm ever so glad you came today,' she said, holding the toasting-fork to the flames. 'It's funny how things turn out. When you first met up with our Rose I was that jealous you'd never believe. I wouldn't go to market because she was taking you there.'

'I was jealous of you too,' Muriel confessed.

That was a surprise. 'Straight up?'

'Oh yes. Ever so jealous. You were so happy, you see. A real happy family. When I was little, I'd have given anything to be part of a family. And when Bertie said he wanted to marry me, I . . .' But then she had to stop because she was suddenly too close to tears.

Netta leant towards her and kissed her. 'Well now you are part a' the family anyway,' she said. 'You're an honorary Boniface.'

The honorary Boniface was still in Ritzy Street when Rose came home with the cloth, which was a lightweight wool in a very pretty shade of blue grey. So naturally, having been given permission to stay out as long as she liked, she spent the rest of the evening with her adopted family, helping to pin on patterns and cut out the first of the four dresses.

'It's like a factory,' she said, as Rose piled the newly cut sections onto a chair.

And, given how shocked they still were, a surprisingly cheerful one. The work gave them something to concentrate on and – when the first dress was finally finished – to be pleased about.

'Shall we get them done in time?' Netta worried, when they were still hard at work on Wednesday evening.

'Yes,' Rose said with determination. 'If I have to sit up all night.'

'I could stay off school again,' Mabel hoped. 'I could couldn't I?'

'I'd stay off work,' Rose said, 'only I'd get the sack and we can't run that sort of risk just yet awhile.'

'They will sell, won't they, our Rose?' Netta asked, still anxious.

Now that the day of delivery was so near, Rose was anxious herself, but she didn't let the others know. 'Course they'll sell,' she said. 'Like hot cakes. Once people know about them.'

The four blue dresses looked lost on Mrs Tuffin's rail and much smaller than they'd done in the house.

'Come back tomorrow,' Mrs Tuffin advised, 'and see how they've done.'

It was the slowest tomorrow they'd ever known and Mabel made it worse. 'D'you think they've sold our frocks, Netta?' she asked over and over again, until Netta got fed up with her and shouted at her to 'put a sock in it.'

Nancy Cartwright popped in later that afternoon to see how they were. 'If I was you,' she said to Netta, 'I'd nip down the Walk and take a peep. Then you'll know won'tcher.'

It was bad advice. For a start, what with the raw patches on her back and that terrible cough, the long walk was very difficult for Netta. And then, when they got to the stall, they found that all four frocks were still on the rails.

'It ain't gonna work,' Netta said when she'd struggled home again. 'We made a mistake.' Her back hurt and her throat was sore and she felt ashamed to have spent all that time producing things nobody wanted to buy. 'We was wrong.'

'It's early days, yet,' Rose said when she came back

146

from work. 'We'll make another one, a different colour. Something nice and bright. Eye-catching. Maybe that blue was too dull for people to notice.'

'We'll just be pouring good money after bad,' Netta said miserably. 'I'll have to get another job, that's all.'

'We'll give it a fortnight,' Rose decided. 'Three week-ends. If they still ain't selling after that, then we'll think about it. I'll get the cloth Monday and we'll run it up on Tuesday evening.'

But Miss Monk had other ideas.

'My brother and his wife will be coming to visit me tomorrow,' she said when Rose brought in the coffee on Monday morning. 'So I shall need you and Daisy in the evening.'

Rose was annoyed but she made the correct response. 'Very good, ma'am.'

'He's had a nasty shock,' Miss Monk went on, shifting Chu-Chin into a more comfortable position on her lap.

Rose wasn't concerned. 'Oh yes.'

'He's suffered a great loss,' Miss Monk confided. 'In that dreadful explosion. The one that was in all the papers.' Cedric had telephoned her the previous evening to tell her all about it and, although his call had upset her, she was full of importance at being able to claim a family connection with a tragedy.

'You don't mean the TNT factory?' Rose asked. 'Not Brummer Maud's?' Now that *was* interesting.

'That's the one. A terrible loss. That's why they're coming to London.'

'For the funeral,' Rose understood.

Miss Monk looked puzzled. 'What funeral?'

'Of the person he knew, ma'am. The person he's lost.'

What an odd girl she is, Augusta thought, to be talking about funerals. 'Oh, no, no,' she corrected. 'It's not that. Well I suppose he did know some of the people who died. He must have, being on the board. Not the work people, naturally, but foremen and people like that. Oh no, it's *capital* he's lost. Capital. A great deal of money.'

Her callous attitude made Rose too cross to hold her tongue. 'Sixty-nine *work people* got killed,' she said. 'One of them could've been my sister.'

That was such a shocking piece of news that it jolted Augusta out of her self-importance. 'I'm sorry,' she said, with honesty and some humility. 'I had no idea. She wasn't hurt was she?'

'Cuts and bruises,' Rose said. 'And hoarse from the fumes of course. She's had a lot of trouble breathing these last few nights and she's got an awful cough. But she could've been killed. All the others were, poor devils. That TNT's shocking stuff, Miss Monk. Poisonous. It turns them yellow. Did you know that? Like mustard. And their hair goes ginger, or sort of green. And they're always having tummy upsets and being off work sick and bad, without pay. And now she's coughing and gasping most of the time. Your brother should think himself lucky it's only money he's lost.'

It was no way for a servant to address her mistress, but for once, Augusta didn't scold. This whole business was so awful it would have made any sort of rebuke look petty. Still, I'm glad I know about it, she thought. When Cedric starts putting pressure on me for more capital, I shall have one up on him.

'I think Chu-Chin needs his little run,' she said. 'Put him out in the garden will you, Rose. Oh, and give this menu to Mrs Biggs for me, will you.'

When I first came to this house, Rose thought, as she led the puffing animal out into the garden, I would never have dreamt of answering the missus back like that. I *have* changed. But she asked for it. She really did. She shouldn't have been talking about people being killed as if it was nothing. As if *they* were nothing. '*Work people.*' It was ugly.

Mrs Biggs wasn't impressed by the proposed menu. 'Where's she think I'm going to get all this stuff?' she asked. 'They can have plum duff and like it.'

Winifred didn't like it at all. Plum duff was a great deal

too plain for her taste. 'I feel so sorry for you, Augusta,' she said, picking at it, 'living here in London with all these shortages. At least we *eat* well out in the sticks, don't we Cedric.'

'There's a war on,' Augusta pointed out. 'We all have to make sacrifices.'

'Don't I know it?' Cedric complained. 'If it hadn't been for the war, I shouldn't be out of pocket.'

'Oh!' Augusta said acidly. 'Are you out of pocket? You do surprise me. I thought you'd got a subsidy from the government.'

Cedric ignored that. 'I've been talking to my accountant,' he said, pushing his plate away. 'He says the infallible way to get yourself out of a hole is to spend your way out. Not that I'm in a hole, you understand, but I have lost my investment. His advice is to invest further. Not munitions necessarily. Rifles perhaps. Not so risky.'

Augusta gave him one of her sharp looks.

'It was sound advice, if you ask me,' Cedric said. 'He's a good man. Of course, it was a bad business at Brummer Maud's. I won't deny it. A serious loss. There's a lot to recoup. Bad timing of course. If I'd had the money right away, I could have made my pile and pulled out and I wouldn't have lost a penny. As it is, I'm out of pocket.'

Now is the time to sting him, Augusta thought. 'There were sixty-nine people killed in that factory of yours,' she said. 'That was the loss, if you ask me. Not capital.'

He wasn't stung at all. 'TNT is a volatile material,' he said carelessly. 'They knew the risks. They were well paid.'

'That doesn't help if they're dead.'

'What a horrible thing to say,' Winifred rebuked. 'I hope you're not accusing Ceddy of killing them. It wasn't his fault, you know.'

'People always die in a war,' Cedric said. 'Look at the casualty figures from Flanders. They're losing thousands every day. Sixty-nine deaths are nothing compared to that. They're bad I grant you, but nothing compared to thousands. It's a question of proportion.'

'Proportion or not,' Augusta told him. 'I'm certainly not giving you any more of my capital to waste on TNT.'

'There's no waste of capital,' Cedric answered her. 'We shall get the bulk of it back from the insurance. The problem is going to be finding another site and meeting the new regulations.'

'I should stick to farming if I were you,' Augusta said. 'Because you're not going to get any more capital out of *me*.'

'I fully intend to, sister dear,' Cedric said. He had no intention of demeaning himself by asking her for anything. Not in that sort of mood.

They were both dissatisfied by their conversation. It hadn't given either of them the chance to score any real points at all and now they seemed to have reached an impasse.

Augusta turned to her sister-in-law. 'How are the children?' she asked.

That night, when they left the warmth of the dining-room fire and went shivering upstairs to their chill bedrooms, Augusta felt misery descend upon her with every upward step. The meal had been a deadlocked failure and it was made worse by the fact that, warmed by her expensive brandy, Cedric was now in an expansive mood. They parted on the landing with cold-lipped kisses and he patted her on the head as if she were one of his children.

The gesture irritated her. But what came next was worse.

'Night-night, love-chick,' he said to her carelessly.

The words made her heart contract with anguish. It was what their mother had always said to him when she kissed him goodnight. Augusta had heard it so many times in her childhood and always with the same jealous yearning, the same intolerable sense of being unloved. It was such an affectionate thing to say and she's always said it to *her darling boy*. Always to him and sometimes to Edmund but never to Augusta, although she'd ached for it all through her life.

'They don't love me,' she told Chu-Chin when she was on her own in her bedroom. 'None of them love me. They never have and they never will. You do, though, don't you my darling?' The chow pushed his black nose into her fondling hand and licked her fingers. 'Yes, yes, Mummy knows you do. You're my darling. But those two! They're just after my money. That's all. They wouldn't care if I were to drop dead.' She was riven with lack of love, mournful with self-pity, her jowls, cheeks and eyelids drooping.

The dog jumped up onto the bed, ensconced himself on her pillows and prepared for the night, but Augusta was too depressed to sleep. She sat by the window looking out into the wintry garden as the hours ticked past and the ghosts of her childhood walked in and out of the room – her mother scolding her and petting the boys – her mother alarmed when she was ill and sending nanny with warm towels to cosset her and steaming bowls of porridge to tempt her appetite –servants to make up the fire – she always had a fire in her room when she was ill – her mother walking diffidently into the sickroom with toys to keep her occupied while she was in bed. *'Are you better now my precious? We must look after you, mustn't we. We can't have our darling feeling ill.'*

And she did feel ill. She felt dreadful. Absolutely dreadful. They'd sing another tune if I were to collapse again, she thought, as the hall clock struck three. Oh quite another tune. But I shall have to make sure they know how bad it is. I shall have to show them in a way they can't ignore. Cedric can be very callous when he likes. I'll look up my symptoms and see what I'm suffering from and I'll make sure they notice.

Her faithful medical book was lying on top of the bookcase, where she'd left it on the last occasion she'd consulted it. It was a dependable book and a very weighty

151

one, with the title *The Concise Home Doctor: Encyclopaedia of Good Health* printed across its grey cover. She lit the gas, settled in her armchair and began to read.

Rose Boniface was late getting in to work the next morning but, as Miss Monk had kept her well over time the previous evening, she was prepared with her defence.

It wasn't needed. The breakfast things were set ready, the kettle was on the boil and everything in the room appeared to be normal except for Mrs Biggs. She was sitting by the stove, reading the morning paper with her feet on the fender.

'They're not up,' she explained. 'They're all rolling around in bed being idle.'

'Oh.'

'I ain't complaining,' Mrs Biggs said. 'Suits me fine. You'd better creep up and let that damn dog out though or it'll make a mess. Here's Daisy, coming in. We're all late this morning. She can make us all a cup of tea.'

Rose crept up the stairs as she was bidden and opened Miss Monk's bedroom door as quietly as she could. The dog was waiting for her and came scrambling out of the room as soon as there was a crack in the doorway big enough for him to squeeze through. He was making an odd whimpering noise, so, thinking the missus was awake and cross, Rose put her head round the door and peeped in.

Miss Monk was rolling about in the bed as if she were having another fit, only this time her mouth and chin were flecked with white foam and she was making odd grunting sounds. 'Rose . . .' she gasped. 'Thank God you've come. Get the doctor. I'm so ill . . . Tell Mr Monk . . . Oh I'm *so* ill.'

I can't leave her like this, Rose thought. I'll have to wipe away that foam before she chokes on it. But then she saw the commode and that gave her such a shock that she ran from the room at once to do as she was told. The lid had been left up and the pot inside was full of blood.

'Tell Cedric!' Miss Monk panted.

He came to his bedroom door in his pyjamas, yawning and scratching the stubble on his chin, but as soon as he heard what was the matter he was down the corridor at once.

Within ten minutes a fire had been lit in the invalid's bedroom and the house was organised for sickness; within twenty the doctor had arrived.

He examined his patient carefully, particularly in the area of the kidneys, which she confessed to being rather sore; he enquired into what she'd been eating and drinking the previous day; and finally he gave his judgement. 'I think, dear lady, we had better have you into hospital.'

'Am I bad, Doctor?' Augusta asked faintly.

'No, no,' Dr Felgate soothed, 'But just to be on the safe side I think it would be wise for you to see a specialist. We don't want to run risks with our health, do we? And particularly not with our kidneys.'

'Is it my kidneys, Doctor?'

'Let us hope not. I can telephone from here, I take it Mr Monk?'

Cedric and Winifred had been tactfully gazing out of the window while the examination went on, now he tiptoed back to the bed and took Augusta's hand. 'Of course,' he said. 'I'll show you the way.' And he added to his sister, 'It is for the best darling.' He'd been very alarmed by the sight of all that blood.

'I know,' Augusta said weakly.

'Winifred will stay here and look after you, won't you Winifred. I shan't be long.'

'You're so good to me, Ceddy,' Augusta said, smiling at him faintly. 'I do feel so ill. I thought I was going to die.'

'No, no, no,' Dr Feldgate tried to reassure her. 'We shall have you well again in no time at all.'

But as he and Cedric walked down the wide staircase into the hall, he confessed that he was really quite anxious about the state of his patient and would see to it that the ambulance was called at once. 'Blood in the urine is something we must take seriously,' he warned.

'What about the foaming at the mouth?' Cedric wanted to know. That had alarmed him too.

'That is something of a puzzle,' the doctor admitted, as he picked up the telephone. 'It would have no bearing on the kidneys. Something she ate, possibly. A fit of choking. Something gone down the wrong way. Ah! There you are, miss. Dr Felgate speaking. Could you get me Lambeth Hospital, please?'

The ambulance was sent so quickly that the two parlourmaids hardly had time to put Augusta into a clean nightdress before it arrived. And her going was equally speedy and very noisy. She cried out so loudly when they lifted her onto a stretcher that the other servants could hear her in the kitchen and came running out into the hall to see what was going on.

'Wonder how they'll cope with her up the hospital,' the charwoman said, scratching her elbows.

'Rather them than us,' Mrs Biggs said. 'We got other things to think about.'

'Like what?' Daisy asked, hoping it wouldn't mean too much work.

Mrs Biggs grinned at them. 'Like a nice plate of cold beef and pickles for dinner today. While the cat's away. You two gels go and clean up her bedroom and feller-me-lad can clear out all the grates and Clem can give the hall a quick flick and then we're done fer the day. They won't need fires all over the house, that's one good thing, and everything else can wait till we know where we are.'

So Rose and Daisy took their mops and brooms and polishing cloths to Augusta's bedroom and rolled up their sleeves ready to give it a good turn-out. The first thing they did was to strip the bed, which was full of crumbs, and covered in dog hairs and muddy paw-marks.

'Look at the state of this pillow slip,' Rose said.

But Daisy was looking at something that Rose had dislodged from underneath the pile of pillows. It was a large cake of scented soap and it had obviously been recently used because it was still tacky to the touch.

'Now that's funny,' she said. 'What's a cake of soap doing under her pillows?'

Rose neither knew nor cared. She was thinking about four blue dresses hanging on Mrs Tuffin's rail and planning what she would make with her length of pink cloth and wondering whether any of her creations would sell on Friday or Saturday.

CHAPTER THIRTEEN

It was Friday evening and the start of the third and final weekend of Rose Boniface's designated three. And not a single one of their dresses had been sold.

'If it don't work after this,' Netta said gloomily, 'we'll have to throw in the towel.'

'It'll work,' Rose said firmly. She'd been saying the same thing all week, assuming an optimism she didn't feel. 'Something will have sold. You'll see.'

But the blue frocks were still hanging on the rail as if they were permanent fixtures. She could see them as she walked towards the stall.

'No luck?' she asked, as she arrived.

Mrs Tuffin left her customer mulling over a pile of second-hand blouses and grinned across her counter at Rose. 'Pink one went half an hour ago,' she said. 'One a' my factory gels. Very took with it she was. I reckon you could sell more a' *them*.'

Four more were delivered by Wednesday afternoon, even though Netta was worried about such an outlay. 'We can't spend all our spare cash on material,' she said, coughing painfully. 'That could've been a fluke. What if they don't sell? We'll have *eight* on our hands.'

But by the next Friday evening she had to admit that her sister's gamble had paid off. All four pink frocks were gone and one of the blue had sold too.

'You struck a winner with that pink,' Mrs Tuffin said. 'That's what done it. One of 'em went Wednesday, half an hour after we hung them on the rail. Good eh?'

'How about half a dozen next Friday,' Rose said. 'Assorted colours.'

'Try ten,' Mrs Tuffin said. 'I got the space.'

'We'll never make ten frocks in a week,' Netta said.

But Rose had no doubt. 'Now we've started, you'll be surprised what we'll do,' she said.

'I'll help you,' Muriel offered. 'Many hands make light work.'

The dresses continued to sell as news of their quality spread. There were a lot of young women in Kennington earning good money in munitions and a stylish frock was just what they wanted. By the end of the month Muriel and the Bonifaces had made nineteen garments and sold every one. At a mark-up of ten shillings per dress they were well in pocket, even after Mrs Tuffin had taken her sixpence commission.

'We shall have to start thinking about paying people a wage soon,' Rose said, when they got back to Ritzy Street on Saturday evening after their usual trip to the market. 'Muriel can't go on working for nothing. No, you can't Mu, really. And neither should Mabel.'

'Divide it up according to the hours we work,' Netta said, pricking the sausages. 'Fair shares for everybody.'

'Like a co-operative,' Muriel said, filling the kettle for tea. She was so much a part of the family now that she joined in the chores automatically. 'I was reading about that in one of Mr Edmund's magazines.'

What's a co-operative?' Netta said.

'I'll tell you while we're eating,' Muriel said.

Which she did. They were all impressed by such a scheme.

'Fair shares,' Netta approved. 'That's it. Like I said. We share the profits and the risks and everything. We shall be a firm before we know where we are.'

'What are we going to call ourselves?' Muriel asked. 'If we're a firm we'll have to have a name.'

'Ritzy Clothes,' Rose said at once. 'Because we live in Ritzy Street and we make clothes.'

So it was agreed and the new firm was toasted in wartime tea with a spoonful of condensed milk and a great sense of occasion.

157

'Here's to us!' Rose said. 'Success at last.'

In her side ward in the Lambeth Hospital, Augusta's disease was proving a great deal more complicated than the doctors expected, as Edmund discovered when he went to visit her, late one afternoon, bearing a bunch of drooping daffodils and a fixed smile.

He was profoundly distrustful of hospitals and especially this one, which had been converted from the old workhouse and still showed too many signs of its impoverished past – age-stained tiles on the walls and crusted pipes on the ceiling, high windows and over-scrubbed floors, a general air of ancient decay brisked by disinfectant. But he steeled himself to face the place and its new occupant. She might have cut him out of her will more times than he cared to think about but she was still his sister and, despite what his reason might tell him, his instincts made him feel responsible for her.

A houseman took him into the Sister's office.

'Your sister is quite a puzzle,' he admitted. 'We haven't really been able to ascertain what's the matter with her, to tell you the truth. There has been no further haemorrhage, I'm glad to say, but she suffers regular bouts of extreme pain, which we haven't been able to control.'

'I see,' Edmund said politely. Although he didn't.

'We've given her a course of castor oil to dissolve any kidney stones and there's no distention or fever and no other symptoms so far as we can ascertain, but she still seems to be in pain.'

'Yes.'

'I wondered whether you could account for it,' the houseman hoped. 'Could she have pulled a muscle or something like that? Unaccustomed gardening perhaps.'

'I doubt it,' Edmund said. 'She never gardens.'

'Housework?'

'She has plenty of servants.'

'Ah. It's a mystery.'

'Could it be nerves?'

'Is she of a nervous disposition?'

'She's easily worked up.'

'Yes,' the houseman agreed. 'We saw that when we gave her the castor oil.'

'So what is going to happen to her?'

'We shall keep her under observation for another three days, then if there are still no other symptoms apart from the pain we shall probably allow her to go convalescent. There is certainly no cause for alarm. Apart from the pain she is very fit. You'll want to see her now, I daresay.'

Although she'd been in hospital for more than three weeks, Augusta looked remarkably healthy, sitting up in the white hospital bed, surrounded by expensive gifts – chocolates and hot house grapes from Cedric, a small bunch of spring flowers from Mr Tilling and another, larger and more impressive from the vicar. Edmund offered his own wilting bouquet and winced as she put it on the counterpane without looking at it.

'They're being so kind to me here,' she said. 'Nothing is too much trouble. I only have to ring the bell and they come running.'

Edmund opened her bedside cabinet and peered inside. 'How are you feeling?'

'Terrible,' she said brightly. 'What are you looking for?'

'A vase,' he said, finding one. 'For the daffodils.'

'Come and sit down and talk to me.'

He put the daffodils in water, found a chair and occupied it diffidently. 'I'm sorry to hear you've been ill,' he said. 'But you're better now?'

'Oh no,' she said, helping herself to a chocolate. 'I wouldn't say I was better. I need a lot of care. I very nearly died, you know. If Dr Felgate hadn't rushed me in here I should have been done for. No question of that. It's my kidneys, you see. I had a haemorrhage. Did Cedric tell you? I was in agony. Well you can imagine, can't you.' She leant towards him, her tone confidential. 'I've had the most terrible medicine. Excruciating.'

And made the most terrible fuss about it, Edmund thought, remembering the houseman's words. I'll bet she's being an awful nuisance. I hope I die quietly before I can be a nuisance to anybody.

'Personally I think it's a stone,' Augusta was saying, choosing another chocolate from the box. 'Calculus they call it but that's what it means. Stone in the kidney. Oh yes. It'll either be a stone or a tumour. Either way it'll mean an operation. They're going to make up their minds in a day or two. Would you like a choccie?'

'No thank you. I shall have to be going soon. I've got a late class. Is there anything I can get you?'

'A bottle of my nice claret would be a thought. We only have water with our meals in here. It's the one thing I could fault them for. I'm sure they wouldn't mind.'

'I'll ask someone about it before I go,' Edmund lied, knowing they wouldn't allow it.

'Come and see me again,' she ordered gaily.

But when he returned, four days later, her bed was occupied by another patient and the Sister told him she had gone to Suffolk with her brother to convalesce.

'Rather him than us,' Louella said. 'She'll be an obnoxious invalid, you just see. They'll quarrel as sure as eggs are eggs.'

'Not that they'll tell us if they do.' Edmund said.

'She'll be back within the week,' Louella predicted.

But two weeks passed and there was no sign of her return. And at the end of the third week, Mrs Biggs told all the day staff that she'd had a letter from the missus to say that she wouldn't be back home for quite a while and that everybody except Rose, the char and the bootboy were to be given a week's notice.

Daisy was most upset. 'That ain't very nice,' she protested. 'I been here ages. She can't just sling me out like that.'

But it seemed she could.

'She's saving money, mean old baggage,' Mrs Biggs said. 'That's about the size of it. I should start looking for

160

another job PDQ if I was you, my gel. We'll get all the rooms shut up this morning and then you can cut off this afternoon.'

Rose said she'd like to cut off too.

'Why's that?'

'I've got a lot of work to do at home.'

'Suit yourself,' Mrs Biggs said, sucking in her cheeks. 'We shan't have much work here once it's all shut up, so you might as well.'

They cleaned the grates, stripped the beds, boxed the ornaments, covered all the furniture with dust sheets and closed off all the rooms except the parlour, the kitchen and the scullery. It was as if the place had been abandoned.

'Well, that's that,' Mrs Biggs said, rolling down her sleeves. 'You can stay off now for as long as you like. No point coming in. There's nothing more to do. And good luck to the rest of you.'

'It couldn't have come at a better time,' Rose said to Netta when she got home. 'It'll give me a chance to get on with the frocks.'

Now that spring was on its way, there was a sudden spurt of trade and the orders came in as fast as they could meet them. Their living-room was constantly full of half-finished garments and rolls of cloth. March became April, winter wool gave way to summer cotton, and it wasn't long before they'd doubled their output. And they were still selling.

Netta grew stronger and less yellow by the day. The firm worked well together. Miss Monk was still in Suffolk. The Americans entered the war and the papers were full of articles about what a difference their immense man-power would make to the Allied Cause. Col wrote home every week, long cheerful letters to say he was in the pink and to urge them to keep up their peckers. And from time to time a card would arrive for Rose from Jack Jeary – one of the official ones with ready printed sentences for him to tick to tell her he was well and that he wasn't wounded.

After that last dreadful leave of his, and with all the work she had to do, she had almost given up thinking about him – by day – particularly as he never wrote letters to her, but she still dreamt about him most passionately at night and she was glad of the cards. News, however scanty, kept her hopes alive.

And then, best news of all, Col wrote to tell them he was coming home on leave.

He arrived in time for the Whit Monday fair on Hampstead Heath.

It was an oddly disappointing leave – as they all agreed when it was over – although it was hard to put a finger on exactly what was wrong. Col seemed as loving towards them as ever when he first got back but the idealistic boy had gone. Now he spent most of his time up the pub with his friends and staggered home late at night singing coarse songs and too drunk to undo his boots. His appearance had changed a lot too but they'd half expected that. He was a great deal taller and he'd grown a black moustache and lost two of his front teeth. Worse, he'd developed an unpredictable temper.

When they looked at his missing teeth on that first evening, he fairly snapped their heads off. 'And don't say nothink about me mashers!' he growled. 'It could've been me head.' Even quite trivial things triggered off an outburst of lurid swearing – a broken bootlace one morning – a slow-boiling kettle the next. After two days they were quite frightened of him.

But he took them to the fair on Whit Monday and treated them all to the swings and the roundabouts and was quite his old self out in the open air, teasing and joking like old times. Even so, it was a thin sort of Bank Holiday and nowhere near as good as it had been pre-war. There were stalls selling whelks and cockles and shrimps but no pork pie stalls, no pigs' trotters, no barley sugar sticks, no apples, no thick bars of chocolate. Just wheaten bread and chunks of treacly brown cake and oranges at fivepence each, which Netta said was downright exorbitant.

'It's the war,' Rose comforted as they were journeying home. 'It changes everything, shortages and everybody working so hard and all the men at the front.'

'I wish it would change something for the better,' Muriel said sadly.

'I'm thinking of buying a motorbike,' Netta said. 'That'ud be a change for the better.'

'Good God!' Col said, staring at her. 'Whatever for?'

'To deliver the frocks.'

'You don't need a motorbike to deliver frocks.'

'We do, the number we make,' Rose told him with some pride.

'Quite the business women ain'tcher?' he laughed at them. 'What next!'

'Bigger orders if I've got anything to do with it,' Netta said.

But what happened next was the arrival of a card from Jack Jeary with quite a long message printed on it in block capitals.

'Home on leave. Arrive Waterloo 10.45 a.m. second Wednesday in August. See you soon. Love Jack.'

163

CHAPTER FOURTEEN

'Go and meet him,' Muriel urged. 'You know the train he's on. He wouldn't have told you about it – now would he? – if he hadn't wanted you to meet him.'

'But after all this time with only those printed cards,' Rose said. 'It's been months, Mu.'

'Don't you still love him?' Muriel asked.

'I don't know,' Rose admitted. 'And that's the truth of it.'

The postcard had brought all her muddled emotions to the surface. Since that last short leave of his, she hadn't been certain how she felt about him. She'd been grateful for his kindness then – she remembered that clearly enough – but that wasn't love, was it? The times they'd spent together before he went away to France seemed like part of another life that no longer had anything to do with her. Fantasies about him still troubled her dreams, so that she woke aching with desire for him. But was *that* love? She didn't know and there was no one she could ask, not even Muriel because it was too private. Things might have been different if he'd written to her and told her how *he* felt but all he'd ever done was to send her printed postcards full of ticks and crosses and they didn't tell her anything and could have come from anyone. How could she be sure of anything after such a long time and so little contact and so much grief?

'Go,' Muriel advised, giving her a hug. 'You'll never know if you don't. And if you don't, you might regret it.'

So she went.

It was a such a bubbly day it was easy to feel happy, despite her doubts. A day of bright sunlight, clouds like great white meringues, a strong wind whipping the

Thames to a froth and blowing coats and scarves like flags. Men's trouser legs were pushed against their calves as if they'd been pinned there, women held on to their hats as they skipped before the gale into the great cavern of Waterloo Station. And once inside they continued to scurry, rushing towards the platform as the troop train steamed to a halt, doors opening – clack, clack, clack – like dominoes falling, khaki legs jumping out before the train could stop, leaping and running to leave and loved ones.

Rose and Jack saw one another in the same moment, he running, she peering, and in that instant all her doubts were dissolved in a gale of relief and happiness. She ran towards him as though there were no crowds to dodge and in a final rush they were in one another's arms and he was kissing her, long and hard and hungrily.

'Oh Christ Rosie,' he said. 'It *is* good to be home.'

'I love you,' she said. Oh how wonderful, wonderful to know that it *was* true after all. 'So, so much.'

It takes a lot of kissing to make up for months of separation. When they finally stopped they were both breathless.

'Give us a pinch,' he ordered, standing with his arms still round her waist.

She laughed at him. 'Why?'

'Can't believe me luck, to be back here with you, like this. How about some grub?' He flung an arm round her shoulders and tucked her into his side ready to walk off.

It was such a possessive gesture and so full of affection that she turned to kiss him as they walked. 'Welcome home,' she said.

'You're better then?' he said. It was only just a question because he'd already seen the answer. 'You've got over it a bit.'

'Yes,' she said. 'I still miss him. Dreadfully. I think I shall always miss him but it's – well – a bit easier somehow.'

'Good,' he said. ''Cause I got somethink to ask you.'

She was intrigued. 'What?'

'How about a fortnight's holiday by the sea? Whatcher think?'

The idea took her breath away. 'What you an' me, d'you mean? On our own?'

'Why not? Be a lark. I got a fortnight's leave. We could go to Dover.'

'Stay in the same place, sort of thing?'

'In the same room,' he hoped.

It made her feel weak to think about it.

'What about it then?' he asked.

'I'll have to think about it,' she said.

'Think quick then. I've booked it from tomorrow.'

'Tomorrow?'

'Yep! It's all booked up. I'm staying here the one night an' then I'm off. Give us a kiss.'

Cuddled up against his side like this she was in a state of acute desire for him, wanting to kiss and be kissed, touch and be touched. Whatever would it be like if they were on their own together for fourteen days? I'll ask Mu what I ought to do, she decided. She's always so sensible.

The sensible Muriel was waiting for her when she got home much later that afternoon. 'We've run out of pink cotton,' she said when she saw the state Rose was in. 'Let's take a stroll and get some more.'

They set off to the shops arm in arm, striding through the crowds in the easy way of the city bred. It was the perfect setting for confidences but Rose was hesitant now that the chance had come. This was such a delicate subject to broach that, even though Muriel was her closest friend, she wasn't sure how to begin.

'Well?' Muriel said, pushing her glasses up her nose. 'How did you get on? As if I need to ask.'

'You were right,' Rose told her, smiling happily. 'It *was* the right thing to do.'

'I knew you still loved him.'

They walked on in companionable silence for several yards. Then Rose spoke again.

'Mu,' she said. 'Can I ask you something?'

'Anything,' Muriel said mildly, glancing at her friend. Then she was alerted by the serious expression on Rose's face.

'Suppose Bertie had come home on leave,' Rose began, speaking cautiously so that she could retract anything she said the minute she saw it was causing pain or offence. 'Before . . .'

Muriel's eyes were round and serious behind her glasses. 'Yes. Suppose he had.'

'Well, suppose he'd come home, or he'd wrote to say he was coming home, an' he'd asked you to go away, sort of on holiday with him, would you've gone?'

'What, just him and me, you mean?'

Rose looked her friend straight in the eye and now her expression was decidedly anxious. 'Yes.'

Muriel's heart gave a lurch of anguish. If only she'd had the chance, just one chance, before she lost him for ever. 'Like a shot,' she said.

That was a surprise. 'Would you really?'

'Like a shot. Oh, I know you're not supposed to. I know what they say. You're supposed to wait until you're married and keep yourself pure and all that sort of thing. But that was in the old days, before they took all the men off to be killed. Times have changed with a war on. No, if Bertie had offered me a holiday like that, I'd have jumped at it. I wish he had.'

'And you'd've gone with him? No matter what people said?'

'I loved him,' Muriel said, her eyes filling with tears. 'I'd have done anything for him. I don't think I'd have cared what people said.'

Rose was flooded with sympathy. 'Oh Muriel I do wish you could've.'

'This is about you and Jack isn't it?' Muriel said, blinking her tears away.

'Yes.' The admission was so hesitant it was virtually a whisper. But once made, it was easy to tell Muriel the rest. 'I've promised to give him his answer tonight,' she said. 'At the Music Hall.'

Muriel hugged her. 'You go,' she advised. 'Have a lovely time and stay with him as long as you can. Life's too short to waste.'

'You make it sound so simple,' Rose admired.

'It is simple. You love him. He loves you. What could be simpler than that? You go.'

'I'll have to nip in and ask Mrs Biggs first,' Rose said. 'I can't just walk out on her, can I? I need the job.'

Mrs Biggs was quite happy about it. 'Can't see any harm in it,' she said. 'She ain't back, when all's said an' done. Holiday is it?'

'Yes.'

'You won't get paid.'

'No. I know. That's all right.'

'Okay then. Go ahead.'

Now, Rose thought, I shall have to tell Netta and Mabel. And her heart quailed at the thought of what they might say. She'd have to find some way of breaking it to them – sort of gently – so as they weren't shocked.

But Muriel had done her work for her. They knew and approved. And hugged her passionately to show it.

'Mu told us,' Netta said. 'You go our Rose. Holiday'll do you good. You've earned it, all the work you've done. We can manage here.'

So Jack was told that evening and spent the rest of it kissing her and telling her how wonderful she was. 'I'll call for you tomorrow morning,' he said, as he kissed her goodnight on the doorstep. 'We'll have the time of our lives.'

Rose had very few doubts about it and when they arrived at a station called Dover Marine, she was quite, quite sure.

It was the first time in her life she'd ever been further afield than the West End of London. And now here she was, not just at the seaside but in a port, with a strange salt tang filling her nostrils and her ears full of sounds she didn't recognise. The sky arching over her head was the highest and bluest she'd ever seen and full of great fat gulls that mewed like cats and flew so close to her that she felt she could put out a hand and touch them. What a place!

There was every kind of ship crowded into the harbour, from liners to ferries, and a great many more out at sea, waiting to enter or ploughing white furrows in the blue-green water as they headed back to France. She scanned the confusion, listening to the steady chug and purr of the engines and the occasional whoop of an approaching tug, her excitement growing. It was all new to her and wonderfully strange, masts like winter trees; smoke stacks belching black and brown fumes; decks crammed with soldiers, smoking and swearing and packed about with kit; mooring ropes wherever she looked, snaked side to side, tar-stained and creaking; a non-stop bustle of dockers and troops and bellowing sergeants.

The jetty was thronged with soldiers all carrying full kit, some sombrely waiting to board, others striding to the freedom of a well-earned leave. There was a hospital ship being unloaded at the far end of the quay. She could see the waiting ambulances, their red crosses bold in the summer sunlight, and a dazzle of white caps above the long grey capes of the nurses. As she watched, the first stretcher was eased slowly down the gangplank. And that made her think of Col. And Bertie, oh my poor dear Bertie!

'Come on,' Jack said, taking her arm. 'Come an' see our digs.'

The place he'd chosen was on the promenade in a long terrace of three-storeyed hotels and boarding-houses. It was a bright white-stuccoed building with a slate-blue roof, window-boxes crammed with marigolds and orange awning shading all the windows. And it was run by a rather dishevelled lady who introduced herself as Mrs Albert Brown and said she made a speciality of men in His Majesty's Armed Forces and had obviously taken a shine to this one.

'I've put you in a room with a view, Mr Jeary,' she told him, 'being as you got your wife with you.'

It was a very big room and dominated by a high double bed, which Rose made an effort not to look at, although it made her heart beat faster just to know it was there. A very big, grand room. The wallpaper was in a pattern of forget-me-nots and pink ribbons, the wardrobe and chest of drawers were made of some dark wood that Rose couldn't recognise, the wash-stand had a marble top, there were even two cane-bottomed chairs and a little round table beside the window. 'Some of my ladies and gentlemen prefer to take breakfast in their rooms – for a slight extra charge.'

'Yes,' Jack told her. 'That'ud be A1.'

They looked out on the sloping grey-brown shingle of the beach and the peaceful blue of the incoming tide. To their right, several beach huts were drawn up in a line at the water's edge ready for use, like red and blue boxes on wheels, to their left a pier jutted into the sea and the cliffs rose snow white against the blue sky. There were families sitting on the pebbles watching the waves, or strolling the promenade with their perambulators and parasols. The war was a million miles away.

'You'll find all the other information you need on the card,' Mrs Albert Brown said, trying to tidy her hair and failing. 'I hope you have a very happy leave, Mr and Mrs Jeary.' And left them.

They stood in the sunlight and kissed one another – at length and with growing pleasure.

'We ought to find this card of hers,' Rose said, stepping back from him to catch her breath. 'I'll bet we ain't supposed to stay in the room during the day.'

He was daring her with his eyes. 'I'll bet we ain't supposed to do a lot of things.'

She answered dare with dare. 'Like what, Jack Jeary?'

'I'll show you, Rose Boniface,' he promised.

And did.

So the card didn't get read until much, much later in the

day – after much love-making, a pie and a pint in the local pub and a stroll along the promenade in the evening sun. And then it was Rose who read it out and he didn't even look at it. And anyway it was a little late to discover that their landlady *'would appreciate it if her guests could vacate their room after breakfast and return to it after high tea.'*

'Well there's a war on,' Jack said easily. 'She can't expect miracles. Anyway, she won't say nothink. I betcher.'

The holiday itself was a miracle, offering them one pleasure after another. They made love into the small hours and slept late the following morning. When they felt the need of company they strolled down to the pubs and joined the throng at the bar, where Jack made friends with all comers, stood drinks and was treated in his turn, and sang rude songs at the piano to ribald applause.

> *'I don't want to be a soldier,*
> *I don't want to go to war,*
> *I'd rather stay at home*
> *Around the streets to roam*
> *And live on the earnings of a – lady typist.*
> *Don't want a bayonet in me belly,*
> *Don't want me bollocks shot away,*
> *I'd rather stay in England*
> *In merry, merry England*
> *And fornicate me bleedin' life away.'*

'What's fornicate?' Rose asked when they were safe in the privacy of their room that night.

'What we've just been doing.'

'And is that what soldiers really sing?'

'That and worse,' he grinned. 'Don't let's talk about the war. I've left all that behind.'

But war has long tentacles and that night it crept up and found them again.

Not long after they'd fallen asleep, Rose woke to the

sound of thunder. Drowsy though she was, she got up to close the window before the rain began. Her going woke Jack.

'Where you off to?'

She explained.

'Come back to bed,' he told her. 'That ain't thunder. It's the guns.'

She was astonished. It couldn't be. 'D'you mean we can hear them *here*?'

'When there's a push,' he said laconically. 'It's only fifty or sixty miles. Sounds travel at night.'

'Oh Jack!' she said. 'It must be an awful noise if you're right next to it.'

'Yes,' he said shortly. 'It is. Are you coming back to bed or have I got to come and get you?'

The sound of the barrage kept her awake for more than an hour that night, wondering and imagining and pitying. When she woke in the morning Jack was already up and washing himself.

She watched with affection as he soaped his arms and chest and swung the flannel across his back. Such broad shoulders, she thought, admiring him, and such brown skin. Then she became aware that there were raised red bumps all round his waist and down his sides, and that some of them were scabby.

'What are all those?' she asked.

He answered casually. 'Bites.'

'Bugs?' They certainly looked angry enough. But there wasn't any bugs in this bedroom, surely to goodness. It was all much too clean.

'No,' he said, scratching one of them. 'Jerusalem cattle. Lice.' And when she grimaced, 'We all have livestock in the trenches. It goes with the job. Don't worry. You won't catch them. They disinfect us before they let us home.'

She was filled with pity for him but she could see from the stern expression on his face that she wasn't to say any more about it. 'I'm just going down to see Aunt Jane,' she told him and tiptoed out of the room to the WC.

When she got back, he was fully dressed and their breakfast had arrived. 'How about a trip out in the country?' he said. 'It's gonna be a lovely day.'

It was a beautiful day and they forgot the war and enjoyed every minute of it. And the next day was just as good. And the next. But when Rose woke up on their fifth morning, the room was much darker than usual and so muffled that she thought someone had come in during the night and drawn the curtains. Then she realised that the windows were obscured by white mist.

She got up, threw her blouse round her shoulders because it was decidedly chilly and walked to the window to look out. It was as thick as a London fog out there, only pure white and smelling of salt. Sea, sky and horizon had completely disappeared and the beach and promenade were visible only in patches, as swathes of mist came rolling off the hidden sea as if it were boiling.

'You trying to catch the pneumonia?' Jack shivered. 'Come back in the warm this instant. I shan't love you with chilblains.'

'I bet you would,' she said. 'Look at this mist.'

'I'd rather look at you.'

'Tell you what. Let's go out and have a walk in it.'

'What for?'

'To see what it's like. I'd try anything once.'

'Try sommink else first,' he suggested.

So they went for their walk after breakfast, striding out into the mist and crunching across the pebbles until they found the edge of the sea, white as glass under the swirling vapour and totally calm. Now they could see that there were gulls brooding on the breakwater like dark grey statues, and at the water's edge an inch-high wave fell, lip, lip, against the sand. It was awesomely quiet and they seemed to have the place to themselves.

'There y'are,' Jack said, putting his arm round her shoulders. 'You've seen it. That's all there is. Now can we go up the town?'

'Let's walk along the prom. See how far it goes.'

'Daft hap'orth.'

'No go on. Let's.'

'You're not right in the head, you.'

They walked along the promenade arm in arm in the chill air.

'It ain't half quiet,' he said.

'Shush!' she said. 'There's someone else out there.'

Below the squeak of their boots on the promenade they could hear the faint lick of the sea and, above that, a distant crunch of feet on pebbles. There *was* somebody else walking on the beach. And a strange voice calling.

'Fishermen,' he said.

'In this weather?'

The crunching sounds continued, and as they strained their ears to hear what the voice was saying, a thick cloud of white mist rolled off the beach and engulfed them like the smoke from an explosion. For a few seconds they couldn't see anything at all, then it rolled away towards the cliffs, thinning as it went, and in the grey air behind it the strand was full of soldiers. They were marching in uneven ranks, grouped in fours, their faces pale with cold and concentration. One or two looked like old contemptibles, but the majority were raw recruits, awkward in their stiff, ill-fitting khaki, their heads rigid under hard new caps, their feet clumsy in black unyielding boots. Further along the beach, a drill sergeant was barking staccato orders at them. 'Me-e-e hi! Lair Ee!' Only the top of his body was visible in the mist so that he looked as though he'd been cut in half and then suspended two feet above the ground. His squad obeyed him meekly and mechanically, their movements muffled by the white shreds of mist that still clung around them. There was something unreal about the scene, as though the war was already producing a new breed of men, at once above and below the normal run of humanity. They were so quiet, so controlled and so distant.

Rose was standing alone on the coarse pebbles a few yards ahead of Jack, her chin sunk into her collar,

174

watching with awestruck fascination. She didn't say a word when he came and stood beside her.

The squad formed fours and began to march away. They watched as one by one the rigid bodies and pale faces disappeared into the mist. Within four minutes they had all vanished without a sound or trace, as if they had never existed.

Rose was shivering. 'They were all so young,' she whispered. 'Not much older'n our Col, most of them.'

'Bleedin' war!' Jack said. His voice was so bitter that she turned to look at him.

'Jack?'

'Marching away to be killed,' he said. 'That's what they're doing. All the lot of them, poor buggers. *Form fours! Right turn!* That's just fuckin' ridiculous.' His voice was full of hatred, sneering and mocking. 'A load of bollocks. You go over the bags, you don't stand a chance. It's just slaughter. That's all it is. Bleedin' slaughter. Them stupid buggers don't know the half of it.'

Before such terrible passion Rose couldn't think of anything to say. She put her arms round his waist and held him.

He tucked her head under his chin, hiding her face from the fury of his eyes. He was shaking with anguish.

'Is it so bad?' she whispered, remembering the bites on his back and the sound of those awful guns.

'It's the worst thing in the world.' He gave himself a shake, pushing the evil memories away. 'Don't let's talk about it, eh?'

'No,' she agreed, rubbing her face against the rough cloth of his tunic. 'We won't. I promise.'

So they continued their holiday and deliberately put the war behind them. When the guns thundered at night, they didn't listen; when he washed, she noted that his scabs were healing and didn't mention them; when the newspaper placards shouted of a battle at Passchendaele, they walked past. The sun shone on them so they paddled in the sea, the breeze blew so they ran off to their friends in the pub. They took a trip to Canterbury where they ignored the cathedral and found a music hall and another to Ramsgate where they ate cockles and saw the Pierrots. And all too soon it was their last day and time to part.

'Don't come to the jetty,' he said.

She would have preferred to stay with him until the very last moment but she went along with what he asked for. 'All right. If you don't want me to.'

'I couldn't bear to say goodbye to you with all that bellowing going on,' he explained. Now that his leave was so nearly over he was beginning to realise how much he was going to miss her.

They kissed goodbye on the platform just before he put her on the train.

'Come back soon,' she begged as she leant out of the window.

'Soon as ever I can,' he promised. 'You know me.'

'Yes,' she said. 'I do now.' And she was thinking, this is what it's like being married, happy as sandboys when you're together and torn in half when you have to say goodbye. The train was blowing steam. 'Write to me,' she said.

'I will. I promise.' It surprised him to realise that he meant it. She looked so pretty framed by that window with her cheeks so pink and her hair the colour of cob nuts and her eyes huge with love for him. His darling Rosie. He'd never felt this way about any other girl in the whole of his life. Ever. I love her, he thought. She's mine and I love her. It was suddenly, wonderfully, searingly obvious to him. He must have loved her all along and never known. He'd never told her either and now it was almost too late. 'Oh Christ Rosie,' he said. 'I can't bear this.' There was just time for him to leap on the running-board and snatch one last kiss. 'I love you,' he said passionately. 'You're my gel. I love you.'

She hung about his neck, prolonging the kiss until the train pulled them apart. Then she hung out of the window and waved until the engine whistled into the tunnel.

When she last saw him he was standing with his kit at his feet, his cap on the back of that tousled head, smiling and waving.

CHAPTER FIFTEEN

Rose spent the journey home in a happy dream, reliving her holiday and warm with love. It came as quite a shock to her to see how grey and dreary London looked under the same summer sun, its tenements soot black, streets smeared with horse dung, trams and buses spattered with dust and grime. And so many women in mourning, patiently standing in the food queues in their dark, drab clothes. Why've I never noticed them before? she wondered, as she climbed aboard her tram outside Victoria Station. Or has it got worse while I've been away?

It was good to be home, just the same. She took the stairs two at a time, calling happily to her sisters. 'Coo-ee! I'm back!'

But there was no answering call and when she opened the door she knew at once that something was terribly wrong. Netta and Mabel were sitting on the rag rug on either side of the empty fireplace, very still and with their heads down, staring at the hearth. Neither of them looked up when she came in and neither of them moved. It was as if they'd been frozen.

'Oh God!' Rose said. 'What is it? Tell me quick.'

And at that Netta looked up at her and began to cry.

'It come the day after you left,' she said. 'We didn't like to spoil your holiday. I mean, we thought . . .'

'A telegram?'

'Yes.'

'Col?'

Netta nodded with the tears tumbling out of her eyes. 'It come the day after you left.'

All joy drained away like blood from a wound. There

was only horror and death and loss. 'No, no, no!' she cried. 'It ain't true. It mustn't be true. No! Please!'

Netta was fumbling in one of the dresser drawers, turning, holding the awful yellow telegram towards her. But she couldn't see straight. The print was jumping and flickering as if the paper were on fire. 'Not Col too!' She was stunned at the malignancy of it. Both their brothers. 'Not Col too! There won't be anybody left.'

Mabel rubbed her back as she wept. Netta made a cup of tea and handed it to her tenderly. But tea was no comfort in the face of such distress. One death had been terrible enough. Two were too appalling to accept or comprehend. She was stuck in denial, begging to be told it wasn't true, unable to accept.

'Miss Monk's back,' Netta remembered, when they'd cried to a halt at last. 'They sent a letter for you yesterday.'

'I'll go in tomorrow,' Rose said vaguely. But it was unreal. It was as if their own lives had stopped too, as if all three of them had lost the ability to feel any emotion at all, except this endless, aching grief, as if Miss Monk and Mrs Biggs were part of some distant story that didn't have anything to do with them.

Rose went in to Monk House the next morning just the same. There wasn't anything else for her to do. But she worked in a daze and simply did as she was told without thought.

Miss Monk was in a very bad mood. She'd spent ten weeks convalescing with Cedric and nearly eight with Edmund and neither of them had treated her properly, even though she'd made it very clear how ill she was. Now she felt aggrieved and irritable and was ready to find fault with everyone.

'What's this I hear about you going on holiday?' she said, crossly, when Rose brought up her coffee.

The holiday had receded so far that Rose had to make an effort to remember the lie she'd planned to tell. 'Yes, ma'am,' she said. 'I went to stay with my cousin.'

'How long for?' Miss Monk said sharply. 'Mrs Biggs said it was a fortnight.'

'Yes, ma'am. I got back yesterday.' Was it only yesterday? It felt like months.

'I'm not at all pleased!' Augusta said, as she spooned sugar substitute into her coffee. 'You should have asked my permission first. Servants can't just take holidays whenever they feel like it.'

'No, ma'am.'

'I don't know. What's the world coming to?'

'Will that be all?' Rose asked wearily.

'More than enough, I should say,' her mistress declared, munching into the first of her six biscuits. 'I hope you're not going to make a habit of it.'

'I wish she wouldn't eat those biscuits like that,' Rose said when she got back to the kitchen. The sight of those busy jaws, munching open-mouthed and spilling crumbs in all directions, had made her feel nauseous.

'You all right are you gel?' Mrs Biggs said, alarmed by her pallor. 'There's tea in the pot if you'd like a cup.'

But Rose was bolting for the WC, her hands over her mouth.

As the weeks dragged by, she and Netta were often sick. Netta was used to it. Ever since the explosion she'd suffered from a recurring cough and several bouts of vomiting. She called it 'sicking up the fumes' and endured it without fuss. But it was a new thing for Rose and she found it debilitating although there didn't seem to be anything she could do to stop it.

The next three weeks were numb with misery. But then, one day when she got home from work, she found a bulky letter lying on the hall mat. It was from Jack, written in a scrawling sort of handwriting and telling her that he'd had a good crossing and was safely back in France, that he loved her more than he could say and couldn't wait to see her again, that he was going up to the line in a day or two and would write again when he got back to the support trenches. He'd signed it 'Your ever *loving Jack'* and there were twenty firm black kisses drawn in a pattern along the bottom edge of the paper. He'd forgotten to write his address at the top and he hadn't given her his number either, so she couldn't write back, but to have a letter from him was such a joy she didn't mind. He'll do it properly next time, she thought, tucking the letter into her brush and comb drawer. Dear Jack!

Meantime she and her sisters got on with their work, and there was plenty of it because the dresses were still selling. Their hearts weren't in it but they worked as well as they could. Muriel came over three times a week to help with the sewing and to try to cheer them, which was a very hard job. Mabel was prone to fits of howling and needed a lot of comforting, Netta was depressed and, although the letter had cheered her a little, Rose was listless and obviously unwell.

'I don't like her being sick all the time,' Netta confided on the quiet to Muriel.

'Are you?' Muriel asked her friend.

'Every morning for the last six,' Mabel told her earnestly.

'That won't do,' Muriel said. 'If it goes on you'll have to see a doctor, you know Rose.'

'What's the good of that,' Rose said sadly. 'It won't bring them back to life, will it? None of them.'

'I tell you what,' Muriel said. 'There's a special service at St Peter's on Sunday. Nancy Cartwright was telling me. A service for peace. Why don't we all go? That might help a bit.'

'It might,' Netta agreed. 'Pass me the scissors, Mabel, there's a good girl. It could be a way of saying goodbye to them, sort a' thing. Like a funeral.' The lack of a formal farewell had been one of the most difficult things for her to bear. Whatever else you might think about a funeral at least it was a day to mark the end of grief and the beginning of memory, as she knew from Mum's all those years ago. And Dad's before that.

So they all went to the service together, along with most of the other inhabitants of Ritzy Street. Miss Monk was also there, very grand in the front pew.

St Peter's Church was always a chilly place in the winter and on that November morning, it was cold and sombre – apart from the frozen fires of the stained-glass windows above the high altar. The altar itself, distant beyond the choir stalls, looked antiquated and foreign, carved like some huge oak chest and picked out in complicated patterns of giltwork and red and blue mosaic. The crucified Christ who hung upon it was just a poor, torn, naked body, forlorn behind the glitter of candles and gilt. Sitting quietly beside her friends, Muriel began to question the wisdom of attending. There was nothing about the scene before them to comfort Rose or either of her sisters.

The vicar had gone to a great deal of trouble to find a text to help his grieving congregation. 'We are here to commemorate our glorious dead,' he told them, 'who have gone from us into life everlasting, where there is no pain and no sorrow and no war. Now more than ever we need our faith. We must hold on. Hold on to the love of God, to the sure and certain hope of the Resurrection to eternal life, through our Lord Jesus Christ. For the Lord says, Behold I show you a mystery. We shall not all sleep, but we shall all be changed, in a moment, in the twinkling of an eye, at the last trump (for the trumpet shall sound) and the dead shall be raised incorruptible and we shall all be changed.'

But it was neither hope nor change that filled most minds in that cold church on that grief-charged morning. It was the dead, shot or gassed or drowned. It was Collum and Bertie, and all the millions of others. What's the good of praying? Rose thought, as the congregation knelt obediently. Prayers won't stop the grief of all these widows, or pay their rent, or keep them fed. The smell of mothballs rose pungently around her as winter coats were gathered under the knees of the worshippers. And anger

grew in her for the first time since she'd heard about Col –
against the war and the politicians who wanted to keep it
going and the generals who couldn't bring it to an end.
Anger and the familiar sickness.

She just had time to say "Scuse!' to Muriel and then she
had to make a very quick exit, reaching the south door
just in time to be sick on the path. Wiping her mouth with
her handkerchief, she staggered off to sit on the wall and
give herself time to recover. What a way to go on in the
middle of a church service, she thought. Perhaps I did
ought to go to a doctor.

She became aware that there were two misshapen shoes
standing just inside her line of vision. Nancy Cartwright.

'You all right gel?' that lady said.

'Yes. I'm sorry I . . .'

Nancy sat down on the wall alongside her and put an
arm round her shoulders. 'You ain't gone and fell have
you gel?'

'Fell?'

'For a baby,' Nancy explained. 'You ain't in the family
way?'

A baby, Rose thought. Oh God! It could be. That
would explain all the other odd symptoms she'd been
feeling lately. But she denied it at once. 'No. Course not.'

'It's none a' my business,' Nancy said. 'I could be
speaking out a' turn, but it *was* your young man you went
on holiday with, wasn't it? I shan't say nothink to no one
else but it was, wasn't it?'

'We was only away a fortnight,' Rose said. 'I mean, I
couldn't have . . . It wouldn't've been . . .'

'It only takes the once,' Nancy said comfortably. 'My
ol' man only had to hang his trousers on the bedpost and I
fell.'

A baby, Rose thought again, absorbing the idea with
shock and wonder and looming terror. A love child,
wasn't that what people said? They *did*, didn't they? But
they said bastard too and being a bastard was the worst
thing that could happen to you. But a baby. Think of it. A

183

baby coming to her now, out of that loving holiday and in the middle of all this awful grief. Why hadn't she thought of it before? It was wonderful. And terrifying. How could she possibly have a baby when she wasn't married? It *would* be a bastard, poor little thing. They'd have a terrible life of it. And yet she knew she wanted it – oh so much – Jack's baby. Oh God! she prayed. Dear God! What am I going to do?

Nancy Cartwright was still pursuing her own practical thoughts. 'When was you last on?' she asked.

'I can't remember,' Rose admitted, embarrassed by such an intimate question. 'Before I went to Dover I think.'

'There you are then,' Nancy said. 'Not much doubt about it, if I'm any judge. You'll be nearly three months gone. Due in May. Just in nice time for the fine weather. That sickness'll pass presently. It never lasts more than three months, leastways not in my experience. You'll have to get your young man to marry you on his next leave. I suppose he will?'

Rose was quite certain about *that*. 'Yes. Course he will.'

'If I was you,' Nancy advised, 'I'd get a ring on my finger. There's some right old mouths round here and you don't want gossip, do you. Best be on the safe side, eh? Write and tell your young man and get him used to the idea but get yourself a ring first. An' a married name.'

Rose was too stunned to take in what she was saying. 'I'd better go home,' she said.

'I'll walk you,' Nancy said.

First thing I'll do when I get back is write to him, Rose thought, as she walked into Ritzy Street. I know his regiment even if I don't know his number. That ought to find him. It's worth a try. I can't tell him about the baby – not yet and not with the censor reading everything –but I could say I'd got something to tell him when he's next home on leave and he might guess. I'll write the minute I get in.

She was still pen in hand when Netta and Mabel came charging back from the church, full of anxious excitement because Mrs Cartwright had told them the news.

'Is it true our Rose?' Mabel demanded. 'Have you got a baby?' She looked happily round the room, expected to see it already in its cradle.

Rose was in too much of a state for patient explanations. 'Yes,' she said shortly and turned to Netta. 'Ain't it awful! What am I going to do?'

'Get a ring on your finger PDQ.'

'That's what Mrs Cartwright said.'

'And quite right too. You could wear Mum's. We've still got it in the drawer. Give yourself a bit of protection.'

'I ain't entitled,' Rose said tearfully. 'It'ud be telling a lie.'

Netta looked her straight in the eye. 'Maybe it's necessary,' she said.

Rose turned away from such uncomfortable directness, glancing at Mum's sampler for support. 'How about *Living with Dignity*,' she asked. 'That means don't lie. Tell the truth no matter what.'

'But it ain't you that'll suffer,' Netta insisted. 'Is it? It's the baby. If Jack don't come home and marry you before it's born, it'll be a bastard and you know how they treat bastards round here. Remember poor Toby? And that Johnson kid? They made their lives an absolute misery. Well we all did.'

'Yes,' Rose admitted. 'I know.' Wasn't it an exact echo of her own thoughts?

'There you are then.'

But Rose still hesitated, too confused to be able to think straight.

'If you say something that ain't exactly true,' Netta said, 'and you know it ain't exactly true, but you do it to protect someone that needs protection, someone that can't protect theirselves, then I don't reckon that's a lie. Not the way most people mean it, anyway.'

It was a persuasive argument. 'Perhaps you're right.'

185

'Course I'm right,' Netta said. 'We got to look after this baby of ours. I ain't having no one call *him* names, I can tell you. Or her, if it's a her. You wear Mum's ring and call yourself Mrs Jeary. And another thing. You ain't to go queuing for no more food or nothing. *We*'ll do all that. We been talking it over on the way home, ain't we our Mabel?'

Mabel nodded vigorously.

'So,' Netta said sternly, 'that's the end of you standing in line. And you ain't to go traipsing round the streets lugging great parcels about neither. We got to look after you.'

'They're no weight,' Rose protested.

Netta overruled that at once. 'Yes, they are,' she said. 'And they're bulky.'

'They'll be bulky for anyone to carry.'

'Not for me,' Netta said. 'I'm gonna buy that motor-bike.'

'We can't afford a motorbike,' Rose protested. 'They cost the earth.'

Netta deferred her dream – temporarily. 'All right then, a push-bike. We could afford that. One of them tricycle things with a goods box, like a "*Stop me and buy one*". I could get it on the drip. I'll work out how many more frocks we got to sell to pay for it and I'll go round and rustle up the orders for them and then I'll get it on the drip. High time I pulled my weight round here.' Now that knowledge of the baby had galvanised her, any sacrifice or action was possible. 'It's gonna be lovely having a baby.'

She was as good as her word, although it took her nearly a fortnight to find the tricycle and to get the extra orders she wanted. But at last it was done and the vehicle was hers. It was a clumsy looking thing and the goods box was rather battered but she assured them she could knock all the dents out and that it would 'paint up lovely'.

For the next two days she deserted her sewing-machine to hammer out dents and paint the goods box bright red, coughing all the time but working with a will. Then, just as

186

Rose was cooking the tea, off she went again. This time on foot.

'Now what's she up to?' Nancy Cartwright called down from her window. 'I never knew such a gel.'

She was gone such a long time that Mabel was home from school and the tea was made before she got back.

She was wearing a man's trench coat and an Australian hat. 'Whatcher think?' she said.

'Very smart,' Rose admired. 'What you done with your hair? Is it tucked up inside?'

For answer Netta whipped off her hat. The mass of her long thick hair was gone and in its place was a neat curly shingle. It made her look quite different, boyish and rakish and very modern. For a few seconds her sisters simply stared at the transformation. Rose wasn't sure whether she liked it or not but Mabel was impressed.

'My eye!' she breathed. 'You *are* a swell, our Netta.'

She was also an amazingly good driver, handling her heavy tricycle with skill almost from the very first day. Half the street turned out to watch as she put on her new uniform and loaded up her first delivery. And they cheered as she drove away, yelling, 'Ritzy Street for ever!'

The baby had changed their lives, giving them something to look forward to and plan for. Just to talk of it provided them with hope and blunted the terrible cutting edge of their misery. They spoke of Col and Bertie too, nearly every day, gradually moving towards acceptance, memory by memory. This second death was at once more difficult to endure and more easy. This time they knew how grief progresses and consequently didn't fight it so hard. This time they were more skilled at comforting one another. There were anxieties, naturally, about getting enough orders, or work being done to time, or the shortage of food, but they were all things that kept them occupied and could be tackled – except for the worst anxiety of all, which was that Jack hadn't written any more letters after the first one. There was no answer to Rose's letter, even after three weeks.

'Write again,' Muriel advised. 'It could have gone astray.'

'Ain't he got a family round here somewhere?' Netta asked. 'Why don'tcher write to them?'

'I don't know where they are,' Rose said. 'He never said nothink about them.'

'Didn't he talk about them *ever*?'

'No. I wish he had.'

'Never mind,' Muriel consoled. 'Write *him* another letter.'

The second letter was a great deal more difficult than the first. The long silence was beginning to make Rose feel fearful, despite her outward cheerfulness. What if something had happened to him? It chilled her with fear to think about it. But she comforted herself that he couldn't be killed. Not after Bertie *and* Col. It was against the law of averages. Two were enough for any one family. But even so – the war was so dreadful and so many men were being lost. '*Please write soon,*' she begged. '*I have got some good news to tell you and I worry when there is no postcard.*'

The weeks passed. December started and she was beginning to show and there was still no reply, even though she wrote again. And again. She took to following the course of the war in the daily paper, anxiously watching for news of the campaign. But the papers were full of the revolution in Russia and the effect that was going to have on the war. She scanned the columns of the local paper just in case there was some mention of him there. But there was never any news to help her. And the weeks passed.

'You'll have to book the midwife soon,' Nancy Cartwright said. 'She's a nice woman – marvellous when it comes to it – but she needs a bit of notice. I suppose you ain't heard nothing from your young man yet?'

'No. Not yet,' Rose admitted, trying to put a brave face on it. 'I've written quite a few times but I don't think my letters are getting through. I don't know his number, you see.'

'Ah well!' Nancy said, wanting to be positive although secretly she was growing more and more pessimistic. 'No news is good news. Wait and see, eh?'

Waiting had become part of Rose's existence now, waiting and accepting. Pregnancy was not only altering her appearance, it was changing her nature. As her waist expanded she became more and more placid, settling into weight and responsibility as easily as a child snuggling into a feather bed. There was an uncomplicated fatalism about her thoughts these days. What was to be would be. There was nothing she could do to change the war or to alter events. All she could do was endure them, living day by day, hoping for peace and looking forward to the baby. If Jack was alive somewhere he would come home eventually and find her. If he was a prisoner he would come back when the war was over. If something had happened to him, she would face whatever it was when she had to. But not now. Not yet. There was enough grief in her life without going out of her way to find more. At night, she yearned to see him again, to be held in his arms and to weep about Col and tell him her good news. By day she simply got on with her work. It was the only thing she could do.

Chapter Sixteen

Nobody in Britain had the heart to celebrate the arrival of 1918. The war had been going on for three and a half years now and the slaughter in France was never-ending. The third battle of Ypres had cost two hundred and forty thousand British casualties alone between August and early November. Thousands of homes were bereaved, the hospitals were full of wounded soldiers, and, as an additional and daily irritation, the shortage of food was parlous. There was very little dairy produce, meat was in short supply and usually of poor quality, rabbits had disappeared off the market, sugar was virtually unobtainable. The Food Ministry mounted an economy campaign but that only made matters worse. The posters that appeared on the hoardings urging people to '*Eat Slowly. You Will Need Less Food*' were seen as a mockery.

Netta spent hours of every day standing in the inevitable queues while Mabel trailed after her, sometimes singing, but more often grizzling and complaining. Netta accepted it philosophically, being used to hard work and limited food and Mabel's peculiar ways, although she was privately annoyed that she had to waste so much time when it ought to have been spent at the sewing-machine.

Augusta Monk, on the other hand, took the shortages as a personal insult.

'It's all very well for that stupid Winston Churchill to say we must fight to the finish,' she complained to Louella on one of her weekly telephone calls. 'He ought to get us some decent food if he wants us to go on fighting.'

'Quite right, darling,' Louella agreed, holding the receiver away from her ear. Augusta always spoke much too loudly and it could give you a headache if you listened too closely. 'I must rush, Augusta. I'm off to my class in a minute.'

'What class?'

She never listens, Louella thought. 'The one I told you about. The art class. You remember. The one I started in October. "The Challenge of Synthetic Cubism". *This* year I'm going to have a painting accepted. I've made my mind up to it.'

Augusta wasn't interested in Louella's ambition. 'If they could just arrange for us to have enough sugar,' she grumbled. 'Surely they could manage *that*. Sugar's so important and you can't get it for love nor money. My grocer says he can't send any up because there isn't any to send, if you ever heard of anything so ridiculous. It's a scandal.'

'I've just seen the time, darling,' Louella interrupted. 'I shall have to fly. See you Sunday.' And hung up.

'She doesn't listen,' Augusta said to Chu-Chin, feeling aggrieved at being cut off so abruptly. 'None of them listen. They're all the same.'

The dog licked her fingers as she stooped to pet him. Beyond his shaggy coat, she saw the approaching feet of her parlourmaid. And the feet gave her an idea.

'Ah Rose!' she said. 'Just the one. Come into the parlour a minute, will you.'

Rose had been making up the fires so she was still in her morning uniform and none too clean. She wiped her hands on her apron as she followed her mistress into the parlour.

'It's about the sugar shortage,' Augusta said, settling herself into her armchair by the fire. 'It can't go on, you know. It's getting serious. Now what I want you to do is this. Leave the housework for the moment – you can do it later, can't you? – get down to the shops and see if you can find somewhere that's got some sugar.'

'You have to queue for sugar, ma'am,' Rose told her.

'Well you wouldn't mind queuing, would you, a great strong girl like you.'

The baby was moving again – flick, flick, flick – reminding Rose of its presence. She looked at the greedy bulk of her employer and thought of Netta and Mabel and the way they'd done all the queuing for the last month, ' *'Cause we got to look after our baby, ain't we our Rose.*' And anger stirred her out of her pregnant lethargy. 'Yes,' she said. 'I would mind actually.'

Augusta was astonished. 'Well now I've heard everything!'

'I been meaning to come in and see you for quite a while,' Rose said, speaking politely but firmly. Now that she'd started this, she found she had the energy to see it through. 'I want to hand in my notice.'

Augusta couldn't believe her ears. 'What for?'

'I've got another job.'

'Doing what, pray?'

'Making frocks.'

Augusta dismissed such foolishness with a wave of her ringed right hand. 'Don't go into the rag trade,' she warned. 'That's just sweated labour. You're much better off with me. You won't make any money out of frocks.'

I could argue, Rose thought as her energy flagged again, but it wouldn't be worth it because she wouldn't listen, and anyway it would be undignified. 'I shall be leaving at the end of next week,' she said.

'You can't,' Augusta said. 'Don't be so stupid. Who'll look after me? Have some consideration.'

But the consideration was over and the decision was made.

Back in Ritzy Street that evening with her feet on the fender and a mug of cocoa in her hands, Rose told Muriel and her sisters what she'd done.

'I hope it was the right thing,' she worried. 'I know she don't pay good money but it *was* regular.'

'We've made a profit every week since November,'

192

Muriel told her. As their book-keeper, she knew the state of their finances better than any of them. 'Except for two weeks after Christmas and nobody was buying anything then so we can't count that. Don't worry, Rose, if we can get the material, Ritzy Clothes will keep us all. It'll be spring frocks soon, don't forget.'

'If we can get the material,' Rose sighed. Getting the material was the most difficult part of the business these days because cotton cloth was in short supply along with everything else.

'You leave that to me,' Netta said. Since she'd appointed herself champion-in-chief of the coming baby she was full of energy. 'Now I got the bike I can go further afield.'

She went as far as Clapham and Croydon and was out on the road every day of the next week. And one way or another, by flirting or bullying or simply being saucy, she got the cloth. At one stage there was so much of it in their living-room they couldn't close the door.

'If you get any more,' Rose laughed, 'we shall have to rent another room to keep it all in.'

'Not a bad idea,' Netta said. 'There's old Mr Grosch's room been empty for weeks. Why don't we have that? I'll bet we could afford it.'

'It's the second floor back,' Rose said. 'Be a lot of carrying up and down stairs. And Mrs MacLaren might have another tenant in mind.'

'No harm asking,' Netta said. 'Try her Sat'day when she comes up for the rent.'

But when Mrs MacLaren came up for the rent that Saturday *she* had something to tell *them*.

'I'm off to Scotland next month,' she said, when she'd taken their money and signed the rent book. 'I'm going to live with my cousin. They've got a smallholding up there, you see. It's not grand but at least they feed well and they've asked me to go and live with them. I can't stand all this queuing. It's making me ill. So there it is. I thought you ought to know. You'll be having a new landlord pretty soon.'

It was a blow but one that any sub-tenant had to fear at any time.

'Do you know who it's going to be?' Rose asked.

'No one yet,' Mrs MacLaren told her, 'because I haven't told them. I shall do that this afternoon.'

'How about us?' Netta offered. 'What if we was to take it on?'

Rose had been thinking the same thing – the whole house instead of just an extra room. Perhaps this was the opportunity they needed, a chance to expand, to have a workroom as well as living space. If only it wasn't such bad timing.

Mrs MacLaren was surprised by such an ambition. 'What? Be the tenant, you mean?'

Now that she'd made the offer, Netta had no doubt about it. 'Why not?' she said.

'We need more room and we're good payers,' Rose explained. With extra sub-tenants it might just be possible. It was worth a try and if it didn't work they could always go back to the old arrangement. 'You could vouch for us, couldn't you, Mrs MacLaren.'

'Willingly,' their landlady said. 'If that's what you want. But I should warn you, it's a lot of responsibility. Not all sub-tenants pay on the dot like you, you know.'

'We'll do it,' Netta said. 'Won't we Rose.'

It came as quite a surprise to them that the rent of the entire house was only just over twice what they'd been paying for their two rooms. With the rent from old Mr and Mrs Marchbank who occupied the second-floor front, and the first-floor back let to a new tenant called Miss Pozzi, they found that they could manage, even without increased sales and even without letting Mr Grosch's room.

Within a fortnight, Rose had left work at Monk House and she and her sisters had taken possession of the basement kitchen and the first two floors of the house. It was an invigorating step upwards. Now they had a wash-house of their own and a kitchen with a constant supply of water, where they could wash up in a sink and cook meals in a range, to say nothing of two living-rooms and a bedroom each if they wanted such luxury. In fact they decided to share their original two rooms as bedrooms, Netta and Mabel in one and Rose and the baby in the other. Then they turned the back parlour into their workroom and stored the completed garments in the second-floor back, all neatly packed away in cardboard boxes and nestled into tissue paper, ready for delivery.

'Tell you what,' Netta said, 'I reckon we ought to get ourselves some business cards. Name an' address. That sort a' thing. They do 'em cheap up The Cut. I'm sick of people dithering. If they had a card they could write and tell us when they needed another order an' we could get it off to 'em that day, instead a' waiting for the next time I call. What d'you think?'

Rose was growing more lethargic as her girth increased but she agreed that the cards were a good thing and so they seemed to be. Their trade gradually increased all through February and into March. It wasn't spectacular but it was undoubtedly steady. By the time Mabel left school, they decided to treat themselves to a second-hand treadle machine, which speeded up the work and led to even better trade. And in March, when Rose was seven months pregnant and growing weary, the government came to a helpful decision too. Food was to be rationed – at last.

The system covered butchers' meat and bacon, butter, margarine and lard and two cards were issued to every consumer, one for meat and bacon and the other for the fats. Each card contained detachable coupons allowing for a weekly fifteen ounces of meat, five ounces of bacon, and four ounces of fats, and what was even better, meat prices were fixed at one shilling and tenpence per pound for beef and mutton, two shillings and tuppence for steak and one shilling and eightpence for chops. Within a week or two, food queues in London had virtually disappeared.

Netta was delighted. 'Now we shan't have to waste no

more time standing in line,' she said to Rose. 'And we can feed you up good and proper. You're much too thin.'

'With this?' Rose joked, smoothing her smock over her belly.

'The rest of you's skin an' bone,' Netta said.

'We're all thin,' Rose told her. 'That's the truth of it. Only the rich are fat in wartime. Look at Mu.'

Muriel Spencer had been growing steadily thinner and thinner all through the winter. As they all agreed, it was high time she stopped losing weight. But the next time she came to visit them, she wasn't just skinny, she was visibly cast down.

'What's up?' Netta asked. She was brushing her hair at the mirror over the mantelpiece ready for their evening out.

'Nothing much,' Muriel said, and retreated behind her empty expression.

'Yes there is,' Netta said in her trenchant way. 'You ain't coming out with us with that sort of gob on. Spit it out.'

Muriel grimaced at them. 'Oh all right then,' she said. 'I'm a bit hungry, that's all.'

'Have a bit of bread and marge,' Rose suggested and was off to the kitchen at once to get it.

'Well you were hungry and no mistake,' Netta said, as Muriel ate her impromptu meal. 'Don't they feed you at Chelsea?'

'Well, not properly,' Muriel admitted.

'How d'you mean, not properly?'

Muriel sighed, the last quarter of her slice of bread still in her hand. 'It's the rationing,' she said. 'You believe in fair shares. It's different in Chelsea.'

To Rose's loving ears this sounded serious. 'Different, how?' she asked.

'Well it's worse since the rations came in,' Muriel confessed. 'She eats them all herself. She has the ration books you see. She sort of gives me what's left over. I'm for ever hungry. I can't help it. I eat the make-weight bread on my way back from the shops. I only get a decent meal when I come to see you and that's not fair because it's your rations I'm eating.'

So it *is* serious, Rose thought. They're starving her. No wonder she's so thin. 'Um,' she said, rubbing her belly. 'So that's what's been going on. I knew there was something. You've been so quiet. What does Mr Edmund think about it?'

'I don't know,' Muriel said, returning to her bread and marge.

'Ain't you told him?'

'No.'

'Well you ought to.'

'He's in enough trouble without that. She's entering her work for three exhibitions, you see, and it's getting her in a state. She's so cross he can't talk to her without getting his head bitten off, poor man.'

'Well I tell you one thing,' Netta frowned. 'She can't eat your rations. That ain't fair.'

'Fair or not I shall have to put up with it, if I want a roof over my head,' Muriel said. 'At least I can get on with some sewing of an evening. I've got to model for them again.'

'Them?' Rose asked. 'They're not both going to draw you, are they?'

'That's what they say. I don't mind. It's better than washing her clothes and emptying her slops.'

'Don't the maids do that?' Rose asked. This story was getting worse and worse.

'There's only me and Cook,' Muriel explained. 'The maid went months ago.'

'If you ask me,' Rose said, seriously, 'you ought to go too. Hand in your notice like I did.'

Muriel made a grimace. 'What would I do instead?'

'Get another job,' Netta said.

'I'd have to find somewhere to live too, don't forget. There aren't many live-in jobs these days. Not since the shortages.'

'I tell you what,' Rose said, her tone suddenly changing to a new intensity. 'Why don't you come and live here with us and work for the business full time?'

It was such an obvious solution that they all recognised the sense of it at once.

Muriel's face was lifted by smiles, her hollow cheeks rounding, the glint returning to her eyes. 'Could I?'

'Why not? We got the room. You'd have to share with me and put up with the baby when it comes but if you wouldn't mind that . . .'

'I wouldn't mind it a bit,' Muriel said, flinging her arms round her friend's neck. 'I'd love it. If you're sure I wouldn't be a burden.' And she looked at Netta and Mabel to check their opinion.

'We shall get on like a house afire,' Netta promised. 'Which ain't to say I shan't yell at you now and then, because I yell at everyone.'

'She does,' Mabel said with feeling. 'She's awful sometimes. You have to yell back.'

So Louella Monk lost her companion and was none too pleased about it. And Muriel brought her few belongings over to Ritzy Street, treated herself to a bed of her own, and settled in with Rose.

Mabel was delighted and trotted upstairs at once to help her unpack and make the bed. 'Are you gonna live with us for ever an' ever?' she said. 'Are you our Mu?'

'If you'll have me,' Muriel told her seriously. 'If I'm not a nuisance.'

'You keep saying that,' Rose said. 'You won't be. I told you.'

But two nights later she found out why Muriel was so worried about it. She'd been sound asleep, dreaming that Jack had come home and that they were going to get married, when she was woken by somebody screaming and crying. She sat up in bed at once, greatly startled, her heart pounding. And realised that the awful sounds were coming from Muriel who was sitting on the edge of her bed with her arms round her knees and her face distraught, rocking to and fro.

Rose was out of the bed in a second, bulky though she was. 'Mu! What is it? What's the matter?'

'Oh please! Please!' Muriel wept. 'Don't send me away. I'll be good. Don't send me away.'

'You're dreaming,' Rose realised. 'Wake up. Come on Mu! Wake up. You're having a nightmare.'

It took quite a long time to rouse her. And then she began to apologise and went on apologising for a very long time, although Rose assured her it didn't matter.

'You've had a nightmare,' she said, rubbing Muriel's back. 'That's all it was. I'll bet it was the cheese.'

'I wish it had been,' Muriel said ruefully. 'I'm sorry Rose. I should have warned you. I get a lot of bad dreams. I knew I'd be a nuisance.'

'You ain't a nuisance,' Rose said firmly. 'So we'll get that straight for a start. You can't help having bad dreams now can you?'

'That's just it. I can't help feeling I ought to. Or I could if I knew what was causing them.' She was quite rational now so Rose decided to risk a question.

'What are they about? Can you remember them?'

'Oh I can remember them right enough,' Muriel said with feeling. 'They're always the same, you see. I'm back at the orphanage and they're sending me away and I can't bear it. They were always sending people away. It's like that when you're in a home. They moved you around. You have to get used to it. The trouble was I never did. If I'd had brothers and sisters it would've been different, but there was only me, so I got moved on my own. That's what I dream about. It brings it all back, you see, making friends with someone and then being moved on. It always felt like the end of the world. It still does. In every dream it feels like the end of the world. They used to say "You can write. Don't fuss." But it wasn't the same. You can't keep it up, writing, can you, not when you're little. It took me ages to make friends anyway, being shy. So I never

. . . There was always . . . And then there was being so ugly. I couldn't expect to have lots of friends the way I looked. If you're pretty it's different.'

'You ain't ugly,' Rose said. 'You've got a lovely face. And you've got a lot a' friends too, a whole family.' The story had touched her so much she was almost in tears herself.

'I'm sorry to be silly,' Muriel said, trying to smile.

'You ain't silly neither,' Rose told her. 'It must've been awful to be all on your own with no family and no friends, being moved around all the time. I'd've hated it. I'm not surprised it gives you nightmares.'

Muriel began to apologise again. 'I'm keeping you awake.'

'That's all right,' Rose comforted. 'I don't sleep so good these days anyway, to tell the truth. This baby keeps waking me up, heaving about all the time. If you're going to wake up an' all we shall be good company.'

Which, as the weeks progressed, they were. Soon Rose had grown quite accustomed to comforting Muriel after her dreams and the night had become a time for the sort of confidences they wouldn't have dared by day.

Muriel talked about her life as an orphan, remembering the kindnesses as well as the pains, and Rose talked about Jack.

'He's got to be alive, hasn't he Mu?' she said. 'I can't bear to think of him being dead. Not with this baby coming and everything. He could be a prisoner of war couldn't he? I'll bet they don't let them write home. That would account for it, don't you think?'

'He could be,' Muriel sympathised. 'Anything could have happened. How would you know?'

'I do so want him to see this baby. I can't bear the thought of it being born and him not here to see it.'

'I know it's not the same,' Muriel tried to console, 'but you've got us, haven't you. *We*'ll make ever such a fuss of it.'

'Sometimes,' Rose admitted. 'I just want to sit in a corner and cry.'

'If you want to cry, my darling, you just go right ahead,' Muriel advised. 'Nobody would mind.'

But Rose didn't cry, no matter how near to despair she felt. She had made one of her secret pacts with the Maker. If she could carry this baby without a fuss and give birth to it without crying or screaming, she felt sure He would reward her and let Jack come home. And any effort would be worthwhile if she could achieve that.

CHAPTER SEVENTEEN

Rose's labour began on a warm afternoon at the end of May and her first pains were so mild she thought she'd eaten something that hadn't agreed with her and went on sewing sleeves until it was time to go down to the kitchen and start the tea. Netta was out on the bike collecting material from the drapers and Mabel and Muriel were upstairs finishing off buttonholes in the better light from the bedroom window.

But when Rose called to them, there was such an urgent note to her voice that Muriel threw down her sewing at once and ran down the stairs to see what was the matter, with Mabel clattering behind her.

Rose was standing beside the table, leaning on it with both hands, her eyes shut and her mouth open, panting. They waited until she'd recovered enough to open her eyes and look at them.

'I think it's the baby,' she said when the pain had passed. She was perfectly calm about it and looked quite herself again. 'I been havin' pains all afternoon but that was a big one.'

Mabel was wide-eyed with awe. 'Shall I go for Mrs Towser?' she asked.

'Not yet,' Rose said. Now that the moment had come she was full of confidence, as if that first long pain had put her in command. 'We'll have tea first. Netta'll be back in a minute. The chops are nearly done.'

'Sit down and take it easy,' Muriel said. 'We'll do the rest. Why didn't you call us? You shouldn't've been on your own.'

'Don't fuss,' Rose smiled at them. 'I'm all right.'

In fact she made a better meal than any of the others

who were too anxious to eat with any relish and watched her like cats, all round eyes and sharp attention. Netta ate hardly anything at all because she felt guilty at being out when it all began.

'I should've been here,' she said, scowling. 'You should've said.'

'Well you're here now,' Rose said, cleaning her plate with a chunk of bread. 'You're all here now. So you can stop fussing.'

'Shall I go for Mrs Towser *now*, our Rose?' Mabel said.

'She'll only say it's too soon,' Rose warned. The one thing she *did* know about having a baby – because Mrs Cartwright had told her – was that you had to wait to call the midwife until the pains were coming thick and fast.

But Mrs Towser, who was fat and comforting, was firmly of the opinion that 'young Mabel' had done the right thing in calling her out. 'Can't be too careful with a first,' she said. 'I brought me knitting, so there won't be no time wasted. Have you had anythink to eat?' And when Rose nodded. 'Very sensible. That'll keep up your strength. You got the bed made up, 'ave yer dearie?'

'Will it be long?' Rose asked as she climbed into the bed.

'It's a long process dearie,' the midwife said. 'You can't rush nature. That's something you'll have to accept.'

It was something they all had to accept, as the evening hours ticked slowly past and the pains came and went equally slowly and nothing seemed to be happening. Midnight struck and they all had cocoa sitting round in Rose's bedroom while she lay quietly on her side in the neatness of Mrs Towser's firmly tucked sheets and blankets.

One o'clock passed – two – three – four – as the three putative aunts sat it out in the living-room, their eyes pricking with fatigue and their legs wrapped in blankets because it was cold without a fire and they didn't want to waste the coal ration by lighting one. Whatever else they had to do, they were determined not to go to bed just in case Rose needed them.

Rose was fully occupied riding her pains. Mrs Towser chattered endlessly, about the neighbours and her patients. '. . . And I said to her, I said, that boy of yours has never been and caught his head in the railings again because that I never will believe. Weals on his neck as big as tramlines . . .' But her voice was just a background noise. What was important to Rose was to be in control, to breathe through each pain as it came, to feel on top of it. If she could manage that she knew she would manage everything else. Between pains she thought of Jack and wondered where he was and if he was thinking of her. But she didn't talk and she didn't cry out, she simply concentrated, thinking, if I can do this well, he'll come home.

'The dawn's coming up,' Mrs Towser said from the window. 'I'll draw the curtains for you.'

The oblong of the window was filled with strange, rich colours. A pale sea-green washed behind the black silhouettes of the houses opposite to merge into a dusty blue still studded with white stars. The quiet was uncanny, as if they were all underwater, or in some other world magically distant from the work and worries of wartime London. Rose lay on her back and enjoyed it, while she waited for the next pain to take hold. And the first bird of the dawn chorus began to pipe from the trees in Miss Monk's distant garden. Within seconds birds were singing everywhere, the sound swelling and rising as the next pain rose, blackbirds in full-throated melody, thrushes repeating each lilting phrase, robins high, sweet and shrill. They were still singing as the pain died away. If I can do this well, Rose promised herself again, I shall see him again.

Mabel was almost asleep when the baby gave its first mewing cry. But she woke up at once and jumped to her feet with the others. 'Can we go up?' she whispered, as the baby cried again. 'Are we allowed?'

Daylight was streaming in through a chink in the curtains. They could hear Mrs Towser's feet walking about overhead, a murmur of voices.

'We'll wait on the landing,' Netta decided.

But the door was opened to them as they came upstairs and there he was cuddled up in a shawl in his mother's arms, clear as clear in the brand new daylight, the dearest little boy with a mass of damp dark hair, a wrinkled forehead, enormous eyes and the smallest hands they'd ever seen.

'He's lovely, our Rose,' Mabel breathed. 'Look Netta, he's got nails!'

'Six and a half pounds,' Mrs Towser told them. 'A nice strong baby. Ain't she the clever one?'

It wasn't her cleverness that put them in awe at that moment. It was her beauty, sitting up against the pillows with the baby in the crook of her arm, her hair bushed about her face, her cheeks pink and her grey eyes shining with love.

'Bertie Collum Jeary,' she said, turning the baby towards them, 'meet your aunties.'

CHAPTER EIGHTEEN

Making a bargain with God is disarmingly easy. We do it instinctively in moments of terror or danger and we usually believe – like the bargainers of myth and fairy tale – that we have it in our power to control the outcome. Not so. Not so. Our lives are complicated by their very nature, and keeping such a bargain is a further complication, as Rose Boniface found out in the anxious weeks following her baby's birth.

Feeding baby Bertie wasn't the simple matter she'd expected it to be. He was always hungry, crying for another feed less than an hour after he'd been suckled and settled to sleep, but however often she fed him, he was never satisfied. After a few days, his incessant demands began to make her feel inadequate and guilty. It frightened her that he was doing so badly and that she had so little energy, despite the fact that she was lying in and being waited on hand and foot by her three devoted nurses. She snatched what sleep she could while he was quiet, fed him whenever he cried and prayed that things would get better. But once she got up and started to work again, she was perpetually exhausted.

'Maybe we should get him a little titty-bottle,' Netta suggested.

Rose wouldn't hear of such a thing. 'No,' she said. 'I'll feed him. He must settle sooner or later.' It was part of her bargain to breast-feed this baby and she'd done everything else so well, she couldn't fail now. If fatigue was the price she had to pay, then so be it

But there was a further price and a painful one. Bertie sucked both her nipples raw and even though Mrs Towser produced a breast shield to protect her a little, feeding him was often exquisitely painful. It wasn't until he was six weeks old that her skin toughened sufficiently for her to suckle him without distress and he was still ravenously hungry. Sometimes, when she was bathing him, she thought his little face looked quite gaunt and his arms and legs were much too thin.

'She needs feeding up,' Mrs Towser told Muriel. 'No nourishment. That's what it is. She can't make enough milk poor girl. And fretting too, I shouldn't wonder. When's that husband of hers coming home on leave?'

'We don't know,' Muriel temporised.

'Write and tell him to get a move on,' Mrs Towser advised. 'Get a bit of compassionate or something. Make all the difference that would.'

But what made the difference eventually was a subterfuge, in the shape of a feeding-bottle full of watered-down condensed milk, cooked up and administered by Netta and Muriel while Rose was out shopping. Bertie was a bit sick after he'd scoffed it down but, when they'd cleaned him up and settled him, he slept for nearly three hours – which was unheard of.

'Right, my lad,' Netta said to his sleeping body. 'We'll hide the bottle, so's your Mum don't know, and we'll top you up whenever we can.'

From then on they gave him at least one bottle every day and sometimes managed two. He began to put on obvious weight and, as a result, Rose relaxed and produced more milk; as a result of that, he fed with gusto, smiling at her most lovingly, his stomach round as a drum.

'That's more like it,' she said, kissing his newly plump cheeks. 'Ain't you the lovely one.'

Netta and Muriel were very pleased with themselves. 'Shall we tell her?' Muriel wondered, when she and Netta were on their own in the workroom.

'No fear,' Netta said. 'Let her think it's all her good work. 'Cause it is, mostly.'

The baby grew prettier by the day and it wasn't long before Rose was blooming too, her harassed expression gone at last and her face recovering its lovely serenity. It was a private turning-point. And not long afterwards there was an international one.

'Have you seen the papers?' Muriel said, bursting into the living-room with an evening paper fluttering in her hand. She'd been down to The Cut for the evening shopping while the others were finishing off the day's work. 'The Allies have opened a counter-attack and broken through the German lines. It could be the end of the war.'

'Never!' Netta exclaimed, threading her last length of cotton. 'Let's have a look-see.'

'*Yesterday morning,*' the paper said. '*July 18th, Allied troops opened a counter-attack with the support of 346 Renault tanks on the western flank of the Chemin-des-dames near Amiens. Early this morning they were joined by troops from the United States of America who attacked from the South. Latest reports say that both armies have broken through the enemy lines and that the German army is in retreat.*'

Is it the end? Rose hoped. Oh please, please let it be. Then Jack can come home – because he can't be dead, not after all this – and he can see his baby – oh won't he just love this baby – and we can all be together again. The long months without word were going to come to an end. If he was wounded, he would be sent home, if he was a prisoner they would set him free. It was all possible. At last.

In the more reasonable part of her mind she knew that her bargain was unreal and that some time soon she would have to face whatever truth was waiting for her, but for the moment there was still hope. And like everyone else in Britain, her hopes grew as the summer campaign continued and the news improved. Soon it was obvious that the terrible stalemate of the trenches really was over at last. By August 8th the Allied armies were advancing along a fifteen-mile front and over six hundred tanks were being used to provide cover for the troops. Three days later they had re-taken ten miles of occupied territory. On

August 21st another Allied attack was opened, this time between Albert and the Somme. By the end of September, when Bertie was four months old and prettily plump, the Germans were conceding defeat. On October 3rd, they asked for an armistice.

It was very, very nearly over. Only a matter of weeks, people said.

In fact, it took more than a month to bring the fighting to an end and the last few weeks of the war seemed to be drawn out for ever. 'Soon!' people hoped. 'It must be soon!' The yearning for release was almost too intense to be borne. 'Soon, please God. Let it be soon. All they've got to do is sign the paper.'

But at last it was the eleventh hour of the eleventh day of the eleventh month of 1918 and all over London the maroons were fired to give notice of that last, long-awaited all clear. The years of pent-up anxiety exploded into a passion of relief and excitement.

Crowds poured into the streets, laughing and cheering. Ritzy Street was instantly full of women, tumbling from every house, still in their aprons, their long skirts tangled about their legs, some carrying babies, some trailing toddlers, shouting to one another in excitement. 'Is it really over?' 'Have they signed?'

Muriel and the Bonifaces ran out of number 26 with all the rest, Rose carrying baby Bertie, Mabel whooping with joy. The guns were still firing – thud, thud, thud, flat and heavy and without reverberation – but now there were other sounds too, a steam train whistling joyously as it crossed the embankment, tugs on the river Thames whooping like deep-throated birds, church bells pealing in an unrehearsed tumble of tinny notes, ringing out over the City for the first time in four long years of war.

'It's over!' Muriel shouted in triumph over the din. 'No one's ever going to killed ever again.'

'Lissen to them bells!' Netta said, her dark face glowing with excitement. 'Ain't it a day!'

Rose could hear children's voices. 'They've let the kids out a' school,' she shouted.

'And the people out of the factories,' Muriel shouted back. 'There's Marigold, look. Everything'll close down today.'

Within five minutes the street was packed. When the maroons sounded it had been dark and empty except for two of Mrs Docherty's kids who'd been playing flying angels on the lamp post at the far end. Now it seethed with life and colour and excited movement. Mrs Docherty carried a stool into the middle of the road where she sat with her old trilby hat on her head and her muffler round her shoulders, playing her accordion for the dancers and grinning so broadly it was a wonder she didn't crack her cheeks. Streamers stretched across the street from house to house, sills were hung with bunting and someone had draped a Union Jack out of the first-floor window of the house immediately opposite the Bonifaces. It was frayed at the edges and faded along the creases where it had been folded away all through the war but it struck a bold bright note against the sooty brickwork of the house.

As they cheered and danced, Mr Fassbinder came hobbling out of the corner shop carrying a tray full of paper flags which he distributed to all the children as they arrived in the street, so that the pavements were a-flutter with red, white and blue, as if flowers had suddenly bloomed there.

'Ain't it grand gels?' he called out to Muriel and Rose. 'No more war!'

Nancy Cartwright was dancing on the pavement, clutching four bottles of beer to her chest. 'There y'are mate,' she said, thrusting one of the bottles at Rose. 'Get that down you. This is the life eh? I been up the off-licence. There y'are Mu. Here's to peace eh? And lots of it!'

They drank to peace as well as they could in the jostle. Then still clutching their bottles, they plunged into the dance, baby and all, as Nancy began to sing, 'Come an'

210

ave a drink wiv me, dahn at the old Bull an' Bush – bush
bush!'

It was riotous and uninhibited. Dancers kicked their
legs in the air with total abandon. Strangers kissed as they
passed. The pavements rattled with empty bottles. It was
the biggest street party they had ever known and it went
on and on. Darkness fell and they were still dancing as the
gas lights blazed from every window in the new bright
light of peace. Midnight struck to resounding cheers and
the dance went on.

The next morning they slept late and rose to eat what little
they had or could. Then they returned to the streets. Muriel
and Netta decided they all ought to go up to Whitehall and
see what was going on there. The trams were still running,
dangerously overloaded, sporting Union Jacks front and
back and hung about with red, white and blue bunting, so
they bought tickets and joined the throng. And found that
Westminster was a city in carnival.

They spent the whole day dancing. First outside
Victoria Station, then in Whitehall, then in the gardens of
Parliament Square. Bertie was bounced from one to the
other, fed in doorways and slept tied to his mother's back
in a shawl. They ate buns and pies, and fish and chips, and
drank more beer than they'd ever done in their lives. And
they were all kissed by so many men that Netta said her
lips were quite sore – but added, 'Ain't it a lark!'

By the third morning they were all exhausted.

'Quiet day today,' Muriel suggested as they came
downstairs to the living-room. The Ritzy Street party was
beginning again as she spoke but she hadn't the energy to
join in. 'I'll light the fire, shall I.'

'Quiet morning anyway,' Rose agreed as Muriel started
to clear the grate. 'We need to get our breath back. And
Bertie could do with a nice long sleep in his cot.'

'I'll get the coal,' Mabel offered, heading off to the
cellar with the empty scuttle.

'I'll get the stove alight and rustle up some breakfast,'
Netta said.

Once the fire was lit, it was wonderfully warm and peaceful in their living-room. They sat round the fire, with Bertie sleepy in his mother's arms. And as their excitement subsided they remembered the dead.

'It's all going to be very different,' Rose said seriously. 'When you think how everything's changed. All the men who won't come back.' She looked up at the mantelpiece where their two treasured portraits stood side by side, Bertie and Collum, stiff and formal in their khaki, their young, dead faces bright with eager innocence. The sight of them made her yearn with grief and cringe with the shame of having forgotten them in those two wild days of rejoicing. 'We should've thought of them first,' she grieved. 'The men who won't come back.'

Muriel was feeling ashamed of herself too. 'They would have understood,' she hoped. 'It was the relief. We were bound to go a bit wild. Everyone was a bit wild.'

'It won't bring them back though, will it?' Rose said. 'All the dead. Millions and millions. You think of all the widows. Fifteen in this street alone. Fifteen to my certain knowledge. Look how many women are in mourning. Half the population. It's all very well us cheering and dancing, we're going to be a generation without men.'

It was a sobering thought and Muriel didn't know how to respond to it. She gave Rose's arm a squeeze of sympathy.

'At least it's over,' she tried to comfort. 'And that's one good thing. There won't be any more young men sent away to be killed. It'll never happen again.'

'Rose's right though, Mu,' Netta observed. 'There's going to be a lot of women on their own.'

'If Jack don't come back,' Rose said, admitting the possibility out loud for the first time, 'I shall be one of them.'

'Yes,' Netta agreed, sympathetically. 'You will. There's no denying it. You will. But so will all the others. So will we.' Her tone changed as she tried to encourage her poor sister. 'I tell you what. We'll all be old maids, together, won't we gels? All four of us. So what? We're young, we got our health – more or less – we're still alive.'

'Alive and kicking!' Mabel said, beaming at them. All this serious talk had gone over her head. 'Alive and kicking eh Rose!'

'So there you are,' Netta said, looking hopefully at the others. 'We'll be all right, won't we our Rose.'

'We'll be more than all right,' Rose promised. She felt she was making a pledge to the future, no matter what it might hold. 'We've got Ritzy Clothes.'

'And Bertie,' Mabel said, stroking his dark head. 'Don't forget our Bertie.'

The baby was a comfort to them all in the first difficult year of the peace. And particularly to his mother. As the armies were gradually disbanded, the wounded discharged and the prisoners of war released, she lived in a conflict of impossible emotions, fluctuating between the lift of anguished hope that she would see her Jack again and the drop into bleak despair when others returned and there was still no word from him.

The returning men were much in evidence and much changed. Many were scarred and prematurely aged, some had perpetual coughs because they'd been gassed, others were amputees with empty sleeves or pinned up trouser legs where their limbs should have been. Even the men who had come back without injury were withdrawn and unnaturally quiet. But seeing them only convinced Rose that she would be glad to see her Jack again no matter what sort of state he was in. But the weeks passed and there was no news, just an awful daily yearning that was never answered. The sight of Bertie's innocent good health was the one dependable and wholesome thing in her life. And even that was at risk in that first awful winter.

The returning troops had unknowingly brought a plague back with them. Nobody knew where it had originally come from, but it had been rife in the rat-infested warrens of the trenches and had festered in barracks and hospitals wherever the armies moved. Now it came to the cities in full and terrible strength. It spared no one and there was no cure. It was called the Spanish 'flu.

It was Netta who fell victim to it first, cycling home late one afternoon as pale as putty with the sweat standing on her forehead in drops as big as rain. She was hot to the touch and coughing terribly. Her eyes were plainly sore and she said her bones were aching.

Greatly alarmed, they put her straight to bed and sent young Billy Cartwright round for the doctor. But it wasn't Dr Felgate who came. It was a strange, sandy-haired man with a Scottish accent.

'Is Dr Felgate not. . . ?' Rose asked.

'Dr Felgate has the influenza, the same as everybody else,' the Scottish doctor told her gruffly. 'So ye'll need to mek do with me. We're no immune from it, d'ye see. Where's my patient?

'There's not a great deal I can do for her,' he confessed when he'd taken Netta's temperature and felt her pulse. 'You could give her a wee blanket bath, if you're careful. That might bring down the fever. Aspirin'll help maybe. It has to run its course, d'ye see. Soak a sheet in disinfectant and hang it over the door. Make sure you wash your hands in disinfectant when you've been attending to her. And keep that babby right out of the way. Call me if she gets any worse.' His face was lined with fatigue.

Rose didn't know what alarmed her most, his stern warning about Bertie or the fact that Dr Felgate was ill. But she took his instructions very seriously.

'I'll make a separate bedroom for Bertie,' she said. 'In the second-floor back. He'll be safer up there.'

So the house was re-arranged and the three of them took it in turns to watch over Netta, eight hours on and sixteen off, round the clock.

She was very ill. By the end of that first day, she was delirious, calling out that Collum was coming home from

214

work and she had to get his tea. Sweat poured from her in such quantities that her sheets were damp within an hour of being changed. Rose and Muriel gave her a blanket bath, as well as they could, and held a glass of water to her lips whenever she asked for it, but for most of the time she sweltered in fever, tossing and groaning and far beyond them.

On the third day she rallied a little and they fed her some Brand's Essence to keep up her strength. But on the fourth she was worse and that afternoon Rose found Mabel slumped in the wicker chair in the kitchen, too ill to stand.

'Now it's just the two of us,' she said to Muriel when they'd put their second patient to bed alongside the first. 'We'll have to take it turn and turn about.' But she was thinking, How shall we make out if we get ill too?

'We'll manage,' Muriel promised. 'I never catch things. You'll see.'

It was an anxious and impoverished time. They were exhausted by nursing and, to make matters worse, their trade was badly down because they had little time and energy for making frocks and there were very few people out in the markets willing to buy them. Most women did their shopping as quickly as they could, visiting the food stalls and then rushing home again. Browsing was too risky even with Christmas coming. Rose and Muriel dipped into their reserves and prayed that the epidemic wouldn't go on too long.

But they counted their blessings too. At least they had reserves to dip into. They could still just about pay the rent and keep themselves fed. Bertie hadn't taken the infection and neither – to their private surprise – had they. And eventually, Netta and Mabel got over the worst of the illness and began to recover. They were both very weak and slept a great deal but their fever was down and Netta was well enough to sit up and eat whatever Rose and Muriel prepared for her. By the end of the second week, she insisted on getting out of bed and sat at her sewing-machine for most of the afternoon, pale and bad-tempered but determined not to be a burden any longer.

That night as Rose and Muriel turned out the gas-light in their bedroom and climbed wearily into their beds, they felt the worst was over.

'I don't know how I'd've managed without you,' Rose said, settling back on her pillows.

Muriel took off her glasses and set them on her bedside table, fumbling in the darkness to be sure she didn't drop them. 'Just as well I was here, then.'

'Yes.'

'For two women on our own,' Muriel said into the darkness, 'I think we've made a very good job of things.' She spoke with justified satisfaction but her words reminded Rose of the misery she'd pushed to the back of her mind while they'd been nursing their invalids.

'He's not going to come back, is he?' she said sadly.

Muriel decided on honesty. 'No,' she said. 'It doesn't look like it.'

'I feel as if I've been mourning him for months. Half mourning and half hoping.'

'I know,' Muriel said, speaking gently because she could hear how near the tears were. 'I've watched you.'

'It ain't fair,' Rose wept, her control breaking at last. 'I've waited so long and hoped so hard. I've kept on and on telling myself he can't be dead. And now they're all home and he ain't back. It's the not-knowing that's so awful. The not-knowing.'

Muriel was across the floorboards in two strides and had her arms round Rose's shaking shoulders.

'Oh dear, oh dear,' Rose wept. 'I'm sorry to cry, Mu. I shouldn't cry. What's the good of crying?' But her grief was too extreme for her to stop.

Muriel drew Rose's head down onto her shoulder as if she were a child and held her tenderly. 'Cry all you like, my dear, brave darling,' she urged. 'It's been a long time coming. You need to cry. Cry all you like.'

'He *is* dead, ain't he?' Rose wept. 'He is. Oh dear God,

216

he is. I've known it all along really. I shall never see him again. Never. He's as dead as Col and Bertie only I never got told. Oh Jack! Jack! I can't bear it.'

It was more than an hour before her first awful grief was cried away and another before she could talk or listen with any semblance of reason but Muriel held her and comforted her all the time and when she was recovered, reminded her of the one person who could begin to restore her.

'No matter what else,' she said, 'you've still got Bertie.'

'Yes,' Rose agreed, smiling at last. 'Thank God for our Bertie.'

CHAPTER NINETEEN

In the summer of 1923 young Bertie Jeary celebrated his fifth birthday. There was no end to the delights of the day, an iced cake with five candles, a trip to the zoo, and four of the best presents he'd ever had.

'Ain't you the lucky one?' Aunt Netta said, kissing him. 'A whip and top, a hoop, a diabolo *and* a hobby horse! My stars!'

Bertie agreed with her happily. He'd always known how lucky he was. He knew he didn't have a Daddy because his Daddy had been killed in something called The War but that was simply a piece of information he stored away in his mind. It didn't concern him at all. Why should it, when he had a Mummy and *three* Aunties?

He was a handsome little boy with his father's dark hair and stocky build and his mother's heart-shaped face and fine grey eyes, and, being much loved, he was happy and learnt fast. He could write his name and count up to twenty by the time he was three and, now that he was five, he was learning his letters and had begun to read, picking out the words from his story books as he sat on one lap or another, listening to the story.

There was always a lap for him to sit on and always someone to listen and talk to him. Mum was the best of all, that went without saying because she was always there and always the same. If he woke at night and felt afraid it was Mum's bed into which he crept. He would lie in the mounds of her mattress with her arm under his neck and twine his fingers in her lovely soft hair and breathe in the lovely warm scent of her neck until he fell asleep again. He loved his three aunts very much, but he adored his mother and felt entirely safe in her presence. Although no

218

one had ever told him so, he knew that she was the power in the house. She was the one who worried when there wasn't enough money – you had to kiss her and stroke her hair then – and the one who told the others what frocks they were going to make – you had to keep out of the way then because of the scissors – and the one who decided what you were going to do. 'How about a trip to the fair?' she'd say or, 'How d'you fancy a day by the sea?' and off they would all go.

But at the end of that fifth birthday, she suddenly said something that worried him. 'You'll be off to school come September.'

'I shan't,' he said, his face fearful. School was for big boys. Johnnie Tufnell went to school.

She smiled at him. 'Yes, you will,' she said. 'Everybody has to go to school. You'll like it. I'll make you a nice new pair a' trousers and Aunty Muriel'll knit you a nice jumper. You'll be a real swell.'

But Bertie didn't want to be a swell. He wanted to stay at home, where it was safe.

'If you go like a good boy, you shall have a sugar stick,' Aunty Muriel promised.

'He don't want sugar sticks,' Aunty Netta said. 'He ain't a sissie are you sunshine? He'll go like a good'un.'

As there didn't seem to be any other option, that's how he went. And discovered that he rather liked school. Miss Garthorpe was ever so nice. They did things called sums and she said he was a clever boy. And when she found out how many words he could read and that he could write his name on his slate, she drew a great big star in one corner and said he was 'First Rate'. There were lots of big boys there, and they *were* rough, just as he'd feared, but there were other boys too, much the same size as he was, and they had all sorts of games going when you went out in the yard at playtime. After a week he had a best friend called Sonny Richardson and came home to tell his mother that school was 'All right'.

By the time he'd been there a month, he'd discovered

that you learnt all sorts of things at school. Not just reading and writing and sums but how to make a Guy and a Grotto and what was on at the pictures.

'Mine of information ain'tcher?' Netta laughed at him, when he told them there was a circus coming. 'Now I suppose you want to go and see *that*.'

'Yes, please,' he said eagerly, 'and can Sonny come an' all?'

In the spring of 1924, when he'd been at school nearly two whole terms and had a Christmas in between, he came home babbling with news of a 'nexibition'.

'A what?' Netta laughed.

'A nexibition. Sonny's brother says. It's got a railway you can go on and a lake with boats and swings and coconut shies and everything. It's ever so good. Can we go?'

'He means the Empire Exhibition at Wembley,' Muriel explained. 'It's in all the papers. There was an article about it yesterday.' She was searching through the pile of papers as she spoke. 'Look here.'

'*The Empire Exhibition bids fair to be the largest of its kind ever staged,*' the article said. '*It will have the largest scenic railway in the world and a mock mine. There will be models of Tutankhamen in Egypt. There will be a lake at its centre full of pleasure boats with specially planted flowers upon its banks, and pavilions from every part of the Empire, including Malay and Ceylon. There will be a West African village, an Australian building with a fishery, a South African building in the Dutch style with a characteristic stoep and loggia, and possibly most dramatic of all, an Indian pavilion with a model of the Taj Mahal.*'

'Sounds all right,' Netta said. 'I reckon we ought to go. Can we afford it, our Rose?'

In the five and a half years since the end of the war, their trade had rarely been good. When the new coat-frocks came in, they'd sold well for a year or two but other frocks and blouses were hard to shift. The firm had struggled on, putting aside sufficient cash for rent and housekeeping week by week, and urging their goods on all the local shops, but it had always been difficult and this year was the worst yet.

Sales had been badly down ever since Christmas and the cost of material had gone up, so they were very short of money. To make matters worse, most of the shops they supplied had cut their last two orders by a third, saying there wasn't the demand. Gertrude's hadn't taken a single frock in the last month. In fact, if it hadn't been for old Mrs Tuffin and her stall, they would have been hard put to it to pay the rent. Rose was very worried about it and for the last month she and Muriel had been racking their brains to think of some way to increase sales and doing the accounts twice a week to be certain that they didn't overspend. Now, she scanned the report to find out how much they would have to pay for admission.

'Perhaps by Easter,' she decided. 'If we sell enough.'

Bertie's face fell visibly.

'We'll have to wait for the rain to stop anyway,' Muriel said, to console him. The weather had been very bad for the last few weeks. 'It should be better by Easter.'

'We'll manage, Sunshine,' Netta said, ruffling the child's hair. 'We always do. I'll go out on my bike first thing tomorrer, and see what I can do.'

But in the event it wasn't Netta who found the money, it was Muriel. Two days later, the postman brought her a letter. It arrived at breakfast time and made her laugh out loud.

'Monks to the rescue!' she said and handed the letter across the table to Rose. 'What d'you think of that?'

For a second Bertie expected a gang of tonsured men to come rushing in through the door, habits flapping.

'But that's your money Mu,' Rose said. 'We couldn't . . .'

'My treat,' Muriel said, smiling all over her face.

'Well tell us!' Netta urged.

'Mr Edmund wants me to sit for him again. He's offered

me ten guineas for two portraits. And he sent me a five-pound note in advance. Look!'

Mabel was open-mouthed at such a fee. 'My eye, Mu!'

'So we're all going to the Exhibition,' Muriel announced. 'First day of the holidays as ever is. How about that Bertie?'

Bertie threw his arms round her neck. 'You're the best Aunty in the whole wide world,' he said.

'Won't it be a lark eh?' Netta put in.

It was more than a lark. It was an adventure. From the very start Bertie was enraptured. The sun shone for them, which Aunty Netta said was an omen after all that rain, and they travelled by Underground, on the Bakerloo Line all the way from Waterloo to Wembley, which was very exciting because the trains were round – 'to fit the tunnel,' Aunty Muriel said. There were so many people on the platform when they got out at Wembley that they couldn't walk properly but had to shuffle to the exit one step at a time and Aunty Mabel made a dance of it and they all sang.

And then there it was. A great white building, ever so modern, with a huge flight of steps leading up to it and lots and lots of entrances and flags flying everywhere and boys in odd-looking uniforms selling programmes. Aunty Muriel bought one at once and it had a map inside to show you where to go and there *was* a lake and a mine just as Johnny Jones had said.

'What d'you want to see first?' Mum asked him.

'Everything!' he said rapturously.

They went to the Canadian pavilion which was guarded by Mounties in scarlet and gold uniforms. There was a model of the Niagara Falls inside. It looked just like water, but Aunty Muriel said it was really a huge piece of gauze running round and round on electric rollers.

They saw the Palace of Industry, where there was a safe so large you could walk about inside it and fires lit by gas that you could just switch on and light up and they'd warm you at once – Mum and Aunty Netta thought they were 'Just the ticket' – and the Palace of Engineering where they walked through the cab of the Flying Scotsman. But Bertie thought the naval pavilion was the best because they had sea battles, like the Armada and Trafalgar, actually going on before your eyes, with cannon shooting and lots of smoke and ever such a noise.

They finished the morning in the Wembley Amusement Park where they saw the Witching Waves and rode on the Giant Caterpillar and took a punt out on the Magic Mill, where you had water splashed all over you by a huge wheel as you went past and they all screamed like billy-oh. They played 'Break up the Happy Home' where you threw wooden balls at a dresser heaped with cups and saucers and broke as many as you could – and Mum won a teddy bear. They went in the Palace of Beauty, where they saw Helen of Troy, Cleopatra, Scheherazade, Dante's Beatrice, Nell Gwynne and Miss 1924. Aunty Mabel said they weren't a patch on 'our Rose', which Bertie said was quite right. And Aunty Netta had her fortune told for sixpence by a dark gentleman in flowing robes, who said her lucky day was Tuesday and that she would soon meet a tall dark stranger who would change the course of her life. At which Aunty Netta laughed and said, 'Chance 'ud be a fine thing.'

By that time it was well past midday and they were all hungry so they went back to the centre where all the cafés and restaurants were and see if they could find themselves something to eat. 'There's a Joe Lyons,' Muriel said. 'I saw it on our way across. That will be all right.'

There was a bandstand in the central garden and crowds of people sitting in deckchairs listening to the music. The cafés and restaurants were all facing out into the square and alongside one of the biggest there was a wall covered in scaffolding.

'What's going on there?' Netta said. 'Let's have a look-see.' And she took Bertie by the hand and pushed through the crowds until they were standing beside the wall.

Perched on the scaffolding, there were about a dozen young women wearing paint-daubed smocks and khaki breeches. Some of them had thick woollen stockings on their legs and some were in gum boots and they were all hard at work painting the wall with enormous brushes. Not just ordinary wall painting either but pictures of blue and white dolphins leaping and multi-coloured fishes swimming in a forest of curling weed painted in several shades of green and gold and red. Bertie was fascinated.

'How do they know how to do it, Aunty Muriel?' he asked.

'They have to learn,' Muriel told him. 'People like Mr Edmund teach them.'

'Who's Mr Edmund?'

'The man who's going to paint my picture,' Muriel said.

'On a wall?'

'On a canvas,' Muriel started to explain, but as she spoke there was a commotion immediately above their heads. One of the artists was yelling, 'Look out!' and another was screaming. They looked up at once and there was something falling from the scaffold, something large and dark, turning in the air, its arms outstretched.

'Gracious!' Netta said, starting forward. 'It's a man!'

He landed at her feet, hitting the ground with a thud that made Bertie feel quite sore. But then he went on moving – rolling forward with his head tucked into his chest as if he were a ball – coming to a halt – panting as he lay on the grass with his head between his hands.

'Ho-say!' one of the artists called down. 'Ho-say! Say something!'

Netta was on her knees beside the young man. 'Are you all right?' she asked, touching his shoulder.

'Yes,' the man said, still panting. 'Winded. Breath back. All right. In a minute.'

'D'you want a doctor or anything?'

'No,' the young man said, opening his eyes and looking at her. 'No bone broken. I all right.' He spoke with an odd sort of accent and now that they were so close and he was actually looking at her Netta realised that his appearance was foreign too. His face was pale but his eyes were very dark brown, almost black and so was his hair which was thick and strong and longer than most of the other men she'd met. How odd it was to be looking straight into a man's eyes at such close quarters. It made her feel most peculiar. Who did they say he was?

'You're Ho-say, aren't you?'

'José Fernández,' he said and now he was smiling at her, recovering. 'I all right.'

'Stay there,' Netta commanded. 'I'll get you something. Don't move.'

Then she turned to her sisters. 'Look after him,' she said. 'I'll be back in two shakes.'

Despite his protestations the young man was too shaken to get up and walk. He sat up, gingerly, and pressed his hands on the grass beside him to support his seated weight but otherwise he did as she'd told him. By now some of the artists had climbed down from the scaffold and were gathered round him, asking him how he was. He stretched out his arms and legs to show them no bones were broken.

'You could've been killed,' one of them said.

'So!' he said. 'I am not. You see!'

Netta was pushing her way back through the crowd. She had a glass of brandy in her hand and was carrying it carefully so as not to spill any. 'There y'are,' she said, putting the glass into his hand. 'Get that down you. It's good for the shock.'

He drank it gratefully and smiled at her again, as the colour came back into his face. 'You are very kind,' he said. 'T'ank you.'

This time the impact of his dark eyes was unmistakeable. It was as if he was tugging at her, pulling her towards him from some hidden hook, deep in her belly.

'Yes, well,' she said, gruffly. 'Had to do something.'

He finished the brandy and stood up, brushing himself down with both hands – strong hands, Netta noticed, with short broad nails. He was nearly a head taller than she was and even more handsome standing up than he'd been sitting down.

'What your name?' he asked. 'I must buy a drink for you. In return.' And he looked at the glass.

'You won't do nothing of the sort,' she said, quite crossly. 'It was medicinal.'

'What your name?' he insisted.

She opened her handbag and found one of her cards and gave it to him, blushing slightly. 'We're the Boniface family,' she said, indicating the others with a nod. 'That's my sister, Mrs Jeary. I'm Netta.'

He took the card and bowed to her, rather stiffly. 'Please to meet you,' he said.

Even a meal in a very big Joe Lyons was an anticlimax after that. They talked about it all through their cold meats and salad and were still discussing it as they set off for the Stadium and the afternoon's entertainment.

'I thought he'd have a broken leg at the very least,' Muriel said. 'I never thought he'd get up and walk away. He must be made of india rubber.'

'What d'you give him a card for?' Rose wanted to know.

' 'Cause he's foreign,' Netta said. 'I was being polite.'

'Polite my eye!' Rose said, taking her arm. 'You took a shine to him.'

'No I never.'

'What'll you do if he turns up on our doorstep?' Muriel asked.

'He won't,' Netta said, tossing her head. Would he? Would she like him to?

'Well you've met your tall dark stranger and no mistake,' Rose said.

There was something about this talk that made Bertie want to butt in. He knew they were teasing Aunty Netta and he knew she didn't like it, because her face was dark and she'd drawn her eyebrows together the way she did when she was upset. 'Are we nearly there?' he demanded,

226

pulling at his mother's arm. 'We been walking for *ages*. I thought we was going to the Rodeo. *Are* we?'

He'd been looking forward to it all through dinner, which they could have had a lot earlier if only that silly man hadn't fallen out of the scaffolding.

'There it is,' Mum said. 'And it looks as if we'll have to queue to get in.'

Which they did. But it didn't matter because once they were inside and the show had begun, it was so amazing it put everything else out of every head there – except Netta's.

First there was a parade of ponies, ridden by cowboys and cowgirls in fringed leather jackets and fringed leather trousers and cowboy hats and things called chaps over their legs. They whooped and yelled and drove the ponies so hard Muriel said it was a wonder they didn't fall. But after the ponies, Tex Austin and his bucking broncos roared into the stadium, kicking up clouds of sand and the rodeo began.

Within seconds, the gates at the far end had been opened and the arena was full of huge horned cattle – 'Steers' Muriel said – all charging about and looking really alarming. But Tex Austin and his bucking broncos had everything under control. First they rode their horses at speed alongside the biggest steers, then Tex took up a huge coil of rope from his belt and began to swing it in the air, round and round until the loop at the end was as big as a hoop. And suddenly, without warning he threw the rope at the nearest galloping steer and it snaked out and caught him round his legs and pulled him to the ground. And then four cowboys jumped on him and held him down, big though he was, and tied him up so that he couldn't move. Mabel felt sorry for the poor creature, but Bertie thought it was the most thrilling thing he'd ever seen. And that wasn't the end of it. Soon steers were being lassoed and wrestled to the ground all over the arena and the crowd was cheering so loudly it made your ears sing.

'I'm going to be a cowboy when I grow up,' Bertie

decided when the show was over and they were all walking back to the pavilions.

'You and every other kid in the stadium,' Netta teased.

'And why not?' Rose said. 'You'd make a lovely little cowboy. What d'you want to see next?'

'*Is* there anything else?' Muriel laughed. 'I should think we'd done it all.'

'My dogs are barking,' Netta complained. And she took off one of her shoes and rubbed her foot.

'Time to go home,' Muriel suggested.

'One more thing,' Rose said. 'There's a Hall of Cotton, it says here. I'd like to see that. Might give me some ideas.'

'I'm for a deckchair and ten minutes off me feet,' Netta said.

'Me too,' Mabel agreed. 'I got achy feet too, our Rose.'

So Netta and Mabel limped off to the bandstand with Muriel and Bertie and it was only Rose who went to the Hall of Cotton.

It was well worth the visit. She'd never seen so much material on display, stretched out in great swathes from floor to ceiling, and in a dazzling array of colours, plain, striped, checked, patterned and floral. The smell of new cloth was sumptuous and the colours were lovely.

It wasn't long before she realised that apart from casual strollers most of the people in the curtained aisles were business men in smart suits. I'll bet they're buyers, she thought to herself. And that gave her an idea. Perhaps I ought to buy from the manufacturers too with all this choice. I'll bet if I made a few blouses in that lovely blue muslin they'd sell like hot cakes.

The lovely blue muslin was draped above a counter labelled '*Philips of Manchester*', where three buyers were talking to a middle-aged man in a grey suit, with a gold watch-chain suspended across his waistcoat. He's the boss, she thought. That much was evident. An imposing man, tall and with the sort of face that expected obedience – square chin, determined mouth, strong nose, deep-set eyes, heavy eyebrows and a formidable moustache, brown flecked with grey like his hair.

She waited until the buyers had moved on, and then feeling rather daring, walked up to the counter and addressed him.

'I was interested in the blue muslin,' she said. 'How much does it come out at?'

He was momentarily taken aback to be questioned by a woman, but he recovered quickly.

'Would you care to see the price list,' he said, handing it across.

Rose took the lists and examined the prices, which were better than she expected. Then she stretched out her hand to finger the cloth, rubbing the nap with her thumb.

'It's good quality, madam,' the man said. He'd been dealing with buyers all day but they'd all been men, naturally. To have a woman interested in his wares was something new and presented difficulties. For a start, he wasn't quite sure of her status and that made him momentarily indecisive. Her coat-frock was quietly fashionable and very well made; besides the wedding ring on her finger she wore no other jewellery at all; he would have expected some had she been a manufacturer's wife.

She was testing another length of cloth. 'This is better.'

She knows her cotton, he thought. 'Are you in the trade, ma'am? If you don't mind me asking?'

His respectful tone provoked a sudden and uncharacteristic pride in Rose Jeary. It was a mark of what she had achieved in the long years since the war. It hadn't escaped her that he'd been assessing her clothes and trying to work out who she was. He thinks I'm in the rag trade, she thought, like all the others in their swanky suits. Well that just goes to show how good my clothes are. 'In a small way,' she said, and she spoke with dignity.

'With your husband, I daresay?'

'No,' she said seriously. 'My husband was killed in the war. I run the firm on my own.'

229

'In that case,' he said, 'allow me to introduce myself. Name of Philips. My card.'

'Name of Jeary,' Rose said, beginning to enjoy herself. She found one of her own cards in her handbag. '*My* card.' She was so well used to the name she'd taken all those years ago that she used it as though it really *were* her own.

'Well now, Mrs Jeary,' Mr Philips said. 'Let me see if I can be of service.'

They talked for nearly quarter of an hour, examining various cottons and discussing weight, weave, wearability and costs. Mr Philips satisfied himself that she *was* a manufacturer – of frocks and blouses – and Rose grew steadily more convinced that buying direct could make all the difference to her business. No one in Kennington would have seen even half these designs, she thought, and they're much nicer than anything I could get locally. I shall have to raise a loan from the bank and that would mean paying back interest. But if we start really selling again, it would be worth it in the long run. The only trouble was that she couldn't give him an order there and then, which was what he was obviously expecting.

Fortunately, she was rescued from having to admit her shortage of cash by the approach of two buyers who knew Mr Philips and greeted him loudly as 'Henry, old thing!'

Mr Philips was torn between pleasure at the approach of certain trade and annoyance that his *tête-à-tête* with this beautiful young woman was suddenly over. 'I shall be back in the mill immediately after Easter,' he told her as his colleagues bore down upon him. 'If you're in the vicinity, why don't you call in and see me? I could show you our full range. I'm sure you'd find exactly what you wanted then.'

'Yes,' Rose said. 'Thank you. I might do that.' Then she got out of the way before the buyers stood on her feet.

This could be the answer, she thought, as she walked out into the sunshine. Different patterns and different styles. Something fresh. We've got dull, always using the same old stuff. That's probably why we're not selling. What a good job we came here. Now I've seen what's the matter, I can do something about it.

The family were lolling around in deckchairs in front of the bandstand. Netta had taken off her shoes and was lying with her face turned towards the sun and her eyes shut. Mabel was playing cat's cradle with Bertie. Muriel looked up as she approached.

'How d'you get on?' she asked.

'I think I've found a way out of the doldrums,' Rose replied.

CHAPTER TWENTY

Rose Jeary wasn't the only one planning a change to her life in the spring of 1924. On her father's farm in Suffolk, Miss Ethel Margarite Monk was facing the unpalatable fact that she would be twenty-one in four months' time and she still hadn't found herself a husband. Her brother Percy was up at Oxford, giving himself airs, and baby brother Hereward was due to follow him there in October, but, as far as she could see, there was no future for her at all. Nor would there be unless she took matters into her own hands.

However, she was an exceedingly modern young lady and quite capable of organising her own life. Everything about her gave evidence of that. Not for her the frills and flounces of her mother's generation. Nor the curves. She preferred her dresses to be well cut and perfectly straight and she went to considerable pains to achieve the effect she desired, even to tying down her too adequate bosom with several yards of crêpe bandage. She was given to long beads, elegant cigarette holders, smart straw hats with turned up brims, silk stockings and outfits in scarlet and navy blue or two shades of lilac. Her hair was modern too, cut short and permed into fashionable waves. And she had the vocabulary to match her appearance.

'Angels!' she drawled when her friends arrived to stay. 'How divine of you to drop by.'

To her parents she was firm and severe, and especially now that she'd decided to take action.

'You must hold a May ball, Daddy,' she said to her father. 'It's time I was properly launched.'

At first, her father dismissed the suggestion out of hand. 'Can't afford it,' he told her. 'I've had enough expense with Percy and there's Hereward going up in the autumn.'

'Exactly!' his daughter said acidly. 'So it's high time you spent something on *me* or people will start to say I'm not your daughter. And I'm sure you don't want *that*. I've written out the guest list. I thought we might invite the Quennells.'

'We hardly know them,' Winifred demurred. The Quennells might be virtually next-door neighbours but they were county and well above mere cattle farmers.

'Yes, we do,' Ethel told her coolly. 'Evelyn is one of my dearest friends.'

That was an understatement. The young man was actually her quarry. He wasn't a very prepossessing specimen, being eighteen months younger than she was and rather weedy, with lank fair hair, no chin and an enormous Adam's apple. But the dashing and handsome were all in short supply and weed or not, this man's father owned the estate that bordered onto Daddy's farm. There was a lot of money *and* land for him to inherit come the right time – and no brothers to queer his pitch.

She'd befriended him three weeks ago on a wild trip to London that one of her richer friends had organised. They'd all gone up to see the Empire Exhibition and stayed in town all night on a pub crawl. Evelyn had been very sick and had ended up lying in the gutter and refusing to move, saying he'd just as soon die there as anywhere else and would they please go away and leave him. They'd brought him home in the car with them, naturally, and left him on his doorstep. She'd gone out of her way to be kind to him but he'd probably been too drunk to notice. Since then he'd been a marked man, although luckily for his peace of mind, he didn't know it. He greeted her whenever they met in the village but he was too shy to say more than 'How'd'ee do' and 'Toodlepip.'

'So you'll invite him, won't you Daddy dear,' Ethel insisted. 'I can depend on you, can't I?'

Her boldness won Cedric over, as it generally did. 'Well

if you think he'd accept, I suppose I will,' he conceded. 'But I'm not forking out for a lot of extravagant ball gowns. You needn't think that.'

'You fix the ball, Daddy dear, *I'll* provide the clothes.'

'What with?' her mother asked when Cedric had gone back to his accounts.

'I shall ask Aunty Moneybags.'

Winifred was caught between admiration for her daughter's daring and shame at her outspokenness. She laughed guiltily and tried to scold. 'You mustn't talk about her like that.'

'Why not?' Ethel said coolly. 'You do.'

'Now come!' Winifred rebuked. 'You've never heard me call her names.'

'Don't be a hypocrite, Mother dear. If you don't say it you certainly think it. We all do.'

'Well maybe,' Winifred allowed. 'But you can't ask her this time. Your father wouldn't hear of it. They're in the middle of a row.'

'Then he needn't hear of it,' his daughter said, lighting her first cigarette of the day. 'You needn't tell him.'

That afternoon she donned her new scarlet coat-frock, eased her new straw hat over her carefully weaved hair, stretched her new kid gloves over her expensive rings and telephoned for a taxi to take her to the station.

She was surprised to find her aunt out in the garden supervising the planting of a rose bush in a new flowerbed down by the vegetable garden.

'My dear child!' Augusta said, when she saw who had arrived. 'What's brought you here?'

Ethel answered carefully. 'I thought you might like to see me.'

'Well, you're the only one,' Augusta said rather crossly. 'The others don't care.'

'I care Aunty,' Ethel said with glowing insincerity.

'You're a dear girl,' Augusta said, watching the gardener as he lowered the little spiky bush into the hole he'd dug for it. 'But I've always said so, haven't I?'

Ethel paused – but only slightly. On the last occasion they'd met, her aunt had called her a heartless wretch, but this wasn't the time to remind her of it. 'Always, Aunty dear,' she agreed.

'He didn't suffer you know,' Augusta said. The rose bush was keeling over as if it were fainting. 'My poor dear boy. They did all they could for him.'

Ethel didn't know what she was talking about but she knew how to respond. 'I'm sure they did,' she murmured, wondering who the boy was.

'It was a peaceful end. He didn't suffer.'

'That's a blessing.' So he's dead, whoever he is.

Augusta picked up the small wooden cross that had been lying in the grass and stuck it in the earth in front of the rose bush. '*CHU-CHIN*,' it said. '*Died 20th April 1924. Rest in Peace*.'

Oh for heaven's sake, Ethel thought, it's that damn silly dog of hers. But she kept her face under perfect control and went on making sympathetic noises. 'Poor dear Aunty,' she soothed. 'I do feel for you. I positively do.'

Augusta smiled sadly.

Ethel felt she ought to try to cheer her. 'You've still got the cats though haven't you.'

'Don't talk to me about cats,' Augusta said. 'Nasty selfish things. I've got no time for cats. They're no company at all. Erasmus scratches you if you so much as *look* at him.' She'd pulled the smaller of the two cats onto her lap for a bit of comfort that morning and he'd sworn at her and clawed her hands and kicked her with both feet when she tried to hold him down.

'I tell you what,' Ethel said, seeing her opportunity. 'Why don't you come out shopping with me. That would cheer you up no end.'

'There's nothing I want,' Augusta sighed, looking down at the grave. 'Except Chu-Chin.'

'Exactly,' Ethel agreed in her jolliest tone. 'Get your chauffeur organised – you *have* still got a chauffeur haven't you? Yes. We'll go to Harrods. They've got the best pet department anywhere in town. You'll be amazed.'

Augusta had decided to be totally miserable all day but under such unexpected pressure, she changed her mind, did as her niece suggested and went to Harrods. But she refused to be amazed.

There were plenty of dogs in the pet department, but most of them weren't chows and the few that *were*, weren't Chu-Chin.

'How would modom like a wire-haired terrier?' the salesman offered. 'They're all the rage this season.' The little dogs were very appealing, plump and big-eyed and trembling in their wire cage.

But modom wasn't tempted. She didn't like the cats either. 'Too stand-offish.' Nor the foreign birds, bright-feathered in their cages. 'Too small.'

'Something a bit special,' the salesman said, beginning to understand his customer. 'I think I may have just the thing, if modom would care to follow me.'

He led them to the other end of the department, where there was an African parrot, majestic in a gilded cage, a dapper, pearl grey bird with a scarlet tail, nibbling its claws and looking at them with amber-coloured, baleful eyes.

'Who's a pretty boy then?' the parrot squawked and began to side-step along his perch, swinging his head like a bell. 'Scratch a poll. Scratch a poll. Scratch a poll.' Having reached the side of the cage nearest to Augusta, he ducked his head close to the bars and waited.

'He likes having his head scratched,' the salesman explained. 'He seems to have taken to you modom.'

'He won't bite will he?' Augusta enquired rather apprehensively.

'Oh no,' the salesman assured her. 'He's very gentle.'

Augusta put out a tentative finger and scratched the parrot's feathers. It was a curious sensation to have a bird as big as this waiting so meekly for her attention.

'Aark!' he said and ruffled his neck feathers at her.

'He likes you,' Ethel flattered. 'You've got a way with birds, I can see that.'

'He does seem to,' Augusta said. What a sense of power it gives you to have a parrot bowing his head for you. She felt like a queen. Perhaps this *was* the right sort of pet for her, a creature with style and class, something out of the ordinary. She'd never find another Chu-Chin, so why not go for something completely different? 'How much is he?' she asked.

It was a great deal more than she'd intended to spend but he was irresistible.

'There!' Ethel purred when the purchase was made. 'What did I tell you Aunty dear? Wasn't I right?'

Augusta had to admit that she was. 'You must let me buy you something,' she said. 'A little reward.'

'Oh no, no, no,' Ethel protested, all wide eyes and flicking red-tipped fingers. 'I didn't do it for a reward. I did it because I love you so much and I couldn't bear to see you unhappy.'

That decided the matter. 'All the more reason my dear,' Augusta said. 'Now what would you fancy?'

'We-e-ell,' Ethel drawled. 'I suppose you couldn't run to a little dress could you?'

They headed off to the designer gowns, and Ethel chattered all the way so that Augusta couldn't change her mind. 'Daddy's being absolutely foul to me,' she confided. 'He says I'm not to have an evening dress. He says it's an extravagance. He can't see how important good clothes are to a woman. *You* understand, don't you Aunty darling.'

Aunty darling supposed she did and was hugged and kissed and told she was a regular sweetie. Then her niece rushed upon the gowns.

'Oh, look at that!' she shrilled. 'Isn't that just divine. The most heavenly colour.'

It was a dress made of scarlet silk and seemed shockingly short to Augusta.

'With a double string of pearls!' Ethel said. 'Wouldn't it be just too divine.'

'It's very expensive,' Augusta demurred.

Ethel looked at the price tag. 'Yes, I suppose it is,' she said. 'What about that one?'

That one was pink, had an embroidered jacket to match and was even more expensive than the scarlet silk. 'I couldn't try them on could I?'

She's like a child with a new toy, Augusta thought, and remembered how excited she'd been herself – even as a baby – whenever her mother gave her new clothes. 'Oh all right then,' she said. 'But don't be too long. I want to take this bird home. And I've got to find a name for him.'

'I'll be two shakes of a lamb's tail,' Ethel promised.

It was a formidable lamb. Half an hour later she was still trying on dresses and no nearer to making a decision. 'It's so *hard*,' she explained. 'They're all so darling.'

Augusta had been sitting by the counter for much too long. Her bottom was quite numb and her expression had hardened to a blank of boredom.

'Darling Aunty,' Ethel said, her face all tender concern. 'How vile I'm being. I'm keeping you and you want to get home.'

'Well yes,' Augusta admitted. 'I do.'

'You go on and leave me,' Ethel said. 'It's going to take hours yet. I've got to be certain, you see, haven't I? Perhaps they could send the bill to you later.' And she turned to the assistant. 'You could, couldn't you?'

The assistant spoke directly to Augusta. 'Of course, madam. That would be no trouble at all.'

She's terribly flighty, Augusta thought, looking at the bobbed hair, the red mouth, the bright nails, and I never knew anyone take so long to make up her mind, but she means well.

It was an opinion she was to revise with some venom three days later when the bill came. It was over one hundred pounds and was for a positive wardrobe of clothes, ball gowns, hats, a pair of shoes, even a suit. It took her several minutes before she could comprehend it and when she did she burned with anger. I never gave her

238

permission to buy all that, she thought. One dress, I said. That's all. Not all this. The effrontery of it. Well she can just take it all back. I'm not paying a bill that size, and she needn't think it. And she went straight out into the hall to tell her so.

It was Winifred who answered the telephone. 'Augusta my *dear*,' she said. 'We were just talking about you.'

'That doesn't surprise me,' Augusta said and took a deep breath ready to begin her complaint. 'Have you any idea what your daughter's done?'

Winifred had had a sneaking suspicion ever since Ethel got back from her expedition but she pleaded ignorance. It didn't help her.

'It must have been a misunderstanding,' she said, when Augusta had finished her diatribe.

'Misunderstanding, my foot. Well let her understand this. Tell her from me, she's to send them all back.'

'I don't think they'd take them,' Winifred said.

'Why not?'

There was a long pause and when Winifred spoke again her voice was embarrassed. 'She's worn them all, you see. Well you can imagine, can't you. She's been in and out of them ever since, showing them off to her friends.'

'Crafty little baggage!' Augusta cried. 'She's caught me out good and proper. All that money! And I've *got* to pay it. Well that's taught me a lesson. I'll never go shopping with Ethel Monk again. You haven't heard the last of this,' she promised. And put the phone down.

Later, when she'd summoned Mr Tilling to attend her on the following afternoon, she stood beside the parrot's cage and watched as he held a peanut in one curved claw and shelled it delicately with his great black beak. The sight of him comforted her. He really was a beautiful creature and looked quite perfect between her red velvet curtains. The good thing about animals was how dependable they were, always a joy to look at, always there when you wanted them, always the same. Which was more than you could say for human beings.

239

The parrot winked one amber eye at her, very slowly and deliberately and dropped the empty shell into the debris on the floor of his cage.

'I shall tell Mrs Biggs to expect Mr Tilling,' Augusta told him, 'and she can send someone to give your cage a good clean-out. We must look our best for company.'

Mrs Biggs was aggrieved by both pieces of information.

'What with bloody silly wills,' she said, 'and bloody silly birds, we shall all be driven out of our minds. Keeping all on! She wants to give it a rest.'

For the first time in many years, that was Mr Tilling's opinion too. He was in the middle of a protracted and lucrative divorce case and he had become so intrigued by the 'goings-on' of his clients that he was loth to set it aside. Nevertheless he turned out dutifully to take instructions for yet another will and to eat the statutory scones, pausing at the door for his last-minute command to write to Cedric Monk.

Augusta began as he expected. 'Before you go, Mr Tilling . . .' But then she said something he didn't expect at all, 'you must come and see my new pet. I call him Argus because he's got such beautiful eyes.'

Mr Tilling had no desire to see a pet, new or otherwise, but as his instructions weren't yet completed and they both knew it, there was nothing he could do except comply. He looked at the parrot and pretended to admire it but he was thinking what a nasty, spiteful-looking thing it was, with that hooked beak and those awful claws. It was clinging bodily to the bars of its cage and far too close for comfort.

'Yes,' he said. 'Very colourful.'

'Well, will you look at that, Mr Tilling,' Augusta bridled, as the bird raised its crest. 'He wants you to scratch his head. He doesn't do that to anybody else except me. It shows he likes you, you see. They always know, wild creatures. They are *simpatico*.' That was her latest word, gleaned from an article in a woman's magazine. 'He won't hurt you. He's the gentlest bird

240

alive. Aren't you Argus? Who's a pretty boy then? Scratch his head, Mr Tilling.'

Mr Tilling leant forward stiffly and placed one white forefinger against the ruffled grey feathers of the parrot's neck. If it bites, he thought, I shall sue for damages.

But the parrot didn't bite. It lifted its head, pushed its beak through the bars and before either of them could stop it, dragged Mr Tilling's fountain pen out of his breast pocket and bit the end off. Blue ink spattered in every direction, onto the perch, the bars of the cage, the table, the carpet, all over Mr Tilling's outstretched hand and the dazzling white cuffs of his shirt.

For the first time in his life he was too angry to be logical or diplomatic. 'Stop him!' he commanded. 'He's got my pen.'

But Augusta was laughing. 'Look what he's doing!' she chuckled and pretended to scold. 'You bad, bad boy.'

Having failed to produce anything edible from his peculiar catch, the parrot was beating his head with it. The left side of his face was royal blue and dripping ink.

'Never mind his face!' Mr Tilling said. 'Look at my shirt! It's ruined!'

Augusta was still laughing and paid no attention to him at all. 'Look at him Mr Tilling! Will it come off?'

'No,' Mr Tilling told her, looking at his shirt cuff. 'It's indelible.'

'If he goes on like this, I shall have to call the vet,' Augusta decided.

'I think you should take him straight back to the shop and exchange him for something docile,' Mr Tilling suggested acidly. 'Like a tortoise.'

Now and rather too late, Augusta realised that her solicitor was as badly stained as her pet. 'Oh dear,' she said. 'He has made a mess of your shirt. I'm *so* sorry Mr Tilling. Will it wash off?'

'No. I told you. It's indelible.'

'Yes, so you did. I'm so sorry. You must allow me to

buy you a new one. You bad boy Argus. Look what you've done to our nice Mr Tilling.'

Being patronised was the last straw. 'I shall draw up the will according to your instructions, Miss Monk,' the solicitor said, with icy politeness. 'My clerk will bring it in for you in due course. I can see myself out. Good afternoon.'

'You were right about Miss Monk,' he said to the younger Mr Fordham when he got back to the office. 'She *is* impossible. Look at my shirt! This is the last time I dance attendance on *her*.'

'Give her to the junior,' Mr Fordham advised, when he'd heard the tale. 'He can handle it well enough. After all, her instructions are always the same, no matter how many times she changes her mind. It's either one member of the family or another.'

That was Ethel's view of it, when her father received his customary letter.

'Let her get on with it, darling,' she said. 'Uncle Edmund will do something to annoy her sooner or later and you'll be back in favour before you know it. *We*'ve got a ball to organise.'

It was arranged for the second week in May and everything was going according to plan. Percy and Here-ward had invited several of their 'chums' down for the weekend to attend. And because two of his closest friends had urged him on – at Ethel's instigation – Evelyn Quennell had accepted his invitation too. Oh no, she really hadn't got time to bother about Aunty Moneybags now.

The ball was a very grand occasion, with flowers in the hall to welcome the guests, a buffet supper laid out in the dining-room and a three-piece band playing in the drawing-room for dancing. Ethel was resplendent in scarlet silk and at her most vivacious.

'Help yourselves to drinkies, darlings,' she urged her guests as the drinks' trays were carried round. 'There's plenty more where that came from. Try the cocktail, Evelyn. I shook it with my own fair hand.'

242

Evelyn guffawed and spluttered and said he was sure it would be a cracker, as his hostess flamed off to inspire the next arrivals. He was very unsure of himself in company and tended to cling to the wall, where he felt safe, and talk to his friends, who wouldn't mock him too unkindly.

'Not much of a one for dancing,' he confessed, when the girls came waving their cards at him. And that was usually sufficient to warn them off. But this girl Ethel was different.

'Yes,' she said. 'I know. Olga told me. But I've got something important to tell you so do you think we could sort of stagger round for a while?'

'Something important?' he asked rather fearfully as she led him into the middle of the room. 'Is it a waltz? I'm hopeless at this you know.'

'I'll lead you,' she said. And did. Straight round the room and out of the French doors into the conservatory.

'Oh I say!' he protested.

'We'll have to be very quick,' she said urgently. 'I don't want the parents to see us. Mummy's got eyes like a hawk.'

He was even more alarmed. 'What is it?' he asked, his own eyes popping.

She gave a rippling laugh. 'It's so embarrassing,' she confessed. 'Really. I hardly know how to tell you.'

That made his ears blush.

'It's the parents,' she said. 'This is all a put-up job you see, this party. They think they're throwing us together.'

He gulped. 'Throwing us together?'

'Match-making,' she explained. 'Isn't it just too ridiculous?'

He agreed that it was. 'My parents?' he asked. 'Or yours?'

'Both probably,' she said and added disparagingly, 'you know what parents are like. Mine are foul. They've been planning this for aeons.'

'You mean they want us to start – um – going out together or something?'

'That's about it. Isn't it a *bore*?'

It was terrifying. 'What are we going to do? Keep apart?'

'Well we could,' she said. 'Trouble is, I think that would make them worse. Parents do so hate being proved wrong. They'd keep on arranging things for us, wouldn't they. It would be a sort of challenge.'

He supposed it would.

'It's such a ghastly bore,' she said gaily. 'You don't want to marry me – why should you? – and I'm sure I don't want to marry you. I don't want to marry anybody. But you know what parents are. It's all they ever think of.'

He was biting his lip. 'What *are* we going to do?'

She laid one red-tipped hand on his arm. 'We're going to outwit them,' she said positively. 'Play them at their own game and make monkeys of them. Which will jolly well serve them right. I've got a plan.' She looked around her nervously. 'I say. There isn't anyone listening is there?'

The thought made him jump. He checked but there wasn't.

'I think we should pretend to go along with everything they suggest. Sit beside one another at supper. If they arrange a picnic or a theatre trip or *anything*, we should say 'Oh lovely!' and pretend it's just what we want. We don't have to stay together once we're out of the house. It'll just be to fool *them*. If they think we're interested in one another, it'll keep them quiet and we can go our own way and they won't know. What do you think?'

He was open-mouthed at the daring of it. Fancy outwitting one's own parents. 'I think it's super!'

'We'll have to put on a bit of an act,' she warned. 'Bill and coo a bit, when they're on the look-out. That sort of thing. But it could all be a bit of a lark really. Knowing we've got them running round in circles and all for nothing.'

He felt quite enthusiastic. 'When shall we start?'

'Oh tonight I think. Don't you?'

So that night they sat together at supper and she fed him from her plate and made eyes at him until he blushed and danced with him several times, holding him very close and crooning in his ear. He found it quite thrilling – in a daring sort of way.

As they parted she whispered, 'You know that oak on the boundary, the big one down by the river. Well, if anything happens, I'll leave you a sort of message there. There's a hollow on your side. High up.'

'Cloak and dagger stuff!' he whispered back.

'What are you two up to?' one of her friends called to them.

'Never you mind,' he called back, emboldened by conspiracy. And was bucked when she winked at him.

There was a message for him the very next evening. *'Super success!'* she wrote. *'They think they've made a match. We're supposed to be going to Norwich on Saturday with Catherine and Bob and that lot. Can you make it?'*

How could he refuse?

CHAPTER TWENTY-ONE

As the Manchester express set off from Euston through a complication of rails and a clatter of freight trains, Rose Jeary couldn't help feeling excited. It had taken her a long time to persuade a loan out of her bank manager but she'd done it at last and now she had enough cash for three rolls of cloth, the train fare and even a bit extra, and she was on her way. In every sense of the words, she was heading in a new direction, looking for new materials in a town she'd never seen before. I'll have a root round in the department stores up there, she decided, and see what sort of things they're selling. That might give me ideas too.

Being on her own with time to think was an unusual experience for her. She was so used to living in the demanding chaos of family life that she'd forgotten what it was like to sit and dream. Or to sit and remember.

As the train gathered speed through the green fields of Hertfordshire, memories of Jack Jeary suddenly filled her mind – walking her home from the Halls, kissing her in the Kennington twilight, comforting her when Bertie was killed, singing in the pubs in Dover, warm and loving in the bed they'd shared for such a short, short time. Dear Jack, she thought. I *did* love him. So much. It was ages since she'd thought about him like this but time and distance still hadn't dulled her yearning for him.

The train whistled into an unfamiliar world of canal barges, endless fields and slag heaps as big as hills. How odd life is, she mused. When I was a littl'un, I always thought I'd marry and have lots of kids and live happy ever after – more or less – like Mum and Dad. And now here I am, an old maid with an illegitimate son, living with three other old maids. It ain't exactly happy ever after.

But then it ain't unhappy ever after either. We've made a good life for ourselves, despite everything. We get on well together – most of the time – we understand each other. You can't ask for more than that.

One canal was following the railway as if there were an underground link holding them together. She watched the brown water idly. At Stoke the red-brick station was dark under a glass roof, grown opaque under years of grime. At Macclesfield she had a glimpse of narrow streets hemmed in by giant buildings, mottled black and pink like shrimps. There was an ornate pub, grand on a corner, and a church as black as coal. Then they were out in the countryside again and passing a narrow river as it frothed through bleak fields.

Now that she was close to her destination Rose offered up a private prayer for success. But she didn't bargain. That seemed childish to her now – and futile. Whatever happens today, she thought, as they pulled slowly into Manchester Piccadilly, I shall make the best of it. And she walked out of the station into the smoky air of the city to find a bus or a tram that would take her to Ancoats and Mr Philips' mill.

It was an enormous building and a very ugly one, rising sheer and black above the brackish waters of a canal, five forbidding storeys topped by chimneys belching dark smoke. The contrast between this scene and the sumptuously coloured drapery in the Hall of Cotton couldn't have been more marked.

There was no one about but the entrance was easy to find, so she went in, moving in two strides from the sooty smells of the street to an atmosphere so charged with cotton dust and damp that it made her sneeze. There were machines wherever she looked, their bobbins ranged in long rows, some white, some coloured, threads running out endlessly before them. The workers all seemed to be women, wearing old-fashioned skirts and blouses. They worked with their sleeves rolled up above their elbows in the heat, their hands deft among the threads, the smell of their sweat rising pungently into the aisles. Above their heads the belts growled like thunder as the machines clattered and clacked. None of them took any notice of Rose at all.

For a few seconds, she wondered where to start looking for Mr Philips in such a chaotic place. Then she saw him, standing beside one of his machines, deep in shouted conversation with a man in holland overalls. She walked down the aisle until she was within shouting distance herself and then waited.

'It'll do for the time being,' Mr Philips shouted.

The man shouted back. 'Aye. Happen it will.'

Then Mr Philips turned and saw his visitor. The sight of her was so charming that it filled him with unexpected pleasure. She really is a beautiful woman, he thought while remembering her, and she dresses superbly. That suit is perfect, quietly fashionable, good-quality wool, and the colour's exactly right, light beige with wide revers and wide cuffs and every edge trimmed with red braid. He noticed everything about the entire outfit – T-strap shoes to show off her neat ankles, a box-pleated skirt continuing the line of the jacket, and such a pretty hat, just a shade darker than her suit and trimmed with the same red, worn low on her forehead and with the brim curling round that lovely thick hair as if they were both part of the same design. She has style, there's no mistaking it. He strode forward to greet her and shake her hand.

'Mrs Jeary. How good to see you.'

Rose was surprised to be remembered.

'Let's get out of this racket,' he boomed at her.

He led her to his office down at the far end of the building and closed the door after them to shut out some of the din.

'You've come to see the sample book,' he said, pulling it from the shelf and setting it on the desk before her. It was two feet long and bound in leather and the samples were arranged in cloth type – from cambrics to muslins – each small square of cloth overlapping the next like tiles on a roof. 'You'll not mind if I leave you to it for a few minutes? There's a jacquard needs setting.'

'No,' she said. 'Of course not.' It was the first time she'd spoken since she entered the mill. 'It'll take a bit of time to absorb all this.'

He was back in the office before she'd examined more than half the samples.

'What do you think?' he asked. 'Have you found what you want?'

'There's so much,' she responded. 'I like the florals.'

'They're a new line.'

'Nice strong colours.'

'Look,' he said. 'It's getting on for dinner time. I suppose you wouldn't care to have some lunch with me, if you're not in a rush? I usually ask my customers back to Fallowfields for a bite to eat, especially when they've come a long way.'

That was nothing less than the truth. The difference was that he'd never invited a lady back to lunch because until that morning all his customers had been men. But there was no need to tell her that.

So she agreed to go to Fallowfields, wondering where and what it was. He made a telephone call to his housekeeper to forewarn her, then he took his visitor out into the delivery yard where his new Rolls Royce was waiting for him and drove her out of the city, following the tram route south.

Fallowfields, as Rose soon discovered, was a suburb of the city. It had been built among farms and fields and was green with trees and so quiet that once they were off the main road, she could hear birds singing as they drove through the streets. The houses were enormous, built in the Victorian style and set behind low walls and well-established hedges of privet and laurel. Some of them had stables and coach houses but there were very few carriages out on the roads and even fewer cars.

They passed a wooded park with two lodge gates on either side of an entrance wide enough to take six carriages all at once and drove on into yet another wide street, hushed by foliage. Elm trees, limes and chestnuts arched over the road, the chestnuts bright with the carved candles of their pink and white blossom. Every garden was guarded by low walls, iron railings and an abundance of shrubs. There was hardly anybody about. Two uniformed nannies, deep in conversation, pushed their perambulators along the pavement and a lone dog trotted in the middle of the road in the perfect confidence that he wouldn't be disturbed.

'Here we are,' Mr Philips said and turned into the drive of one of the larger houses.

It was even bigger than Monk House and a great deal grander, built of sand-coloured stone and impressively double-fronted. On either side of the front door, there were wide bay windows topped by even wider gables, and beyond them two tiers of lesser windows all framed by identical green curtains. There was expensive tiling everywhere. The front path was set in a mosaic pattern of blue, buff and chocolate, the garden beds edged with curved terracotta, the roof shining with blue-grey slate. It looked like the sort of house that would stand for a thousand years.

'Welcome to Elm Tree Villa,' Mr Philips said proudly.

The interior was equally impressive, rich with patterned carpets and heavy oak furniture, the walls hung with flock paper and real paintings. Not for this man the sentimental prints of Miss Augusta Monk. *He* had landscapes. And he knew how to keep his servants. The place smelt clean, newly washed and polished, and there wasn't a speck of dust anywhere. No wonder he's proud of it, she thought.

Mr Philips was wondering what he ought to do to entertain his guest until lunch was served. He usually invited his customers into the study and offered them a drink. The decanters of whisky and brandy were laid out ready, as he knew. But it would be indelicate to offer spirits to a lady. Better to be on the safe side. 'Would you care to take a turn round the garden?' he offered.

They strolled out into the sunshine and ambled across the lawn to admire the goldfish swimming in his pond. There was an orchard at the far end of the garden, where fruit trees were thick with blossom but he said that might be a little muddy yet and steered her to the rose arbour where new red leaves were beginning to brighten the trellis and the beds were fragrant with wallflowers and sky-blue with forget-me-nots.

'I've got a good gardener,' he told her, 'as you see. Good eye for colour. Knows how to bring out the best in things.'

'It's a lovely garden,' she said, thinking how rich and lucky he was.

Her admiration made him want to brag. 'There were stables here one time,' he said. 'Stables and potting-sheds. We ran a carriage before I bought the car. My wife liked the carriage. After she . . . after I bought the car I had them converted into a garage and moved the sheds down by the vegetable garden. More convenient.'

His momentary hesitation revealed more than he intended. So he's a widower, Rose thought, and felt instant sympathy for him.

'There's the gong,' he said, turning his head towards its distant reverberation. 'Lunch!'

Despite good food and a bottle of French wine, it was a difficult meal because neither of them was entirely sure of the other and that stilted their conversation.

They talked of cloth types and the variety of weaves. They discussed fashions. They commiserated with each other on the state of trade. And as the sweet course was being cleared, Henry Philips tried to find out more about Ritzy Clothes.

'You run your business on your own, I believe you said.'

His interest was so marked she felt she ought to let him know how small that business was. He'd been treating her as if she were a big buyer ever since she arrived and it wasn't fair to let him go on expecting a big order.

251

'It's a very small business,' she said bluntly. 'Just me and a friend and my two sisters. We supply the local shops.'

He tried not to show his disappointment. 'You have a workshop,' he hoped.

She was honest about that too. Much better to let him know the true state of affairs. 'No. It ain't big enough for that. We work from home.'

Hope of a good sale was gone but he couldn't stop being interested in her. 'So you're looking for new lines to increase your trade,' he said. 'I could put a few bargains her way, he thought, bewitched by those fine grey eyes. In the sunlight streaming through his dining-room window, they were so warm they almost looked brown. She really *is* a very pretty woman and we ought to help the small producers now and then.

'Yes,' she said.

'We'll have our coffee,' he told her, 'and then we'll go back to the mill.' Now that he'd made his decision, he couldn't wait to help her. 'I've got a few special lines you might like to see.'

The special lines were in a small storeroom – some twenty rolls of cloth in various types of cotton and equally various colours.

'How many rolls were you thinking of buying?' he asked.

'Two or three, depending,' she said, looking at the stock. 'Three probably.'

'How about these?' he said, pulling down two rolls from the shelves.

They were both checks, one in beige and the other in rose pink and they looked a good weight. But were they too good for her to afford? she thought, looking for the price.

'Those would retail at two and eleven three a yard,' he told her.

'So little?' she asked, thinking what a bargain they were. But then she unrolled the rose pink and saw why.

252

The material was flawed. 'They're seconds,' she said.

He was pleased to see how well she understood his offer. 'And at an excellent price,' he beamed. 'You could make a good profit on cloth like that. Of course, you'd lose a little in the cutting, but that's reflected in the asking price.'

'Mr Philips,' she said speaking calmly because she felt so offended. 'I never offer my customers seconds. Never have. Never will. I got a reputation to think of.' Despite her control, her pride and anger grew as she spoke. How dare he offer her damaged cloth. She might be poor but she did have some standards. 'If they buy from Ritzy Clothes they know what they're getting and it ain't seconds.'

He saw that he'd made a mistake and tried to retract it. 'You've misread my intentions,' he said. 'I thought I could be helpful to you. I didn't mean to insult you.'

'Well you have,' she said bluntly. And turned to leave the store. 'I came here for the sort of cloth I saw in the Hall of Cotton, not seconds.'

'The florals,' he said hopefully. 'You liked the florals.'

'No,' she said. 'I'm not sure I even like *them* now. I shall have to think about it.'

'Would you care to see them again?'

'No,' she said and the word was firm and final. There were lots of other mills in this city, where she wouldn't be treated like a poor relation. She'd try some of them.

He escorted her to the exit, saying he hoped he could be of service on some other occasion, and she shook hands in a civilised way and said goodbye politely. But his mistake had opened out like a gulf between them and, as he watched her walk away, he recognised that it wasn't just her custom he wanted. God damn it all, he thought angrily. How was I to know she'd be proud? And yet even that was endearing. The flash of those eyes when she said she'd got a reputation to think of. For a few ridiculous seconds it had made him feel young and free, as if he were twenty and could follow her to the ends of the earth.

Now he couldn't even follow her to the end of the street. He watched her as she walked away, small and straight-spined and determined in her pretty suit and that red-trimmed hat. God damn it all, what a thing to happen!

Rose walked her temper away before she was back in the centre of the city. The sun was shining, she was well fed, there were other mills. There was also a fine shopping emporium called Lewis's on one side of that central square. She'd noticed it from the tram. Time to do a bit of browsing and see what they had on offer. She might even find out where they got their stock. Manufacturers printed their names on the rolls so it shouldn't be too difficult.

It was a very grand store and the luxury of the goods on display transformed her mood. One day, she told herself, letting her pride warm her, they won't be offering me seconds, they'll be selling me suits by Chanel and pure silk underwear. The clothes here weren't quite as fashionable as Chanel but they were well made and the underwear was gorgeous, all in silk and in deceptively simple styles. She strolled past stand after stand, admiring chemises and petticoats, casting her professional eye over cut and finish. If I could afford one of these, she thought, I should feel like a queen.

But the rolls of cloth were no help to her. They were all made by Lewis's itself.

'Are these all your own lines?' she asked the shop-girl.

'Yes ma'am. Won't they suit?'

The girl had such an open face that Rose decided to confide. 'To tell you the truth,' she said. 'I ain't a customer. I'm looking for a manufacturer.'

'You want Watts Warehouse, then. They have all sorts there.'

'Where is it?'

'Just along Portland Street,' the girl said. 'The other side the gardens. You can't miss it.'

She was right. Nobody could have missed Watts Warehouse. It was enormous, filling the space between one side street and the next with five storeys of flamboyantly carved grandeur like some gigantic Venetian palace.

Everything's so big in this city, Rose thought, as she walked through an entrance high enough to admit an elephant. They certainly like size. The foyer of the place was dazzling, lit by a chandelier as big as a diving-bell, and with a huge cantilevered staircase rising in the centre and curving right and left through all five storeys towards a high glass roof.

She stood before it impressed but perplexed, thinking it was just a little too grand for her purposes. But there was a polite young man at her elbow, welcoming her and asking what materials she would like to see. So she allowed herself to be led to the floor labelled cottons and rayons, where there were rolls of cloth displayed on wide shelves in labelled bays that ran the length of the building.

'The rayon's down the far end of this bay, madam, if you're interested,' the young man explained as they passed.

'What's rayon?' she asked, never having heard of it.

The answer was a surprise. 'Artificial silk.'

'Is it new?'

'Not to us, madam. We've had it for years. It's used for artificial silk stockings mostly. Would you care to see it?'

Why not? she thought. It wouldn't take a minute and after admiring all that gorgeous underwear in Lewis's, she was vaguely intrigued by the thought of a substitute for silk.

But when she saw it, she was more than vaguely intrigued. She was very decidedly interested. Even from a distance the long rolls had a silken sheen to them, a look of luxury and glamour. The assistant took down the nearest roll and flipped out a couple of yards for her inspection and she lifted the cloth and let it fall over her hand, pleased by its elegance. The material was more shiny than silk and a lot more slippery, which would make working it tricky, but it was soft to the touch and it looked beautiful.

255

'What's it made of?' she asked.

'Wood pulp,' the assistant told her. 'Pine and spruce mostly. We think this one is particularly good. The yarn is made by Henry Bronnart & Co. of Princes Street and they have small quantities woven locally. They call it lustro-silk. Courtaulds produce several different types of yarn too in their Coventry works. There's some of that on the next shelf. Of course it's still rather in the experimental stage. The local manufacturers tend to shun it so not a great deal is made up.'

It would make beautiful underwear, Rose thought. Chemises and petticoats. 'Is it locknit?' she asked.

It was and in a choice of three colours, snow white, pale peach and ecru. But what was even better about it was the price. With material like this she could make underwear just like the stuff she'd just lusted for in Lewis's, petticoats that would look like silk and sell at an eighth of the price. White cotton underwear was so boring and only the rich could afford *crêpe de Chine*. With this rayon, everyone could have a bit of luxury.

She ordered two rolls, one in white and the other in ecru. Then she went back to Lewis's and bought a petticoat and a chemise to use as patterns.

It was late by the time she got back to the station and all her money was gone. But her plans were made.

CHAPTER TWENTY-TWO

As Rose was admiring the silk petticoats in Lewis's, the postman made his last delivery of the day in Ritzy Street. There was a postcard for number 26 addressed to Miss Muriel Spencer.

'*I should like to start work on the first portrait tonight,*' it said. '*Would that be possible? About 7.30. Regards, E. M.*'

'He's got a sauce!' Netta disapproved. 'Who does he think he is? Ordering you about. You ain't his skivvy now. Write an' tell him.'

Muriel surprised them both by leaping to his defence. 'He's not ordering me about,' she said. 'It's not like that at all. He wouldn't order anybody about. He's much too much of a gentleman for that. It's only a suggestion. And he *has* paid for it.'

Netta wasn't persuaded. 'Well he should give you more notice,' she growled. 'He can't expect you to be forever at his beck and call.'

'I don't mind going tonight,' Muriel said. 'I haven't got anything else to do, now have I?'

That was the truth, as Netta conceded, but she still didn't approve. 'Won'tcher get bored?'

'No,' Muriel said, smiling now that their threatened spat had passed. 'I quite enjoy it, in a way. It's peaceful.'

'Well rather you than me,' Netta grinned. 'I'd be bored out of me mind.'

Mabel and Bertie were setting the table for tea and they were more interested in knowing when Rose would be home.

'Presently,' Muriel told them. 'She won't be long now. We'll have our tea and she'll be back before you know it.'

In fact she put her key in the door just as Muriel was adjusting her hat in the hall ready to go out. She was carrying an expensive-looking parcel and was flushed with excitement. 'I've got such a lot to tell you,' she said. 'Where's the others?'

Muriel was in such a hurry that she didn't notice the flush or the excitement. 'Tell me when I get back,' she said, heading for the door. 'I'm modelling for Mr Edmund. Must rush or I'll be late.' And she was gone before Rose could say another word.

After two long journeys and the high emotion of her extraordinary day, Rose had expected a very different welcome. Now, left alone in the hall with the breeze of Muriel's departure still stirring the air about her, she felt as though her friend had hurled cold water in her face. That's not like Mu, she thought, feeling hurt. She could at least have asked me how I got on. But, being Rose, she pushed the hurt aside, tucked her purchases under her arm and strode into the living-room to show them to her sisters. The family would be different.

Bertie was sitting in his chair beside the new bookcase with a copy of Aesop's Fables on his lap, absorbed in the tale of *The Owl and the Eagle's Daughter*. He jumped up at once to run to his mother and hug her. 'Ain't you late Mum. I thought you was never coming.'

The embrace restored her. 'Hello my Bertie,' she said, kissing him. 'Have you been a good boy? Yes, 'course you have. 'Lo Mabel. Now then, look what I've got here!' And she began to open the parcel with Bertie leaning lovingly against her.

She'd hardly undone the string before there was a knock at the door.

'It's all go tonight,' Netta pretended to grumble and went out to see who it was.

Standing on the doorstep, cap in hand, neat and presentable in a brown jacket and grey flannel trousers, his chin newly shaved and patched with papers, his thick hair greased into obedience, was José Fernández.

'I come to take you out,' he said, giving her the full benefit of a white-toothed smile. 'I owe you a drink.'

It was such a surprise to see him, it made Netta's heart race. She'd thought about him every night, dreamt about what she'd do if they ever met again, but she'd never seriously imagined he would actually come to Ritzy Street to see her. 'What? Now?' she asked.

'Now. Tomorrow. H-when you like. I in the neighbourhood.'

'So I see,' she said, grinning at him. 'Well you'd better come in for a minute. See what my sister says.' She led him into the living-room. 'Look who's turned up.'

He was just the sort of company Rose didn't want. No! she thought. Not now! Not just as I was going to tell them. But she controlled her annoyance and managed to be polite.

'You got over it all right then,' she said, 'your fall.'

He was very polite too. 'Yes, thank you.'

'He's asked me out for a drink,' Netta explained.

'I bring her back safe and sound,' he promised, making eyes at Netta.

'What, now?' Rose asked.

Netta was putting on her hat. 'You don't mind, do you?'

It would be all the same if I said I did, Rose thought rather bitterly. All that effort, all that way, and you run off and leave me the minute I get home. You're as bad as Muriel. Can't you see I've got good news for you? She was weary with disappointment, her neck and shoulders aching.

But there was no stopping Netta. Within five minutes she was out of the house, talking nineteen to the dozen and holding the young man's arm as they strode off down the street.

Mabel watched them with admiration. 'Ain't he lovely, our Rose. Did you see his hair? All curly. I love curly hair, don't you? Dark curly hair, our Rose. I'll bet it's soft. Ain't he lovely?'

Bertie was scowling. 'I don't like him,' he said.

It was such an exact reflection of her own feelings that Rose could have hugged him, but that might have told him more than it was good for a child to know. So she merely asked mildly, 'Don't you? Why not?'

'He was looking at things.'

So he was, Rose thought. His eyes were everywhere. 'A cat may look at a king.'

'He was looking at *everything*. It was nasty how he was looking.'

'He's all right,' Rose said, feeling she had to defend him – for Netta's sake. 'Bit flash – but that ain't a sin. Who's for cocoa?' If she kept busy she could pull herself out of the miseries.

But once she'd put Bertie to bed and quietened Mabel's incessant babble by giving her a barley-sugar stick to suck, the evening stretched before her, desert empty. She unpacked her parcel, unpicked both garments and began to make her brown paper patterns, thankful that at least she had something to occupy her. But for the first time in her life, the work felt like a burden. She was aware of the weight of her responsibilities, the dependence of her family and, worst of all, she knew she was resenting poor Mabel for babbling, which wasn't fair because she couldn't help it.

By ten o'clock she was so weary, she took herself off to bed. So it wasn't until breakfast the next morning that she had a chance to tell anyone her news and even then it had to wait until Netta had entertained them all with the tale of her evening out.

'Never mind going fer a drink,' she said, grinning at them. 'We went to the pictures. He's a caution. He don't half make you laugh. You should hear some of the jokes he told me.'

Rose was in no mood for jokes but Muriel and Mabel were all encouragement so the jokes were told. And were still being told when the table was cleared and they were getting ready to start work.

Then, and at last, Muriel asked her friend how she'd got on in Manchester.

Disappointment and a lingering sense of rejection still rankled in Rose's mind, despite the clarity of morning. 'We-e-ell,' she said, smiling at them, half teasing, half rebuking, 'if you can tear yourselves away from José Fernández for two seconds, I'll show you.' And she took her new paper patterns and the dismantled underwear from the dresser drawer.

Netta and Muriel exchanged grimaces, conveying in a second that they knew they'd annoyed her, that they knew how and that they wished they hadn't. But the minute they heard what she'd got planned they saw how they could make amends.

'That's brilliant!' Netta applauded. 'Cheap silk undies. They'll sell like hot cakes.'

'If the shops'll take them,' Rose said, smoothing out a pattern.

'They'll take 'em,' Netta promised. 'Leave that to me. How soon could we make up a sample?'

'It'll be difficult material to work,' Rose warned. 'It ain't *exactly* like silk.'

'We'll manage,' Muriel said, seeing her chance to make amends too. 'I think it's a marvellous idea, Rose.'

'We could have some leaflets printed,' Netta suggested. ' "*Luxury lingerie at bargain prices*." Whatcher think?'

It was just the sort of response Rose had hoped for the previous evening and none the less welcome for being late. 'Half a gross,' she decided. 'Then we'll see.'

Netta went to the printers that morning and the leaflets were delivered the following afternoon, just after Rose's order arrived from Manchester – two rolls of rayon, sewing-thread to match and an assortment of lace for trimmings. The four women couldn't wait to get started, although as Rose had foreseen they soon discovered that artificial silk wasn't easy to sew. Simple seams tended to come apart, French seams were too bulky, run-and-fell took twice the time. But by the end of the day, and after considerable experiment, they had made up their first four garments to the standard they wanted, two petticoats and two chemises, one in each colour. Now it was up to Netta to sell them.

She was loading up the goods box on her tricycle early the next morning when José strolled round the corner.

She didn't even give him the time of day. 'Can't stop,' she yelled as she drove past him. 'Got a job on.'

'I see you tonight,' he yelled back.

She waved as she turned the corner. 'What sort of answer is that?' he asked Muriel who was coming out of the house, shopping basket over her arm.

'If I were you, I'd come back tonight and see,' she suggested. 'We're all rather busy just now.' And she walked off, thinking what a turn their lives were taking, with new stock to sell and Netta courting and the business changing overnight. It made her wonder what on earth would happen next.

Netta's business was grittily determined. Until that morning she'd limited her selling to local shops and small street traders. Now, as an apology for rushing off with José like that and leaving Rose on her own, she was going to tackle a department store.

The store she'd chosen was Arding and Hobbs, which was one of the largest and in a prime position down by Clapham Junction station. It was a daunting place with well-to-do customers, expensive fittings, windows shaded by blinds and packed with classy merchandise and a considerable carriage trade. It made her heart pound just to look at it, but she was going to brave it, daunting or not.

Once she'd left her tricycle by the kerb and walked into the shop she felt better, because she looked like a customer and didn't feel so out of place. But getting a shop assistant to take her seriously was hard work. She was passed from junior to senior until she reached an impressive lady with ginger hair and tortoiseshell glasses, who made her wait until she'd finished with a customer and was then haughty and dismissive.

'I'm afraid our buyers don't see people without an appointment,' she said.

'He'll see me,' Netta said, with more confidence than she felt. 'This is a new line, see. Silk lingerie at bargain prices.' She spread all four items on the counter and waited.

The assistant was still haughty. 'We already have an excellent line in silk lingerie. As you can see.'

'Not at these prices you don't,' Netta insisted. 'He'll come down for these, I'd lay money on it. These are new. They look like silk and sell like cotton. Send one a' the leaflets up to him an' see.'

'He won't come down.'

'Oh well, suit yourself,' Netta said, folding up the ecru petticoat. 'I just thought I'd give you first refusal, that's all, seeing your reputation. There's plenty of other stores.'

Her confidence made the assistant dither. 'Well,' she said. 'I'm not sure. It's highly irregular.'

'Give me back me leaflet then an' I'll be off.'

'There wouldn't be any harm just sending it up, would there?' the assistant wondered, feeling the white petticoat.

Her change of tone was the best encouragement Netta could have had. 'Nothink venture,' she said, speaking for both of them.

So the leaflet was dispatched upstairs with a message written on the bottom. And then there was a very long wait.

Netta did her best to appear nonchalant but as the minutes passed it became more and more of a strain. She arranged her wares ready for him but then there was nothing else to occupy her. She felt as if her smile had been glued to her face and her heart was beating so violently it was moving her blouse and she was afraid the assistant would notice.

But at last an elderly man wearing striped trousers and a black jacket came walking towards her through the

263

shoppers, looking stern. Lost, she thought, reading his expression. He'll never buy from the likes of me. He's much too posh. But she determined to put up a good fight anyway.

It wasn't necessary. 'A new cloth, I believe,' he said, picking up the ecru petticoat. 'I've heard of it, naturally. They use it for artificial silk stockings but I've never seen it used for lingerie. How does it wear?'

'Depends how it's made up,' Netta told him. 'We use run-and-fell seams and a rolled hem.'

He examined both, his face thoughtful. 'Were I to give you an order,' he said, looking at her sideways, 'how soon could you deliver?'

Netta said the first thing that came into her head, too stunned for calculation. 'Friday week?'

'Two dozen assorted,' he said and turned to walk away.

Now the smiles were real, the excitement too great to be contained. As soon as he was out of the department, she ran from the store at full pelt, to the astonishment of the shoppers, leapt on her bike like a circus turn and pedalled home so fast she made her legs ache, triumph burning in her brain.

'Two dozen! From Arding and Hobbs!' Rose said ecstatically. 'How did you manage it? You clever thing!'

Muriel was impressed but anxious. 'We'll never do it,' she said. 'Not by Friday week.'

'Yes, we will,' Rose said, her cheeks pink with excitement. 'I'll start tonight.'

'We'll all start tonight,' Netta said.

'What if your young man comes back?' Muriel wanted to know. 'I told him he could.'

'When?'

'This morning.'

'Then he'll have to go away again,' Netta said, tossing her head. 'I ain't at his beck and call and he needn't think it.' She certainly wasn't going to make the same mistake twice.

But when he arrived just after seven o'clock with an

armful of flowers, her resolution wavered visibly.

'For you,' he said, thrusting the flowers towards her. 'If you can come out with me, I would like. If you can't, I grin and bear it.'

'You're a case,' she said.

'Is being Spanish,' he explained. 'We go out?'

'Can't be done,' she told him, brusque with the pull between temptation and the determination to resist. He was so handsome. It really wasn't fair. 'I got work to do. There's a rush on.'

He argued briefly but she was adamant, her jaw set.

'I come back Sat'day,' he promised, making eyes at her. 'I not go away.'

'Sat'day week,' she said implacably. 'Can't do nothink till then.'

Netta's decision left Muriel in a quandary, a private one because it wasn't something she could discuss with the others, but a quandary nevertheless. Far from being a peaceful occasion, her first sitting with Mr Edmund had actually been rather difficult. He'd been depressed, nothing had gone right and he'd finished by tearing up all three of the sketches he'd made and cleaning his brushes with the air of a man doomed to failure. She'd been torn with such sympathy for him that she'd offered to sit again, whenever he liked. Now she would have to write and tell him that she'd changed her mind.

She wrote that evening, choosing her words with care, and was relieved when he wrote back by return of post to say that of course he understood and that his portrait might well benefit by being delayed for a day or two and would she please write back and let him know as soon as she was available again.

Just as well I got that out of the way, she thought, as she settled down to her third day at the new work. The pile of cut garments looked formidable and they were only a third of the way through the order.

Netta was standing beside the dresser, busily writing something in block capitals on one of her leaflets. 'There y'are,' she said, waving it at them. 'Whatcher think a' that? "*As supplied to Arding and Hobbs, Clapham.*" That'll bring 'em in!'

'Just as long as you don't go mad when you're promising delivery dates,' Rose joked. 'Remember we've got to make 'em. We're working all hours as it is.'

'Time off Sat'day week,' Netta said.

'We'll have earned it,' Rose told her.

But by Saturday week, Netta had got so many orders that they couldn't see how on earth they would get through them.

And José arrived early.

'It *is* all right, ain't it?' Netta asked as she put on her hat. 'I'll do twice my whack tomorrow.'

'You done more than your whack *today*,' Rose told her. 'You cut off and enjoy yourself.'

'Ain't it romantic, our Rose?' Mabel breathed when the couple had gone. 'I knew he'd come and ask her out again. D'you reckon they're courting?'

The idea wasn't welcome. 'I hope not,' Rose said. 'Not with all this work coming in. We've got too much to do.'

And that puts paid to my visit to Chelsea, Muriel thought. I shall have to write and tell Mr Edmund to find someone else because this could go on for a very long time.

Mabel pressed her snub nose against the windowpane. 'Will he come back tomorrow, our Rose?'

'I shouldn't think so,' Rose hoped. 'He can't take her out every night, can he?'

But apparently he could try. He came back evening after evening, sometimes with flowers, sometimes with chocolates, once with a length of ribbon to trim her hat, obviously courting hard. And Netta, relaxed by the success of her sales and seduced by so much flattering attention, went out with him more and more frequently.

A week went by and their '*luxury lingerie at bargain prices*' began to sell in larger quantities. Edmund Monk wrote back to Muriel to say that he would prefer to use her as his model and was prepared to wait for her. And José told his 'lovely **Netta**' that he would have to leave her for a week or two because he had a job erecting scaffolds in the Midlands.

'You miss me, eh?' he instructed as he kissed her goodbye.

He was gone for nearly four weeks and she missed him very much. They wrote to one another every other day and his letters were full of affectionate promises. '*I be back soon to love you.*' '*I never love nobody like I love you.*' '*I love you till I die.*' But he didn't ask '*Will you marry me?*' which was what she was hoping for. Never mind, she thought, as she hid his letters away in her bedroom, he'll ask sooner or later. He loves me too much not to. And she tried the words out for size. '*Husband and Wife.*' '*Till death us do part.*' It was going to happen to her after all. Meantime there was plenty of work to keep her occupied while he was away.

At the beginning of July, she pedalled her tricycle to the Old Kent Road and got sizeable orders from three linen drapers there. Rose sent off for double the quantity of white and ecru rayon and took an extra roll of peach-coloured cloth too. By the end of the month, when José was away in Kent on yet another job, their orders had trebled and they were struggling with more work than they could manage.

'We shall have to take on more workers,' Rose said, when Netta came back from Arding and Hobbs with the biggest order yet. 'I'll put an advertisement in Mr Fassbinder's.'

'You mean employ people?' Netta said. 'Like a boss.'

Put like that it seemed an extraordinary step for them to be taking. But that *was* what she was thinking of doing.

'What'll you pay them?' Netta asked. 'You'll have to think it all out.'

'I shall pay the going rate,' Rose said. 'And we'll have bonuses shared between us when trade's good.'

'Like a co-operative,' Muriel said.

'The going rate's about twelve shillings a week,' Netta told them. 'I seen it in the paper.'

'Then we'll offer fourteen and bonuses,' Rose decided. 'And we'll take our time. Make sure they're people we can trust. We've all got to work together when all's said and done. It's a big step to take.'

The advertisement was written out and taken down to Mr Fassbinder's corner shop that afternoon. And the first person to answer it was their old friend Nancy Cartwright.

'I ain't exactly a dab hand with me needle,' she confessed, 'but I could work a machine. You'd only have to show me what you wanted. And I need the work, I tell you straight. Specially when he's at sea.'

They hired her instantly and with great relief at the thought that they'd be working with a friend.

'Start Monday?' Rose said.

'On the dot,' Nancy said. 'How many more d'you want?'

'Why?' Muriel asked. 'Do you know someone?'

'My Marigold'ud jump at the chance,' Nancy said. 'She's been making packing cases down at Dingwall's since the kids went to school. Half past eight in the morning till seven at night, for twelve shillings a week. Terrible work. She's like a dead thing some nights.'

So Marigold was hired too. Soon the back room was heaped with half-completed garments and their living-room was full of boxes. Their success was a daily pleasure to them but the concomitant muddle was not.

'We need a handyman to shift all this stuff about,' Rose decided.

'Specially them rolls a' cloth,' Nancy agreed.

'You could have my Charlie,' Marigold said, 'if he wasn't just off to sea.'

So a second advertisement was put into Mr Fassbinder's window and this one was answered by a stranger, a rather dusty looking man with grizzled hair and badly scarred hands.

He said his name was Mr Thomas, that he was an old

268

soldier and that he'd never been a handyman before, and added, with a grin, that he wouldn't mind putting his hand to anything, 'providing it's legal'. They hired him on a week's trial. By the end of his third day he was part of the firm, amiably tackling any job that needed doing. He fixed shelves, changed gas mantles, packed and unpacked, carried their great rolls of cloth about, even made tea in the middle of the afternoon. He was perpetually cheerful, whistling as he worked, and very reliable. By the end of the week they couldn't think how they'd managed without him.

José Fernández came back to London five days later. He was deeply impressed by all the changes. 'I turn my back five minutes,' he said, 'an' you're running a workshop.'

'What's all this about five minutes?' Netta teased. 'You was gone nearly five weeks.'

'You miss me, eh?' he hoped, making eyes at her.

'No,' she said, her expression belying her words.

They had been to the pictures that evening and now they were strolling along the embankment admiring the Thames by moonlight. Behind them the traffic made its usual racket – trams buzzed busily along the middle of the road, their lights ablaze, cars snorted and tooted as they jostled for position – but the scene before them was magical and peaceful. The river glittered with reflected light and the Thames barges were mystic blue shapes, huddled side to creaking side, their russet sails furled and subdued. The obelisk of Cleopatra's Needle was as white as if it had been newly carved and all the arches of Westminster Bridge were edged with silver. Even the dolphins on the lamp standards had acquired silver fins.

Netta traced the line of one bulbous head and its upwardly curving body. 'I love these little dolphins,' she said.

'I love you,' he said, putting his arm round her and pulling her towards him.

She kissed him with one hand still on the dolphin's snout. 'Likewise,' she said lightly.

'I wish I didn't have to keep going away,' he said into her neck.

She was dreamy with the sensations he was rousing, bewitched by moonlight and desire. 'Um,' she said.

'I wish I work in Ritzy Street. Be with you all the time.'

'Um.'

'You get me job in Ritzy Street, eh?'

The question was too pointed to be ignored. She made a great effort and stirred out of her trance. 'You mean work for me and Rose?'

'Why not?'

'What as?'

'Handyman?' he suggested. 'Driver. I could drive the bicycle.'

'We've got a handyman,' she said. 'Mr Thomas. Didn'tcher see him? An' *I*'m the driver.'

'Something else then,' he said, pulling her back towards him and kissing her neck. 'You ask eh? Then we can be together all the time. I shan't have to keep going away.'

It was tempting, she had to admit that. Not very likely but very, very tempting. If she could get him a job with the firm she could see him every day. And that would bring the possibility of marriage that much closer. She *did* so want to get married. 'I'll ask tomorrow,' she promised.

And was kissed most passionately as a reward.

Unfortunately, Rose gave her exactly the answer she expected. 'There ain't the work,' she said. And joked, 'Unless he wants to turn his hand to sewing.'

'I can't see him doing that,' Netta joked back. It was a cover for her disappointment, as Rose suspected. But neither of them said any more about it, Netta because she couldn't see any point in it, Rose because she didn't want to be told how serious this courtship was becoming. There was something about José Fernández that worried her, something that didn't ring true. She couldn't explain what it was and she kept her opinions to herself, naturally, because she didn't want to upset Netta. But knowing that he was after a job in the firm made her even more suspicious of him. It didn't seem proper somehow for a man to be pushing his sweetheart to get him a job.

José saw nothing improper in it at all. 'Ask again,' he urged, when Netta told him what Rose had said. 'You got lots of orders – you tell me so – so all right, there plenty of work. You find me a job, eh? Then I not have to go away. I stay with you all the time.'

'*All* the time?' she asked.

'Why not?' he said. 'If I have a job. We could get a little flat, maybe. Three rooms. That the sort of flat for married people.' And he put his arms round her ready to kiss her.

'Is this a proposal?' she asked.

He kissed her before he replied and his voice was warm and loving. 'You would like, eh?'

She was breathless now that the longed-for moment had almost arrived, but she tried to be sensible. 'Could you afford it?'

'Now – maybe not,' he said. 'Later? I don' know. With a good job, who knows? A job with a good firm. When I not in rooming houses all the time.'

It worried her that he would keep harping on about working for the firm, because there was nothing she could do about it. But he'd proposed. That was the great thing. They were going to get married. She wasn't going to be an old maid for the rest of her life.

'Oh,' she said, 'I do love you.'

Happiness skimmed her through the next three lilting days. She sang as she pedalled her tricycle through the dust of the streets, hugging her secret to herself, her head full of happy anticipation. But it was an ephemeral happiness and she knew it. José was still pushing her to get him a job, there was still too much sewing to be done, the house was still too full of people.

On the fourth day, the weather was hot and muggy with a storm threatening and, just as she was struggling into the hall with the latest batch of petticoats for delivery, their next consignment of cloth arrived. Blinded by her pile of boxes, she tripped over two rolls that were propped up against the hat-stand.

'There ain't room to swing a cat in this house,' she said, and she was only half joking. 'Why couldn't he put that lot straight upstairs?'

'He's doing his best,' Rose said, defending her handy-man. 'He can't carry them all up at the same time.'

'You should've employed José,' Netta said. 'He'd've done 'em in seconds.'

Muriel was working the treadle machine and was hot and tired and annoyed that José was being pushed at Rose yet again.

'If you want them upstairs so much,' she said, wiping the sweat from her forehead, 'you put them there. We've got enough on our plate without hauling great rolls of cloth up and down stairs.'

'And what's that supposed to mean?' Netta said, putting her head back inside the room.

Despite Rose's warning grimace, battle was joined. 'If you were to pull your weight,' Muriel said, 'we shouldn't be in such a mess all the time.'

'I do pull my weight. Who d'you think gets all the orders?'

'But who goes out every night of the week?' Muriel asked.

'I do *not* go out every night of the week.'

'Every night bar one in the last six.'

'You're just jealous, that's your trouble.'

'No, I'm not, as it happens.'

'You're jealous,' Netta insisted. 'Anyway, why shouldn't I go out once in a while. We all need time off now and then, for Gawd's sake. It don't do you no good to be working all the hours God sends. You need a break now and then.' Then she began to cough, the way she always did when she was upset.

Muriel was upset by the cough but she fought on. 'Now and then, yes,' she said. 'Not every night of the week.'

They were bristling at one another as if they were going to come to blows.

'We're all tired,' Rose intervened. 'There's too much work to do. *That*'s the trouble.'

'Well p'rhaps I shouldn't get so many orders then,' Netta said. It was a cheap sneer and she knew it but she was too cross to keep her feelings under control.

Now Rose was cross too. 'Don't be silly.'

An earned rebuke was more than Netta could bear and it made her cough more than ever. 'Oh silly is it?' she yelled. 'First I'm told I can't go out with my young man and now I'm being silly!'

'Nobody said you couldn't go out with him,' Muriel corrected. 'I just said it was a bit much to have you gallivanting off every single night.'

'Gallivanting?' Netta roared. 'I ain't gallivanting. I *never* gallivant. And what about you? You're off to Chelsea whenever that artist feller so much as cocks a finger for you. But I suppose that ain't gallivanting.'

'Now look!' Muriel said, pale with anger, 'I went there once, that's all, and ever since then I've been putting him off.'

'You never told us,' Rose said, much surprised. 'You didn't have to do *that* Mu.'

'Well no, maybe not, but I did it. So we'll have a little less about me gallivanting, if you don't mind. I went out *once*.'

'Once, twice, it's exactly the same if you ask me,' Netta said, still bristling at her. 'You got no right to go criticising me. I got a right to go out. José and me are going to get married.'

The words hung in the air, alerting them all. Marigold looked up, ready with congratulations, but then caught Rose's eye and changed her mind. Mabel took it in slowly, her smile and her understanding growing together. Nancy was watchful, Muriel guarded, knowing what a mistake she'd made to quarrel now. But it was Rose's reaction they were all waiting for.

She didn't flinch at the news, as she'd feared she might, but she couldn't smile either. 'When?' she said.

Such an abrupt and unloving response tore Netta's feelings into tears. 'I thought you'd be pleased,' she said, controlling them with anger. 'It ain't every day of the week your sister says she's going to get married.'

'We are pleased,' Muriel said, changing her tone at once. 'It's marvellous news. Isn't it Rose.'

Rose turned the garment she was sewing and tried to smile. But her movements and expression were too weary to fool her sister. 'Yes,' she said. 'It is. We're all . . .'

'You're all nothing!' Netta said, her anger breaking. 'I can see how it is. You don't have to tell me. You don't want me to get married. That's the size of it.'

'That ain't true,' Rose said, anguished that they were on the brink of a row, embarrassed because it was happening in front of Nancy and Marigold, guilty because Netta's cough was getting worse. 'You know it ain't Netta. It's just . . .'

'You want us all to go on being spinsters for the rest of our lives,' Netta said, coughing violently. 'That's the truth of it. You can't stand the idea of any of us getting married.' She was steaming with anger. 'It's all right for you. You got Bertie. And the firm. And everything. Well I tell you straight, I don't care what you think. José loves me and I'm going to marry him, the minute we got the money for it. Soon as I earn that bonus I shall put it in the bank ready.'

And she stormed out of the house, coughing as she went.

For a second there was an embarrassed silence in the room, then Rose finished the seam she was working, bit off the thread and stood up. 'We can't go on like this,' she said calmly. 'It's ridiculous.' And she walked into the hall, took up her hat and left them.

Her departure was so abrupt and unexpected that nobody knew how to cope with it.

'Shall I go after her?' Muriel wondered.

'Better not,' Nancy advised. 'Let her get over it for a bit.'

'Our Netta's going to marry the pretty man,' Mabel said, beaming at them. 'I knew she would. He's got ever such pretty hair. All curly. I like curly hair.'

CHAPTER TWENTY-THREE

The storm broke as Netta left the house but she was too angry to care – and, anyway, thunder was appropriate. She pedalled furiously towards the Old Kent Road, scattering dogs and pedestrians right and left, her thoughts boiling. How dare they criticise her like that! I got *some* rights, she thought angrily, as the thunder growled again. I got a right to a life of me own. And so has he. It ain't his fault he's courting at the wrong time.

By the time she reached the first store on her list, the rain was falling like needles and the streets had mushroomed umbrellas. The air was noticeably cooler and so was her temper. I shouldn't've shouted at Rose, she thought, as she carried her boxes damply into the shop. And she made up her mind to put things right the minute she got back to Ritzy Street.

Because of the storm, it took her longer than she expected to deliver all her goods. It was well past four o'clock before she got home. And Rose wasn't there.

'Haven't seen her since you left,' Nancy said. 'She went out straight after. We thought she might have been with you.'

Muriel had been holding her anxiety at bay all afternoon, now she worried. 'You don't think she could've had an accident, do you? She *did* rush out.'

'Not our Rose,' Netta hoped. 'She's too sensible.'

'Then where is she?'

Netta was all for going out on her tricycle again for a quick search but Muriel pointed out that she wouldn't know where to start looking and said she'd be better employed running up the next batch of chemises. It was the right decision. Just as Nancy was threading the hand machine for the second time and Netta was packing the last four completed garments, their missing person returned. They looked up anxiously as she came through the door, but to their relief, she was smiling and seemed to be pleased with herself.

'Get your hats on, you lot,' she said. 'Where's Bertie? Is our Netta back? I got something to show you.'

They trooped out of the house obediently and followed her down the street, round the corner, past Mr Fassbinder's shop, and along Vauxhall Walk. By now they were all agog with curiosity but no one dared to ask what was going on until she turned the corner into Old Farm Street and then it was Bertie who voiced their question.

'What we going down here for Mum?'

'Take a look at that,' Rose said, stopping in front of an empty warehouse.

They looked. It was like most of the other buildings in the street, a single-storey brick construction with a corrugated iron roof and long barred windows. She took a bunch of keys out of her pocket and opened the double gates that led into the yard.

'It's ours,' she said. 'Our new workshop and store-house. I've just rented it. We're going to make some changes. For a start we ain't working all the hours God sends. Netta's right. We need time off. All the lot of us. We shouldn't feel guilty if we ain't working night and day.' She picked out another key from the bunch and opened the back door to the workshop. She was full of cheerful energy. 'Come in and see it.'

Muriel's brow was furrowed with anxiety. 'Can we afford it Rose?'

'No,' Rose said cheerfully. 'But we've outgrown Ritzy Street. We couldn't go on as we were. Not in that crush. It's no wonder we got ratty. Stands to reason when you think about it. So we're moving. We'll earn enough for it in time. You'll see. It'll be a pinch to start with but we'll do it.'

277

The others weren't worried at all. They were caught up in the excitement of possession and ran up and down through the dust, jumping to look out of the high windows. Netta lifted Bertie up so that he could see too, as Rose walked round for the second time that day, full of the pride of ownership, telling them her plans.

'We'll have our workshop up this end,' she said, 'where the light's better and we'll store the cloth down the other end, all neat and tidy. There's gas laid on so we shall be all right for light in the winter and I thought we'd get one of them gas fires we saw in the Exhibition. We could have it up this end and group the work tables round. Later on we'll have a wall built for the storeroom with a little office next to it so's Mu can do the accounts in a bit of peace. We might even run to a telephone. Wouldn't that be grand?'

'We can have our sign on the wall outside,' Netta said. 'I can see it now.' She was so excited, she'd quite forgotten her anger.

'It'll be hard work moving in,' Rose warned.

'He's going away Friday,' Netta said, answering the question she hadn't asked. 'Got another job in Luton. Three weeks. I'd have told you only . . .'

It was time for apologies which were lovingly given and accepted. 'I'll work like anything from now on,' Netta promised.

'I'm sorry I shouted at you.'

'I'm sorry I was so lukewarm when you told me. I *am* glad about it. Truly.'

'I know. We was all worn out and hot. It's better now.'

It was. A great deal better. Although it meant a lot more work. It took them three days to have shelves and lights fitted and to get the place clean. And despite all the extra work, their sewing had to continue because orders were still coming in. On the fourth day they took delivery of six trestle tables and their sign was put up, bold and red along the outside wall. On the fifth they hired a barrow and wheeled the sewing-machines round from Ritzy Street.

'Now,' Rose said to Muriel, 'you're to finish sitting for poor Mr Edmund. He's waited quite long enough, especially when you think he's half paid for it already. Write and tell him.'

That night, when they got home to Ritzy Street, dirty and bone-tired, there was a package for Rose from Manchester.

She was so exhausted she had to sit down before she could open it – a rare thing for Rose Jeary. It was a letter from Henry Philips and a small book of samples.

'*I owe you an apology,*' he wrote. '*It was remiss of me to assume that you would be looking for inferior cloth. I had no business to think such a thing and regret that I did. Can I hope that you will forgive my clumsiness?*

I enclose a book of samples showing our latest floral cottons in the additional hope that you might find something to suit. I look forward to your reply.

Assuring you of my earnest endeavours,

Henry Philips.'

'Who's he when he's at home?' Netta asked. In the rush of their sudden success she'd forgotten why Rose went to Manchester in the first place.

'He's the man Rose went to see,' Muriel remembered. 'The man from the Hall of Cotton.'

'What's all this about inferior cloth?' Netta wanted to know.

'It's a long story,' Rose said. 'I'll tell you when I ain't so whacked.'

'Let's have a gander at them samples,' Netta said, picking the book from the table. And when she'd looked, 'They're nice, our Rose. Look at that one with all the peach and blue flowers. That'ud match our peach undies.'

'So it would,' Muriel said. 'And look at that one. Two shades of green and red and the background's ecru. They're *made* for us, Rose. I can see the leaflets. "*Frocks to match your lingerie.*" '

Tired though she was, Rose saw the possibilities at once, and realised that if these garments sold as well as the underwear, she wouldn't have to worry about the rent for the warehouse. 'We could sell them in companion pairs,' she said. 'They might even put them in the windows. That would be a draw, wouldn't it. Where's the price list?'

Her '*esteemed order*' arrived from Henry Philips, Manchester, almost by return of post. By the end of the following week Netta was offering companion pairs to all her best customers. And on Friday morning, Muriel had a letter from Edmund Monk.

He was considering a full-length portrait '*for the first time, such is my cowardice*' and wondered whether he could prevail upon her to be his model on Saturday mornings. '*I should like to paint you in a red dress against the russet curtains in the drawing-room. You know the ones. An autumnal study suitable for the time of the year. Most of the work would have to be done on Saturday mornings because of the light. Would this be at all possible?*'

'Why not?' Rose said. 'There's no need for you to work every Saturday. We could spare you now an' then.'

'I haven't got a red dress,' Muriel said.

'We'll make you one,' Rose offered at once. 'Something gorgeous. What about that heavy cotton that came in last week? It's patterned but it's a lovely colour. He'd like that.'

'Bloody Edmund Monk!' Netta said suddenly. She was cutting bread with the loaf held against her waist and the knife was moving dangerously close to her body. 'Why should we put ourselves out for *him*?'

All three women looked up at once, alarmed by her anger, Mabel puzzled, Muriel upset to think that her new dress might be the cause of it.

But Rose understood it. 'We'll make your wedding dress first, if you like,' she said easily. 'You've only to say.'

Netta's expression changed, irritation smoothed away. 'Thought you'd forgotten,' she said, and began to grin.

'As if we would,' Rose grinned back. 'Soppy hap'orth!

You're going to have the best wedding dress anyone's ever seen. And the top brick off the chimney an' all.'

Netta grinned again. 'So I should think,' she said. 'Quite right.' And she put the loaf and the newly cut slice down onto the bread board with great satisfaction.

It was a moment to talk. 'You got a date fixed yet?' Rose asked, as casually as she could.

'Won't be till March or April,' Netta told her. 'Another six months at least. He's saving up for a flat and I got me bottom drawer to get. I was thinking of going to Arding and Hobbs tomorrow, matter a' fact. To see the linen.'

'We'll all go,' Rose said. 'You can't buy your bottom drawer on your own.'

'All except Mu,' Netta pointed out. 'She'll be sitting.'

'Not till the dress is made,' Muriel said. 'This Saturday I shall be with you.'

Muriel's red dress turned out extremely well. They made it in the very latest style, with a dropped waist and the new short hemline. It was the first time any of them had ventured into short skirts and they were amazed by how youthful it made her look. With her dark hair cut in a fringe and trimmed to just below her ears, her newly revealed legs elegant in artificial silk stockings and her skin glowing with excitement and the reflected colour of the dress, she could have been seventeen rather than twenty-seven. Edmund Monk was bewitched by her.

'The dress is perfect,' he said, as she took up her position against the faded folds of his russet curtains. 'But I shan't be able to call this an autumnal study. You make me think of spring.' Of spring and the eternal promise of youth. Bright new colour against the faded grandeur of this musty room. Bright, new hopeful life in her fascinating face, dark eyes smiling at me impishly from behind those silly little round glasses. Oh if I could catch all this, what a picture it would be. She so bright and modern and the room so old-fashioned and dowdy. Like me.

'You must tell me when you get tired,' he warned as he took up his brush. 'I shall take a long time over this. It's

281

not a picture to be rushed. Not that I could rush it if I wanted to. It's a foolish time to start a picture really, at the beginning of autumn, just when I'm beginning to lose the light.' And he sighed at his folly. 'Anyway,' he resumed, 'what I'm saying is, you must rest whenever you need to. A standing pose can be very tiring.'

'Yes,' she said, gazing out of the window as he'd told her to. 'I will.'

It was very peaceful in the room on that September morning. Louella was out somewhere, the servants were busy below stairs, even the view was obscured by mist. It was as if they were cut off from the rest of the world.

Edmund worked happily, his confidence growing as the outline of the picture took shape. And Muriel began to dream. Of Bertie and how dear he'd been to her, of the love they could have shared if only the war hadn't taken him away.

The wistful longing on her face was something Edmund had seen there before. He sketched it quickly, aware of how transient an expression can be, but it endured and the longer it lasted the more intrigued he became.

At last he ventured a question. 'What are you thinking of?'

She answered him honestly. 'The man I was going to marry.'

'Ah!' But of course. What else would have provoked such yearning tenderness? 'You loved him very much, I think.'

'He was killed in the war,' she said. And sighed.

'I'm so sorry. It must have been dreadful.'

'Yes,' she said calmly. 'It was. But there you are. I wasn't the only one. It happened to lots of women. Look at all the spinsters there are.'

It wasn't something that had occurred to him until that moment. 'What a waste war is,' he said.

'Yes.'

She looked so bleak he had a sudden urge to take her in his arms and comfort her. He picked up his brush instead and painted busily, his thoughts racing. What a waste of a good woman. She's much too loving to be a spinster. She'd make a beautiful wife.

And then his own wife came crashing into the room and the spell of this girl's charm was broken. And so was his concentration.

'I think that's enough for one day, Miss Spencer,' he said. 'We'll leave it until next week, if you're agreeable.' He could have worked on for a great deal longer but his appetite for painting was gone now that Louella was home.

She was reading a letter she'd just opened. 'We're invited to a wedding,' she said, as Miss Spencer left the room. 'On New Year's Eve, apparently. Ethel's going to get married. Imagine that!'

But Edmund wasn't paying attention. He was imagining how his portrait would look when it was finished.

The painting took a very long time, as Muriel had known it would. October began and it still wasn't finished.

'If we was as long-winded as him,' Netta mocked, 'we'd never get nothink done.'

'Just as well we're not then,' Muriel said.

Ritzy Clothes was still doing extremely good business, the companion pairs selling almost as well as the lingerie. By the middle of October they had enough capital to pay out their first bonus, to build the walls to the storeroom and their quiet office, to buy a good stout table for cutting out *and* to have a telephone installed.

Nancy and Marigold were thrilled with their sudden riches.

'I shall buy mesself a new bed,' Nancy decided. 'My old one's been giving me gyp for ages.'

'I'd like a new bed and all,' Mabel said to Rose. 'Ours is all lumps.'

But in the event it wasn't just a new bed she got but a new bedroom.

At the end of the month, when Netta was miserable because José had been back for less than a fortnight and had gone away on yet another job, old Mr and Mrs Marchbank came downstairs one evening to tell Rose that they were going to leave Ritzy Street and live with their niece and nephew in a ground-floor flat in Peckham.

'We can't manage the stairs no more,' Mr Marchbank confessed. 'Specially in the cold weather with the coal and everything. We're getting on a bit, that's the trouble. Bit creaky in the old joints. We thought we'd better tell you in good time, seeing as Miss Pozzi's gone and we're your only tenants.'

'It ain't that we ain't been happy here,' Mrs Marchbank said. 'You been ever so good to us. Well I mean to say, look at the way your Mr Thomas fixed that cupboard for us. He done it lovely. It's just old age.'

'We shall miss you,' Rose said. 'You must write to us.'

They were gone at the end of the week, their small belongings packed up in less than a day and wheeled away to Peckham on a coster's barrow.

Now, for the first time since their arrival in Ritzy Street all those years ago, the Boniface family had an entire house at their disposal and were earning more than enough to pay the rent without the need to sub-let. It felt luxurious.

'We could have a room each if we wanted,' Rose said. 'It's high time Bertie had a room of his own.'

'Can I have a room too, our Rose?' Mabel asked. 'Bags I one on the top floor. Can I paint it pink?'

But Rose said there was a lot of work to get through before she could think of decorating, even in Bertie's little room. And when Mabel appealed to the others, Muriel didn't answer because she was thinking how lovely it would be to have a room of her own and neither did Netta because she was daydreaming about José and wondering how soon he would get back.

'When you got time then, our Rose,' Mabel pleaded. 'When there ain't so much work. Can I have it pink then, our Rose?'

But although they didn't know it, there was even more work coming their way and of a rather prestigious kind.

Augusta Monk had begun to plan her outfit for Ethel's wedding the minute she received her invitation. After the disgraceful way her niece had behaved in Harrods, she had a few scores to settle, and what better place to do it than at a wedding.

She decided she would wear a dress, that it would be made of velvet, as befitted her status, and that it would be the boldest colour she could find, so that nobody could fail to notice her. She chose a really splendid heliotrope and bought accessories to match. Then she wrote to summon her dressmaker. To her annoyance, the silly woman wrote back to tell her she wasn't taking on any more commissions until after Christmas.

'It's most exasperating,' she complained to Louella during her next telephone call. 'People have no sense of responsibility these days.'

Louella couldn't see that there was a problem. 'You'll have to find someone else, that's all,' she said. 'What was the name of that parlourmaid you used to have? She sewed, didn't she?'

'Rose,' Augusta said, and suddenly remembered her clearly, sitting on the bedroom floor altering that green dress all those Christmases ago. A nice patient sort of girl and very quick. I wonder whether she'd . . .

'That's the one,' Louella rushed on. 'Why don't you ask her. Look, I must go. The meat's getting cold.'

She might be the answer, Augusta thought, as she put the telephone down. I'll ask Biggs if she knows where she is.

So a message was sent.

'*Dear Rose,*
I have been invited to a family wedding on New Year's Eve. Unfortunately my usual dressmaker is unable to complete my wedding outfit in time. I have bought all the materials. I believe that you are now employed as a

*dressmaker. I remember how handy you were with your
needle. Would you care to undertake a special commission? I would naturally remunerate you generously.*

A. A. Monk.'

It provoked Netta to roaring. 'Ain't that just typical?'
she shouted. ' "*Handy with your needle*." Patronising old
bat! You ain't a dressmaker. You run a firm. Write back
and tell her.'

'No,' Rose said. 'Let her come to the workshop and see
how well we're doing. I'd enjoy that.'

'See you make her pay, then.'

'Oh don't worry,' Rose said. 'I will. And handsome.'

So Augusta's note was answered with the suggestion
that if she cared to visit the workshop, it might be possible
for some arrangement to be made. She arrived the next
morning, red in the face from her unaccustomed walk and
bearing a Harrods' carrier bag full of material.

She was visibly disconcerted to find herself in a factory,
particularly when the first thing she saw was a pile of
boxes that Netta had deliberately left in her way and that
were prominently labelled '*Arding and Hobbs – special
delivery*.' And she scowled when she discovered that Rose
and her sisters owned the place.

'We don't normally make dresses to order,' Rose
explained as she led the way through the workshop. 'Most
of the work is for local department stores, as you can see.'

Miss Monk's face was a study of annoyance.

'You *have* done well,' she said acidly. 'But then I'm
sure you always had it in you. Even when you were my
parlourmaid. Didn't I always say so?'

You won't cut me down to size like that, Rose thought.
I've gone far beyond that sort of trick. 'Come into my
office, Miss Monk,' she said, opening the door. 'When
we've agreed on my fee, I'll send someone in to measure
you.'

The fee had doubled under Augusta's deliberate insult
but it was agreed because the lady didn't want to appear
mean in front of one of her ex-servants. However the

knowledge that she was paying over the top made her very disagreeable and she took her bad temper out on poor Marigold when she came in to take her measurements. She fidgeted and fussed and complained, thrusting out her bosom and pulling in her stomach every time the tape measure came anywhere near them.

'I like a good fit,' she said. 'I trust you understand that.'

'All our clothes are a perfect fit, madam,' Marigold said, noting down her customer's hip size. 'We're renowned for it.'

And despite this customer's difficult bulk, the dress was an excellent fit. Even Augusta had to admit that, although she couldn't bring herself to praise it.

'I don't know how you done it,' Nancy Cartwright said, when the dress had been delivered and the bill paid.

'It's the cut,' Rose told her. 'That's the secret. You got to let cloth flow.'

Plenty of cloth flowed through their factory as Christmas approached. Their profits grew, steadily if not spectacularly. In the middle of November, Rose wrote to Mr Philips to order more of his stock for a special line of party blouses, and feeling very proud of herself, put her new telephone number at the head of the letter.

Two days later he telephoned her to report that her letter had been received and to tell her that her order was in hand. And that wasn't all.

'I shall be in London at the end of the week,' he said, casually. 'All on my own, as I usually am in your city. I suppose you wouldn't care to have dinner with me?'

She was surprised and flattered to be asked. An evening out away from all her work and worries was very tempting. The others took time off so why shouldn't she? An evening out with a business acquaintance. And why not? She *was* a business woman. 'Well yes,' she said. 'I think I might. That's very kind of you.'

'Would Friday be in order?'

She agreed that it would.

'I'll call for you at seven.'

'Do you know where I live?' she asked, mindful of how vast London was.

'I shall find you,' he said.

CHAPTER TWENTY-FOUR

The arrival of a Rolls Royce in Ritzy Street on that misty November evening caused a great stir. Curtains twitched all along the street, lollipop faces were amazed in every window, some neighbours even strolled out onto their doorsteps, chill though it was, pretending to put out milk bottles or call the cat. Speculation was instant and intense. 'That's never our Dr Felgate with a new car!' 'No, someone for Miss Monk, more like, took the wrong turning.' When the great car came to a halt before Rose Jeary's door and a wealthy man emerged from its opulence, they were sharp-eared with curiosity, and when Rose herself came out of the house, wearing a new blue coat and a very pretty hat, to be greeted by the stranger like an old friend and driven regally away, they buzzed like bees. 'We *are* going up in the world,' they said.

Henry Philips took no notice of any of them. A Rolls Royce is the sort of car that attracts admiration – that was one of the reasons why he ran it – and as a successful business man he was used to being the centre of attention. But it was a new experience for Rose. She found herself smiling at the faces watching her departure and knew she was feeling pleased with herself.

'There'll be tongues wagging tomorrow,' she said, making a grimace.

He smiled at her. 'Will that worry you?'

She considered for a second, in her careful way. 'No,' she said. 'I don't think it will. It's rather nice in a way. Makes me feel special.'

'And so you are,' he told her. 'If you don't mind my saying so. There's not many women around who run factories.' Particularly when they live in a place like Ritzy Street.

'That's necessity,' she said. 'I got a family to support.'

'Well, allow me to admire you for it, notwithstanding.'

'I shall get a swollen head,' she warned, laughing.

He answered her seriously. 'Oh I think not. You work a deal too hard to be conceited.'

That was a novel idea. 'So that's the cure for a swollen head is it? Hard work.'

'The other way about, in my experience. Lack of it is the cause. All the most conceited people I've ever known have been idle. Idle and full of their own importance.'

That made her think of Miss Monk. 'You could be right,' she said and told him about the special commission.

'My point exactly,' he said. 'And if you look round you tonight, you'll see a lot more women who are just the same.'

He was taking her to one of his favourite restaurants, a place called Merrystone's, right in the heart of the West End. He had chosen it for the food rather than the clientèle, but now that he'd seen where she lived, he felt he ought to warn her about the company. His wife had been quite touchy about being in the right company.

Rose took it in her stride, handing her coat to the waiter and following him through the restaurant as if she'd been doing such things all her life. And when she was handed the menu and discovered that it was written in French, she coped with that too.

'You'll have to translate for me,' she said, holding it up towards him. 'I can't understand a word of it.'

Her honesty was refreshing. 'I can't understand all of it myself,' he admitted. 'We'll need to work it out together.'

Choosing the meal took a long and pleasurable time, as they discussed each dish in turn and how it was cooked and whether or not they would like it.

She knows her own mind, he thought, as the choices were finally made. And she likes her food.

290

'We'll have a bottle of your best claret,' he told the wine waiter. But then turned to Rose to ask, 'Unless you'd prefer champagne.'

'I've never had champagne,' she confessed.

'Then both,' he decided. 'We've got something to celebrate.'

She was surprised at that. 'Have we?' she asked when the waiter had left them.

'Your new factory. My new mill.'

She looked her question but didn't say anything.

'I've decided to go into rayon production,' he told her, 'as it seems to be the in thing. There's a mill come up for sale just along the street. I've made them an offer. I've been thinking of making patterned rayons. Courtaulds have a new yarn, out last month, guaranteed to take a dye. If it'll take a dye, it'll take a pattern.'

'Florals,' she said at once, visualising it. 'Roses and forget-me-nots. I could use that for blouses *and* lingerie.'

'Precisely what I had in mind.'

She smiled at him. 'You must send me samples.'

'It will be my pleasure.'

They talked shop all through the meal and, although the range of cutlery beside her plate confused her and the champagne made her giggle, Rose enjoyed herself immensely. Soon, warmed by good food and dizzied by champagne, she was talking freely.

'It don't seem possible the Empire Exhibition was only seven months ago,' she confided. 'I seen so many changes since, it seems like years.'

'All good I trust.'

For a second she was on the verge of telling him about Netta. But she checked herself in time, feeling disloyal even to have thought of it. 'Most of them.'

The little hesitation told him more than she realised, as did the frown wrinkling her wide brow before it was deliberately smiled away. It made him feel protective. 'My wife always used to say, it's not change that's important, it's the way you cope with it.'

291

'Very true,' she said. It was the first time he'd made any reference to his wife but, as his face was inscrutable behind the glow of the candles, she didn't know how she ought to respond. 'You must miss her very much.'

'Yes,' he agreed. 'I do.' But looking across the table into those lovely grey eyes, he was thinking, not so much now.

She wondered whether she ought to say anything else and decided against it, not wanting to pry.

'She was ill for nearly three years,' he told her briefly. 'Cancer. In the end she was in such a state it was a merciful release.'

Now she could sympathise. 'It must have been awful.'

'It was. Well you know how awful. Losing your husband, I mean. It must have taken you a long time to get over that.' This was the first time he'd spoken so intimately to anybody since Margaret died and he was surprised to find it so easy. Something to do with that calm expression of hers. Or the attractive way she listened.

Their intimacy edged her towards a confession. 'I ain't over it yet, if the truth be told,' she said sadly. 'It's the not-knowing, you see. If you get a telegram, it's awful but at least you know. That's how they told us about my brothers. But with Jack I've never really known. I know he's dead but that's all. I don't know how he died or where or anything. That's the hard bit, the not-knowing.'

'Yes,' he said, aware of how much it was making her suffer simply to talk of it and wishing he hadn't opened the subject. 'It must be.'

'Yes, well,' she said, shrugging her unhappiness away. 'No good making a song and dance about it. You just got to get on with your life, that's all.'

He led her to a safer topic. 'So you started the firm.'

'Yes.'

'During the war?'

'1917. A lifetime ago.'

'Seven years.'

'It's funny how things turn out. If anyone had told me

292

then that in seven years' time, I'd be sitting in a place like this eating food like this, I'd never've believed them.'

'And there's still the sweet to come,' he smiled, wanting to pet her. 'They serve profiteroles here. All cream and chocolate. You wait till you taste them.'

'It's been a delightful evening,' he said when they were back in Ritzy Street. 'We must do it again the next time I'm in town.'

'It'ud be a pleasure,' she said. And meant it.

He was back in town '*unexpectedly*' ten days later. So they dined at Merrystone's again. Over their coffee he told her that his bid for the mill had been accepted and that he was investigating the cost of the new machinery.

'I shall be back again in a week or two with the fabrics for spring,' he said as they parted. 'Same time, same place?'

So luxurious evenings became part of Rose's life that November and December. She was a bit worried by their frequency, afraid that she was shirking her responsibilities, but her sisters told her to go ahead and enjoy herself and not to be a chump. And she had to admit that his company did her good. He was so easy to talk to and so generous.

But on his third visit she invited him into the house for a few minutes to meet her family. Bertie was playing out and missed him, Netta and Muriel were carefully polite, Mabel was thrilled with him and kept trying to touch his hair.

After they'd gone, Netta and Muriel had a serious conversation.

'He's courting her,' Netta said. 'Don't you think so, Mu? He wouldn't've come all this way to see her else.'

'He's very handsome,' Muriel said. She'd been very impressed by him, with that strong face and those nice broad shoulders and that nice thick moustache. 'He's got an air about him.'

'Oh he's a looker,' Netta said trenchantly. 'I'll grant you that. But handsome is as handsome does. I don't like him coming after our Rose.'

But does *she*? Muriel thought. That's what will count in the end.

CHAPTER TWENTY-FIVE

The Angel Inn in Bury St Edmunds is the perfect setting for a wedding reception. Standing foursquare above the Abbey Gardens, steeped in history, its ivy-covered façade important among the lesser buildings that face the slope of Angel Hill, it could withstand any function, no matter how prestigious.

For the new Mrs Evelyn Quennell, superb in a *crêpe de Chine* gown with her bridegroom's gift of pearls about her neck and a bouquet of hothouse roses on her arm, it had exactly the right ambience.

'I'm so happy, my darling,' she said, squeezing Evelyn's arm. 'Isn't this divine?'

The groom was still in a state of shock after the amazement of his courtship and the rigours of the ceremony. It was all he could do to say, 'Oh yes! Jolly dee!' as the guests filed past him with kisses and congratulations. But Ethel's mind was acutely active, noticing the wealth and sophistication of her new relations, wondering whether a small house in Bury was going to be good enough for her and Ev and watching out for Aunty Moneybags because she looked as though she was up to something.

There was a stir at the entrance. Someone important had arrived. Who is it? Ethel thought, turning the wired pearls of her headdress ever so slightly to peek through her veil.

It was a woman in a man's suit and not just an ordinary grey suit either but pillarbox red. And what a hat! A brown felt cloche with a red belt tied around it, buckle and all. Good God! 'Who on earth's that?' she whispered to Evelyn.

He blinked. 'She's the artist,' he said, as another guest bore down upon him. 'Fancy Something-or-other. She's come with one of my cousins, I think. Hello Poppy. Yes. Jolly dee.'

Fancy Something-or-other was guzzling champagne and talking to Ev's mother in a loud booming voice. 'But you *must* see it, my dear. It's outstanding. Bernard Shaw at his absolute *best* and Sybil Thorndike is *astounding*. You'll kick yourself if you miss it.'

I shall have to cut her down to size, Ethel thought, as the red suit joined the line, or she'll steal the show. Who does she think she is?

'Fancy Pepperell,' the lady said as they shook hands. 'I paint.'

'How nice for you,' Ethel drawled. 'You must meet my aunt and uncle. They're artists too. Standing over there by the high table. The lady in the feathered cloche. He's a Professor of Art, actually.'

'Poor sod,' Fancy commiserated. 'I sympathise with him. The things we artists have to do to earn our living!' And she went straight across to make herself known.

Louella had been feeling rather miffed since her arrival. Her long pale face was still pinched from the cold of her journey, nobody had taken any notice of her and Augusta had been queening it all over the room in a dress made of heliotrope velvet – of all colours – and those damned family pearls of hers. So when a dashing young woman in the most unconventional outfit came up to a make her acquaintance, she brightened considerably.

'Yes,' she admitted. 'I do paint a little. In a modest way.'

'Glad to hear it,' the lady said. 'They're all Philistines here. Are you a Pre-Raphaelite or a Modern?' She was a stunning looking woman. Her eyes were green as glass and ringed with black kohl, her mouth was a scarlet slash under a straight Roman nose and her hair was straight too and as black as dye could make it, clubbed short to show the lobes of her ears and with one curving kiss-curl attached to her right cheek as if it had been stuck there.

'Oh a Modern,' Louella said, gambling that it was the right answer.

'Well thank God for that,' Fancy nodded. 'I was beginning to think I'd have to make an excuse and leave early. I can't stand country bumpkins at the best of times and especially at a wedding. Half these clodhoppers haven't even heard of Bernard Shaw – can you credit it? – leave alone Picasso and Miró. Is this your husband? How de do? Haven't you got any champagne?'

From then on she ignored Edmund and took Louella under her scarlet wing, snatching glasses of champagne for them both whenever a tray came anywhere near her long fingers and shepherding her to the lesser table to which they'd both been undeservedly demoted with raucous remarks about the lack of style on the top table.

'*Who* is the apparition in the heliotrope?' she boomed.

'My sister-in-law, I'm afraid,' Louella laughed.

'Relations are the curse of human existence,' Fancy sympathised, 'and absolute death to art. Absolute *death*. I ran away from mine at the first opportunity. I advise all my friends to do the same. It's the only possible way to live. What does Madame Gargantua do apart from eat?'

Louella found her new friend's irreverent humour quite wonderful. 'She cuts people out of her will,' she said, enjoying herself. 'It's the work of a lifetime.'

'Ah!' Fancy understood. 'Food and money, eh? Greed on legs. I'll bet she suffers from chronic constipation. People like that always do. You should paint her, my dear. As an object lesson if nothing else. Tell me, what are you working on at the moment?'

They talked about themselves and their art all through the meal, while Edmund, forgotten on the other side of the table struggled to make conversation with two women he didn't know. As time went by, he stooped closer and closer to his plate with boredom and embarrassment.

On the high table, as Fancy had noticed, Augusta had

contrived to sit between her two attentive nephews and was now dominating the proceedings. The Quennells might be wealthy and were decidedly overbearing but she was a match for any of them, especially in this dress. She told them about her splendid house in town 'it's been in the family for generations you know' and her parrot 'such an aristocratic bird' and her dressmaker 'a London couture house, naturally.'

Young Hereward was being perfectly sweet to her, saying all the right things, almost as if she'd primed him, complimenting her on her splendid appearance and her beautiful dress.

'You're the best-looking woman here,' he told her as the vegetables were served.

'You'd better not let your sister hear you, if you're going to say things like that.' She made eyes at him, happily.

'Hard cheese to her!' he said, making eyes back. The fact that Ethel was glowering at him gave the situation an added piquancy. She might be the bride but she should learn to treat her brothers properly. 'Between you and me, Aunty darling, I think you knock her into a cocked-hat. Don't you, Percy?'

Percy was slightly drunk but he played up gallantly. 'I should say so!'

All very satisfactory, Augusta thought. And there was better to come when a certain score was settled. She had only to choose her moment.

It came at the end of the meal when the bride and groom were posed down at the far end of the room beside the three grand tiers of their wedding cake, ceremonial knife in hand, waiting to have their photograph taken. All the guests were gathered before them, ready to applaud and Ethel was simpering.

Perfect, Augusta thought, and she rolled her eyes as high into their sockets as she could get them and let out a long pitiful groan. Then, as all heads turned in her direction, she fell gracefully to the floor in a swoon, dragging the edge of the tablecloth down with her and breaking a considerable quantity of china and glass in the process. The fall was even better executed than she'd dared to hope. She landed with the jagged stem of a broken wine glass immediately under her hand and, in the muddle of tumbled linen and crockery, contrived to pull the glass along her calf and open a splendidly dramatic wound.

There was instant uproar, as guests and waiters ran to see what had happened. Somebody yelled, 'Fetch a doctor!' and another voice answered. 'Make way! I *am* a doctor.' Then strong hands lifted her into a seat and she opened her eyes – after another long groan – and looked up to see concerned faces all around her.

'Oh dear!' she said in a weak voice. 'I'm so sorry. What a thing to do. What must you think of me?'

'She needs air,' the nearest face said with authority. So *he*'s the doctor. 'Stand back please. There's no cause for alarm.'

'I shall be all right presently,' she said, looking pitiful. 'You mustn't let me trouble you.' She could feel the blood oozing through her stockings and dripping onto the carpet. 'Oh dear! I seem to have cut myself. What a trouble I'm causing.'

'It's no trouble, dear lady,' the doctor said. Oh he *was* a nice man. 'I'll just bind up that cut for you, *pro tem*. You don't want to spoil your dress. Clean table napkin someone! Then I suggest we get you through into the lounge and I can take a better look at you. Has this happened before?'

'Once or twice,' she admitted coyly. 'It's not serious, is it Doctor?'

'I shall be better able to judge that when I've examined you,' the doctor said. 'It could be gallstones.' Gallstones were his speciality. He diagnosed them frequently. 'Have you had any pain recently?'

Under his instructions she was carried out of the dining-room, chair, improvised bandage and all. She had a vague impression of people running about and Ethel and her silly husband standing on their own beside the cake, looking foolish. Then she was in the quiet and safety of a nice empty lounge.

Ethel was so angry that the tears rose in her eyes. That hateful old Moneybags! she thought, clutching the knife furiously. Never mind the cake, I'd like to use this on her. I really would. She did that deliberately. I knew she was up to something. She's ruined my wedding.

'Don't cry sweetie,' the groom urged, wiping away her tears. He could just about cope with her when she cried and it was natural for her to cry now – being worried about her aunt and everything. 'You musn't cry on your wedding day.'

She threw her arms round his neck and kissed him passionately. 'You'll look after me, won't you my own love?' she begged.

'Yes! Yes!' he promised, between kisses. 'I will. You mustn't cry!'

Then their friends gathered around them, offering commiserations and thumping their shoulders and Mrs Quennell arrived to tell Ethel that her aunt had recovered and to suggest that she and Evelyn ought to go ahead and cut the cake now that the 'little crisis' was over. So the celebrations resumed and the bride became the rightful centre of attention again.

But I shan't forgive her, she thought as she and Evelyn led the dancing. She'll have to leave me lots and lots of money to make amends for *this*. And she smiled with brittle sweetness at another dancing couple.

In the quiet of the lounge, where the bridal music was a distant thumping, Vermont examined his new patient.

'That's a nasty cut you've got on your leg,' he said. 'I'm afraid it needs stitching.'

Augusta was meek and happy under his ministrations. 'Could you do it for me, Doctor?'

'I could.'

'Here? Or would I have to go to hospital?'

'No, no. I can do it here, if you can stand the pain.'

She shrugged and looked long-suffering. 'I'm used to pain.'

'But of course,' the doctor told her gravely, 'the real trouble is those gallstones of yours. It's just as well we've caught them when we have. Gallstones can be very tricky. If you'll take my advice, dear lady, you'll allow me to admit you to my hospital as soon as possible and have the nasty things out.'

An operation! Augusta thought, thrilled by the drama of it. But she answered him meekly. 'Anything you say, Doctor, of course. When do you think it ought to be? I'm supposed to be travelling back to London on Monday.'

'Then if I were you, I would travel to the hospital instead.'

'You are very kind,' Augusta said. 'Who would perform the operation?'

'I would.'

Augusta sighed with relief. 'Then I shall be in good hands.'

'Now let's get that cut attended to,' the doctor said with great satisfaction. 'I'll get my bag.'

So on Monday afternoon, when Cedric would have preferred to be resting after the wedding, he had to drive his sister into Bury St Edmunds again and deliver her to the hospital.

'She's nothing but a damn nuisance,' he said to Winifred on his return home. 'First she makes a scene at the wedding breakfast and now she's got to be carted about all over the county. I shall be glad to see the back of her. Gallstones indeed. I thought it was her kidneys that were bad.'

'Perhaps it's both,' Winifred said, trying to be charitable.

'Between you and me,' Cedric said, 'I don't care what it is. Just so long as she doesn't expect to come here to convalesce.'

That was Edmund's opinion too. 'I hope you won't go

301

dragging her back here,' he said to Louella. 'We had quite enough of that last time. If she needs some sort of convalescence let her go in a home or hire a nurse. She can well afford it.'

Louella was reading a letter from Fancy Pepperell. 'No, Edmund my dear,' she said. 'I shan't drag her anywhere. She's on her own this time. I've got other things to do.' Fancy's letter was an invitation to join her artistic circle. Imagine that! *'We meet every Tuesday evening at my house here in Little Venice. Breaks for New Year and suchlike. We start up again on January 6th. You would be more than welcome. Canvasses and paint provided, bring your own easel and brushes. Can't wait to see your work. I feel we are soul-mates already.'*

'We shall have to break it to her gently,' Edmund worried, feeling guilty now that he'd made his decision. 'Perhaps I'll go down and visit her. When she's got over the worst of the operation. I do feel sorry for her, poor old thing. It can't have been much fun having gallstones. I shouldn't have liked it. It's just that I can't face her being in the house all the time.'

To his relief, the operation went very well although, in the privacy of the operating theatre, it was a surprise to the surgeon to discover that the gall-bladder was entirely innocent of stones.

'This does happen occasionally,' he explained to his team. 'Phantom symptoms, you see. However, better safe than sorry.'

'Caught in the nick of time,' he told his patient when he did his rounds the following morning. 'Now we must take great care of you and nurse you back to health and strength.'

He took very expensive care of her indeed. When he heard that neither of her sisters-in-law were able to look after her, he arranged for two nurses from his private agency to travel to Kennington and live in at Monk House for the next – and vital – six weeks.

For the first few days of her highly organised convalescence Augusta felt too ill to complain. She slept a lot and ate a little and welcomed each stern injunction as a sign that she was being well and truly cared for. But, given her nature and her powers of recovery, a change of opinion was inevitable. It began when the parrot was removed from her bedroom as *unhygienic*. From then on doubts and suspicions crept through every crack until she was seeing an insult behind almost every medical action.

'Why must I be washed every five minutes?' she complained. 'It isn't as if I'm dirty?' And when her invalid diet was explained to her for the umpteenth time, 'I don't see why I can't eat what I fancy. A little of what you fancy does you good. I'll have steak and kidney pudding tomorrow and a bottle of claret.'

Matters came to a head over food. When a large box of chocolates was carried out of the room as if it were something nasty, with stern-faced mutterings about *inadequate nourishment* she rose from her sickbed, sturdy with rage and wrote to both her brothers.

'*I need the care of my family,*' she said. '*I shall make a poor recovery with two martinets to look after me, if that is what they can be said to be doing. I have very grave doubts. My chauffeur could drive me over as soon as you say. When it comes to it, nothing can beat being in the bosom of one's family. One's family is so important. Haven't I always said so? Please write back to me as soon as you can. I am very ill and need your help.*'

'I shall go to whichever one answers first,' she said to Mrs Biggs, 'and then I can dismiss the martinets and get back to normal life.'

They answered in the same post. And they both said 'no', Cedric because he was '*too busy with the farm*', Edmund '*because he and Louella would both be out of the house too often to give her the care she needed*'.

'It's perfidious!' Augusta said to Mrs Biggs when she came to remove the tea things. 'Absolutely perfidious! Their own sister and they can't lift a finger to help me. Well, I know what I shall do about *that*. Phone Mr Tilling and tell him I want to see him.'

'We mustn't get ourselves upset, now must we?' the day nurse said in her disapproving voice.

But her patient was adamant. 'We'll do what we damn well like,' she said. 'And while we're about it, we shan't need your services after tomorrow. We're perfectly recovered.'

'That is *not* my professional opinion,' the nurse said, her voice as starched as her apron. 'But if that is what you want, it's entirely up to you.'

'Oh yes,' Augusta said, grimly. 'That's what I want, you can depend on it. I always know what I want.'

She knew what she wanted when it came to re-writing her will too, although she was a little annoyed when it was the younger Mr Fordham who turned up to take instructions and not her dear Mr Tilling. This time she cut out both her brothers and bequeathed her money to Percy and Hereward.

They were delighted with such a potential windfall. Hereward bought a magnum of champagne on the strength of it. But his brother was more cautious and said he'd believe it when he saw it.

'The old dear's got to die first,' he pointed out. 'And if you ask me she's as fit as a flea. I never saw anyone put food away like she does, and she got over that operation PDQ.'

'Dad won't enjoy this,' Hereward said, grinning. 'I'd like to have been a fly on the wall when he opened *his* letter this morning.'

It had sent him into paroxysms of rage. 'She's gone off her head,' he roared to Winifred. 'Leaving it to those two. What's the matter with the woman? They'll spend it like water and it's *my* money for Christ's sake. Where's my pen?'

The letter he wrote sputtered with anger. '*Don't you understand what you've done? Those boys will waste my inheritance. And it* is *my inheritance. Make no mistake about that. It always was and it always will be. I've worked and struggled all my life and all they've ever done is swan* around Oxford and spend my hard-earned cash. How could you be so stupid? You've done some damn silly things in your time but this takes the biscuit.' And on and on through four pages of fury.

His letter charged Augusta with righteous indignation. She left her sickbed at once, dressed in her warmest clothes, ordered a huge meal and came downstairs to the parlour where she sat by the fire to compose an answer.

'In case it has slipped your attention, let me point out to you that the money and property you are talking about belongs to me and has done ever since our father made his will. That being so, it is up to me how I bestow it. I don't have to ask your advice. If you had been anything like a brother you wouldn't be in this position now. You have only yourself to blame . . .'

By the time the letter was finished to her satisfaction she was ready for anything and sat down to her steak and kidney with relish. 'There's nothing like a battle for giving you an appetite,' she said to the parlourmaid as the plates were cleared. 'I hope there's cream with that pie. Has Mr Edmund sent me a letter yet?'

In fact, Edmund had taken the news cynically and hadn't bothered to reply to it.

'She'll change her mind in a month or two,' he said to Louella. 'Once they ring up and ask for a sub, they won't be the blue-eyed boys any longer. It's the old, old story, I'm afraid.'

And for once, Louella didn't comment, because for once she wasn't thinking about Augusta's money.

CHAPTER TWENTY-SIX

Compared with the drama at Bury St Edmunds, Netta's wedding to José Fernández was a very quiet affair. For a start it was on a chilly day in April rather than in the hubbub of the New Year. And there were far fewer guests, since José said he didn't have 'a *relative in the world*' and Netta could run to only two sisters, a best friend and a nephew. But they invited all the Cartwrights and Marigold and Charlie and their two little boys and old Mr and Mrs Marchbank came over from Peckham to join them and Mrs Tuffin left her nephew in charge of the stall so that she could attend and Mr Thomas was the best man and provided moral support for everybody. So they made a lively party if not a particularly large one.

'It'll be a right knees-up, if I'm anything to do with it,' Nancy Cartwright said. 'I'm really looking forward to it. High time we had a knees-up in this street.'

So the firm closed down for the wedding day, Marigold wheeled her new gramophone down the road to provide the music, Mr Thomas blew up balloons, hung decorations, shifted furniture and generally made himself useful, Nancy Cartwright collected the wedding cake, the bride and her sisters provided the food and drink, and they were all happily busy together, even though Rose still had serious – but private – misgivings and Muriel was secretly concerned and worried about Rose.

True to her promise Rose had made Netta the most beautiful dress she could devise, in Mr Philips' new cream rayon with a boat-shaped neckline, low waist, short gathered skirt and long bishop sleeves all trimmed with scalloped lace. With a headdress made of real orange blossom and a shoulder-length veil, she glowed like a pearl in the half-light of St Peter's Church. The bride-groom was on top form too. He made his responses boldly at the altar rail and, once they were all home again in Ritzy Street for the reception, he poured beer and darted about with plates of sandwiches, swift-footed and darkly handsome. And Mr Thomas stood before the fire and gave what could only be described as an unusual speech.

'They've asked me to say somethink,' he began, producing a crumpled piece of paper from his pocket and squinting at it, before making his first joke. 'Seems I'm the best man for the job. Don't ask me why! Anyway I got to make a toast so here it is. Happiness to the bride and groom. You come through the Great War, the pair of you, so marriage'll be a doddle after that. An absolute doddle! So here's to you! Happiness. That's about it.' And he raised his glass, beamed at them and sat down.

Despite her anxiety, Rose was glad to see her sister so happy and she had to admit that José Fernández had done his best to get the marriage off to a good start. He'd found a nice flat for them – three furnished rooms in the Kennington Road – and had bought one of the new gas cookers on the 'never-never'. Perhaps I've misjudged him, Rose thought, watching as he hugged Netta against his side and kissed her neck. He's certainly very loving. Perhaps it will work out. Well, it's got to, now they're married, so there's no point in worrying about it any more. In any case there were too many other things to think about at the moment. Like her own unexpected holiday in Manchester.

Ten days ago – was it really ten days? It felt like less – Mr Philips had telephoned her late in the afternoon to ask her out to dinner in London.

'When?' she'd asked, thinking how nice it would be to have some time away from all the preparations.

It was Friday, the evening before the wedding.

'Oh dear,' she said. 'That's the one evening I *can't* manage.' And explained why.

He changed his plans at once. 'In that case,' he said,

'why don't you come up to Manchester as soon as the wedding's over and spend the rest of the weekend as my guest. You'll need a rest by then, if I'm any judge. We could go to the theatre.'

It was such a tempting offer she accepted there and then. It was only after she'd put the telephone down that she wondered about the propriety of it.

'Perhaps I shouldn't've,' she said to Muriel. 'Staying in his house, I mean.'

'I'll come and chaperon you,' Muriel offered, grinning at her. 'I could do with a holiday too.'

'I wish I'd suggested it,' Rose said and she was only half joking.

'You go,' Netta advised. 'You've earned it. You'll have a lovely time. Take Bertie if you need a chaperon. You could hardly come to grief with a nipper in tow.'

'I ain't expecting to come to grief,' Rose laughed. 'He's very nice. A gentleman. Well, you seen him, so you know. He ain't the sort to try anything on. Nothing like that. It's just I thought it wouldn't look good.'

So she arranged for Bertie to share her holiday and now the two of them were packed and ready to leave as soon as the wedding was over. Which it was, surprisingly quickly. It seemed no time at all before they were all standing at the door, waving goodbye to the new Mr and Mrs Fernández as they set off for their weekend by the sea.

'We'd better be off and all,' Nancy Cartwright said. 'It was a grand wedding Rose. You got the gramophone Marigold? Mind you look after them bunions, Mrs M.'

'Goodbye Rose love,' Mrs Tuffin said, kissing her. 'See you Friday. Don't forget the ecru.'

The flurry of leave-taking left Rose feeling stranded and a little too aware of how profound this change was going to be.

'I can see why mums cry at weddings,' she said to Muriel.

'You haven't lost her,' Muriel understood, putting an arm round her shoulders.

'It feels as though I have.'

'She'll be back in the workshop on Monday.'

'I know. But it ain't the same. She was right what she said when we had that row, you know Mu. I didn't want her to marry. I couldn't stand the thought of things changing. I liked them the way they were. All four of us living there together. I suppose you're my family. That's what it is.' She tried to make a joke of it. 'I didn't want any of you to break up the happy home.'

'*I'll* never leave you,' Muriel promised.

'I don't think I could bear it if you did.'

'No fear of it,' Muriel said. 'I shall be here for good and all. I promise. I shan't ever leave you. Ever. You're stuck with me. We shall be two old maids together.'

'That's what we always said we'd be, didn't we? Right at the start of all this, when the war was over and we was dancing in the street.'

'That was years ago,' Muriel pointed out. 'Our Spaniard hadn't fallen out of the scaffolding then. Here, look at the time, for heaven's sake! You and Bertie had better go or you'll miss your train. You can't leave your nice Mr Philips waiting on the platform.'

Henry Philips had been waiting on the platform for nearly half an hour when their train finally arrived, late and breathless and hissing steam. He'd been watching out for it, dapper in his grey suit, his watch-chain gleaming in the gaslight.

'I've got the car outside,' he said, taking their case in his courteous way. 'Did you have a good journey? How did the wedding go?' Then he noticed Bertie and tried to find something to say to him too. 'And how's your little man?'

It sounded patronising and was certainly too avuncular, as he realised the moment the words were out of his mouth. Bertie cringed into his mother's side, muttering 'Very well, thank you.'

'That's right,' Henry said, trying to improve things by patting Bertie's head. But that only made him cringe again. And at that, Rose caught the child's eye and sent

309

him a warning glance that he was to keep quiet and not say anything else. What's the matter with the child, Henry thought. Why do children always have to be so difficult. And he led the way out of the station, resenting the little boy's presence.

On the way back to his house, he played safe by talking about the new mill and the next batch of cloth he was going to produce. 'Six new colours,' he said. 'I've brought the sample book home to show you.'

Rose had been rather surprised by the way he'd spoken to Bertie at the station. She hadn't expected him to be so touchy nor to discover that it diminished him in her eyes. He's not used to children, she explained to herself, as she gave him the answer he wanted. 'I can't wait to see it.'

'I'll show it to you after dinner,' he promised, as they arrived at the house. 'Mrs Murray's got something special planned. I told her to pull out all the stops. Now then, I put you in the Morris room because it has the best view. I hope that's all right. We've moved in a little single bed for the lad.'

It was a very grand room, with patterned wallpaper in swirling shapes of pink, blue and brown and a blue Wilton carpet on the floor. The towels on the wash-stand were thick and fluffy and there was a cake of scented soap in the dish and hot water steaming in the ewer. Real luxury, Rose thought, taking it all in. What more could anyone want? But Bertie was still looking anxious.

Mr Philips paused at the door to say. 'Half an hour to dress for dinner. Will that be sufficient?'

'We *are* dressed,' Bertie said when he'd left them. 'An' what's he mean "dinner"? We've had our dinner. We had sandwiches. What's he on about?'

'Dinner's what we call tea,' Rose explained. 'You have to change into different clothes before you have it.'

'What for?'

'It's what you do when you live in a house like this.'

The explanation didn't satisfy Bertie at all. 'Well I

reckon that's daft,' he said. 'We don't change our clothes to eat at home.'

'Well we do here,' Rose said, wearied by the argument. 'Come on.'

He allowed her to wash his face and put him into a clean shirt and the new jacket she'd made for him. Then he sat on the edge of his bed and watched while she got ready. Even in his present rather disgruntled state he had to admit she looked very pretty – in a grey dress with her long red beads.

But when they went back down that enormous staircase and walked into the dining-room, it was so grand it took his breath away.

The table was covered with dishes all made in posh china with patterns on. There were pink glasses with patterns on and knives and forks everywhere and pink candles all alight in great big crystal candlesticks. And eight chairs all ranged up around the table so that you didn't know where you were supposed to sit. He stood by his mother and held on to her skirt and felt alarmed.

'You here, Rose,' Mr Philips said, holding the chair for her. 'And your – um – Bertie here,' taking the child by the hand and leading him right round to the opposite side of the table.

'I always sit next . . .' Bertie tried but Mr Philips wasn't listening. He'd sat himself down in the chair at the head of the table and was talking to Mum about 'our new lines'.

If this is dinner I don't think much of it, Bertie thought. And he thought even less when the food arrived and turned out to be a watery soup that he had to eat with a spoon so big it left trails of liquid running down his chin. But he did his best with it, and smiled at Mum whenever she looked across the table to encourage him, and wiped his chin clean on the back of his hand whenever nobody was looking. When the maid took the plates away he was very relieved and ready to get up and go, but Mum made a little grimace to warn him to stay where he was. Then even more food was carried in – a great joint of meat on a platter for Mr Philips to carve, and roast potatoes and all sorts of vegetables, some of which he'd never seen before. They heaped his plate with so much food he knew he'd never be able to eat it all. So the rest of the meal was simply struggle. The afters was the best – a nice treacle pudding – but by then his stomach was so distended he couldn't do justice to it. He was quite worn out by the time the maid came back to remove the cloth.

'Bedtime for you,' Mum said. 'You're all eyes.'

'Coffee in ten minutes or we shan't be in time for the theatre,' Mr Philips said to the maid.

And then Mum got up at last and walked round to his side of the table and took his hand and led him out of the room and back upstairs. He lay down on the bed they'd given him and let Mum pull off his clothes. 'It's horrid here,' he said. 'When are we going home?'

Poor little man, Rose thought. He don't fit in here at all. Perhaps I shouldn't have brought him. 'Tomorrow,' she said, smoothing his hair from his forehead. 'Now I'm off out for a little while with Mr Philips. You'll be all right won't you. The housekeeper's here. You won't be on your own.'

He assured her that he'd be quite all right but his heart sank at the news. And after she'd gone everything got worse. The house began to creak and groan as if it was full of ghosts and demons and he knew they were all coming to get him. He put the covers over his head and tried to be brave and, after a long trembling time, he fell into a light sleep. But the creaking was still going on when he woke and now the corners of the room were full of heaving shadows. He was very frightened.

'Please God,' he prayed, 'send my Mum home as quick as you can. And make the ghosts go away. For ever an' ever. Amen.'

But his mother was in the theatre and it would be a long time before she came back to Elm Tree Villa.

Henry had chosen a variety show at Leslie's Pavilion. It was very entertaining but Rose found it hard to enjoy.

Her thoughts kept straying back to poor Bertie all on his own in a strange house – except for a housekeeper who didn't know him.

Her anxiety cast a restraint on their conversation. They were as awkward with one another as they'd been at the beginning of their acquaintance. During the interval, they discussed the turns they'd just seen and examined the current state of trade but the intimacy they'd reached in London was so far beyond them it might never have occurred. They were both relieved when the show was over and they could drive back to Fallowfields and the privacy of their separate rooms.

It's been a long day for her, Henry thought, noticing how tired she looked as they said goodnight. That's what's the matter. Things will be better tomorrow.

But there was still another screw-turn of conscience for Rose to endure before she could sleep. As she lit the gas light in her bedroom, a small voice quavered from the receding shadows.

'Mum.'

She was beside his bed at once. 'What's up? I thought you'd be asleep.'

His face was very pale. 'I don't like it here. There's a ghost.'

Oh my poor Bertie, she thought. I shouldn't have left him on his own. 'Come into bed with me and have a cuddle,' she said. 'It'll be better in my bed.' And she pulled back the covers and cuddled him across the room.

It was a great deal better with her protective warmth beside him. 'There *was* a ghost,' he said. 'It was making a sort of groaning noise.'

'There ain't no such thing as ghosts,' Rose said, kissing his head. 'It was the house cooling down. Old houses always creak at night.'

'Ours doesn't.'

'Yes it does, only you don't notice. Now you just snuggle down and get some sleep, like a good boy. It'll all

313

be different in the morning. You'll like it a lot better then, you see if you don't. It's a lovely place.'

She was persuading them both. And neither of them believed it.

The next day was bright and full of sunshine. And Henry had recovered his spirits.

'Just the day for a walk in the park,' he said. 'You could meet some of my friends. How would that be?'

She agreed. Naturally. He'd gone out of his way to entertain her so it was the least she could do. But she was tired after her broken night and, if the truth had been told, she would rather have gone home there and then.

'Splendid,' Henry said. 'We'll go to Birchfields Park.'

Birchfields Park was where most of the better-class inhabitants of Rusholme and Fallowfields went to promenade on a Sunday morning. It was laid out for the purpose, with wide walks between neatly mown lawns, a bandstand to provide entertainment and plenty of trees for shade. But its great charm was as a place to see and be seen. That morning it was full of people in their Sunday best, most of whom he knew. It was a great pleasure to stop and introduce his companion, particularly as the women were plainly curious about her and the men were full of admiration. One or two were envious, which was even more satisfactory. As the promenade progressed, he became more and more proprietorial, taking her hand and tucking it into the crook of his arm, introducing her as 'my dear friend Mrs Jeary.'

Rose wasn't sure how to take all this attention. There was an edge to it that worried her and made her wonder whether their acquaintance wasn't becoming rather more than just a business friendship. But she pushed the idea aside, telling herself he was just being kind and making a fuss of her because she was his guest. When they got back to the house he was more himself, talking shop again and telling her entertaining stories about the people she'd just met, so perhaps that was just the way he went on when he was with his friends.

But for all the effort he'd put into it, the weekend wasn't restful and, from her point of view, it wasn't a success. She was glad when Sunday evening arrived and she and Bertie were on the train and on their way home. They had a carriage to themselves so she told Bertie he could go to sleep if he wanted. But he said he'd had enough sleeping at Mr Philips.

'Not much fun, was it?' she sympathised.

'It was all right,' he said loyally.

She kissed him lovingly. 'You're a good boy, our Bertie.'

'We won't go there again, will we?'

'I might,' she said. 'But I won't drag you along.'

They travelled on in silence for several miles as the countryside around them congealed into darkness.

'It'll be nice back in Ritzy Street,' he said, 'with all the others.'

But it won't be with all the others, she thought sadly, as the train rocked them onwards. And she wondered how Netta had been getting on and ached to think how much she was going to miss her.

Netta was late to work on Monday morning, out of breath and apologetic. 'We was back so late last night,' she said, 'I'm all behind like the cow's tail this morning. I'm ever so sorry our Rose.'

Before Rose could open her mouth to say it didn't matter José had taken over. 'If they can't allow you a bit of leeway the morning after your honeymoon,' he said, glaring at them, 'they not much cop.'

'It's all right our Netta,' Mabel said. 'We don't mind. Did you have a good time?'

He wouldn't allow them to talk about that either. 'That between Netta an' me,' he said, sternly. 'Mind you back in good time tonight Netta.'

Rose and Muriel grimaced at one another and then looked at Netta fully expecting him to be told off for being saucy. But she'd turned away to set up her machine and didn't seem to have heard him. It was – as they told one

315

another later that evening – the first time they'd ever heard Netta being bossed about.

However, as soon as he'd gone, she was quite her old self again, entertaining them with tales of all the things she'd done during her two days by the sea. 'We went on the big dipper and the ghost train – that was a lark – and Sunday afternoon we went for a trip out to sea. Whatcher think of that?'

But what Rose was thinking about was that Netta wouldn't be coming home to Ritzy Street that night.

José escorted her to work every morning that week and on Friday he arrived to take her pay packet out of her hands as soon as she'd received it. And while Rose and Muriel were still reeling from the shock of that, he took Rose by the arm and walked her down the workshop to confide, 'You ought to buy a van for my Netta, you know that?'

'She's got a van,' Rose said, trying to shake her arm free without being too obvious about it.

'No. No,' he said. 'A *real* van. With a roof. To keep dry in the rain. I get it priced for you.'

'If I want it priced,' Rose said, wanting to put him in his place but aware of Netta's anxious face watching them from the other end of the workshop, 'I can do it myself.'

He was impervious to hints. 'I price it good,' he said. 'Come along, Netta. Time for my tea.'

His arrogance upset Rose more than she wanted to admit. 'He don't listen,' she said to Muriel after he'd gone. 'He just says what he wants and goes his own way. There's no getting through to him. You don't think he *will* go after a van, do you?'

'Not now he knows you don't want one,' Muriel said. 'He couldn't be *that* insensitive, even if he does have trouble with the language.'

But she was wrong. On Monday morning, he and Netta arrived at the workshop in a black delivery van, which he drove with great aplomb, straight into the compound. 'I got it for you cheap,' he said. 'What you think? Good eh? Netta can drive it.'

316

'It's ever so good,' Netta said quickly. 'I been practising with it all yesterday afternoon. Look at the space inside. I could do all our deliveries in one go with this. What d'you think our Rose? It *would* keep us dry.'

Rose didn't like the sound of that 'us' but she didn't know how to refuse the van without upsetting her sister. There was something about the expression on Netta's face that alarmed her, an earnest anxiety she hadn't seen before, and a trick of looking sideways at José as if she were checking his temper.

'Well,' said Rose hesitated. 'I don't know.'

'It'ud increase our trade no end,' Netta urged. 'José's been working it out.'

'It'll increase our costs too,' Rose said. 'We shall have to pay for petrol for a start, don't forget, and hire-purchase don't come cheap.'

José dismissed all her arguments. 'You not regret it,' he bullied. 'You make a mint. I work it out.'

'He has,' Netta said, the anxiety on her face now too clear to be ignored. 'It's a good investment Rose. Honest! Give it a try, eh?'

So despite her better judgement, Rose signed the papers José produced and hired the van.

'We shall have to drum up a bit more trade,' she said to Netta, 'otherwise we'll be in Queer Street.'

'Leave it to me,' Netta said. 'I'll do it. I'll work non-stop.'

But even that was denied her. Two days later José arrived in the yard without her.

'She not come in to work today,' he said to Rose. 'She got headache. I drive for you.'

There were goods that had to be delivered so she had to allow it. But it annoyed her, especially as she knew she'd been outmanoeuvred.

Netta came into work that afternoon, uncharacteristically subdued and got on with her sewing without saying anything.

317

'D'you want to take out the second load?' Rose asked. 'It's ready to pack.'

'No,' Netta said, and she sounded weary. 'I'll pack it, but we'd better let him do it. He's set his heart on it. I got enough to get on with here.'

'He'll want me to put him on the payroll next,' Rose said rather bitterly.

To her surprise, Netta took the joke seriously. 'Oh would you, our Rose?' she said. 'It'ud make such a difference if you did. There's no work for scaffolders anywhere, you see. He's been looking and looking. And he gets ratty when he's at a loose end.'

Put like that it was difficult to deny such a request. 'We'll try him out for a week or so,' Rose said. 'See how it goes. Might not be permanent, mind. There ain't the work.'

So José joined the firm, much to the other workers' annoyance. In just under a fortnight, he'd inveigled his way into the job he wanted and pushed poor Netta out so that he could do it. From then on, she only drove the van when he was out of the yard or when she made a particular stand about it, which was rare. And he became so much a part of the firm that Rose couldn't think how to uproot him.

He bought himself a uniform and spent the time when he wasn't driving polishing his boots or lounging about in the yard, smoking cigarettes and chatting to the passers-by.

'He don't exactly pull his weight, that José,' Nancy Cartwright complained one afternoon when Netta was out of the workshop packing the van.

'He's bone-idle, if you ask me,' Muriel said, looking out of the window. 'He can't even be bothered to help Netta with the packing. Mr Thomas is doing that. He's leaning against the wall with a fag in his mouth.'

'Well we've taken him on now,' Rose said. 'I can't very well sack him, can I? Not when he's married to our Netta.'

But he'd been right about the van. It made an

appreciable difference to their trade. And not simply to the speed of their deliveries either. Shopkeepers were impressed by it and increased their orders on the strength of it, much to Netta's delight.

'What did we tell you?' she said, when the month's accounts had been done and the improvement was obvious. 'Good ain't it. A change for the better.'

'Yes,' Rose agreed. 'It *is* good. Very good.' And was rewarded by the relief on her sister's face.

CHAPTER TWENTY-SEVEN

All through the long hot days of that summer, Augusta and Cedric remained locked in their old, stale quarrel. They wrote abusive letters to one another at least twice a week and grew steadily more self-righteous by the day. Edmund kept himself occupied at work and did his best to ignore what was going on. Louella went for a holiday in Paris with her dear friend Fancy Pepperell.

'Paris in June,' she said rapturously, as the two of them strode down the Champs Elysées, arm in arm. 'Doesn't it make you feel *young*!'

'I *am* young,' Fancy told her. 'A stripling.' Which was true – for she was a mere thirty-two to Louella's forty-six – and she certainly looked it, in a dashing suit made of pale green *crêpe de Chine* with the shortest, most fashionable skirt and a cute little boxy jacket.

'The women here are so chic,' Louella said. 'All arms and legs. Did you ever see such style? Just look at those two over there.'

'You could look just as stylish if you wanted to, my dearest,' Fancy said. 'It's only a matter of image.'

'Change myself do you mean?' Louella asked, letting the idea expand in her mind.

'Why not?' Fancy said. 'You've taken the first step by coming here. Go the whole hog. I dare you.'

Louella threw caution into the summer air. Why not, indeed? 'Where would I start?'

They were approaching a small boutique and an obviously expensive one. The blinds were green and gold, the sign was exquisitely written, there was a single silk dress in the window.

'Here is as good a place as any,' Fancy said.

And so it appeared to be. With Fancy's encouragement she bought 'exactly the right costume', which was a deep pink *crêpe de Chine* with a very short skirt, and matched it with 'exactly the right hat' which was an enormous stuffed halo made of crimson silk, its wide brim woven with pearls.

Then they headed off to Fancy's hairdresser.

'Steady on,' Louella warned when she saw the tariff. 'I'm not made of money.'

'I'll give you a loan if you run short,' Fancy promised. 'It'll be worth every sou.'

The new hairstyle cost considerably more than a sou and when the curlers were removed and Louella saw it in all its glory, she was a bit shaken. All her long tatty brown tresses were gone. Now she had a neat cap of tightly waved, decidedly fair hair. 'It's amazing,' she said, giving it a tentative pat. 'It doesn't look like me.'

'Glad to hear it,' Fancy said. 'Now you can do yourself justice. Release your spirit, my darling. Reveal your true colours to the world. Make-up next. Then lingerie. Then shoes. Then the rest of the wardrobe.'

By the end of that first day there wasn't a trace of the old Louella left, nor a trace of her money. But her image was dazzling, all long, long legs and smart shoes and beautiful colours. 'I never knew I was so tall,' she said, admiring herself in a shop window. Even the length of her face was acceptable in these clothes. And best of all, she looked much younger.

'Elegant,' Fancy said. 'That's what you are. Now you're fit to visit the *Exposition*.'

The Paris *Exposition* was, ostensibly at least, the reason for their holiday. Fancy had advised all the young hopefuls in her Tuesday class to visit it at least once during its six-month existence. 'You will see the best of the new art there,' she told them. 'Everything that is modern and progressive. Go to Paris and let the great designers brush the cobwebs from your minds. Experience the shock of the new.'

321

So naturally, the next morning she took her newly elegant friend through the *Porte d'Honneur* into the exhibition. The visit was to change Louella's life even more dramatically than her new image.

Even the outward appearance of the buildings amazed her, because all the material used in their construction was futuristic – brightly coloured plastic, white concrete, marble, terracotta, even stainless steel dazzling in the sunshine, and all of it decorated with geometric designs unlike anything she'd ever seen before – sunbursts, lightning bolts, spirals and shooting stars. She couldn't wait to walk through the doors and see what was inside.

'Sculpture,' Fancy commanded, heading off through the crowds.

The sculpture pavilion was full of prowling beasts and lithe, leaping girls, carved in ivory and cold-painted bronze and all triumphantly modern. They were the most athletic young women imaginable, short of hair and long of limb – just as she was herself –and every single one was on the move. They pirouetted on plinths of green onyx, leapt through flames, flew through the air above black marble steps, their long pale arms lifted and outstretched, their painted draperies flowing about them like water.

Louella was stunned by them.

Fancy laughed at her. 'The shock of the new, eh?' she said. 'Long flowing lines, d'you see? Nothing fuddy-duddy here.'

To their disappointment there was no pavilion set aside for the art of painting, but they visited the jewellery pavilion and admired the beauty of Lalique's frosted glass and his extraordinary flowing designs; and they took a turn round Le Corbusier's *L'Esprit Nouveau* pavilion, where they saw the latest in modern furniture, which was all straight lines and functional surfaces in steel and plastic and lacquered wood.

Then, well pleased with themselves, they strolled off to the nearest pavement café to be refreshed with coffee.

'Didn't I tell you it would be an experience?' Fancy

said, as the waiters sped between the tables, holding their trays aloft.

'I shall never be able to live quietly at home after this,' Louella said. 'Our furniture is going to seem *antiquated* now. I shall have to change *everything*.'

'I'm very glad to hear it,' Fancy said, lighting a cigarette. 'Shows you're acquiring some style. You go ahead and change it. And while you're at it, you can make some other changes too. You've put up with old anti-quated Fuddy-Duddy quite long enough. High time you stepped out into the wide, wide world.'

Louella wasn't sure she liked hearing poor old Edmund described as a fuddy-duddy. She lit her own cigarette while she thought about it.

'Change him, do you mean?' she asked.

The answer was cool. 'Change him or leave him.'

'Leave him? Good God! I couldn't do that.'

'Why not?' Fancy said calmly, blowing smoke rings through her bright red lips. 'He's no use to you.'

Happy though she was, Louella felt a momentary pang of pity for him. 'He *is* my husband.'

'*That*,' Fancy told her, 'is the most antiquated idea of the lot. Why should any woman stay with a man who doesn't make her happy, when there's a door in front of her, marked "The Future", simply waiting to be opened?'

'But where would I go?' Louella wondered.

'You would come to me, my darling,' Fancy said, adjusting her dark kiss-curl. 'You would live with me. *Garçon! Encore du café, s'il vous plaît.*'

Louella sat in the sunshine, drank her second cup of coffee and admired her friend's insouciance. Life with her would certainly be an adventure. 'Well I don't know,' she said. 'I shall have to see what happens when I get home. Don't let's think about it now.'

'Fun!' Fancy agreed. 'That's what we're here for. Tonight, the *Folies Bergères*.'

'The trouble is, they're all so old-fashioned in England,' Louella said, still thinking of Edmund and

323

Cedric and Augusta while she admired her reflection in the window beside her.

'Old-fashioned and insular,' Fancy agreed. 'It simply wouldn't occur to them to visit such a thing as an *Exposition*. It takes an artist to see the true value of things.'

She would have been surprised to know that, at that very moment, back in England, in his old-fashioned office in Ancoats, Henry Philips was ordering the dispatch of another sample of artificial silk for display in the new materials pavilion in the Paris *Exposition*. He knew – who better? – that international exhibitions are good for trade and had offered his wares at the planning stage of this one. Now he had decided to pop over to Paris to see how things were going and was suggesting to Rose – in his dull and insular way – that she might like to accompany him.

'A fortnight,' he explained to her. 'Saturday to Saturday. Time to see how they've handled the display, and get in a spot of sightseeing. What do you say?'

Rose held the telephone receiver away from her ear and tried to think of the best way to answer him. A holiday in Paris was a great temptation but she could hardly go there on her own with a man, even one she knew as well as Henry Philips.

'I'd love to,' she said. 'But I can't leave my Bertie for a fortnight.'

'Wouldn't your friend look after him? Muriel, isn't it?'

Rose looked through the glass panel of the office to where Muriel was sitting, her dark head bent over her machine. 'I'm sure she would,' she said, 'but I think he'd miss me too much. He's only little. Besides, there's so much work to do.'

'So the answer's no.'

'I'm afraid so.'

'Very well then. I'll take "No" for an answer this once,' he said. 'But be warned. I shall ask you again.'

'Oh dear!' she said to herself as she returned the receiver to its hook. 'Oh dear, oh dear!'

'What's up?' Muriel said, looking through the open door. 'Trouble?'

'No,' Rose said as she walked back to her machine. 'It's nothing really. I mean, it's just . . . That was Mr Philips. He wants me to go to Paris with him.'

'Paris!' Mabel said, from her seat by the window. 'Oh Rose! How romantic!'

'No,' Rose said, flatly. 'It's work. It's to see an exhibition, clothes and materials and things like that. Anyway I'm not going.'

'Why not?' Muriel asked. 'It sounds just the ticket. I'd jump at it if it was me.'

The machines were making enough noise to cover a personal conversation. 'It'ud be just him an' me going,' Rose explained. 'I don't think that's a good idea, now do you?'

'Ah!' Muriel understood. 'What you mean is, he's getting serious about you.'

'No,' Rose said at once. *Was* that what she meant? 'I don't think he is. No, I'm sure he's not. He's too old. No, no, it's not that. He spoke without thinking, that's all.'

But the idea stuck in her mind long after the conversation was over and returned to plague her late at night when the others were asleep. Were his intentions as honourable as she'd been trying to think? Or was his interest in her more than mere business? She remembered their walk in the park and how he'd taken her hand and slipped it through the crook of his arm and how uncomfortable she'd felt about it at the time. What if it hadn't been just a courtesy? Could Mu be right? Could he be interested in her in that way? She had to admit it was possible, old though he was. Possible and flattering, but did she really want it? What on earth would she say if he proposed? Or started to talk about love? No, she decided, he wouldn't. And anyway, the whole idea was ridiculous. He was a rich man, the owner of two mills. He lived in a grand house, with servants to wait on him, while she was little better than a servant herself. She was reading too much into it.

And while she was struggling with all these unwanted thoughts, the memory of her dear, long-dead Jack suddenly took possession of her mind, with his handsome face and that warm, beautiful mouth kissing her so tenderly, and those warm tough arms wound so lovingly about her – and loss and yearning pushed the problem of Henry Philips into the shadows.

Two days later she had a business letter from him about her latest order. It was so formal and correct that she felt quite relieved and told herself that she could stop worrying.

'I was reading too much into things,' she said to Muriel when she showed her the letter.

'Or it's because his secretary typed the letter,' Muriel told her sagely. 'See what he has to say if he writes to you from France.'

He sent four postcards and although they were all about the exhibition and how well his goods had been displayed, they were signed '*Yours, Henry.*'

'What do you think?' she asked Muriel.

'Hard to say,' Muriel hedged. She wasn't quite sure how Rose felt about this unwanted courtship – if it was a courtship. Best to play it down while things were still ambiguous. 'Maybe it's a sort of shorthand.'

But what happened next could neither be interpreted as shorthand nor explained away. A small, well-wrapped parcel was delivered to 26 Ritzy Street addressed to Mrs Rose Jeary. It had been posted in Paris and contained a bottle of French perfume, exquisite in a blue and gold case lined with amber-coloured velvet. The card attached to it simply said, '*With my fondest thoughts.*'

'I don't think there's much doubt about it now,' Muriel said. 'He's courting you!'

Rose's reaction was instant and unequivocal. 'Well he'd better stop. I shall send it back and tell him so.'

'Oh don't do that, our Rose,' Mabel protested. 'I'll have it if you don't want it. It's gorgeous.'

'I know it's gorgeous but that ain't the point,' Rose

326

said, 'He should'nt've sent it.' The little box lay on their old chenille tablecloth like an accusation. It made things look bad for her, as if she'd been encouraging him. 'I can't keep it.'

'It wouldn't be kind just to send it back,' Muriel said. 'Wait till he's home again and then write and thank him and drop a hint that it's a bit too personal for a business friendship. See what he says.'

It was a sensible suggestion but it left a problem. 'What shall I do with the perfume?'

'Give it to me,' Mabel urged. 'Give it to me our Rose. Please!'

'What d'you think?' Rose asked Muriel.

'Let her have it,' Muriel advised. 'You don't want it, so why not?'

So Mabel took the pretty bottle up to her bedroom and hid it away under the pillow. And the next morning when it was time to wash her face and hands, she emptied it into her wash-basin and used it instead of water. The smell in her little room was so overpowering it made her eyes water and it wasn't long before the rest of the household came running up to her bedroom to see what had happened.

'Pooh!' Bertie said. 'It don't half pong in here. What've you *done*, our Mabel?'

Rose burst out laughing. 'You idiot!' she said with exasperated affection. 'You're supposed to dab it on, little dabs here an' there, not wash in it.'

What with bewilderment and the strong smell, Mabel was crying in earnest. 'Will it come off, our Rose? I didn't mean to. I thought . . . What I mean is . . . Oh Rose, will it come off?'

Rose was still laughing at her. 'Not for years I shouldn't think.'

Even when they opened all the windows it was still so strong they could hardly breathe.

Muriel was laughing too. 'Thank you very much, Mr Philips!'

327

'I knew it was a mistake,' Rose said, fanning the fumes out of the window. 'I should've sent it back.'

By now, Mabel's mouth was trembling. '*Will* it come off, our Rose?'

'Come here, you daft thing,' Rose said, taking pity on her, 'and we'll see what we can do.'

They washed her three times in clean soapy water but the smell was still very strong.

'It's the heat. Everything smells worse in the heat,' Muriel said, wiping the sweat from her forehead. 'Hot weather's all very well if you can go on holiday and sit on a beach all day . . .'

'Or stroll about in Paris,' Muriel grinned at Rose.

In fact, Henry's stroll through Paris had finished that afternoon. He was on his way back to Dover, wondering how his gift had been received and travelling on the same cross-channel ferry as Louella Monk and Fancy Pepperell.

As soon as they arrived in Victoria Station, he headed off for the hotel he always used when he was in London, ordered a meal and made a telephone call to Ritzy Clothes, coming straight to the point in his usual forthright way.

'Hello. I'm back. Did you get my present?'

'Oh dear,' Rose said, trying to remember what she'd planned to say about it. 'Well yes, I did. Thank you very much. But there's been a bit of a mishap.' And she told him what Mabel had done.

He laughed out loud. 'Not quite what I had in mind,' he said. 'Never mind, I'll buy you another one next time.'

'I'm not sure you ought to,' Rose said, struggling to find the right words to explain this to him without hurting his feelings. 'I mean it's very generous but I'm not sure it's . . . I don't think I ought to be taking presents like that from you . . . I mean . . .'

He swept her objections aside. 'Of course you should. You wear perfume, don't you?'

'Not as a general rule, no.'

'Then you should start. Give me a chance to spoil you. How's trade?'

I handled that very badly, Rose thought, as she put the receiver down. Not only had she failed to make him understand that she thought his present was compromising, she'd agreed to meet him for dinner when he came back to London in September. I'll have to talk to him properly then, she thought, make the position clear. It'll be easier face to face. He hardly let me get a word in edgeways on the telephone. But she was making excuses for herself and she knew it. She ought to have made more of an effort.

It was a relief to her when Nancy Cartwright put her head round the door of the office to ask if she wanted the new florals brought down. That, at least, she could cope with.

Louella Monk and Fancy Pepperell parted at the entrance to Victoria Station.

'Now don't forget,' Fancy said. 'Stand your ground. Let him see you've got a will of your own. Show him how much you've changed.'

He'll see that the minute I step in through the door, Louella thought. Now that she was back in England she wasn't quite so happy about her new appearance. In Paris it had seemed modish, almost natural. Here it was making people stare. If he says anything I'll fight back, she told herself. Fancy's right. I ought to make a stand. Hiding my feelings is foolish. He ought to know what I think. But she was tense with apprehension to be so close to a row.

By the time her taxi delivered her to Chelsea, she'd worked herself up into such a state she was ready for anything, shock, outrage, even bad temper.

Edmund was out in the garden, working on his portrait of Miss Spencer, and when he looked up and saw her he was so appalled by her appearance that he didn't know what to say. But he held on to his self-control and managed not to comment. It was too late for criticism and he knew that unless he could praise her and sound as though he meant it, he would only upset her. So he merely smiled briefly before he returned to his painting.

His apparent indifference angered her. It was almost as if she hadn't changed at all. 'I suppose you're going to ask me how I got on?' she said sarcastically.

'You had a very good time,' he said, as if it were obvious.

'Yes,' she said, crossly. 'I did, as it happens.' That stupid Miss Spencer was deliberately not looking at her. Unpleasant woman, she thought, frowning back into the house. And what *does* she think she's wearing? A white dress is totally unsuitable for a woman like her. And so is the pose, standing there with one foot in front of the other. It's so static.

I did that well, Edmund thought as he painted in the shadows of the apple tree that curved over Muriel's dark head. I wasn't provoked. I hid my surprise. I was calm. But even while he congratulated himself on his self-control, he knew that the real reason for his ability to control himself was that this painting was too good to be marred by ugly emotions. It was the best thing he'd ever done, and the knowledge was lifting him into a sense of well-being that was very nearly impregnable.

The first full-length portrait of this girl had been good – standing by the window in her scarlet dress hooking the russett curtain into a long swathe – the dawn rosy before her – light flooding through the window into the musty room – that yearning expression on her funny little round face, hopeful and tender. He'd called it *spring* and knew that the title was as good as the work. But this one, which was going to be called *Summer*, was better – all greens and golds and the white blaze of that diaphanous dress – thick foliage, tangled and interwoven like the arches of a church – and she striding down the aisle almost like a bride. The expression on her face changed so often he hadn't decided which he would finally use but he knew it would be fitting when he found it. And in the meantime

330

there was the pleasure of painting and the ease of her intelligent company. Even Louella's appalling appearance couldn't break the spell he'd created.

But she could criticise the painting. And did, the minute he carried it into the house.

'Oh Edmund!' she said and the words sounded like a rebuke. 'It's so old-fashioned. So *static*. You really must try to get some movement in your work you know. Movement is *de rigueur* these days. You ought to go to Paris. Then you'd see.'

'We all have our own style,' Edmund said mildly, setting the portrait on his easel. 'And the figure *is* walking.'

'Walking!' Louella scoffed. 'That's no good. She should be leaping through flames or balanced on one leg at the top of a mound of Elephantine.'

Edmund gave his wry smile. 'I don't think I've ever seen Miss Spencer balanced on one leg on a mound of Elephantine.'

'Try not to be troublesome,' Louella told him. 'You know what I mean. The world is *changing*, Edmund. And while we're on the subject, we shall have to change the furniture, you know. I really can't go on living with all this old-fashioned stuff.'

'We've lived with it for nearly twelve years,' Edmund said mildly. 'It's comfortable. It's practical. There's plenty of wear in it. I can't see the necessity for change.'

'Exactly,' she said crossly. 'That's just what I mean. It's so fuddy-duddy. Well I *can* see the necessity. I shall order a new dining-room suite tomorrow. We'll have the whole room made over. You won't know yourself.' She patted her new blonde hair with her new red finger tips admiring her image in the studio mirror.

The gesture betrayed her intentions. In that moment he realised that she was going to alter the house to suit her new image and that she would have to be opposed.

'No, Louella,' he said quietly. 'You will do no such thing. You may change the front parlour if you wish. That has always been your domain and I see no reason why you shouldn't alter it, providing you keep within the budget. But the rest of the house is to stay as it is.'

She was furious. 'How can you be so selfish? I'm offering you the chance to move out of the nineteenth century, for God's sake.'

'You're offering me the chance to make my house uncomfortable,' he said mildly.

They were very close to a quarrel now and Louella's heart was beating painfully. 'You know nothing about it,' she said.

'Possibly,' he allowed and then, feeling sorry for her flushed throat and bolting eyes, 'I will reserve judgement until I've seen what you propose to do with the parlour. How will that be?'

She flounced out of the room, silk stockings swishing.

The next six weeks were acutely uncomfortable for Edmund Monk. First a team of removals men arrived and hauled all his familiar furniture out of the front parlour and up two flights of stairs to the spare room. Then the decorators moved in. He watched in misery as the room was transformed, winced as the skirting-boards were painted black and the picture rails emerald green, was given an instant headache by the terrible zigzag design of the wallpaper –black, red and green flashing like lightning across an oatmeal background – and dropped into a gloom when an equally ugly carpet was laid. Worse was to come when the furniture was delivered. As he confided to Miss Spencer in the garden that Saturday, he had never seen anything more hideous.

There was a cocktail cabinet made of chrome, a side table that looked like a skyscraper – long and narrow and painted green – an indescribable bookcase, an oblong sofa and two cubic chairs made of planks of black wood and upholstered in mock zebra skin.

'It gives me backache to look at them,' he said to Muriel, 'leave alone sit on one.'

'I like something cushiony,' Muriel admitted,

diplomatically but honestly. Her own back was beginning to ache from too much standing.

'The only good thing about it is that it's very nearly finished,' Edmund said. 'Could you just walk towards me once more?'

The painting was taking much longer than he'd expected. There were several days when the weather was too bad for it and more when he couldn't face it because of Louella's ill temper.

'I'll phone the workshop and let you know about next Saturday,' he said, as he cleaned his brushes. It had become a habit to forewarn her these days because he'd had to cancel so often.

'Is there much more work to do?' she asked.

'Oh I do hope not,' he said, misunderstanding her. 'She's talking about changing the fireplace now, so who knows?'

But no amount of change could satisfy Louella's passion. One room, stylish though she'd made it, was nothing when she had to live and sleep in the rest of a fuddy-duddy house.

As August drowsed from one hot day to the next she began to nag. 'You really ought to let me make the bedroom over, you know Edmund. This is so dull.'

He weathered her pressure as well as he could, turning her insistence aside with wry jokes, ignoring the catalogue she placed before him, explaining patiently, over and over again that fashions were ephemeral, that their existing furniture was well made and should last for years, that *he* had to live in the house too.

'One room dedicated to Art Deco is sufficient for any man,' he said. 'Even an artist.'

'You're impossible,' she told him. And went to Little Venice to visit her friend.

Their inhibited quarrel dragged on. Although they would never have admitted it, it was as bitter as the one being waged so openly between Cedric and Augusta. And it damaged them both – although Edmund had little idea how badly until one Saturday morning late in August.

He came home from a visit to his suppliers to find Louella busy in her bedroom, flinging her clothes into a large valise.

'Ah!' he said. 'You're packing.'

She froze him with a glance. 'I should have thought that was patently obvious.'

His apology was almost a reflex action. 'I'm sorry. That was crass of me.' A weekend was it? She must have told him about it but he couldn't remember. 'Will you be away long, my dear?'

She pulled her underwear drawer right out of the cabinet and tumbled the contents into the bag, pushing them down with fingers so stiff and frantic that the sight of them frightened him. 'I'm leaving you,' she said. 'I'm going to live with Fancy Pepperell.'

He heard the words but couldn't make sense of the meaning. 'How long will you be gone?' he asked.

'For ever,' she said wildly. 'Don't you understand what I'm saying? I'm leaving you.'

His mind stopped, wouldn't move forward, stayed with the question rather than accept the answer. 'When are you coming back?'

'I'm not,' she said and her voice was shrill. 'I'm leaving you.'

It was too ridiculous to be taken seriously. 'Oh come on, Louella,' he said, struggling to be reasonable. 'People don't walk out on their husbands. Not in the middle of a Saturday morning.'

'Saturday. Friday. What does the day matter? I'm going to live with Fancy.'

'But why?'

'She understands me.'

'I understand you.'

'She *values* me. She knows what it is to be a woman and an artist. We have to stick together, support one another— as artists and women. We can't be dragged down, don't you see. We have to be free spirits, free to paint when we choose, free to catch the bird of inspiration on the wing.'

She's talking like a Modernist pamphlet, Edmund thought. 'Is it about decorating the house?' he said. 'Is that it?'

She screamed at him. 'You don't listen to a word I say. Get out of my way. There's the cab! I can't stay here a minute longer or I shall suffocate.'

She hauled the bag off the bed and struggled out of the room with it, banging it against his legs as she went. He heard her crashing down the stairs and bumping through the hall.

This isn't happening, he thought. It can't be happening. We don't do things like this.

Then she was gone, banging the front door behind her.

CHAPTER TWENTY-EIGHT

'I'm off then,' Muriel Spencer said. 'I shan't be long.'

She and Rose had eaten their sandwiches that lunch time sitting on the workshop steps in the sunshine. Netta was still out with the van and José was nowhere to be seen, so it was peaceful out in the yard. Mr Thomas had carried their tea out to them on a tray, teasing that it was 'all right for some!'. But now the church clock was striking one and it was time for Rose and the others to get back to work and for Muriel to head off to Chelsea and the nearly finished portrait.

'Mind how you go,' Rose said automatically, smiling at her.

'I hope he gets it finished today,' Muriel said, as she wrapped herself up in her coat and took up the bag that contained her flimsy white dress. 'Come September it's going to be too cold for standing about in that garden of his.'

'Wear a cardigan,' Rose suggested, pulling hers around her shoulders.

'He'd hate it,' Muriel laughed. 'It would spoil the picture.'

But for the moment the weather was fair. As she stood on the doorstep at Chelsea waiting to be let in, the sun was warm on her shoulders.

Betty, the parlourmaid, gave her an odd look when she opened the door and for a second Muriel was disconcerted. Had she got the wrong day? No, surely not. He'd rung the workshop yesterday afternoon to confirm the sitting. But Betty's lowered glance alerted her. There was something up and they knew it below stairs.

'Is he out in the garden?' she said.

'No, Miss,' Betty said. 'He's in the studio.'

Muriel climbed to the top of the house, moving quietly, in her neat, contained way, and wondering what was going on.

When she first walked into the studio she thought Betty had made a mistake and that he wasn't there after all. Then she saw him. He was standing beside the window with his forehead resting against the pane and he was unnaturally still.

'Mr Edmund?' she said, stepping towards him.

He started as if he'd been struck, turned and looked at her. His face was haggard with misery.

She ran to him, all instinct and pity, to put her hand on his shoulder for reassurance. And before either of them was fully aware of what was happening he groaned and fell forward into her arms.

She held him as if he were a child, patting his shoulder and murmuring comfort. 'What is it? Tell me what it is. You poor man. You mustn't be upset. Tell me what it is.' She realised that she was treating him in exactly the same way as she treated young Bertie when he was upset, using the same words but she was working intuitively and couldn't think of anything else to say. 'There now, don't cry. I've got you.'

He put his face into her neck. 'She's gone Muriel. Gone. Walked out. Left me.' His voice was changed too, thickened by unshed tears and muffled by her consoling flesh. 'After all these years she's walked out and left me.'

Ah, so that's it, she thought, without surprise. Well it had always been on the cards. Was it just a tiff or had she really gone? 'She'll come back,' she comforted.

His reaction to that was almost violent. 'Oh no. She won't. She's taken all her things. Even some of my books. She packed up a great trunk. Carter Pattersons collected it. She had it all thought out. No, no, she won't come back. After all these years, all this effort. I can't understand it. What did I do wrong?'

How could she answer that? 'I'm sure it wasn't all your

337

fault,' she said, trying to reassure him. 'There are always faults on both sides, aren't there.'

'It's such a shock,' he said. 'I can't take it in. What will people think?'

'The same as they've thought all along I expect,' she told him, deciding to be frank. 'We all know what you've had to put up with all these years.'

He didn't move his face out of her neck but she could feel that he was listening intently. 'How do you know?' he asked, misery momentarily stopped. 'Who. . . ?'

'They know below stairs,' she told him. 'They always do. You can't live in a house with someone without knowing what's going on.'

The information made him groan again. 'Oh God!'

'We all know how good you were to her. You never quarrelled with her, now did you?'

He lifted his head and moved away from her to look out of the window again. 'Perhaps I should have done,' he said bitterly. 'Perhaps all that self-control was a waste of time. Perhaps I was doing everything wrong.'

She asked him a direct question, going to the heart of the matter. 'Do you want her to come back?'

The bitterness receded from his voice. 'No,' he said. 'I don't. Not really. Not if I'm honest. We've never been exactly happy together. This is hurt pride, that's all.' He turned to give her his wry smile, joking to regain his self-control. 'The bubble reputation. That's what I'm worried about. What people will say about me. That and the feeling that I can't bear it.'

'You'd be surprised what you can bear when you have to,' she told him. 'As I should know.'

'How could you?' he said, bitterness returning. 'Your man didn't walk out on you.' And then with a moment's doubt, 'Did he?'

'No,' she said and decided to tell him a little truth so as to pull him away from self-pity. 'My dad walked out on me.'

Her shock tactics worked. He turned his head and

338

looked straight at her for the first time. 'You never told me that,' he said.

'There's wasn't any reason,' she said and as he was obviously waiting for her to say more, 'I was an orphan. I was brought up in a home.'

He forgot his own distress in sympathy for hers. 'I'm so sorry.'

Now she felt she might have told him too much and began to cover up. 'I got over it. You do get over things.'

Her expression had changed with the words, hardening and becoming the deliberate blank he'd seen and wondered about so often. After the warmth of her sympathy he felt as if she were deserting him. He leant towards her, put his hands on either side of her face and held it. 'Don't leave me,' he begged. 'Don't close me out. You're the only person I can talk to now.'

Her eyes behind those round glasses, shifted and focused on his face. Gentleness returned. Light was reflected. She was herself again, looking at him lovingly. Was it lovingly? Had he any right to hope for love? They were so close to one another that he could see every eyelash, could note the depth of colour at the centre of each brown pupil, the way it shaded out into lighter and lighter brown and was finally edged with sea blue. Delectable eyes, he thought, and the beauty of them made his heart clench with unbidden pleasure. 'If you shut me out too,' he confessed, 'it *would* be more than I could bear.'

She was suddenly breathless. 'I try not to shut anybody out,' she said. But he was kissing her before she could finish the sentence, his mouth pleading, holding her so close she could barely breathe. And she was kissing him back, surprised and yet not surprised, tremulous with sympathy for him, her fingers in his ridiculous fringe of hair, loving him, as pleasure began and extended and extended.

The kiss went on for a very long time as sensation held them both in thrall. When he finally stopped it was because they were too breathless to continue. He tucked her head against his chest and held it there so that she couldn't look at him. 'Don't say anything,' he panted. 'Not yet. Wait till I . . .'

She waited, listening to the pounding of his heart and wondering.

'I've loved you for years,' he said. 'From a distance because I never thought . . . being married, you see . . . It wouldn't have been . . . I didn't think you could ever . . . You're the loveliest woman I've ever known. Lovely by nature. Lovely in appearance. I tried to show you that in the portrait but I couldn't catch the expression I wanted. You've been the one good thing in my life in all these months. The one and only good thing. Looking forward to your visits kept me sane.' He released her so that she could lean back and look at him. 'Well there it is,' he said, shrugging his shoulders. 'I had to tell you. Now you can scold me if you like.'

'I wouldn't scold you,' she said, touched by the hopefulness on his face. 'Ever. I'm honoured.'

'I may love you?'

That made her smile. 'I can hardly stop you now.'

His desire for her was so strong it was turnng him pale. 'Oh yes,' he said with perfect seriousness. 'You may stop me at any time. Any time at all. You must understand that. I would never do anything you didn't want me to.'

She took his hand and placed it on her breast, giving him permission, her face intense.

'I've been celibate for a very long time,' he warned her. 'If I start now it will be very hard to stop. Although I will stop if you want me to. I promise you that. But if I start now . . .'

'Start now,' she said. She was amazed by how cool she was and how clearly her mind was working even though she was aching for him to go on.

His caressing hand made her tremble but she was still sensible. 'You'd better lock the door,' she said between kisses. And when he went off to obey her, she thought,

340

I've given him permission now. It will happen. But if this is seduction, it's what I want. It all seemed natural and inevitable, and she couldn't deny it was desired. Then he was back again and kissing her so passionately she was too caught up in the pleasure of it to think at all.

Love was no surprise to her, although the strength of the climax he gave her was a storm compared to what she'd expected from the hints she'd gleaned from Nancy and Marigold. It was the peace that enveloped them afterwards that was the surprise. She lay beside him on the musty coverlet and listened to a blackbird singing in the garden below them and was happy beyond words. A beam of sunlight shone through the high window and spread in a sloping column towards the polished wood of the floor. It was full of motes that jumped and swirled like live things. It's magic, she thought, now you see them, now you don't, and it seemed to her that everything was magical that afternoon, and that she was seeing things more clearly than she'd ever seen them in her life. He loves me, she thought, listening to his sleeping breath. I never thought anyone else would love me after Bertie died. But this man loves me. I have a lover. Me, plain Muriel Spencer. And the wonder of it filled her mind as she drifted to sleep beside him.

When she woke it was late afternoon and she could just about see him without her glasses. He was sitting beside the window, sketching, his long face serious. 'They're on the table,' he said. 'I put them there for fear of getting them bent.'

She found the glasses and restored her sight. 'How long have I been asleep?' she said.

'A hundred years and woken by a kiss,' he smiled and put down his sketch pad to suit the action to the word. 'I love you very much.'

She accepted the kiss dreamily. 'It feels very late,' she said. 'What's the time?'

'I've no idea,' he said, sitting in the chair beside her. 'Don't let's bother about the time. I want to talk to you.'

So she sat on the edge of the bed and waited to hear what he had to say. When he finally began to speak it was as if he were making confession.

'I ought to warn you,' he said. 'You're making a bad bargain. I'm a married man – unless she'll agree to a divorce and I can't be sure about that. I'm fifty-two. I'm a mediocre painter. An inadequate teacher. A worse husband, apparently, if her opinion is anything to go by. In fact, taken all in all, I'm not particularly good at anything very much. I haven't got a lot to offer you.'

'That's all right,' she smiled at him. 'I've never expected much. Love will do to be going on with.'

It was a perfect answer. 'You're an amazing creature,' he said, putting out a hand to stroke her cheek. 'I'm a very lucky man.'

She laughed. 'That wasn't what you were saying when I arrived.'

'That was before . . .' he said. 'Everything's changed now, hasn't it?'

She was beginning to realise the enormity of what had happened, of how great the change to her life would have to be. I can't just go back and live in Ritzy Street, she thought. Not now. I shall have to stay here with him. At least for a little while.

He was reading her thoughts. 'You will stay with me, won't you?' he begged. 'You won't go.'

'Is it important for me to stay?'

'Very,' he said seriously.

'I shall have to tell Rose and Mabel,' she said, frowning. 'They'll be wondering what's become of me. And there's my clothes.'

'So what do you want to do?' he asked, trying to be practical about it. 'Would you like me to drive you over?'

'No,' she said. 'I'll go on my own. This is my problem, not yours. And I *will* come back. *I*'m not running out on you. It's not in my nature to walk out.'

'I know that,' he said, 'and I'm very grateful for it. You are happy about this, aren't you?'

'Yes,' she said and that, at least, was the simple, inescapable truth. 'Very happy.'

But problems would have to be faced in Ritzy Street. She would have to find some way to explain to Rose and Mabel without upsetting them. And how on earth was she going to do that, after all these years and all the promises she'd given? As she left the house, anxiety descended on her and she grew more and more agitated the nearer she got to Kennington. What *could* she say? Whatever else, I mustn't upset them, she thought. They've been so good to me and I love them so much. Oh God, why is life so complicated?

Rose and Netta had had a trying afternoon. Just as Netta was about to set off with her van, a brewer's dray lost a wheel at the entrance to Old Farm Street. Traffic was held up for over an hour while the beer barrels were removed and rolled round to the pub and then the wheel had to be botched together again and re-attached. Netta's second delivery was delayed so long they were afraid it wouldn't get out in time for the evening trade and just when the road was finally clear, José appeared, blurry eyed, smelling of beer and belligerent.

'You should be home getting my tea,' he said. And he turned to Rose to complain to her too. 'It no good she work here so late.'

'We couldn't help it,' Mabel started to explain, but he wasn't listening.

'Come down out a' there,' he said to Netta. 'I drive now.'

For once Netta fought back. 'No,' she said. 'I drive of a Saturday. We agreed.'

'Come down,' he insisted. 'You get my tea.'

'I ain't got time for this,' Netta said. 'I'm late enough as it is.' And she crashed the van into gear and drove off.

He was enraged. 'Come back,' he shouted, running after the van. 'You come right back, you hear!'

'Back to work,' Rose ordered Mabel. 'If he's going to make a scene, he can do it on his own.'

But he followed them into the workshop. 'Now look here,' he said to Rose. 'You make her mind her husband. She not to drive the van so late. It not right. She got my tea to get. She got duties.'

Until that moment Rose had never argued with him. She'd felt it wasn't her place and she didn't want to upset her sister. But now, such a direct challenge could be answered.

'Netta's got a job to do,' she said. 'We pay her good money for it and she does it.'

'Then maybe she should leave this job, eh. Maybe she shouldn't work. Have you thought of that?'

'That's up to her.'

'Oh no,' he said. 'That up to me. She *my* wife. Okay then. She leave the job. *I* do it.'

So that's it, Rose thought. Artful beggar! But she stayed calm. 'There's something you ought to know, José,' she said. 'You're on the payroll simply because you're married to our Netta. If she leaves the firm, you leave too. There won't be a job for you.'

'What you mean, there won't be a job?'

'What I say. I won't employ you.'

'But who drive the van?'

'I'd hire someone else. Someone who'd do a good day's work for a good day's pay. Which is more than you do.'

He ignored that. 'But how I manage?'

'That's your affair. But you wouldn't work here. Make no mistake about that. I wouldn't want you.'

His face was suffused with rage. 'You a hard-hearted woman. You got no heart.'

'No,' she said. 'I've got a lot of work to do. And now I'm going to get on with it, if you don't mind.'

For a few seconds he stood where he was, looking so threatening she wondered whether he was going to hit her. Then he turned and banged out of the workshop.

'Good riddance!' Mabel said.

'I hope he don't take it out on our Netta,' Rose worried.

'He wouldn't do that, would he?' Mabel said, her face puckering at the idea.

'You saw him,' Rose said. 'Yes. I think he would.' And she thought, he'll make trouble out of what I said too – if he can.

Netta was obviously worried about how he'd react too. When she got back with the van, she packed up as quickly as she could and rushed off home.

'I wish she hadn't married him,' Mabel said as she and Rose walked back to Ritzy Street.

'So do I,' Rose said. 'But it's no good crying over spilt milk. What we got for tea?'

Mabel had done the shopping that morning. 'Haddock,' she said. 'Me an' Bertie got a really nice bit. The fishmonger said it was the best bit on the slab. The best bit. And I said . . .'

'Mu'll be back by now,' Rose said interrupting the flow. 'I expect she'll have put it on. Give our Bertie a yell, will you?'

So Bertie was collected from his friend's house and they all went home arm in arm. But the house was empty. 'That's odd,' Rose said. 'Where's she got to? It's not like our Mu to be late.'

They were setting the table when they heard Muriel's key in the lock.

'There she is!' Bertie called, rushing out into the hall to greet her. 'Come on Aunty Mu, we're starving.'

'Ain't you been a long time,' Rose called. 'We'd almost given you up for good.'

Now, Muriel thought, as she walked into the living-room holding Bertie's hand. Now I've got to tell them. The room was at its most enticing, warm and welcoming. The gas lights bloomed softly behind their yellow mantles, the tea things were set in their usual order, teapot under its cosy, bread and butter spread like a fan, milk jug wearing its little gauze cover, the coloured beads catching the gaslight as if they were jewels. Home, she thought and the sight of it made her yearn with a new and exquisite pain. This is what I've got to leave behind. This is the price I've got to pay.

'What kept you?' Rose said. 'Mabel's got us a lovely bit of haddock. Done us proud ain'tcher Mabel?'

Muriel's courage failed her. I can't say anything now, she thought. Not when they're all waiting for their tea. It wouldn't be fair. And not with Bertie around either. But it was very hard to eat as though nothing was the matter and she was sure Rose knew, because she looked at her several times during the meal with the oddest expression on her face. But nothing was said until the table was cleared and Mabel was upstairs putting Bertie to bed.

Rose took her sewing-basket and settled down by the fireplace to darn Bertie's socks but Muriel stayed on her feet, taut and uncertain.

'Come and sit down,' Rose said to her. 'It's been a long day.'

Muriel stayed where she was. 'No,' she said. 'I've got to pack.'

'Pack? What d'you mean pack? Where are you going?'

'It's Edmund,' Muriel said.

'Edmund?' She's never called him *that* before. It's always been Mr Edmund. Oh God Mu! Not you too!

'Mr Edmund,' Muriel corrected herself. She could see from her wary expression that Rose already suspected. Now the confession came out with a rush. 'Louella's left him. He's terribly upset. I said I'd go and stay there for a little while. Keep him company.' That sounded lame but that else could she say?

Rose wasn't impressed. 'Whatever for? He's a grown man. He's got servants. He don't need you to look after him.'

'No. You're wrong,' Muriel said tremulously. 'He's in a terrible state. He *does* need me. Very much.'

Anger made Rose sarcastic. 'And we don't I suppose?'

'Yes,' Muriel pleaded. 'You do. I know you do. It's just . . .'

Rose put her sewing aside. Weary though she was, this needed her entire attention. 'What's been going on?'

'He's in a state. He needs someone with him.'

346

'But why you?'

Muriel couldn't answer but her shame-faced expression spoke for her. 'It's just . . .'

'Oh for heaven's sake!' Rose said angrily. 'Don't tell me what it's just. I can see what it's just. I'm not blind. He's been feeding you a line – telling you he loves you, ain't that right? And you've fallen for it. He's got round you, that's what he's done. It's the oldest trick in the book. I thought you was above being caught by that sort of thing.'

To hear him being accused of duplicity was more than Muriel could bear. 'It's not a line,' she cried, her face anguished. 'He wouldn't trick anybody. Really. It's just . . . Well, he loves me. And I love him. I can't help it Rose. I do.'

Mabel ambled back into the room. 'What's up?' she asked, catching the atmosphere. 'Is it about the van? It was ever such a crash our Muriel. All the barrels went everywhere . . .'

'No it ain't,' Rose said brusquely. She was too upset to be gentle. 'Muriel's leaving us. She's going to live with Edmund Monk.'

'She ain't,' Mabel said, denying it at once because that was the only form of defence she knew. 'She ain't. She can't live with *him*. He's a Monk. And anyway he's *old*.'

The familiar, terrible sense of loss and rejection dropped like ice into Muriel's blood, clogging her power to think and depriving her of speech. What was the good of saying anything? She was bound to lose, whatever she said. She always lost and she was always hurt. It was inevitable. There was no hope, only this overwhelming sense of being caught up in events she couldn't control and couldn't avoid. She was so far withdrawn into misery she didn't know where to look. But she managed a whisper. 'I must go. I've given him my word.'

Her blank expression was more than Rose could bear. Even though she knew the reason for it and had seen it often and with sympathy, especially in those tricky early days, this time it felt as deliberate as a blow to the face. It had to be fought and fought hard. 'Go then,' she said bitterly. 'See if we care. It's no good shutting your face against us. That'll only make matters worse. It won't help you.'

This time, Muriel turned her face away and wouldn't even look at her.

'You're the same as all the others,' Rose cried, torn by anger and rejection. 'First Netta and now you. You're all the same. A man only has to beckon and you drop everything and go running off to live with him. It's horrible. How *could* you? We made promises to each other. You forget that. We said we'd stay together, look after one another, work together, "women without men" we said. Remember? We was going to stay together for ever and ever. That's what we worked for. To be together. What happened to all that?'

Muriel was too far gone to talk at all.

'And what about our Bertie? You been with him all his life. He'll be cut to bits if you walk out on us. You don't think of him, poor kid.'

Muriel was quite rigid now, standing before them as if she were tied to a stake.

The sight of such acute distress should have roused Rose to pity, but it didn't. The combination of the day's fatigue, Muriel's rejection and her own terrible, sudden anger were too powerful. 'Well if you're going to pack, you'd better do it,' she said. 'We're not stopping you, are we Mabel? Only don't think we'll take you back once you've gone. If you're going to *him*, you're going for good an' all, understand that. We shan't want you.'

And at that point Mabel began to scream.

'She ain't to go!' she yelled. 'She ain't!' Then she was running and kicking, wild-eyed and red in the face. 'Make her stop! Stop! Stop! Stop!'

Both women ran towards her, instinctively, but Rose put out a hand and held Muriel off. 'Leave her!' she said

348

furiously. 'She's my sister. *I*'ll deal with her. You've done enough damage for one day.'

Mabel flung herself across the table, pounding it with both fists and shrieking.

Rose controlled her fury with a superhuman effort. 'Come on, our Mabel,' she said, seizing her hands and holding them hard. 'Calm down. I'm here. Let go of the tablecloth, there's a good girl.' Then she looked up briefly at Muriel and spat words at her as if they were enemies. 'If you're going,' she said, 'go!'

Muriel caught her breath, swayed, gathered her strength. Then she turned and ran from the room, stumbling up the stairs to the bedroom that was no longer hers. Quick. Quick. Pack and get out. You're not wanted.

Once in the bedroom, she realised that she didn't possess a case. The one she'd brought with her when she moved in had disintegrated long since. There were three carrier bags at the bottom of the cupboard but that was all. Frozen-faced, she took what clothes she could and pushed them into the bags. Hair-brush, talcum, books. What else? She'd have to take her coat and skirts over her arm. But that was nothing new. It was how she'd moved from home to home as a child.

Downstairs, the tantrum was still going on. She could hear kicks and screams and Rose's voice soothing and placating. She took her bags and stumbled down the stairs, struggled through the door, walked away down the street.

She was still frozen with misery when she got back to Chelsea. But Edmund had acquired a new and instinctive understanding that day and knew what to do. He took the bags out of her hands, set them on the floor and gathered her into his arms. 'Cry if you want to,' he said. 'There's no one to see you now.'

Permission was all she needed. She put her head on his chest and burst into tears. 'My poor dear love,' he said, stroking her hair. 'Was it so awful?'

Between tears she told him how awful. 'There's always

a price to pay,' he said sadly. 'No joy without pain, they say, and I've always found it to be true, I'm afraid. I only wish it weren't. I'd have given anything to be the one to pay the price this time.'

His tenderness warmed her. 'I know,' she said.

'I'll make amends to you, my darling.'

'You don't have to.'

'Oh yes,' he said. 'I do.' And kissed her, very gently.

The kiss reminded her of the extraordinary happiness of the afternoon. 'I do love you,' she said. 'We *shall* be happy. You'll see. I'm sorry to make such a fuss.'

'That's all right,' he told her. 'Make as much fuss as you like.'

But there was a worse fuss to come. After the strong emotion of the day, the ogres of her childhood returned that night to stalk her dreams. She woke wild-eyed and distraught, crying not to be taken away. 'I can't bear it,' she wept. 'I love them so. Don't move me. I'll be good. I promise.'

It took him a long time to coax her back to the world again.

'It's all right,' she said, when she was calm. 'It's nothing.'

So this isn't the first time, he understood. 'Does it happen often?'

'Sometimes,' she admitted but modified the confession at once. 'Not often. I haven't had one as bad as that for a long time.'

'What was it about?' he asked. 'Can you remember?'

'Oh yes,' she said bitterly. 'I can remember. That's half the trouble. I wish I couldn't.'

'Tell me,' he said.

'It's horrible. You won't want to hear it.'

'I want to know all about you,' he told her. 'Everything. Warts and all. And I want you to know all about me. Warts and all. So we'll start with this nightmare. What was it about?'

Bit by bit she told him the story of her life in the homes,

of her terror at being taken from her friends, her sense of isolation, her belief that nothing good would ever happen to her. And he listened and questioned and held her in his arms. They talked until it was dawn.

'I shall change your mind,' he told her. 'You'll see. And gradually, as your mind changes, the nightmares will go.'

She didn't tell him that Rose and Mabel and Netta had worked that cure once already. It would have undermined him. But the knowledge took the edge from his promise.

After his long failure with Louella, life had given Edmund a second chance to do well by a woman. He took it with joyful responsibility. During the next few days he treated her as though she were recovering from a long illness. He ordered invalid food for her and bottles of fortified wine; he took her for a walk down by the river in the twilight; he drove her to Richmond to be healed by the peace of a little open countryside. They admired the reddening oaks and watched the deer as they browsed in a halo of sunlight, twitching their flanks against the last of the summer flies.

The nightmares returned every night just as she'd feared they would but with diminishing power. And by day there was love to sustain them. On their third morning together he was kissing her when his house-keeper came in with their lunch. Muriel was shamefaced to be caught in a compromising situation but he merely looked up and smiled.

'Let them know,' he said, when she voiced her doubts. 'They do anyway, if what you said was true. Let them see how happy we are.'

So she kissed him to show she agreed. It was silly to be prudish. They were still kissing when the telephone began to ring.

CHAPTER TWENTY-NINE

'I don't like the sound of Edmund,' Cedric Monk said, scowling at his wife. He'd just put the telephone down and was rubbing his right ear to relieve the pressure he'd been putting on it. He always clutched the receiver too tightly and shouted into the mouthpiece. 'Don't like the sound of him at all.'

Winifred was in the farm kitchen making blackberry and apple jam. She lifted a spoonful from the preserving pan and dropped it onto a cold plate to test it. 'I shouldn't have thought you'd heard enough of him to form a judgement,' she said, tilting the plate. 'You were doing all the talking.'

'Exactly,' Cedric said. 'That's just my point.' He squeezed himself into the rocking-chair and fitted the tips of his fingers together, one after the other, carefully. It was a gesture he often used to assist his thought processes. 'He let me talk. He listened. And he hasn't done that since this awful business with Augusta began. He's always fobbed me off. Well you know how he's fobbed me off. There's something going on and if you ask me it's something to do with Louella. When I asked him how she was, he said "All right, I suppose." What sort of an answer is that? He says he hasn't seen Augusta for weeks. Says he's been busy. Well I can't believe *that*. He's only a teacher, for Pete's sake. When is a teacher ever busy? It's not as if he does anything important. Like farming. No, you mark my words, there's something going on.'

'You don't think she's changed her will again and not told us,' Winifred worried.

'I wouldn't put it past her. I wouldn't put anything past her. But there's definitely something going on and

Edmund knows what it is. I think we ought to go up to London straight away and see for ourselves.'

'Quite right,' Winifred said, stirring the bubbles. 'So do I.'

'We'll go on Friday,' Cedric decided. 'I can see old Johnson at the same time. Kill two birds.'

'The boys are coming home from France on Saturday, don't forget.' Now that they'd both acquired degrees, Percy and Hereward had spent the entire summer on the continent. 'I hope your sister's going to pay for it all. They've been spending money like water.'

But for once Cedric wasn't interested in his sons' profligacy.

'Friday,' he said, looking up at her. 'I'm not going to be outwitted by Louella. Not after all these years.'

It was rather a shock for Edmund Monk when Cedric and Winifred were announced on Friday afternoon. He made them welcome but only because he couldn't think of an excuse to avoid their company. He and Muriel had just sat down to afternoon tea so there was nothing for it but to get Muriel out of the way by sending her for extra cups and plates and to invite his unwanted relations into the dining-room to join him at the table.

Winifred came straight to the point. 'Where's Louella?' she said.

Edmund coughed with embarrassment. 'I'm afraid Louella has moved,' he said.

Cedric was so surprised he blinked. 'Moved?' he said. 'Moved where? I suppose it's Monk House. Is that it?' The news infuriated him. I can see the game they're playing, he thought. She's gone to flatter Augusta and get her to change her will.

'No,' Edmund explained with patient trepidation. 'She's gone to live with a friend of hers. Fancy Pepperell. They met at Ethel's wedding.'

'Oh I see,' Cedric said heavily. Does he really think I'll believe that? 'How long for?'

'Well, for good, actually.'

That *was* news. 'Good God! You don't mean she's left you.'

''Fraid so.'

'Well, go after her. Get her back. She can't just walk out on you.'

'I'm afraid that's exactly what she has done. She's very strong-minded, you know. I can't tell her what to do.'

'She wants horsewhipping,' Cedric began. But then the door opened and Miss Spencer came in with the tea-tray, so he waited until the table had been set, scowling at the fire but saying nothing because private matters should not be discussed in front of a servant. He was horrified when this particular servant actually sat at the table and began to pour the tea as if it were her place to do so. Good God! Now what?

Edmund was compelled to explain. 'This is Muriel Spencer,' he said. 'I daresay you remember her. She's come to keep me company. She – um – lives here.'

That was such a shock to Winifred and Cedric that neither of them knew what to say. Winifred murmured 'How d'ye do', wondered whether she ought to shake hands and thought better of it. She was so upset to have her tea poured by Louella's ex-companion that the cup and saucer rattled in her hands as she received it. Cedric glowered at his brother whenever he could catch his eye. And Edmund, ash-pale with distress, couldn't look at him because Muriel had withdrawn behind her listening face.

They made fatuous conversation – about beef prices, the cost of holidays abroad, the Prince of Wales, last month's Olympic Games in Paris, the fall of the German mark, anything rather than talk about Louella's departure and Muriel's arrival. Cedric couldn't wait to get out of the house and shoot off to Kennington to break the news to Augusta.

Edmund stood by the window and watched as his brother drove his classy new Packard rapidly out of the street. 'I'm so sorry,' he said to Muriel.

She stood beside him, slipping her hand through the

crook of his arm. 'It was bound to happen sooner or later,' she said. 'We can't keep it hidden, can we?'

He was relieved that she was taking it so well. 'They'll tell Augusta, of course,' he said sadly, his heart sinking at the thought.

'I thought they were quarrelling.'

'This will stop it. They'll both turn their guns on *me* now.'

'Yes,' she said, 'I suppose they will but there's nothing they can do to stop us, is there? Not really.' And she was thinking, what does it matter? The Monks are always quarrelling with somebody or other. It's not *their* quarrels that are important, it's mine with Rose. How could we have parted like that, after all those years? How could we have said such things to one another? Is there any way I can ever put it right? And the bleakness of loss made her heart contract.

Augusta was none too pleased when Cedric and Winifred arrived. 'Tell them I'm out,' she said, when the parlour-maid put her head round the door to announce them.

'No you're not,' Cedric said, pushing into the room.

'You're not welcome here,' Augusta said, bristling at him.

'Just wait till you hear what we've got to tell you,' Winifred said. 'Then see if we're not welcome. Edmund's got himself a fancy woman.'

'He's what!'

They told her the story with gusto. 'What do you think of that?' Cedric asked.

Their quarrel was forgotten, just as Edmund had foreseen. 'They must be stopped,' Augusta said. 'I shall go there at once and tell him so.'

She arrived like a storm at nine o'clock the next morning, pushing past Edmund's maid and blustering straight into his parlour. She was wearing a purple dustcoat and a black cloche hat and·looked larger and more formidable than he'd ever seen her.

'Hello Gussie,' he said, deflecting his alarm with kindness. 'Have you come to breakfast?' In one way this early arrival was opportune. Muriel was out shopping so they had the parlour to themselves. If he was quick he might get rid of her before too much harm was done.

She steamed into the attack at once, tossing her hat and gloves into the nearest chair.

'Are you living with this woman?'

He answered her quietly. 'If you mean Miss Spencer, yes I am.'

'Well you can't. You must stop it at once.'

'Oh I must, must I?'

'Yes you must. Of course you must. Oh for heaven's sake, don't you understand what you are doing?'

'Yes Augusta,' he said gravely. 'I think I may say I understand exactly what I'm doing.'

She snorted at him. 'You're bringing disgrace to the family name.'

Edmund surprised himself by how clearly he was thinking. 'Oh come now, Augusta,' he said. 'That's a bit strong, don't you think. We're not royalty.'

Augusta stormed on. 'You can't go on like this.' There was an hysterical note to her voice and her top lip was beaded with sweat. 'She's your wife's companion, for goodness' sake. You can't set up house with your wife's companion. It isn't done. You must give her up. At once.'

'Sit down,' Edmund said firmly. 'You're getting yourself into a state.'

'And whose fault is that?' Augusta cried. 'You know how delicate I am. You never stop to think.'

Edmund took her by the arm and led her to the nearest armchair. 'You might not like this, Augusta,' he said, 'but I'm a grown man. My life is my own affair, not yours.'

'It's a family affair,' Augusta panted. 'Don't you care about your family?'

'Have I ever had a family?' Edmund wondered.

'Oh don't talk nonsense,' his sister scolded. 'Who do

you think I am, if I'm not family? Why do you imagine I'm here?'

Because Winifred and Cedric ran straight to Monk House last night to tell tales, Edmund thought.

'You'll be a laughing stock,' Augusta warned. 'People will talk.'

He could take this calmly now. 'I daresay they're talking already.'

'Don't you care?'

'No,' Edmund said, giving her his wry smile. 'I don't really. I'm happy for the first time in my life.' He was surprising himself by how easy this was.

Augusta was open-mouthed. 'How can you say such a thing?'

'Because it's true, I daresay.' It was a beautiful morning. The sky was the colour of a duck's egg above the pewter grey of the roof tiles, the brickwork a splendid rich ochre, the upper windows fiery in the sunlight, like molten metal, almost too bright to look at. The house as a shining shield, he thought, following the curve of the windows . . .

'You're not listening to me,' Augusta said.

'No,' he agreed lazily. 'I'm not. I'm thinking about colour. And sunlight.'

Augusta was outraged. 'I've come here all this way – and you know how ill I've been – I've put myself out purposely to help you and you can't even do me the courtesy of listening to what I've got to say.'

Edmund was still looking out of the window. 'I've heard it all before.'

Augusta snorted. 'You have *not* heard it all before. Don't be so ridiculous. This hasn't happened before. You've never left your wife for another woman before.'

'My wife left me,' Edmund corrected gently.

'You're doing this on purpose,' Augusta said. 'You know perfectly well what I mean. You've *got* to listen to me Edmund. You must give this silly girl up. Now. This instant.'

'Or what?' he mocked her.

'Or I shall cut you out of my will.'

He laughed at her. He actually looked her straight in the eye and laughed at her. 'Again?' he mocked.

'It's no laughing matter,' she said angrily.

This time he smiled at her and his smile was more infuriating than his laugh. 'It's no go, Augusta,' he said. 'We're grown men and women. You can't bully me any more.'

'Bully you? I'm not bullying you.'

'You bully everybody,' he corrected mildly. 'You've always bullied everybody. You've been a bully all your life.'

She was trembling with rage, her jowls shaking. 'How dare you say such a thing! I'm your sister. I've never bullied you. Ever. It's always been the other way about. *You've* bullied *me*. After my money all the time.'

'Ah I see,' Edmund said and now there was no doubt that he was mocking her deliberately. '*That's* what's been happening. *We've* been cutting you out of *our* wills.'

It was too much! How dare he poke fun at her. She couldn't endure it. 'You'll regret this,' she warned, struggling to her feet. 'I came here out of the kindness of my heart – to warn you – make you see sense. I didn't come to be mocked.' She was so angry she could barely breathe. 'Oh the ingratitude of it! That's what I can't stand. I come all this way. With *my* heart. And this is how you treat me. It's scandalous. No. Don't ring the bell. I'll find my own way out. But you mark my words. No good will come of it.' She was nearly at the door. 'The wicked never prosper, Edmund Monk! You will live to regret it.'

As soon as the door banged shut behind her, Edmund began to laugh. Merriment bubbled into his throat like champagne. It was all so totally, gloriously ridiculous.

He was still laughing when Muriel came back.

'What *is* going on?' she asked, running into the room.

'I've just seen off my sister,' he said, beaming at her. 'The dreaded Augusta.'

'That one. I never thought I'd have it in me but that's what I've done. Come and kiss me.'

Augusta carried her grievance home like a brand burning deeper and deeper into her chest. It took her ages to find a taxi and a nasty, smelly, uncomfortable thing it was. The streets were dusty, the air stank of petrol fumes, the fare was exorbitant. It was as if everything were conniving to make her life unpleasant.

By the time she reached Monk House she was twitching with bad temper. She couldn't wait to get inside.

And there in the hall was the wretched charlady, down on her knees scrubbing the floor and making a nasty sloppy mess of it.

'Do you have to do that now?' Augusta said tetchily.

The answer was flat and unfeeling. 'If you wants it done, ma'am. Yerse.'

'How rude!' Augusta said, feeling her annoyance justified. 'That is no way to talk to your employer.'

'Do you want it done, ma'am, or don'tcher?' the woman said, massively patient.

'If you talk to me in that tone, I shall fire you,' Augusta warned. 'And you won't like that.'

The woman tossed her floor-cloth into the bucket, sat back on her heels and waited. If she was going to be fired there was no point in going on with the floor.

'All right then,' Augusta said furiously. 'You're fired.'

The charwoman stood up and wiped her hands on her apron. 'Suits me,' she said.

'Empty that bucket,' Augusta ordered. 'You can't just walk off and leave a bucket full of dirty water in the middle of my hall.'

'You should ha' thought of that before you come the old acid,' the charlady said and trudged off along the corridor towards the kitchen. 'I'm fired. You just said so. I'm off to get me things. That's two hours you owe me.'

Augusta was so angry she could feel the heat rising into her cheeks. She stomped through the hall into the parlour and threw herself into her favourite chair. But her troubles weren't over. After a few seconds she became aware that there was a terrible smell in the room.

'Oh God!' she said aloud. 'Now what?' But her nose was telling her what. One of those foul cats had made a mess on the carpet. She marched to the fireplace, seized the bell-pull and rang furiously.

It took a very long time – and three more furious rings – before anyone answered. And then it was Mrs Biggs, puffing and pink in the face. 'What is it?' she asked brusquely.

Augusta waved a hand at the mess on the carpet. 'One of those disgusting cats,' she said.

'That accounts,' Mrs Biggs said. 'I heard yowling.'

'Then why didn't you let it out?'

'Not my job. I'm cook-housekeeper, in case you've forgot.'

Augusta decided to ignore Biggs' rudeness – for the time being. 'Well get someone to clear it up,' she ordered.

'Who do you suggest?'

'*I* don't know. And clear that bucket out of the hall while you're here.'

'That ain't my job, neither,' Mrs Biggs said heavily.

'Then tell the maid to do it when she's cleaned up.'

'What maid? You sacked the last one yesterday.'

'Well somebody else then. Just do it, for heaven's sake, and don't keep worrying me.'

'There ain't nobody else. You've sacked 'em all. And not for the first time neither. But you never learn do you.'

'What do you mean, I never learn. That's no way to . . .'

'You never learn,' Mrs Biggs said implacably. 'We been through all this over an' over. I hire 'em and look after 'em and get 'em to stay, and you go an' fire 'em. It gets on my wick if you really want to know. Well now there's only me left and I ain't clearing up cat shit, nor carting no buckets about neither. Not if you want yer dinner.'

The time had come to be firm. 'If you go on talking to

me like this,' Augusta warned, 'I shall have to think seriously about whether you're fit to stay in my employ. You wouldn't want me to fire *you*, would you?'

Mrs Biggs folded her arms and stared. She was breathing deeply but she didn't say anything.

'You see!' Augusta sneered. 'You wouldn't like that.'

Mrs Biggs went on scowling at her for a very long time while they both caught their breath. That's got you! Augusta thought. Now we'll see what you've got to say. But what Mrs Biggs actually said was such a shock that she couldn't believe her ears.

'You're wrong,' she said. 'It's just exactly what I would like. I been thinking about it for ages. Off out of it and not having to put up with your nonsense no more. I can't think of nothink I'd like better. You're right. It's high time we parted company. Very well then. I shall be taking me pension soon. Me and me sister's thinking a' packing off to Margate. Being a few months early wouldn't make all that much difference. I got a bit put by. I shan't be beholden to no one. All right then. I'll go tonight if that's what you want.'

It wasn't at all what Augusta wanted, nor what she'd intended when the conversation began. Perhaps she ought to backtrack a little. 'Now come,' she said. 'That's silly. There's no need to be hasty.'

'No need to be hasty,' Mrs Biggs mocked. 'After all these years and the way I've put up with you. If that ain't a need to be hasty, I don't know what is. I'm too old for all this malarkey.' And with that she left the room, banging the door behind her.

She can't mean it, Augusta tried to comfort herself. It's just temper. She won't really go. Not after being with the family all these years.

But no meal was served that evening and there was far too much banging about in the flat. And at a little after seven o'clock Mrs Biggs appeared in the dining-room uncalled for. She was in her hat and coat and was carrying two bulging carpet bags.

'I'm off then,' she said. 'I've took me wages out the housekeeping. Two weeks in lieu of notice. Can't say fairer than that.'

'I hope you realise I haven't had any dinner,' Augusta said, assuming her most pained expression.

That didn't rouse any sympathy at all. 'That's your hard luck,' Mrs Biggs said. 'You know what they say in Russia. Them as don't work don't eat.'

She left with a tremendous stamping and banging of doors, crashing the front door behind her so violently that the lustres jumped and tinkled on the mantelpiece. The silence that washed back into the house afterwards was numbing.

Heartless, beastly creature, Augusta thought. Well I can manage without her. I'll cook my own dinner. I shan't go short. I keep a good larder. And she marched down to the kitchen to make a start.

It was a nasty shock to find that her good larder was bare. There was half a loaf of rather stale bread in the bread bin, a scraping of butter in the dish and two wrinkled potatoes on the shelf, but no meat, no bacon, no eggs, no cakes, no biscuits, not even the odd vegetable. Good God! she thought. Where's it all gone? She can't have taken it all with her.

But that was exactly what her aggrieved cook-house-keeper had done. There was nothing for dinner that night except a slice of buttered toast and a cup of tea, and it took ages to prepare *them* because she didn't know how to work that horrible new-fangled gas cooker. And the bucket was still in the hall and the parlour still hadn't been cleaned.

I suppose I'd better do that myself too, she thought, or the carpet will be ruined. At least I've found out how to boil the kettle. It made her heave but she cleaned up as well as she could, using plenty of disinfectant in the water and feeling martyred. Then she went miserably to bed.

It was a long, empty night and sleep was impossible. She tossed and turned on her feather mattress, brooding and plotting. This was all Edmund's fault. He'd got her in such a state, she hadn't known what she was doing. Well, she couldn't go on like this without anyone to look after her, or she'd be ill. Somehow or other she would have to get a new housekeeper and some more servants. That much was clear. There must be servants somewhere. They couldn't all have disappeared off the face of the earth. She would put a card in the off-licence and the corner shop. That used to do the trick. That was how Rose came to her all those years ago. A good girl Rose. *She* wouldn't have gone on like that dreadful Mrs Biggs. *She* was always sensible. Look how she'd made that dress. And that gave her an idea.

The next morning after a well-sugared cup of tea, she went into the parlour, opened the window to let out the smell of disinfectant, rummaged through her desk to find her writing-pad and sat down to compose a letter.

'*Dear Rose,*

I would appreciate it if you would call on me at the above address at your earliest convenience. I have a proposition to put to you, which would be to your advantage.

Yours faithfully,

Augusta Monk.'

CHAPTER THIRTY

In the miserable days that followed her row with Muriel, Rose deliberately kept herself busy. Work was her proven cure for unhappiness and there was plenty to do. At home she kitted Bertie out with new clothes ready for the start of the autumn term which was only a matter of days away. At work she bought two new machines and hired two more machinists, cousins called Amy and Gertrude, who were nicknamed Pug and Gert and settled in very quickly. She insisted that Netta should deal with all the morning deliveries and she spent hours on the telephone badgering suppliers.

'Yes, I know we're only just out of August,' she said to them, 'but our holiday's over. We've got work to do.'

She was so snappy that her workmates grew wary of her and Netta was most concerned. It upset her to see her sister in such a state and it hurt her to be told so little about Muriel's going. She hadn't expected a long heart-to-heart talk – that wouldn't have been in Rose's nature – but to be held at arm's length was demoralising, especially when she couldn't help feeling that José had been partly to blame for it, sounding off like that because he wanted to drive the van. For a day or two she wondered whether she ought to write to Muriel and try to heal the rift but Rose's touchy mood deterred her. So for the moment, and uncharacteristically, she held her peace, got on with her work and waited.

On Friday morning her patience was partially rewarded. At the very moment that Cedric and Winifred were storming towards Chelsea for their show-down with Edmund, there was a telephone call to the workshop from Henry Philips. It was the third he'd made since his return from Paris and Mabel's *contretemps* with the perfume. The others had been brief and business-like because he'd come back to a great deal of work and, after the business with the perfume, he hadn't been entirely sure of his reception. But this time, catching a new and depressing note in Rose's voice, he talked longer, spurred on by the feeling that she needed comfort and the hope that he might be the one to provide it.

'I'm coming up to London again next week,' he said, when she'd told him how hard she'd been working. 'How about dinner? Sounds as if you could do with a night out.'

A treat, Rose thought. A chance to eat a meal I haven't cooked and talk to another adult, an evening without having to watch out for Mabel's tantrums all the time. But she dithered. 'It would depend when.'

'Monday,' he said, making up his mind at once and rushing her towards a decision. 'Same time, same place.'

So, although there was still some doubt in her mind, it was agreed.

'Quite right too,' Netta approved. 'You been working a darn sight too hard these last few days. Give yourself a break. I'll come over and look after Mabel and Bertie.'

Rose thanked her but as she went back to her cutting-table she was wondering whether she'd done the right thing. What on earth would she and Henry find to talk about? There seemed to be so many things she couldn't tell him now, about Muriel going and José being pushy and Netta subdued and how she felt about his unwanted gift, which would have to be dealt with very delicately – if it could be dealt with at all.

However, ten minutes before the Rolls Royce drove into Ritzy Street, the postman delivered Miss Monk's letter and provided her with a safe topic of conversation. She took it with her to the restaurant and while they were waiting for the first course to arrive, she handed it across the table for him to read. 'What d'you think of that?'

'Sounds like business,' he said. 'Is she rich?'

'Very,' Rose said and told him about the house and the family and the way they all quarrelled over money.

'Then if you ask me, she's going to invest in your firm.'

The idea made Rose laugh out loud. But underneath the laughter she was flattered and pleased. 'That *would* be a turn-up for the books,' she said. 'I used to be her parlourmaid. I can't imagine her investing money in a parlourmaid.'

'Why not?' he asked. 'You're not a parlourmaid now and you're doing well. You'd be a good investment. Maybe it's time for you to expand anyway.'

'I hadn't thought of it,' she told him. 'But I suppose I could.' It gave her a most rewarding sense of worth to sit in this stylish restaurant and think about expanding her business. 'Larger premises, perhaps. If there's capital.'

But not here, he thought, smiling into those lovely grey eyes. Not here and not with that woman. In Manchester with me. 'I've got a better proposition to put to you,' he said, his tone light. 'I'm having a dinner party on Friday. Something special. Friends of mine in the trade. Could be useful to you. How about joining us? You could stay the weekend and have a real break.' Ever since his return he'd been planning to ask her to spend some time with him and now that they were together again and she was looking so delightful he certainly wasn't going to pass up the opportunity.

It didn't take Rose long to decide on her answer. It was *so* pleasant to be with him in their restaurant. He was such good company he'd made her feel quite herself again. She looked across at his determined face – at the set of his jaw, the strong nose, the thick hair and luxuriant moustache – and thought how much she valued his friendship and how sound his judgement was. Meeting other people in the trade could be good business. A weekend like that was just what she needed.

'I'll go and see Miss Monk first thing tomorrow morning,' she said, 'then I'll get everything sorted out at work and then I can take a weekend off with a clear

conscience. Netta'll keep an eye on Bertie. Thank you.
I'd love it.'

The next morning, as she was frying their bacon, Bertie
came down to breakfast squeaking with excitement
because they'd got the sweep in at Monk House and he
knew his mother was going there.

'I seen the cart from Aunty Mabel's window,' he said.
'Can I come with you? Say yes. Can I?'

'What for?' Rose laughed at him.

'To see the brush come out the chimbley.' He'd been
allowed the privilege the last time the sweep came to
Ritzy Street and he couldn't wait for a repetition.

'Daft hap'orth,' she said, ruffling his hair. 'I suppose
you can. You'll have to behave yourself though. Keep out
the way. No larking about.'

So they walked into the grounds of Monk House
together and, feeling very daring, marched up to the front
door.

The sweep's cart was propped up on the side path, its
route through the garden marked by two thick trails of
soot. The name 'J. Taylor Chimney Sweeper' was
prominent on its side but the brushes were gone and there
was no sign of the sweep.

'He's started,' Bertie said, looking up at the chimney
stacks. 'Which chimbley d'you think it'll be? It won't've
come out already will it? Can I stay in the garden and
watch?'

'If you behave,' Rose said vaguely, as she pressed the
doorbell. The front door was wide open but she couldn't
just walk in. That wouldn't have been proper. She waited
on the doorstep while Bertie ran across the lawn to get a
better view. She could see that somebody had been at
work in the hall. The floor was covered with a thick layer
of stained newspaper and the runner had been curled up
like a swiss roll and now stood on its end under the
grandfather clock. But the hallstand hadn't been
shrouded in its usual dust sheet and nobody came to
answer the bell.

367

Presently the dining-room door opened to reveal the sweep's black face under its grimed cloth cap.

'You the 'ousekeeper?' it said, gruffly. 'An' about time.'

'No, I'm sorry,' Rose said, apologising because she could see that the sweep was annoyed. 'I ain't. I come to see Miss Monk.'

'She let me in,' the sweep said. 'Bit of a rum do, if you ask me. Nothink's ready. I had to do the 'all mesself. There ain't a sight or sound of any staff.'

But at that, Miss Monk herself emerged from the front parlour, looking larger than ever in a lime-green suit and her long pearls.

'Ah Rose!' she said. 'I *am* glad to see you. You don't happen to know where the dust sheets are, do you?'

Rose was so surprised she answered honestly. 'In the linen cupboard I expect. That's where they always were.'

'You couldn't get them for me, could you,' Miss Monk said grandly. 'Everything's in such a pickle this morning. The servants haven't come, you see, and Mrs Taylor can't start.'

Mrs Taylor? Rose thought, looking round at the sweep.

'That's me,' the sweep said, stepping out into the hall and obviously female. 'An' she's right. I can't. Not unless you want your furniture all smuts.'

Under such unexpected pressure, Rose didn't feel she could say no. 'All right,' she said. 'I'll get them for you but I ain't got all day.'

She climbed the stairs quickly, noticing details as she went. Dust under every stair-rod, the banisters filmed with it, stains on the landing carpet, chipped paint on the skirting-board, the smell of must and damp stirred up by every step she took. Never mind *the servants haven't come in this morning*, she thought, she hasn't had any servants here for months.

The linen cupboard struck stale too. She took the dust sheets from the top shelf and carried them down to the dining-room, where, as Mrs Taylor seemed to be expecting it, she shook out the first half a dozen and covered the furniture.

'What about the curtains?' the sweep said.

'I ain't dragging curtains down,' Rose told her. 'I only covered the furniture out the kindness of my heart.'

'They'll spoil.'

'Then they'll have to. I've done all I'm going to do. You can make a start now. I'm off to see Miss Monk.'

'I'll do the one chimbley in here, tell her,' Mrs Taylor said. 'Then I'm off. I ain't working without dust sheets. I'll come back another day, when she's more ready-like. You tell her.'

The lady was sitting in her armchair in the parlour beside the empty grate and she didn't seem surprised when Rose walked in without knocking.

'It's a perfect nuisance the sweep coming this morning,' she complained.

Rose wasn't interested. 'You said you had a proposition to put to me,' she said.

'That's right. So I did. Five pounds a month and all in. How would that be?'

What's she talking about? Rose thought. She's surely not offering me a job. I thought she was going to . . . Oh for heaven's sake! What a come-down! But she stayed calm and spoke politely. 'I beg your pardon?'

'I'm offering you the job of housekeeper here,' Miss Monk explained. 'Mrs Biggs has left and I thought of you directly. I think you'd suit me very well. Five pounds a month is over the going rate but I want someone I can trust. The flat goes with it, naturally, and full board and uniform . . .'

Rose looked at Miss Monk's complacent face and didn't know whether to laugh at her or tell her off. The very idea! 'Just a minute,' she said. 'What makes you think I'd want a job like that?'

'It's good money,' Miss Monk said, bristling a little.

'I can earn three times that amount,' Rose told her. 'More if I set my mind to it. I own a company, Miss Monk.

369

Well you've seen it. You know what it's like. I ain't a skivvy. I ain't been a skivvy for years. I employ other people. I've took on two more girls since I last seen you.'

'Oh well,' Miss Monk pouted. 'If you don't want it . . . I thought you'd jump at the chance.'

It's no good talking to her, Rose thought. She don't listen. 'I've left my little boy out in the garden,' she said, walking towards the door. 'He's watching for the sweep's brush. Oh and that's another thing. She says she's only doing the one chimney this morning. If you want the rest done you'll have to make another appointment.'

'She's the same as all the others,' Miss Monk said, with such bitterness that Rose stopped and turned to look back at her and listen. And what the lady said next was so unlike her that she had to go on listening.

'Chu-Chin died, you know. My dear little Chu-Chin. And then everything went wrong. My whole world's turned upside down. Mrs Biggs walked out on me. After all these years. The charwoman wouldn't empty the bucket. The cat was sick and I had to clear it up.' Was this really the great Miss Monk talking in this maudlin way? 'And Edmund's taken up with some awful girl.'

No, Rose thought, I know you're talking rubbish because you're feeling sorry for yourself but you ain't getting away with a thing. 'I know about her,' she said and her voice sounded cross.

Surprise made Augusta sharp. 'How do you know?'

'She's my best friend. And she ain't awful. She's very nice.'

Augusta's thick eyebrows arched with surprise. 'Are we talking about the same girl? Miss Spencer? Louella's companion?'

'That's right,' Rose said, standing her ground. 'My best friend. She's lived in our house for years. He's jolly lucky to get her, I can tell you. He should be down on his knees fasting for a girl like her. You mustn't go round calling her awful.'

Augusta recognised that she'd made a mistake but she

370

didn't apologise for it. 'I don't know about that,' she said. 'I only know what I've been told. The whole world's turned upside down. That's the trouble. You don't know who to trust any more. Nothing's the same.'

You're right about that, Rose thought. Nothing *is* the same. We've all changed – me, Netta, Muriel, every single one of us except Mabel, poor thing. Now you've got to change too. There was a time when you could take your pick of servants, now you've got to ask me to be your housekeeper. And *I've* turned you down.

She realised that Augusta was still talking, gazing into the empty grate and sighing profoundly. 'They've never loved me,' she said. 'Cedric and Edmund and that lot. None of them. They were foul to me when we were children. The boys were so spiteful and Louella lorded it over us all the time.'

Rose wasn't sure whether she ought to be listening to all this but she was fascinated by it just the same. Fancy Miss Monk holding forth about her childhood, she thought, and to me, of all people.

'It was the money you see,' Augusta went on, still looking at the grate almost as if she'd forgotten that Rose was there. 'Louella's father was the elder brother and she was the only child and she thought they were going to inherit. And then at the last moment Grandfather changed his mind for some reason or other and he left it all to *my* father instead. There was such a row. They shouted and swore and threw things about. I can remember it to this day. I don't think they ever forgave us. But we couldn't help it, could we? It was *his* money, he could do what he liked with it. It wasn't our fault that he gave it to us.' She paused and sighed again.

Rose went on listening, because she was too embarrassed to move. She felt she was eavesdropping but she didn't know what to do about it. I never knew they were cousins, she thought. But it explained a lot. Now she could see why they were always quarrelling. She remembered Mrs Biggs saying, 'It's always money with that lot.' Money and a sense of grievance. But she didn't say anything because Augusta was in mid-complaint and now she was talking about Edmund.

'I've always thought it was because of the money that she married poor old Edmund,' Augusta brooded. 'It was one way of getting some of it back. She never loved him, poor man. Still, perhaps I'm being unkind. They were always so unkind to me, I've got into the habit. They used to cut me out of all their games. "Go and play with your dolls," Cedric would say. "Stupid girl." And Louella was always mocking, "Well we know who *won't* inherit." It was horrible. I used to run to Mummy and beg her to help me. She never did though. She was always busy with something else. She used to say "Run along." So heartless. "Run along." You don't know how awful it is to be told to run along. You stand there and you know they don't love you. It's something in the tone of voice. You can't pretend about it any more. You *know* they don't love you and you feel absolutely cold. As if you don't exist. It's a terrible feeling. Terrible. She never loved me.'

'I'm sure she did,' Rose said, feeling she had to contradict such a dreadful statement. 'All mums love their kids. It's . . .'

'No,' Augusta interrupted and her voice sounded resigned. 'My mother didn't love me. The only time she ever gave me any attention was when I was ill. They were all hateful to me when I was well but the minute I was ill they all came running. I had the top brick off the chimney then. Oh yes. A fire in my room, any toys I wanted, lovely food – jelly and ice-cream, breast of chicken, broth in its own little dish, hot bread all wrapped in a table napkin. It was lovely. Nanny used to read to me and Daddy bought me treats and even Mummy was nice to me then. "Poor little pigeon," she used to say. "I can't have my pigeon feeling poorly." The boys had to keep out in case they teased me. If I so much as *cried* when they were near me, they were sent straight to their rooms without any supper. It was *lovely!*' Her face had grown warm with the memory of it.

Rose suddenly remembered the soap in the bed and an absurd idea grew in her brain. 'Did you *like* being ill, Miss Monk?' she asked.

'Good gracious, no!' Augusta said, noticing her for the first time and aghast that such a thing should be said. 'I mean to say, *nobody* likes being ill, do they. Being in pain and having to take horrible medicine. I had to have the doctor to me only last week. I've been in agony sometimes. No, no. Of course I don't like it but . . .'

It was time to take matters in hand. Confession may be good for the soul but you have to know when to stop. 'What you need is a good housekeeper,' Rose said firmly. 'It's no good asking me. You can see that, can't you. You'll have to advertise.'

Augusta made a great effort and recovered her composure. 'Yes,' she said. 'I suppose I will. Well, thank you for coming. And for being so frank.'

'I'm sorry I couldn't help you.'

'I'll see you to the door,' Augusta said. This had been the oddest interview. She couldn't think how it had got so out of hand. Now she knew she needed to bring it to an acceptable conclusion.

Bertie was standing on the lawn talking to Mrs Taylor.

'I seen it come out the chimbley,' he called to Rose as she walked towards him. 'We seen it together, didn't we?'

'We did that, sonny,' Mrs Taylor said. 'Now I'm off to pack me brushes. Did you tell her?'

'Ain't you doing no more?' Bertie asked, his face falling.

'No. That's your lot.'

'But you've only done one,' Bertie protested. 'Why ain't you doing no more?'

'Manners!' Rose warned as she joined them.

'Because,' Mrs Taylor said, cryptically.

Bertie was just going to ask 'why because?' when there was a cough behind them and both women turned at once to see who it was.

There was a very young man approaching them along

the side path, looking at them hopefully. He wore a thirty-shilling suit and a squashed trilby, his face was covered in angry pimples, and he had a notebook in one hand, a pencil in the other and a camera slung over his shoulder.

'Mrs Taylor, chimney sweep?' he asked.

'That's me,' the sweep acknowledged. 'Can't do you till Thursday week, though sonny. I'm that booked up you wouldn't believe.'

'No, no, it's not like that,' the young man said, blushing because he'd been misunderstood. 'It's . . . I'm a reporter you see. With *The Mercury*. I'm doing a piece on valiant women.'

'Oh yes,' Mrs Taylor said dubiously.

'Women doing men's work,' the reporter explained. 'I've got a tram driver and a riveter. I wondered if you wouldn't mind . . .'

'All depends on what I've got to do,' Mrs Taylor said, frowning and rolling up her sleeves. 'Still I ain't exactly pushed for time this morning.'

He quailed a little at the sight of her beefy arms. 'Well . . . I wondered if you wouldn't mind letting me take a photograph and sort of writing something about you. How you came to be a sweep in the first place, for example.'

'Didn't have no option,' Mrs Taylor told him. 'My ol' man went to the war and soot don't sweep itself.'

The reporter wrote her words down verbatim. 'And after the war?' he prompted.

'He come back full a' mustard gas.'

The young man wrinkled his face with concern. 'I see,' he said. 'So you sort of carried on.'

'That's about the size of it.'

'Could you tell me how you feel about being a sweep? What the job's like and that sort of thing?'

'It's a rotten job,' Mrs Taylor said. 'Bloody hard work, filthy dirty, don't pay well.' And when the young man winced. 'Was that what you wanted?'

'Well sort of. Could I take a quick pic d'you think? Standing by the cart. And then ask a few more questions after?'

It took quite a long time to arrange Mrs Taylor to his satisfaction. Bertie watched it all with immense interest, dodging about and listening to every word that was being said. When the last 'pic' had been taken, he pulled at the reporter's sleeve.

'Yes sonny?' the young man said. 'What is it?'

'You know what you said.'

'What about?'

'Valiant women. You said "I'm doing a piece on valiant women." Well, my Mum's a valiant woman and so's my Aunty Netta.'

'Is that right?'

'My mum runs a firm,' Bertie said earnestly. 'And my Aunty Netta drives the delivery van. She's ever so valiant. You ought to take a pic of her.'

'I might at that,' the reporter said and he turned to Rose. 'Would it be agreeable?'

'You'd have to come to our workshop,' Rose said. 'I ain't got time for anything now. Ritzy Clothes in Old Farm Street.'

'Big place, down the end,' the reporter said, plainly impressed. 'I know it. And you run it, you say? Would you and the van driver be there this afternoon by any chance?'

'Off and on,' Rose said. 'You can take my picture if you like, but Netta might have different ideas. She's just as likely to send you packing. I ought to warn you.'

'I'll take my chance of that,' the reporter said. 'I'm used to being sent packing.'

But when he turned up at the workshop that afternoon, Netta was delighted. 'Good luck to you, mate,' she said. 'High time people knew what sort of work we women was capable of.'

'Could I have a picture of you standing by the van?' the reporter asked.

'Why not in it?'

'I wouldn't see enough of you in it,' he explained. 'It 'ud be better standing beside it.'

So she posed beside the bonnet of the van, wearing her Australian hat and her leather coat and looking very dashing.

'One more,' the reporter said.

And José walked into the yard. 'What you doing?' he bristled.

Netta explained. 'He's doing a piece on women doing men's jobs.'

José's eyebrows went down at once. 'Is my job too,' he said. 'She's not the only one.'

'This is my husband,' Netta explained. 'He drives the van an' all.'

'Okay Squire,' the reporter said. 'Stand beside your wife an' I'll put you in the picture.'

Which he did in both senses of the words, explaining his article on valiant women while he took two more photographs. By the second shot, José had been sufficiently placated to stand with his arm round Netta's waist. So all was well that ended well.

'And now,' Rose said, when the newspaper man had packed up his notebook and left them and José had gone whistling back to the workshop, 'perhaps we can get on with our petticoats.'

'What a lark!' Mabel said. 'You an' Netta having your pictures took. He took ever such a lot of pictures, didn't he? Ever such a lot. I liked it when that box went click. It made me jump. Will you be in the paper our Rose? Will you? I'll bet you'll be in the paper. You ought to write to our Muriel and tell her all about it. She'd like to see you in the paper.'

'Yes,' Rose said. 'That's a good idea.' So much had happened that day, there was plenty to write about and a letter full of news might be just the thing to break the ice.

So, after a rather shorter version had been composed to tell Henry what had happened, it was written that night, at length and with undeniable affection. *'Dear Muriel, I've had such a day you'd never believe it. A day and a half. I hardly know where to begin . . .'*

It's a good letter, she thought when it was done. She ought to write back to all that – especially the stuff about Miss Monk. Oh Mu! she yearned. I do so want to see you again. It's awful to be still quarrelling.

But there was no answer. Wednesday and Thursday brought nothing but bills and renewed orders and on Friday there were no letters at all. The long silence felt like a rejection and rejection was worse than the quarrel.

I can't let this go on, Rose thought. And just before she left for Manchester that Friday afternoon she sat down and wrote another letter, shorter and straight from the heart.

'Dear Muriel,
I'm sorry if I upset you when we had that silly row. It wasn't intentional. Please write back. We all miss you so much.
Your ever loving friend,
Rose.'

It was safely delivered, like the first, but Muriel wasn't at home to read either of them. She and Edmund were in Florence, on what Edmund called their 'unofficial honeymoon'.

CHAPTER THIRTY-ONE

The city of Florence lay in its valley between the hills in a haze of September sunshine. From their vantage point in the Boboli gardens, Edmund and Muriel could see it all, the huddle of rooftops, their tiles tawny in the filtered light, the great cupola of the Duomo, pink and white against the blue distance of those wooded hills, the Palazzo Vecchio like an elaborate sandcastle, its minaret rising so high that the tip was silhouetted against the lavender of the sky. As they watched, a flock of pigeons rose with a clatter and flew in a wide parabola around the dome, patterning the sky with wings.

'Exquisite!' Edmund said. 'If I were a landscape artist, this is what I would paint. Over and over again. In all its moods.'

Muriel stood beside him, enjoying the scene as well as she could, but her mind was filled with thoughts of Rose. In a place as beautiful as this, it seemed awful that they should be quarrelling. And she supposed they *were* still quarrelling although there were times when she didn't know what to think about anything. It felt unreal to her to be in a foreign city, unreal to be with Edmund, unreal to be accepted as his wife wherever they went, and although her days were full of sunlit wonders, her nights were plagued by bad dreams. Even after the most tender love-making she woke in the small hours weeping with terror. Last night it had taken him more than an hour to comfort her and they'd both come down to breakfast pale with fatigue.

Now, admiring the view, he was perfectly recovered. 'This is the way life should be,' he said, still gazing at the city. 'Two people on their own together, surrounded by great works of art, with no one to interfere. Let the world go hang, eh, my *orpheline*.'

'Yes,' she said, although she didn't agree with him. The world would still be there waiting for them when they got back to London. The world and her quarrel with Rose. The world and his quarrel with Louella. They were taking time off, that was all. But he was too dear to her now, his tenderness at night too precious, to allow any argument between them. For all her doubts and however much she was missing her friend, she knew it was good to be with him in this beautiful place and to be loved and cared for.

He had turned to look at her, a quizzical expression on his long face. 'Penny for your thoughts?' he asked.

'I was thinking of Rose,' she confessed. 'Wondering how I could put things right.'

Her puckered forehead roused his sympathy. 'You can't let the world go hang, can you my dear?'

'No. I'm sorry. I can't.'

'Send her a postcard,' he suggested.

'Not from here,' she said. 'It would be too casual.'

'Then write to her when you get home.'

'But would she answer?'

'You won't know if you don't try.'

She returned her attention to the scene below them and, encouraged by his sympathy, asked a more intimate question than she'd dared so far. 'Do you ever think of Louella?'

He smiled at her lazily. 'Not now I'm with you. Why do you ask?'

'No particular reason,' she said, smiling back. 'I just wondered.'

'There's nothing left to think about Louella,' he said. 'I think about you now. And all the great works of art we're going to see together. For example, tomorrow we're going to visit the Uffizi.'

She could see from his face that it was important. 'What's that?'

379

'That, my charming ignoramus,' he said happily, 'is what I'm going to show you.'

Dear Edmund, she thought as she took his arm. Despite everything, we *are* right for each other, we can be happy together.

For the first few days of her new life in Little Venice Louella Monk was happy too. Welcomed with kisses and champagne, praised for her courage, fed on steak and salmon, taken amorously into Fancy's tiger-skin bed to be given more pleasure in a night than Edmund had managed in a marriage, she felt she was the heroine of the hour.

Unfortunately, such heated passions burn themselves out by their very nature. After two weeks, the glory began to fade. However charming the view from their sitting-room window – and the canal was very charming with its colourful long boats and all those overhanging willows – the room itself was squalid. Without servants to remove them, dirty coffee cups remained for days where they were hidden and were then impossibly difficult to clean, the carpet hadn't been swept for weeks, the kitchen was so untidy she never knew where anything was, the sheets needed changing. But worst of all, she discovered that her beloved Fancy was fickle and promiscuous.

The first time she dismissed Louella to the spare room and took one of her hopefuls to bed in her place, Louella spent the night in tears. The bed was uncomfortable, the room cold, the night never-ending. She even thought kindly of Edmund and wondered how he was managing without her. He'd never written to her and she'd half hoped he might. It would have been pleasant to be begged to return. Not that she'd have gone. Even in her present misery she knew *that*. But it would have restored her ego to be able to think about it.

At breakfast the next morning, Fancy was her loving self and insisted on Louella's return to the tiger-skin that night, but damage had been done. Louella refused all her advances, saying she was tired, and the next morning she took a small revenge by announcing that she would like to decorate her 'new room'.

'It could be very charming,' she said, 'with the right treatment. Like most people I know.'

'You must do as you please, my darling,' Fancy said carelessly. 'It will have to come out of your pocket, of course. I'm a bit skint at the moment.'

By the end of that first fortnight together it was plain to Louella that she had embarked upon a lifestyle that would contain disappointment as well as pleasure. She realised from telephone calls and the stacks of letters that kept arriving that Fancy's lovers were many and varied and of both sexes. And even though the two she favoured during that fortnight stayed for only one night, they were a threat to Louella's peace of mind. In fact, if it hadn't been for the skip, there were times when she could have been quite unhappy.

She found it in a corner of the studio, where it was being used as an extra seat by one of the hopefuls, and as the lid was awkwardly shut, she opened it to put things right and discovered that it was full of sumptuous costumes – gypsy dresses in bold bright colours, Elizabethan gowns with padded bodices and huge embroidered skirts, Victorian crinolines with horsehair petticoats, Edwardian dresses with elaborate bustles, Pre-Raphaelite draperies that could have stepped straight out of a Burne-Jones painting. They were very smelly because nobody had ever bothered to wash them, but they looked magnificent.

That Tuesday evening she offered to model for the hopefuls in any dress they cared to choose. They found a Pre-Raphaelite gown in lilac and three shades of blue and matched it with two delicately patterned chiffon scarves, one to bind round her hair to disguise its lack of length, the other to wear as a loose belt. Then they arranged her on the *chaise-longue*.

Her modelling début was a great success and did wonders for her self-esteem. She felt reinstated, sure that the delicacy of the gown set off her vulnerability to perfection. And presently the conversation took her into the most pleasurable fantasy.

The two newest recruits were extolling the virtues of the artistic life. 'You have to suffer to understand,' the younger of the two said thoughtfully. 'Art is tempered by anguish.' He was an exceptionally hirsute young man with thick brown hair and a full and shaggy beard. There were even dark hairs on his forearms. But his eyes were small and earnest, peering from the thicket of his face.

'That is true in my life,' she told him. And when he looked up at her with respectful interest, she elaborated, moving effortlessly and deliberately into fantasy. 'I was an unloved child.'

'I could tell it,' the young hopeful said. 'You have the air. Were you very badly treated?'

'Yes,' she said, letting the fantasy flower. 'I'm afraid I was.' And sighed again.

'Could you bear to tell us?' the youngest hopeful urged.

'I'll try,' she said, assuming her most reluctant air.

He waited, brush in hand. It was wonderfully enhancing to be the focus of such masculine admiration.

'It was all to do with money,' she told him, gazing back into the past. 'I should have been an heiress, you see. But my uncle cheated me out of it.'

It was the stuff of fairy tale, a tender heroine, a wicked uncle, a room full of ardent princes. 'My grandfather was a rich man,' she sighed, 'although you wouldn't think it to look at me. But he was. Very, very rich. He had a farm in East Anglia where he raised beef cattle for Smithfields, and a tannery by the Thames and two beautiful houses, one in London, as you would expect. My father was the elder son so naturally we all expected him to inherit. But no.' She stopped and turned to smile soulfully at her enraptured audience. 'It was not to be.'

'What happened?' the youngest hopeful asked.

'Treachery happened,' she told him. 'Darkest and most doleful treachery.' Oh she *was* enjoying herself. 'My uncle inveigled himself into my grandfather's favour as the old man lay dying. God alone knows what lies he told, but lies they most certainly were. It took two days, that's all, two days to push us out of our inheritance and have grandfather's will changed in his favour. I have never forgotten it and I shall never forgive it.'

'And were you poor?' the youngest hopeful asked.

'Desperately.'

'That's the most dreadful story I've ever heard,' the young man said.

Rain was pattering against the window. Louella could hear the fire flickering and the gas light giving an occasional plop. How soothing sounds can be, she thought, as she let her mind drift back to her fantasy world. Soothing and uplifting somehow. Like being the centre of attention.

In Henry Philip's elegant dining-room in Fallowfields, the conversation round the table was so full of nuances that nobody noticed the weather.

Henry had chosen his dinner guests after the most careful consideration. It would assist his courtship if these six people were to signal their approval and, even if they didn't, he owed it to their long friendship to let them guess his intentions. So far, things were going well. His brother Geoffrey had taken to Rose as soon as they were introduced and so had his sister-in-law as far as he could tell – but he wasn't sure about the others yet. Margaret's brother Timothy was bound to be a bit difficult and so was his wife Clara because she and Margaret had been very close; and old Johnnie Smethwick – his oldest friend and the cotton manufacturer whose presence he'd promised – was a wily customer who always played his cards very close to his chest and wouldn't allow his wife to express an opinion until he'd done so himself.

Fortunately Rose was handling the meal as easily as if she'd been the mistress of the house for years. She sat at the centre of the table between Geoffrey and old Johnnie and divided her attention between the two of them without allowing either to feel neglected. She even took time to look across the table and talk to Timothy and his wife now and then. Henry watched her with admiration. If she was aware that she was on trial, she gave no outward sign of it.

He was wrong of course. Although she had hidden her misgivings under a deliberately calm expression, she knew very well that this was no ordinary meal. Henry had given the game away right from the start when he introduced her to his brother-in-law – and smoothed his moustache with his forefinger. She knew him well enough by now to read the signs and that little gesture was an indication that he was worried about something. It didn't take much intelligence to work out what it was nor to realise what was going on. The knowledge worried her but now that she was in the middle of the situation, she felt she had to make the best of it.

'She's given you the go-ahead I hear!' Johnnie Smethwick said, leaning towards his host. 'The new designs have passed muster.'

'I'm relieved to say,' Henry agreed, smiling at Rose in a conspiratorial way. 'A1 seal of approval.'

'But will there be the market for them?' Clara said, responding to the smile with some acidity. 'That's what I want to know. After all it *is* artificial and who's going to buy artificial silk when they can get the real thing?'

'It's not whether they can *get* the real thing,' Henry told her, 'but whether they can *afford* it. It's a different market.'

'I take your point, me dear,' Johnnie Smethwick boomed at Clara. He was a large man with a plump face and a barrel chest and his voice fitted his appearance. 'Will the lower classes want to buy silk of any kind, real or artificial? That's your point, isn't it me dear. Cotton we know about, that's why I've stuck with it, but silk's a different commodity altogether.'

'Would they know the value of it?' Clara went on,

addressing her remarks to Rose like a challenge. 'Because if you ask me it would simply be casting pearls before swine. Poor people do smell so and they never wash their clothes. You've only got to walk past them to notice that. What *would* be the point of clothing them in silk?'

'Quite right,' Johnnie said. 'Casting pearls before swine eh. Very true.' And he turned to Rose too. 'What do you think, me dear?'

Henry smoothed his moustache again, once, twice, his face guarded. They were on dangerous ground, as he'd known they would be sooner or later. He glanced at Rose to see how she was taking it and was relieved that her face was as serene as a Madonna's.

'I think it's to do with taps,' she said.

They were surprised and amused. Even Clara smiled slightly even though she'd been hoping for an argument.

'What is, Mrs Jeary?' Timothy asked.

'Poverty,' she told him calmly. 'It's a matter of how many taps there are in a house.'

'You've got me there,' Johnnie Smethwick said, beaming at her. 'You'll have to explain, I'm afraid. I was never much good at riddles. Even at school. Henry will tell you.'

'When I stay in this house,' Rose said, looking round at them, because they were all listening to her now, 'I can wash in warm water whenever I want to. Or take a bath. There are four taps in the bathroom and a geyser for hot water. And there are three more taps downstairs, in the kitchen, the butler's pantry and the flower room, *and* a range for hot water. That's seven taps and two water heaters for one house and the people who live in it.'

'Right!' Johnnie agreed. 'With you so far.'

'When I was little, I lived in two rooms in a big house in Kennington. That was all my mum and dad could afford, you see. There were five of us kids and he earned about twenty shillings a week. So there wasn't much money for soap, or anything else for that matter. But the real problem was taps. There were six families in that house –

385

must've been about twenty or thirty people – and there was only one tap. Right down in the basement. You had to go downstairs of a morning and stand in line and wait your turn to run a bucket of water and then you had to lug it upstairs – and a right weight it was, I can tell you – and that was all the water you got that day. You had to eke it out, for cooking, tea, washing, everything. And when it was all used up you had to carry the slops downstairs and empty them in the outdoor privy.'

'My dear,' Clara said. 'How frightful!' And she looked askance at Henry. Fancy him taking up with a woman from a background like that. Poor old Henry.

'You're right about clothes too,' Rose said, speaking directly to Clara because she'd understood that glance. 'Our's *did* smell but not for want of washing. Our mum washed the clothes every week. We took it in turns to use the copper. But it all had to be dried in our rooms, you see. There was only a yard out the back and the family on the ground floor had that. So it dried on the fireguard and over the backs of chairs and it took the smell of the cooking.'

'You mean you cooked in one of your rooms?' Timothy asked.

'We did everything in one or the other, ate, slept, washed, cooked, played games, read books, dried clothes. That was how it was. And we always smelt stale. And we always hated it. I remember once, me and my sister Mabel was outside a hotel when a rich lady walked in. She went right past us, as near as I am to you, and the smell of her was lovely, all scented soap and new cloth and perfume. We stood there on the pavement breathing it in. And we both said, "When I'm grown up, that's how I'm going to smell." ' She paused and smiled round the table at their stunned faces, relishing what she was going to tell them next. 'Actually, my sister Mabel *washes* in perfume now.'

'In lavender water you mean,' Clara corrected, her face all disbelief. 'Or eau-de-Cologne.'

386

'No,' Rose said. 'In perfume. From Paris. It was the real McCoy, wasn't it Henry?'

'Oh yes,' he laughed, giving her that conspiratorial look again. 'Expensive stuff.'

The intimacy of their exchange made Clara flush with annoyance. It was evidence – if any were really needed – of how far this relationship had already gone and she wasn't at all sure she approved of it.

'What a magnificent story,' she said, sourly. 'How clever you are my dear. You should write a book.'

The other women followed her lead. 'Yes, yes,' they said. 'Wonderful story. You had us spell-bound.'

Which means they don't believe me, Rose thought. They think I'm making it up. 'Henry's taking me to the theatre tomorrow afternoon,' she said, deftly turning the conversation to a safer topic. 'It's a play by Bernard Shaw. They say it's very good. Have any of you seen it?'

The three men hastened to give her their opinion of the play, and the moment passed. And Henry realised he was feeling relieved.

'A great success,' he said, when their guests had finally departed. 'You made a real hit with my brother. He was eating out of your hand.'

She took it for the compliment it was, knowing that, despite her outspokenness, or perhaps because of it, the meal had been a triumph. 'Thank you,' she said. And teased, 'I gather I passed muster.'

'Is that what it felt like?'

'Most of the time, yes.'

'It didn't occur to you that I might be testing *them*?'

'Were you?'

He didn't answer that but asked, 'What did you think of them?'

She looked at him, wondering how honest her opinion could be and he caught the look and reassured her, 'I should really like to know.'

'I like your brother,' she said, beginning positively. 'His

wife's a bit on the shy side but she seems nice as far as I could tell.'

'And Johnnie Smethwick?'

'He's shrewd,' she said. 'Don't miss a trick. All that booming's just to put you off. He's not so green as he's cabbage looking.'

Her assessment made him laugh out loud. 'You've got him bang to rights there,' he laughed, admiring her more than ever. 'And what about Clara?'

The fly in the ointment, Rose thought. 'Oh well,' she said, 'she's a snob. Probably well-meaning but a snob just the same.'

'You're a breath of fresh air,' he told her. 'That's what you are. A breath of fresh air. Come and have a night cap.' He led her out of the hall and into his study. 'I've got something to ask you.'

'Not another proposition,' she teased.

'No,' he said, picking up the brandy decanter. 'A proposal.'

Her eyes widened but she didn't say anything.

He poured two glasses, one single measure, one double. 'We work very well together,' he said. 'We understand the trade. We make a good team. I think we could make an even better one.'

'Do you?' she said, knowing what was coming.

'Yes. As husband and wife. What do *you* think?'

'I don't know,' she told him. 'An' that's the honest truth.'

He hadn't expected a rapturous assent but her uncertainty was a disappointment even so. Still, a decision like this had to be thought about and she was too sensible to say something if she didn't mean it. He nodded her towards an armchair and waited until they were both comfortably seated.

'Let me tell you what I've been thinking,' he said. 'We already share a great deal, isn't that right. We like one another. We trust one another. We enjoy one another's company. Why not take the next step? I could offer you a very good life here. Fallowfields is a pleasant place, near the town and with countryside at the end of the road. If you were to transfer your business to Manchester – I could find you a good site – I guarantee you could double your turnover in a year.'

Encouraged by good food and brandy, she felt that wasn't just possible but likely. 'Yes,' she said. 'I daresay I could. But what about Bertie and Mabel?'

'They would come with you, naturally. We could hire a nurse to look after Mabel. Or a nurse-companion. And it could be the making of your Bertie. You think how he'd get on in a really good school. He's a bright lad.'

That's true, Rose thought. It was the first time she'd considered the possibility of Bertie being sent to a good school and it was a great temptation. But she didn't say anything.

'I'm not going to rush you for an answer,' Henry said, finishing his brandy. 'I just thought I ought to put my cards on the table. Seemed the fairest thing to do in the circumstances. Especially as I've got a little present for you.'

It was a jewelled brooch in the shape of a butterfly, with a body made of turquoises, ruby eyes and wings set with opals, lying in its original box and obviously treasured and old.

She looked up at him, her forehead creased with the anxiety of being offered such a thing. 'It's gorgeous,' she said. 'But I can't take it. It wouldn't be right.'

'It belonged to my mother,' he said. 'It was the one thing I never handed on to Margaret. I want you to have it.'

'I should've said something when you sent me that perfume,' she said. 'I knew I should. I can't take presents from you Henry. Not when . . . It don't look good. It ain't . . . Well, it puts me in a difficult position.'

'You're in exactly the same position you've always been in,' he said. 'It doesn't matter what your answer's going to be. This is all perfectly proper. I'm offering you a present, that's all. If you like it, take it. It's hardly something I can wear, now is it?'

'Yes, but . . .'

'No buts. If your answer's yes, you can take it as a preliminary engagement present. If it's no, it can be a gift from a business man who admires your business capacity.' And, he thought, would love you if he could.

She took the box in her hand, feeling the pressure of his generosity. 'In that case, thank you very much,' she said. 'But I don't deserve it.'

'You do in my eyes. I'd give you the moon if I could.'

'That 'ud be a bit heavy to wear,' she laughed, glad of the chance to joke.

He raised his glass to her and smiled. 'May this be the first gift of many,' he said. And when she opened her mouth to tell him that she couldn't make up her mind yet, no matter how many presents he gave her, he forestalled her by adding, 'Sleep on what I've said. Take your time. There's no hurry. Just tell me when you're ready.'

It was only after she was in bed and had been trying to get to sleep for nearly an hour that she realised that he hadn't offered to kiss her and that she hadn't wanted him to. Not one bit. How extraordinary that he'd been so correct. He hadn't even held her hand. He'd proposed to her and he hadn't even held her hand. But his offer *was* tempting. There was no doubt about that. He was certainly giving her the taste for a better life. If she married him, she would dine well every evening, live in a fine house in a leafy suburb, be showered with pretty things and never want for anything.

I've been poor all my life, she thought, and she remembered the way she and Bertie had struggled to find the rent and feed the kids after Mum died and how they'd had to pinch and scrape when anyone needed new boots. Oh the nightmare of those boots! And half-bricks in the grate to cut down on the coal and jam bought by the spoonful and carried home on a saucer and the endless darning and patching to keep them all respectable. Now,

for the first time in her life, she was being offered a chance
to escape from all that for ever. A chance of security. And
not just for her either. Bertie would be made by it. He was
quite right about that. A good school meant a good job, a
good house, a comfortable life. It was what every mother
wanted for her child and she had the chance to hand it to
hers with a word. There were problems, of course – like
living in Fallowfields and having to transfer the business
to Manchester – but nothing in life was ever simple and
the advantages in this marriage were very obvious to her
at that moment. Maybe she owed it to Bertie to say 'yes'.
In any event it was an offer that deserved to be given very
careful consideration.

I'm twenty-nine, she thought, and if I stay in
Kennington I shall be on my own. Muriel's gone, Netta's
gone, Mabel's hard work. It'll only be me and her and
little Bertie all by ourselves with nothing to do but work.
This could have come in the nick of time for all of us.
Perhaps it was meant to be. I don't love him. Not in that
way. Not the way I loved Jack. Oh Jack! Dear Jack! If you
hadn't been killed and I'd married you, it would all have
been very, very different. But there's all sorts of
marriages. They don't all have to be the same. Perhaps
this one could work.

Sleep was beginning to wash into her mind. In the
morning, she told herself. See how I feel in the morning.
It's too much now.

But the morning brought a problem she hadn't expected.

She and Henry were finishing the meal, sitting opposite
one another at the breakfast-room table. Mindful of his
promise, he hadn't referred to their late-night conversation but was reading the newspaper and picking out the
choicest morsels with which to entertain her. He'd just
turned the page, giving the paper a little shake to neaten
it, when the telephone rang.

It surprised them both that it was for Rose.

She took the receiver from his hand, feeling a sudden
jolt of alarm.

It was Netta and she was plainly in tears. 'Can you come home our Rose?' she begged. 'I've had this letter.'

'What letter?'

'It's from some woman. She says José's her husband. He's a bigamist she says. She's coming here this afternoon to have it out with me.'

'I'll be right back,' Rose said. 'Don't you worry our Netta, I'll sort it out whatever it is.'

To his credit Henry didn't argue about her change of plan. He questioned her quickly, told her she must go back and deal with it and went to get the car ready while she was packing.

'Telephone me tonight,' he said as the train pulled out of the station. And he tried to make a joke to lighten her tension. 'And don't shoot till you see the whites of their eyes.'

'All right,' she said, but her voice was vague. In her mind she'd already left Manchester behind and was well on her way to Ritzy Street. But at the last moment she remembered to be polite. 'Thanks for everything, Henry. I do appreciate it.'

He smiled at that and waved goodbye. But she'd already pulled in her head and was out of his sight.

CHAPTER THIRTY-TWO

Netta Fernández had been standing on a chair watching out of the workshop window for most of the afternoon, anxiety and impatience making her fidget – up onto the chair and down again – a turn round the room – a prowl into the office in case the telephone was going to ring – up on the chair again. When she finally saw Rose walking into the yard, she fairly fell out of the door to greet her.

'Thank God you've come!' she said, dragging her sister into the workshop. 'I've been worried out me wits in case she got here before you.'

'You'd better show me the letter quick,' Rose said, taking off her coat and hat.

But there wasn't even time for Netta to pull the envelope out of her pocket.

'She's here!' Mabel yelled from her look-out post on the chair.

'Get down!' Rose ordered. 'Everyone to work.'

'What's she like?' Netta called as they all took up their work again.

'Fat,' Mabel said.

And fat she was, a short, stout woman with tightly permed, brown hair, mottled cheeks, a bruiser's arms and a belligerent expression. She moved in to the attack at once.

'Which one of you reckons she's Netta Fernández?'

'I am,' Netta said, squaring up to her.

'My name's Rose Jeary,' Rose said moving between them and offering the woman a hand to shake. 'If you'd just like to come into the office?'

'I'll say what I got to say right here,' the woman told them, standing her ground massively. 'And what I got to

393

say is this. If you think you're married to that man, you got another think coming.' She pulled a large buff envelope out of her massive handbag and emptied the contents onto the nearest worktop. 'Take a look at that!' she instructed. 'My wedding picture that is. November 1913. Recognise the man?'

He was a good deal younger but it was undeniably José.

'And there's me wedding lines,' the woman said, picking another paper out of the pile. 'Joe Smith, that's him. Constance Leadbetter. That was me. Connie Leadbetter I was and I been Connie Smith these past eleven years. Twelve come November. His little gel's ten. That's her picture look, sitting on her daddy's knee when she was only a little thing. Oh no, sunshine, I'm his wife. Make no doubt about that. It's all fair, square an' above board. I writ as soon as I saw the picture in the paper. I knew it was him.' And she smoothed out a copy of her local paper and glared at them both to look at it.

'Tottenham?' Rose said. 'How did it get in a Tottenham paper?'

'Don't ask me,' Connie said. 'But it's just as well it did.'

Netta was scowling at the two images. 'It's a resemblance,' she admitted. 'I'll grant you that. But that don't mean to say it's him.'

'It's him right enough,' Connie said. 'The name'ud give it away if nothink else did. Fernández. That was his mum's maiden name. Spanish she was, you see. He was always showing off about it. Thought it made him special, great daft hap'orth.'

'You're saying he wasn't born in Spain?' Rose asked.

'No! Course not. His mum was. But not Joe. He's a Londoner born and bred. They all spoke funny though, him and his sisters and his mum and his granddad. Now he *was* foreign, his granddad.'

They were all so shattered by the news that for a few seconds none of them knew what to say. Then Rose found a question.

'When d'you see him last?'

'During the war. He come home on leave just before the Somme. I thought there was summink up at the time. He was sort of fidgety like. And then he went back and he didn't write or nothink – not even one of them postcard things they used to send – and there wasn't a telegram so we knew he wasn't dead and he wasn't posted missing or nothink. And that was the last I heard. I had a devil's own job getting me widow's pension. Took for ever. I thought he must have been blowed to bits. Lots of them was. Anyway I just got on with it, like you do, and then blow me, there's this picture on the paper and all about José Fernández driving a van and all. And I thought "Hang about. I ain't having this." And here I am.'

And at that point, the van drove into the yard.

'Is this him?' Connie said.

He strode into the workshop in his cocky way, cap on the back of his head, cigarette stuck to his bottom lip, darkly handsome and very sure of himself. Even when he looked up and saw that everyone was looking at him, he was still jaunty. Then he saw Connie and his expression changed.

'Crikey!' he said, and then he swore in a mixture of Spanish and English. 'That torn it!'

'Joe Smith!' Connie said accusingly. 'What sort of a caper d'you call this?'

'I explain,' he said, backing away from her.

'You'd better. I thought you was dead.'

'Then she's right,' Netta said, stepping towards him too. 'You ain't José Fernández.'

He looked at Netta for the first time and spread out his hands to placate her. 'No. Look I sorry. If you just let me . . .'

But she pressed on. 'And we ain't legally married.'

'Well no, but I explain.'

Rose watched her sister nervously, ready for an outburst of fury, but Netta was white-faced and horribly calm. 'You're a bigamist,' she said. 'You've been living a lie all this time. You've made *me* live a lie. Me! An' I

395

never told a lie in all me life. We always tried to *live with dignity*, didn't we our Rose? How *dare* you do this to me!'

'It not how you think,' he said, his face wrinkled with distress.

'What's up?' a slow voice said from the door. 'You all right Mrs Jeary?' Mr Thomas had come to see if a rescue was necessary.

His arrival had a calming effect on everybody in the room. Work began again, Rose relaxed, Netta stopped glaring.

'We're all going into the office,' Rose explained to him. 'Could you bring us three more chairs, please Mr Thomas.'

'Seems to me,' Connie said to her errant husband, when the three extra chairs had been crowded into the office and they were all sitting down, 'you got a lot of explaining to do.'

José had shrunk into his chair and seemed to have been struck dumb.

'Start with why you never wrote to us,' Connie suggested.

That provoked a growling answer. 'Because I couldn't.'

'Why not? You can still write can'tcher?'

'I'd ha' been arrested.'

'Oh for crying out loud! For writing a letter? I never heard such rubbish.'

'All right then,' he said, his voice suddenly vicious. 'I was deserter, if you must know. If you deserter, they arrest you and then you shot.'

That was such a surprise it stopped them all in their tracks. Rose was very upset. Our Bertie and Col get killed, she thought bitterly, and my Jack's gone for ever and *he* runs away and gets away with it. Where's the justice in that?

Netta was scowling, lost in her own miserable thoughts. I trusted him, she brooded. I believed what he said. I *loved* him. And all the time he was nothing but a deserter. A rotten deserter, leaving his mates and saving his own rotten skin.

396

'You could have come back and told us,' Connie told him scathingly. 'Fine sort a' man you were, leaving us in the lurch.'

'No,' he said angrily. 'Is not possible. I'd ha' been pick up on the doorstep. That the first place they came searching.'

Mr Thomas had been standing by the office door, just in case Mrs Jeary wanted him to run any more errands or if things got nasty. Now, and most unexpectedly, he joined in. 'That's a fact,' he said. 'None of 'em never went home. Not if they had any sense. They'd've been a sitting target – marched off and shot and no questions asked.'

Netta was so angry she was callous. 'An' serve 'em right. They shouldn't've run away.'

'They was all shot,' Mr Thomas said, sadly pursuing his own thoughts. 'All the ones they caught, poor beggars.'

'Picked up, marched off and shot,' José confirmed. 'Once I ran, no going back. That was it.'

'Then you shouldn't've run,' Connie said, agreeing with Netta. 'You should've stayed where you was and fought it out like all the others. I never thought you'd end up a coward.'

'You don' know what it like,' José said with weary bitterness. 'If you been there, you wouldn't talk such rot.'

'To run away!' Connie said disparagingly. 'What a thing to have to tell your kids! You was yeller-bellied.'

His weariness suddenly broke into a terrible anger. 'All right! All right!' he yelled at her. 'So I ran away. I admit. I ran away! You'd ha' done same thing. I tell you for why. Because you couldn't stand it no more.'

'He's right,' Mr Thomas said, speaking with an intensity they'd never seen in him before. 'Nobody back home never knew the half of it. Terrible it was. Never stopped, you see. Went on day after day, hour in, hour out, men being shot, men being blown to bits, men out in no man's land screaming in agony, dying by inches, poor beggars, and you couldn't get to them. The mud was all right. We could manage the mud. And the rats. You could

397

shoot the rats. And the lice. You could burn *them* out with matches and candle ends. It was the dead, you see. The stink of dead bodies all day and every day.'

Rose and Netta listened to him in horror, astounded to think that their cheerful Mr Thomas had seen such dreadful things and never said a word about it until that moment.

'All bloated up they was,' José remembered. 'They use to turn green, the bodies. Then the rats come an' they made nests in their bellies and they run in and out.' It was making him shudder to remember. 'The dead was what it was, all the dead. And you know you the next one to die and nobody can't stop it.'

'There was nothink you could do about it, you see,' Mr Thomas explained. 'You just had to take it, sort a' thing. One a' my mates was blown to bits right next to me. Joints a' meat he was. I'll never forget it as long as I live. That's all any of us was, really. Joints a' meat, running over the top, waiting to be slaughtered.'

'I took it long as I could,' José pleaded. 'Honest Connie. Honest Netta. It just . . . one day I couldn't take it no more. So I run. If that was yeller-bellied, we all yeller-bellied. Every single one.' And he put his head in his hands and began to cry, long terrible sobs that shook every woman in the room to pity.

Netta and Connie ran to him, both moving at the same time, knelt on either side of him, caught hold of his hands, rubbed his bent head, did what they could to comfort him. The horror he'd just re-lived had dissolved their emotions into irrelevance.

Rose took command. 'Pot of tea,' she said to Mr Thomas and when he'd sloped off to make it, she turned her attention to the two women. 'Stay here in the quiet,' she suggested. 'You'll be better here. I'll go and see to things in the workshop.'

'Well who'd've thought it!' Nancy Cartwright exclaimed, when Rose had told them as much as she felt they ought to know. 'A bigamist. What'll happen now d'you think?'

Rose said she had no idea even though her head was spinning with them. But there was no point in speculating. Whatever it was it would have to be decided by the two wives.

'Makes you wonder who else'll turn up,' Marigold said.

'You mean Jack?' Rose said. The thought had occurred to her too, briefly and with a terrible bitter-sweet hope while Mr Thomas was talking. But what was the use in building up false hopes? 'No,' she said. 'If he'd have been going to turn up he'd have done it long before now. I'm afraid he's dead. I shan't ever see him again. I faced that long ago.' And now here she was with a proposal to consider. But she couldn't face up to that. Not yet. Not with all this going on.

Mr Thomas brought tea for all of them and Netta took three mugs at the door of the office and closed the door again.

Meanwhile there was work to be done. 'How's the chemises coming along?' Rose asked.

The tea was drunk, the machines began to whir again, Mr Thomas became his old cheerful self and assembled new boxes to pack the chemises in, Rose cut out the next batch of petticoats, rain began to patter against the windows. It was almost like a normal working afternoon, except for that closed office door and the fact that they worked without gossip. Minutes were sewn into hours, the dusk began to deepen until the corners of the room were lost in shadow, the gas lights were lit in a bloom of golden light to gild their busy fingers and soothe their unspoken worries. And when the last seams were being sewn and the last garments carefully packed in their tissue paper, Netta finally emerged from the office. Her eyes were red-rimmed but she was perfectly calm.

'He's going home with Connie,' she said to Rose. 'We thought that was for the best.'

'Very sensible,' Rose approved. 'We was just packing up. Does he want to wait till we're all gone?'

'I think he'd rather,' Netta said. 'I'll lock up.'

So they all went home and left the final moments of the drama to its three participants.

'What d'you think she'll do, our Rose?' Mabel wondered, as she and Bertie were setting the cloth for tea.

'Come here if she's got any sense,' Rose hoped.

She arrived just as the kettle boiled. And she arrived in floods of tears. 'Oh Rose,' she wept, falling into her sister's protective arms. 'Why did he have to go and do a thing like this? Why couldn't he have been honest with me? I'd've kept it a secret if he'd said. It's so cruel. What did I ever do to him? It ain't fair.'

She was beyond reason and almost beyond self-control, as Rose could understand. She needed creature comforts, to be petted and loved and hugged.

'Never you mind, our Netta,' Mabel told her solemnly. 'You've always got us, ain'tcher. Me and Rose and our Bertie.'

'Yes,' Netta sobbed. 'I know. But it ain't fair. It just ain't fair.'

It took them until past midnight to comfort her into a fit state to settle to sleep and even then she was still so weepy that they moved Muriel's bed into Mabel's room for her so that she would have company during the night. And Rose retired to her own room to write to Henry.

It was a long letter and as informative as she could make it without blackening any characters. '*I had to feel sorry for him,*' she wrote. '*It must have been awful in the trenches. We can't begin to know the half of what they had to endure.*' Then she tried to give him what answer she could. '*I haven't had time to think about your proposition. There's been too much else going on. I haven't talked to the others about it either. I'm sorry. I shall have to take my time over it. Netta is in such a state. I wouldn't like her to think I was running out on her just when she needs me most.*'

The next morning Netta was quiet but back in control of her life. That afternoon, as it was Sunday and they didn't have to go to work, she moved back into Ritzy Street.

'One good thing about being poor,' she said

philosophically as she unloaded what she called her 'bits and bobs' from the barrow. 'If you ain't got much, it don't take long to move house. The gas cooker's coming tomorrow.'

'I got your room all nice and warm for you,' Mabel said. 'I've had a fire going since dinner time.'

'She did it special,' Rose said.

'So here we are again,' Netta said as they took their customary places round the table for tea. 'Women without men. We never said a truer word than that.' She was much more cheerful. Leaving the flat had made her feel she was leaving her marriage and part of her life but being back in Ritzy Street with all her belongings around her was simply coming home.

Mabel didn't answer because she was thinking about the fire and wondering whether she ought to go upstairs and make it up, and Rose was quiet too, because she was thinking of Muriel and wondering whether they would ever patch up their quarrel. Fortunately Bertie filled the silence with one of his practical questions.

'Now you've come home, Aunty Netta, will you help me with my sums?' he wanted to know.

'What sort a' sums?' Netta said cheerfully.

'Short division.'

'Very fitting,' Netta said, giving Rose a wry grin. 'That's just about what it was – a short division. Go an' get your book then, sunshine, and we'll see what's what.'

They'd hardly got the book open when there was a knock at the door.

'Drat!' Netta said. 'You go, our Mabel. We got sums to attend to.'

So Mabel went and was back again so quickly that the door had scarcely shut behind her before she was pushing it open again. She was giggling and chattering and pink in the face because she was holding Edmund Monk and their own dear Muriel by the hand.

'Look who's come!' she shouted. 'Ain't it grand our Rose. Look who I got! Now we're all together again. Look who's come!'

They looked, their eyes bolting with delight and disbelief. But it *was* Mu, right enough, wearing a new beige suit they hadn't seen before and one of Ritzy's floral blouses. And ain't that just typical of her, Rose thought. Dear Mu.

'We've just got back,' Muriel explained as she was dragged into the room. 'Your letters were on the hall-stand waiting for us. We came straight over. I hope you don't mind . . .'

'Mind?' Rose said, her face transformed with smiles. 'Oh Mu! It's *lovely* to see you. I'm so glad. Don't you look well! Where've you been?'

Then what kisses there were and what squeals of delight. Muriel was hugged by all three women at once and kissed until her hat fell off. Mabel danced round the room, kicking her legs in the air. Edmund stood in the midst of it all, caught up in their happiness and smiling so much and so broadly he felt his jaw would crack. And when the first delights had calmed a little, Rose made a fresh pot of tea and they all sat round the table to drink it as they caught up on the news.

There was such a lot of it. Netta described José's bigamy and his wife's visit, Muriel had told them about her holiday in Florence, Edmund made an entertaining story out of Augusta's attempt to bully them, and Rose mentioned, rather shyly, that Henry had asked her to marry him.

'He asked me Friday night,' she said, 'and then Saturday morning I had to rush away before I could give him an answer. It's all been a bit sudden.'

Muriel and Netta raised eyebrows at one another and Muriel looked a question across at her old friend but, catching Netta's warning grimace, didn't ask it. Oh surely not, she hoped. Not when we're all together again. And then she felt she was being selfish even to think such things. If she could set up house with Edmund, Rose had the right to marry Henry if she wanted to. *If* she wanted to. And none of them should be surprised. They'd seen it coming. 'How are things at work?' she asked, tactfully changing the subject.

'First-rate,' Netta grinned. 'Except for the accounts. They're in a bit of a muddle.'

'Who's doing them?'

'I am,' Rose said, grinning ruefully. 'That's why they're in a bit of a muddle.'

'I presume you used to do them,' Edmund said to Muriel, reading her expression accurately.

'Brilliant she was,' Netta praised. 'Never out, not by so much as a penny. I don't know how she done it.'

He smiled his nice, wry smile. 'Then perhaps she ought to do them for you again.'

'You wouldn't mind?' Muriel asked.

'I go to work all week,' he said. 'Why shouldn't you?'

'Well it would be nice,' Muriel admitted.

'Never mind *nice*,' Netta said. 'It'ud be brilliant.'

'Tomorrow?' Mabel hoped. 'Say you'll come tomorrow our Muriel. I could get a cake for elevenses.'

'That ain't fair,' Bertie complained. 'I shall be at school.'

'We'll bring you a bit home, sunshine,' Netta promised. 'Won't we Mu?'

'Oh!' Muriel said. 'It's so good to be back.' And when Edmund pretended to protest, she said, 'You know what I mean.' And he admitted that he did.

It was so good that none of them wanted the evening to end. Bertie was allowed to sit up till nine and Edmund and Muriel didn't get back to Chelsea until long after midnight. But she was up and dressed at seven the next morning so as not to be late for work and, true to form, she was the first to arrive at the workshop.

It was a day pulsing with activity. The machines whirred non-stop and Rose took her first telephone call two minutes after she'd opened the door. Netta was in and out of the yard all day with her van and Mr Thomas' cheerful whistle seemed to be everywhere at once. Muriel sat in the office and took over the accounts. They were in such a mess she hadn't quite sorted them out by the end of the afternoon when the postman arrived with the last mail of the day.

The second letter was for Netta. She opened it as she drank her afternoon tea. It was from José and was a long, anguished apology. She read it through once, showed it briefly to Rose and Muriel and then tossed it in the waste-paper basket.

'Ain't you gonna answer it?' Rose asked.

'No. I ain't,' Netta said. 'He needn't think he's getting round *me*. He's cooked his goose and now he can live with it.'

'Don't you feel just a little bit sorry for him?' Muriel asked, sipping her tea. 'I know I do.'

'You wasn't married to him,' Netta said grimly. 'Pass me the sugar, Mabel. It ain't all it's cracked up to be you know, marriage. Oh all right for some, I daresay. Depends on the man.'

'Yes,' Muriel smiled, thinking of Bertie as well as Edmund. 'It does. Doesn't it Rose?'

'I think it would've done,' Rose said, rather sadly. 'I never really got the chance to find out though, did I?'

Now, Muriel thought, we can find out what she's going to say to Henry. And she started to form a question that wouldn't sound too probing. But Netta was still talking about José.

'He was all right some a' the time,' she said. 'He could be a right charmer when he liked. Well, you all seen that. It was different when he'd had a skinful, that was the trouble. He could be a brute then. And no, I didn't tell you, Rose. What would've been the use? Anyway, I'm out of it. Well out of it. An' we got better things to think about now. I got three new orders this afternoon.'

Rose could see that the matter was closed. Netta had put it behind her. Very well then. So would she. And at that point, as if to remind her that there was work to be done, the telephone began to ring.

It was Henry. 'I'm in a rush,' he said. 'Can you make dinner on Wednesday?'

CHAPTER THIRTY-THREE

Wednesday was an indecisive day. It began with a sudden downpour so that Rose and her workforce scuttled into Old Farm Street under umbrellas, damp, dishevelled and squealing protest. From then on, neither the weather nor their mood could be depended upon. The first rain gave way to sunshine so bright and strong that they were all quite cheered by it. Pavements and horses steamed, and work tables were spot-lit. Mabel sat in a patch of sunlight and said it was making her head 'all warm'. But just as they were enjoying the change, another stinging shower dragged darkness across the windows and cast them and their work into a gloom. And so it continued all through the morning, the afternoon and into the evening.

Netta and Muriel got on with their work as well as they could but they were suffering from indecision too and the weather made it worse. They suspected that Rose was going to give Henry his answer that evening. It seemed just a little too likely, especially as she hadn't said anything about it, so they were both taut with anxiety. They discussed it whenever she wasn't near, but they couldn't bring themselves to ask her any questions or even to throw out a hint that they'd like to talk about it – Muriel because she thought it wasn't really their business, Netta because she was afraid that Rose was going to accept.

By the time Henry arrived in Ritzy Street, Netta was irritable and it was raining again and very dark. The street lamps were lit, their yellow globes misted with rain, the gutters were awash with puddles and even the short sprint from Rose's front door to the passenger seat of Henry's Rolls Royce required the protection of his black umbrella. But as he drove across Westminster Bridge, the weather changed again. The street lights cleared within seconds, colour grew richer, sounds sharper, traffic picked up speed, and the city took on that peculiar quality of shimmering luminescence which so often followed rain.

On the north side of the river the lighted windows of the Houses of Parliament dropped swirling curls of reflected light into the black waters of the Thames, puddles were hissed into white fountains by every passing vehicle and the trams rode the Embankment in convoy, their red sides shining wet, all lights blazing, as big and bright as ocean liners in the dark sea of the street.

In ordinary circumstances, Rose would have given herself up to the enjoyment of it all but now, watching as Henry manoeuvred past two slow-moving trams, she realised that she was feeling too nervous for pleasure. They'd hardly said a word to one another since she got into the car and his unusual quietness disturbed her. It made her feel that he was steeling himself for bad news. And that made her feel guilty. She turned her head away from him to look out of the window.

They rode through Parliament Square and up White-hall where the Cenotaph gleamed like a white ghost and guards in silver helmets sat astride their steaming horses watching the traffic. They edged into the tangle of cars and buses at Trafalgar Square, past the fluted heights of Nelson's Column and the long classical frontage of the National Gallery and came at last to Piccadilly where the neon signs rolled their messages round and round – Bovril – Schweppes – and the flower sellers sat on the steps beside their wicker baskets, shawl-wrapped and black-hatted, their aprons moth-white and their mouths black Os as they called their wares. My city, Rose thought, filled with an ineffable affection for it. It seemed to her that on that night she was taking in the sense of it, vast, sprawling, cosmopolitan, complicated, but, for all that, the simple centre of things, like a great heart beating endlessly. My city.

Sitting beside her thoughtful profile, Henry tried to think of something cheerful and non-committal that he could say to break their silence. Having driven off without a word, beyond a friendly 'Okay' he had reduced himself to wordlessness and now he found their lack of conversation disquieting. From time to time he glanced at her, in an attempt to read the signs. She'd dressed as well as always and smiled at him in her usual way, which could only be to the good, but she wasn't wearing his brooch and that had to be a minus and she'd spent the entire journey looking out of the window. Never a patient man, he'd found waiting for her answer intolerable but he'd vowed to let her take her own time and he was determined to keep his word.

They drew up outside Merrystone's, were ushered into the restaurant and shown to their table by the window. They ordered their meal, chose wine, settled into their usual luxury. And still nothing important had been said.

While they had their soup, he spoke of his plans for the coming season and she told him about Netta's return and their reconciliation with Muriel and how impressed she'd been with Edmund Monk.

'I've misjudged him,' she confessed. 'I used to think he was a boring man. I couldn't understand what Muriel saw in him.'

'And now you can?'

'Yes. I think so. They're happy together.'

This is better, Henry thought, taking another bread roll with appetite and satisfaction. Now we're getting to the point and by a very good route – very positive. 'He's a lot older than her though, isn't he?' he prompted.

'Yes,' she admitted. 'It don't seem to matter though. Not when you see them together. I think it's a love match.'

'So age needn't be a barrier?'

'Well it ain't in their case.'

'And in ours?'

She took a breath before she answered. The moment

407

was coming and she had to handle it delicately. 'I've never seen it as a barrier. No. I suppose being in the same trade makes a difference. Traders being all ages, I mean. Age doesn't matter in trade, does it? I mean, it's experience that counts.'

'I've got the advantage though, haven't I?' he said, smiling at her across the table. 'Your youth to my age.'

It was a challenge and they both knew it but as luck would have it she didn't have to answer him at once because the waiter had arrived to serve the main course. She gave her attention to the food, keeping her expression calm but thinking hard. He's got such a strong face, she thought, looking at him as he was being served. You can see he's used to taking decisions, a tough, dependable, determined face. And she realised that part of her present nervousness was due to the fact that she didn't really know how he would react to what she was going to tell him. Until this moment their intimacy had been restricted to shared meals, visits to the theatre and the factory, one dinner party and the trade they shared. She'd never seen him in a temper or feeling low or playing the fool or stupid with happiness. In fact, if the truth were told, she hardly knew anything about him.

'So what do you say?' he asked, as he cut into his steak. He was secretly annoyed that they'd been interrupted at such a critical moment in their conversation but he was in such perfect control that he gave no sign of what he was feeling.

She put down her knife and fork and wiped her lips with the table napkin. 'Can I ask you something, Henry?' she said.

'Of course,' he said, smiling to encourage her. Now they would get to the point. Now she would tell him one way or the other. And the signs *were* good, even though she wasn't wearing the brooch.

'Do you believe in God?'

The question was such a surprise that it made him blink.

But he answered her honestly. 'I suppose so. I haven't really given it much thought. Why do you ask?'

She picked up her fork again and turned it between finger and thumb, not looking at him. 'When I was little,' she said, 'I used to think God was like some sort of judge, sitting up in the sky somewhere. A grand old man with a white beard.'

He smiled at that. 'It sounds familiar.'

'But always fair. A just God. I used to think if you prayed every day, He'd look after you, see you was all right, protect you, sort a' thing. I used to make bargains with Him.'

He couldn't see where this conversation was leading but he let it ride. 'Did He keep them?'

'Not that I can remember. He might have done over little things but not when it came to the big ones. Not when it came to death. He let my dad die – long before his time – and then Mum. He let them kill both my brothers in the war. And Jack. You can't feel the same about a God who does that, can you?'

'No,' he said, a little stunned to find them discussing such a serious topic. 'I suppose not.'

'You must've been angry with Him when your Margaret died?'

Ah! he thought. So that's what we're talking about. 'No. I can't say I was. I was upset, naturally. Took me a long time to get over it. Years. But anyway her death was different. It had been coming a long time. It was a happy release really. A kindness, if that's not too strong a word. She was in a lot of pain, you see, and she was never going to get better and I couldn't bear to see her suffering.'

She was touched by how tender he was. That was a side of him she hadn't seen before. 'The thing is,' she said. 'I suppose what I'm saying is, I've changed. I don't think about God in the same way. I don't make bargains with Him now. I don't think you *can* make bargains with Him. I ain't the same as I was when I was young. I've had to change. The war changed me for a start. But I've changed my mind about all sorts of things. I've had to stand on my own feet for too long.'

He knew what was coming now but he decided it would be better not to question her. What was going to be said would be said. Let her give her answer and then he would see how to argue against it.

'For example, I used to think I'd grow up and get married the same as my mum and dad. Because everyone did. It was the way life was. But it ain't now, is it. Not since the war. Look at all the spinsters there are. Unmarried women. Left on the shelf because their men were killed.'

'And you want to be one of them? I can't believe that.'

'I *am* one of them.'

'But you needn't be. You've only to say the word.'

She put the fork down and looked across the table at him, her face serious. She looked more beautiful than he'd ever seen her, her grey eyes full of concern. 'I'm sorry Henry,' she said. 'I am really. Ever so sorry. But the war's changed everything, don't you see. How I think. How I feel. How I want to live my life. Everything. What I'm saying is, I can't marry you. It wouldn't be right.'

'There's someone else,' he said, shortly. If she was refusing him outright that's what it had to be.

She rushed to reassure him. 'No. No. Nothing like that.'

He was still stiff-necked with annoyance. 'Then you don't make sense. If there's no one else, you can marry me. I can't see any reason why not.'

This was even more difficult than she'd expected it to be. 'I don't know how else to put it,' she sighed. 'I *can't* marry you. That's all I can say. It wouldn't be right.'

'Why not?'

'I can't leave London, for a start.'

'That's nonsense. You can trade just as well in Manchester as you can here. It'll be a bit of an upheaval moving but once that's over . . .'

'It ain't that. I wouldn't mind the move. It's leaving

London. It's the city, what it means to me. Living here. Being part of it.'

He was smoothing his moustache with his forefinger. 'Manchester's as good as London any day of the week. You move there and you'll soon find that out.'

The anxious gesture made her want to soothe him but even so she couldn't give him the answer he wanted. 'I expect you're right,' she admitted, 'but it ain't just the city. It's everything. Oh, how can I put it? I know I wouldn't be the right sort of wife for you. If I married you it wouldn't be right.'

'Why not?' he asked again.

'Look,' she said. 'I'm very fond of you. Very fond. But I don't love you. Not in that way. It wouldn't be right.'

He leant across the table and caught her hand. Now was the time to persuade. 'But *I* love *you*,' he said. 'We don't have to fall in love, now do we. Love grows. Why can't you let it grow?'

She made no attempt to withdraw her hand but left it where it was, still and unresponsive. 'Because it wouldn't,' she said truthfully.

'That's defeatist,' he urged. 'We could make it grow. Think of all the things we've got in common. It's silly to reject me out of hand when we've come so far. If there's no one else, why shouldn't we make a go of it?'

'I ain't rejecting *you*,' she said. 'You mustn't think that. I'm rejecting marriage. I don't want to get *married*. D'you see? I've been my own boss for too long. I'm used to it. I'd be a rotten wife.'

'Let me be the judge of that.'

She gave him a wry smile. 'I can't, can I? I'd have to marry you for that to happen.'

'Then marry me. For heaven's sake, why not? I love you. Yes, all right, you don't love me, but we like one another. We get on well. Let me support you, look after you and then see what happens. Why not? Why should you have to struggle along on your own when I can give you a good life?'

411

The word 'support' dug into her mind. 'That's exactly it,' she said. 'I don't want to be supported. Not really. Not if I'm honest. Ever since Mum died I've supported the others you see. First it was me an' Bertie – and then when he was killed it was just me. When I started the business it was just me. I used to have kittens every Friday, balancing the books, wondering how I'd make out. But I learnt bit by bit. I managed. By the time I met you I was managing pretty well, all things considered. I *prefer* to manage on my own. It's easier in the long run.'

'But don't you need company?'

I've got company, she thought. I've got Netta and Muriel and Mabel and Bertie, a whole family. But she kept her thoughts to herself, because they would have hurt him. To herself and filling her mind – yearning memories of Jack in their warm bed at Dover, of Bertie being born, of the long struggle to feed him, of her pride in the way he was growing up like his father. She knew that this was what she wanted from marriage, even though she'd had only the briefest taste of it, passionate, loving, instinctive, full of strong feelings, sharing everything with the man you loved, bed and board, work and play, thoughts, hopes, everything. Generous and handsome though he was, she didn't want to share a bed with Henry Philips nor to tell him her most private thoughts and feelings. She knew that her flesh was shrinking from the thought.

'I prefer being on my own,' she said at last, speaking as firmly as she could. 'That's the truth of it. I like my independence.'

Her momentary withdrawal into her thoughts made him recognise that he wasn't going to persuade her. At least not now. 'So it's no.'

'I'm sorry.'

He shrugged her refusal away, smoothed his moustache, became practical. 'We'd better eat this meal then,' he said, 'or it'll go cold. Tell me about your companion pairs. Are you bringing them out again for Christmas?'

412

She was relieved by how deft he was. 'Yes,' she said. 'We've had an order from Arding and Hobbs already. Netta got it yesterday.'

By the time the pudding was served he'd recovered enough to smile at her. 'Should you ever change your mind, you would tell me?' he asked.

'Yes, if I ever did, but . . .'

'And I hope we'll meet for dinner now and then. You wouldn't object to that?'

Now that's generous, she thought, admiring him. 'Yes. 'Course. I don't want to lose you, Henry. I value you too much.'

He raised his eyebrows at that but said nothing.

In the pause that followed, she picked up her handbag and took his brooch from the inner pocket where she'd put it for safe keeping carefully wrapped in tissue paper. Now that they'd both recovered a little, she judged she could give it back to him without it being too hurtful. 'I can't keep this now, can I?' she said, and held it out towards him.

He took it, unwrapped it and walked round the table to pin it on the collar of her dress. 'That's yours,' he said firmly. 'I've given it to you. I told you what it was going to be. A gift from one business partner to another. A gift from someone who's fond of you. I *shall* always be fond of you, you know that, don't you.'

'Yes. I do know that,' she said, looking up at him. 'And I shall always be fond of you.'

'But not enough to marry me,' he said, returning to his seat.

'Too much to marry you,' she parried. 'And that's the truth.'

'Chop logic,' he said and for the first time she could see that he was bitter. 'Still,' he tried to joke, 'half a loaf is better than no bread, eh?'

'Oh dear!'

'You'll keep in touch?'

'I shall be telephoning you on Friday,' she said. 'I've got another order for you.'

413

Her light tone helped him to joke again. 'Half a loaf *and* a telephone call. I *am* spoilt.'

'Spoilt but not ruined,' she hoped.

'That's about it,' he agreed and managed to smile at her. Disappointment and anger would come later and in private. Now, and in public, they were being civilised. And that was a source of pride to him and the means of ultimate recuperation.

Netta was waiting up when Rose got home. She was scowling with anxiety and came to the point at once.

'Well?'

'I turned him down,' Rose told her, taking off her hat and coat. Now that the evening was over she was weary. 'I said no.'

'Thank God for that,' Netta said in her trenchant way. And she flung her arms round her sister's neck and gave her a fierce hug. 'We been on pins all day, worrying, me an' Mu.' Then, being Netta, she began to see things from Rose's point of view. 'You ain't done it because of us though, have you?'

Rose linked arms with her sister as they walked into the living-room. 'I was thinking of Jack,' she explained. 'I couldn't've said yes. Not after loving him and having Bertie. It would've been letting him down. Him and Bertie and Collum and all the others. All the dead. It would've been dishonest to say yes. I had to do the right thing.'

Their mother's sampler hung on the chimney breast immediately in front of them. The roses on the embroidered cottage were faded to the merest hint of pink but her motto was as bold and bright as ever.

'*Live with Dignity,*' Netta quoted, looking at it. 'You couldn't do nothing else, could you?'

'No,' Rose said, relieved to see how entirely her sister understood. 'I couldn't. Not when it came down to it.'

414

CHAPTER THIRTY-FOUR

At Monk House the telephone was shrilling its urgent message into the still air of the hall.

'I hate that dratted thing, Mrs Henderson,' Augusta said to her new housekeeper. They'd been discussing the day's menus when it started up. 'It's such a row. Shriek, shriek, shriek all the time. I wish somebody would stop it.'

Mrs Henderson didn't comment. She'd made it quite clear to this new employer of hers, right from the very first day, that she didn't consider answering the telephone to be one of her duties. 'I will cook,' she'd said, 'I will hire and fire, I will supervise the running of the house, but I will not live in – I got family to consider – I will not light fires and I will not answer the telephone.' She might be undersized and underweight but, as Augusta was discovering, she had a will of iron.

'It's very inconvenient,' Augusta grumbled as she trudged out into the hall. She'd been in a bad mood ever since that awful meeting with Edmund and it annoyed her that Mrs Henderson hadn't taken the hint. Servants these days were altogether too cocky, laying down the law about what they would and wouldn't do. 'I hate being interrupted and I shall tell them so.'

She didn't get the chance however because the caller was Cedric and he was in a worse mood than she was.

'Now look here, Gussie,' he said crossly, 'What's going on? I've been trying to telephone Chelsea and he won't answer. His house-keeper says he's busy. That awful woman hasn't gone either. I thought you were supposed to have sorted it out.'

'How could I?' Augusta said crossly. 'He wouldn't listen.'

'You should have gone back and made him listen. What's the matter with you? Well it can't go on. What are you going to do about it?'

'*I* don't know,' Augusta said tetchily. 'Why ask me? I'm not his keeper. I went and saw him and got abused for it, that's all. If you want something else done, I suggest you do it.'

'I can't leave Suffolk,' Cedric said. 'Those damn boys of mine have been running up bills like nobody's business. I hope you're going to honour them now they're your heirs.'

'No I am *not*. If they're such fools as to run up bills let them deal with the consequences. They're not my responsibility.'

'They're *your* heirs.'

'That,' Augusta said grimly, 'can be changed.'

'You see what I mean,' Cedric said with satisfaction. 'You're the one with the power to change things. The only one. You've got the money and you've got the power.'

'Quite right,' Augusta said. 'I'm glad you realise it.'

'So you're the one to deal with Edmund and Louella. Tell her you'll cut her right out of your will unless she stops all this nonsense and goes back to live with him. That'll do it. You see if it doesn't. She's always been after the money.'

'And you *haven't*?'

'This is different.'

'No, it's not,' Augusta said crossly. 'It's always the same with you, Cedric. It always comes down to money in the end. You and Louella are a pair.'

'Because you will keep messing us about. None of us knows where we are. If you were to settle it for good and all . . . But no, you won't do that will you? That would be too sensible. Leaving it to those two fool boys! I ask you! You're nearly fifty, for God's sake, and you're still playing stupid games . . .'

'You're making me ill,' Augusta said, beginning to pant. But he went on shouting. 'I feel bad, Cedric,' she

416

warned. 'I'm going to have one of my turns.' There was no doubt about it now. Her breathing was dreadful! She might even faint.

But he didn't pay any attention to her. He just went on. '. . . those two fool boys! They haven't got the first idea how to handle money . . .'

Augusta put the receiver down on the hallstand and left it there, with his voice buzzing away inside it like an angry wasp. Then she staggered back to the parlour, checking the mirror in passing to see how flushed she was.

'I feel ill,' she said to her housekeeper. 'The menus will have to wait. He's made me too ill to attend to them. You'll have to call the doctor out. I've left the telephone off the hook.'

Oh no, Mrs Henderson thought, you're not catching me out that way. 'The parlourmaid can attend to it,' she said. 'I'll tell her.'

It was the sixth time in as many weeks that Dr Felgate had been called to Monk House and he was beginning to get tired of it. But he examined his patient as thoroughly as ever and made the sort of consoling noises she expected.

'Try to relax, dear lady,' he said. 'You make matters worse by breathing so quickly.'

'It *is* my breathing, isn't it Doctor?'

'Your breathing is part of the problem,' the doctor told her. 'But your general condition is good. There is no cause for alarm. I will get my dispenser to make you up a bottle of medicine and have it sent up. Rest for a day or two. Light diet. You know the sort of thing. Try to avoid stressful situations.'

Augusta became confidential. 'What have I got, Doctor?' she whispered. 'You can tell me. It isn't just indigestion is it? I know that's what you said last time but it isn't, is it?'

Over the years, Dr Felgate had grown used to this particular ploy. He knew that Miss Monk liked a fine-sounding medical name to apply to any condition she complained of and on this occasion, partly to satisfy her and partly to bring the consultation to a close, he provided one.

'You are suffering from dyspnoea,' he said.

That sounded suitably dreadful. 'How do you spell it?'

After he'd washed his hands and left her, Augusta went up to her bedroom to consult her medical encyclopaedia. At first it wasn't much help to her, merely translating his wonderful medical term as 'Breathlessness'. But when she looked that up too, she found two whole pages of fascinating material. Breathlessness was a symptom of all sorts of illnesses – asthma, consumption, irritable nerves, pneumonia, and weakness of the heart. That's it, she decided, pouncing on the words. That's what I've got. I've always known my heart was weak. Now here's proof positive. So Cedric can stop being so unkind. I shall write and tell him. He ought to know what he's done to me.

'I'm afraid I'm really rather ill,' she warned Mrs Henderson, when that lady came upstairs in answer to her bell. 'I've got dyspnoea, you see. My heart's in a very bad condition. I shall have to take great care of myself. I shall lunch in the bedroom.'

Outside in the garden, the leaves were beginning to change colour and there was an autumnal mist wreathing the Lebanon cedar like white smoke. The melancholy of the season pleased her. It would soon be her birthday and time for her family to make a special fuss of her. I shall be fifty, she thought, and the importance of the figure pleased her too. It's a good age. They ought to give me a 'surprise' party – if they were anything like. But she knew it wouldn't occur to them. If she wanted a party she would have to give it herself the way she always did. But they could provide some extra special presents.

I'll write to them all, she decided, and let them know I'm ill and invite them here for a birthday tea on the Sunday. I might even hint that it's likely to be my last. That'll have them running.

The event took shape in her mind, growing in grandeur.

She would open up the dividing doors between the dining-room and the breakfast room and make one long area to entertain in. She could see herself at the head of the table, beautifully dressed, naturally, but decidedly unwell. Pale and interesting. There would be a cake from Harrods and fancy biscuits and Earl Grey tea. She would put the parrot in the window at the far end of the double room so that her guests could admire him while they ate. Oh she could see it all. It would be splendid.

As her day moved from meal to meal she enlarged upon her fantasy. An occasion like this was the ideal time to put pressure on her family and especially on Louella and Edmund. Ceddie was right about that, at least. If she were to threaten to cut Louella out of her will for good and all it might bring her to heel. Once they're here and sitting round the table, I could tell them all about a new will, fair shares between the three of them if they get back together again. If I invite that Miss Spencer that'll make sure Edmund comes. And if everybody's here and Edmund's pleading with her and we're all putting pressure on her she'll hardly be able to say no. Now that *will* be a triumph.

By the time she'd consumed her supper she'd made all her plans and composed the invitations in her head. Now it was simply a matter of writing them. It took her longer than she expected because each letter had to be adjusted to suit its recipient, but the resulting invitations were little short of masterpieces.

'*I am writing to all of you to invite you to my fiftieth birthday celebration on Sunday afternoon in several days' time, to Cedric and Winifred, and all their children including Evelyn, to Edmund and Miss Spencer, and to Louella. We are none of us getting any younger and I am so ill with dyspnoea that I seriously wonder whether I shall see another birthday. But let us not dwell on disagreeable topics.*

It is time we buried the hatchet and made peace with one another no matter what might have passed between us in years gone by. We have to change with the times.

I mean to change with the times myself. I intend to make a new will immediately after the party to settle my affairs once and for all and fairly. I will tell you what I have in mind when we meet. I feel sure you will approve of my plans, since you will all be involved.

I shall order a special tea for the occasion with a cake from Harrods. Shall we say half past four? Don't forget blood is thicker than water. We should not let the sun go down on our wrath. We should stick together now that we are getting older. Who knows what tomorrow will bring?

Your loving sister/aunt/cousin,

Augusta.'

A full moon beamed approval on her as she took the letters to the postbox and the pavement shone as if it were coated with silver. She was swollen with virtue and importance. Once they're all in my house, I shall be the peacemaker, she thought. I shall make Cedric eat his words. And Winifred too, because she can be pretty horrid when she likes. I shall persuade the boys that my last will really wasn't sensible and that the next one will be better all round. I shall please Ethel and that Evelyn of hers because it won't all go to her brothers now. And I shall bring Edmund and Louella together again. It will be magnificent.

The four members of her immediate family weren't quite so sanguine about it.

Cedric approved. 'She's making an effort,' he said, 'so we'll make one too. It looks as though she's going to disinherit those two fool boys – and not before time – so we might be in the running again. Just so long as she doesn't do anything stupid.'

'I think we ought to go,' Winifred said. 'She *is* fifty.'

Cedric forbore to point out that he and Edmund had both passed *their* fiftieth birthdays without any celebration at all.

'Of course a lot depends on what Edmund and Louella will do,' Winifred said. 'It'll be a bit difficult for them. Do you think they'll go?'

'*She* will,' Cedric said. 'We might have to put a bit of pressure on *him*. We'll telephone in a day or two and see what's what.'

'But you won't make a scene, will you Ceddie.'

'I never make scenes.'

'I know you don't. But you won't make a scene at the party will you. Not on her birthday. Not when she's trying to bring them together.'

'I shall be diplomacy itself,' Cedric promised and went off to check the cattle feed. 'Providing she divides the money in the proper way.'

Edmund was put in a quandary by his invitation. 'I'm not at all sure about this,' he said to Muriel. 'Why is she inviting you?'

Muriel wasn't sure about it either but she didn't say so. She felt it would be churlish to ignore such a strong plea and especially when it was being made on behalf of the family. 'Perhaps she's trying to be kind.'

'Kindness, my *orpheline*, is not in her nature.'

'Well maybe not,' Muriel admitted, 'but I think we ought to accept. She's invited us both so she *is* making an effort and it's more for you than anybody. I think she's giving us a chance to be civilised.'

Privately Edmund thought she was giving them the chance to be castigated but he allowed himself to be persuaded.

Only Louella and Fancy accepted at once and without hesitation.

'I will wear my red costume and smoke a cheroot,' Fancy decided.

'She hasn't invited *you*,' Louella pointed out.

'An oversight. You'd hardly want to go there without me, now would you.'

Louella admitted the truth of that. 'I can't wait to see Edmund's face when we walk in together,' she said. 'He'll have a heart attack.'

'Then I shan't have lived in vain.'

'Fancy!' Louella drawled in admiration. 'Sometimes you're downright evil.'

'Such praise,' Fancy said, blowing her a kiss. 'You'll turn my head.'

So all the invitations were accepted. Now it only remained for Augusta to take a drive to Harrods and order her banquet.

There was nothing she enjoyed so much. The food hall was always so splendid, and this time it was packed with so many mouth-watering delicacies it was almost impossible to choose between them. She spent an hour in the place and worked up such a healthy appetite that she had to go to the restaurant to slake it. By then she was in such an excellent mood that on the way out of the store she decided to take a detour through the pet department. There was just a chance that they might have another parrot and if they did she would buy it and have a pair to entertain her guests, one on either side of the window like book-ends.

But there was no parrot this time, although there were parakeets and budgerigars and kittens and puppies in abundance. And one or two rather nice chows. Was it time to replace Chu-Chin? she wondered as she walked past the cages. Another dog would be company. But then she walked into another section and saw the monkey.

It was sitting on a perch demolishing an orange, eating neatly and with splendid singularity of purpose, flicking the skin aside and spitting out slivers of pith between small white vicious-looking teeth. It was perfectly clean and extremely handsome with a thick mane of golden fur that reminded her of Chu-Chin, small deft paws, a very long tail and a chocolate-brown face. The fur on its body looked as soft as velvet and its eyes were a defiant yellow. It was a princely creature, an animal that no one could possibly ignore. She was enamoured of it at once, recognising it as just the sort of pet she'd always been looking for. It would be the making of the tea party and a splendid fiftieth birthday present to herself.

She bought it there and then and arranged to have it delivered at the same time as her birthday cake. Now, she said to herself, I simply can't fail. Not with an animal like that as a talking-point. I've thought of everything.

So the day of the great occasion arrived and the players gathered for the show, each dressed according to character. Edmund was in his respectable grey because he felt his respectability was going to be challenged, Muriel chose the blue suit she'd worn as a companion because it made her feel less obtrusive. In Suffolk, Ethel decided on a green cocktail dress decorated with blue and gold beads, Evelyn was coaxed and petted into his velvet jacket, Cedric wore tweeds and Winifred had a new dress made and was annoyed because it didn't fit properly.

For her part, Augusta wore a new blue velvet and the pearls in which she'd graced Ethel's wedding. She took a long time over her preparations, wearing just a touch of lipstick and powdering her face into a suitable pallor. Then she took up her position in the hall to welcome them all in.

'So *good* of you to come,' she said to Edmund kissing him on his proffered cheek. 'And – um – (what was her name?) – um – too. Such a *wise* decision, my dear. Oh! And a birthday pressie as well! How kind! And here's Ceddie. Oh and Ethel and Evelyn. Did you all travel up together? How nice!'

Her guests were brittle with nerves, bouncing away from one another after their initial greetings, as though they were being propelled by wires. But Augusta pretended not to notice and went on gushing happily as they were divested of their coats and hats. 'What a lovely lot of pressies! Am I to open them now?'

Hereward and Percy arrived loudly, bearing chocolates and champagne, and Hereward thumped his new brother-in-law between the shoulder blades just as he was about to say something and consequently made him choke. Ethel was wiping his eyes when Louella made her entrance alongside the show-stopping scarlet of Fancy Pepperell's tailored suit.

Augusta was so surprised to see her that, for once in her life, she was bereft of speech. But Fancy took the moment in her scarlet stride.

'I'm gate-crashing,' she said gaily. 'You don't mind, do you darling? We always go absolutely everywhere together, don't we, Lou? Absolutely everywhere. Inseparable you might say. I knew you'd understand. Hello Ev, old thing. What's up with you?' And she thumped him between the shoulder blades for the second time in twenty minutes.

Despite her boisterous greeting, Evelyn was jolly relieved to see her. 'Steady on Peppers, old fruit,' he rebuked. 'You damn nearly cracked my windpipe.'

'Shall we go into the dining-room?' Augusta suggested. 'The tea's ready and I've got a surprise for you. I bought it for myself as a birthday treat. Something really special. I can't *wait* to show you.'

The monkey was an even bigger success than she'd hoped and entirely because of her uninvited guest. Fancy took one look at him and shrieked across the room to admire him.

'But he's gorgeous!' she cried. 'Look at him, Lou! What amazing colours! We must paint him. What's his name?'

'Co-co.'

'Co-co, you gorgeous thing! Miss Monk, I envy you.'

Ethel was eyeing the monkey with some concern. 'Where do you want us to sit, Aunt Augusta?' she asked, hoping she would be as far away from the wretched thing as possible.

Augusta had arranged the table to suit her purposes, positioning her two brothers at the head of the table, one on either side of her with their wives beside them, and distributing the lesser breeds below the salt, where she wouldn't have to pay them too much attention. Louella spent the first part of the meal sending frantic eye signals to Fancy at the other end of the table. But Cedric and Edmund watched their sister.

'Tea first,' Augusta said brightly. 'Winifred dear,

would you pass the bread and butter? We'll all get settled and then I've got something to tell you.'

The meal began with a shuffle of silks and a clatter of plates. Grimaces passed from one to the other with the newly filled cups. Bread and butter was consumed politely, small cakes were selected, scones buttered, tea cups replenished.

'Now then,' Augusta said, brushing crumbs from her skirt and smiling regally around the table at her relations. 'Before I cut my birthday cake I've got something to tell you.'

They gave her their attention immediately.

'I've been giving a lot of thought to Daddy's inheritance. I think I told you in my letter. Well then, what I've been thinking is this. It's about time I settled things once and for all. To make everything fair. We're all relations, when all's said and done, and blood's thicker than water.' Then she turned to look at her brothers and their wives, one after the other, addressing them directly. 'What do you think?'

'You must do as you think fit,' Edmund said, concentrating on a tea cake. But his words were lost because Cedric and Louella were speaking at the same time and both saying the same thing.

'It depends how you're going to divide it,' Cedric boomed.

And Louella said, 'I hope you're going to include me.'

'Well naturally I'm going to include you,' Augusta smiled. 'You're Edmund's wife. You *are* still Edmund's wife, aren't you?'

'I'm Edmund's cousin. That's more to the point. Edmund's cousin. Your cousin. The one who would have inherited everything if it hadn't been for your father and his sneaky tricks.'

'Bygones!' Cedric warned. 'Don't let's dig up old bones. There's nothing to be gained by that.'

'Not for you maybe. There is for me.'

'I say! Look here!' Hereward called from his end of the

table. 'Does this mean we're out of the running? That's a bit tough, don't you think?'

'No,' Augusta told him. 'You're not out of the running. Whatever makes you say such a thing? I shall make provisions for all three of you. I've thought of everything.'

'Oh that's nice!' Louella said sarcastically. 'And what about Edmund and me? If we haven't got children we're to get less money. Is that it?'

'No, no,' Augusta said, raising her voice to regain control. 'It's all perfectly fair. I've worked it all out. Let me explain.'

Louella was still speaking, her voice so cool it sounded insulting. 'What is the point of all this?' she said. 'You're not going to share it out the way you ought. The bulk of it will go to Cedric and his children.'

'Well, thank you very much,' Hereward said, bristling at her. 'You're a fine one to talk – walking out on your husband.'

'Don't stick your nose in where it isn't wanted,' Louella rounded on him. 'You know nothing about it. You're just a child.'

Winifred weighed in at that. 'You leave my Hereward alone. He's right. You *are* a fine one to talk. You're nothing but a – a – a scarlet woman.'

'No, no, sunshine,' Fancy mocked. 'That's me. Or hadn't you noticed?'

'Let's you an' me keep out of it,' Evelyn suggested. 'We're not family.'

'Family!' Augusta cried, seizing on the word. 'That's exactly it. That's what it's all about. Family. And if you'll listen instead of shouting, you'll see how fair it's all going to be.'

Edmund was looking round the table, sending eye signals to the others. 'Give her a chance,' he urged. 'At least hear what she's got to say.'

Muriel understood her own particular signal instinctively and acted on it at once. 'Perhaps it would be easier if

Fancy and I withdrew for a little while,' she suggested. 'As we're not family.'

Augusta should have been pleased that Edmund had restored order for her but in fact she was annoyed and irritable. 'Yes,' she said, bluntly. 'It would. You do that. I'm sure you won't mind, will you Fancy?'

'Actually,' Fancy said. 'I do mind but,' catching Louella's anguished expression, 'I'll do it out of the kindness of my heart and to oblige my darling.'

Augusta ignored the provocation of the last drawled word and waited while the two young women took their cups and walked down to the other end of the room where they sat in the window between the parrot and the monkey.

'Thank heaven's we're out of that,' Muriel whispered as Augusta began to speak again. 'I was beginning to feel a bit embarrassed. Weren't you?'

'No,' Fancy said coolly. 'I was enjoying it. I like a scrap.'

'Well I don't. I hate it when people argue.'

'I shall eavesdrop,' Fancy decided. 'It'll keep me amused. I need a lot of amusement. Or I might take this monkey out of its cage for a while and see what it's like to hold. That fur looks superlative.'

The suggestion made Muriel nervous. 'Do you think you should?'

'Never do what you should,' Fancy advised, stroking the monkey's head through the bars. 'It's the quickest way to boredom.'

Augusta was addressing her now attentive family. 'So let me tell you what I have in mind. I propose to make a small allowance for Ethel and the two boys and then I'm going to divide the rest into three equal amounts, one each for Cedric, Edmund and Louella.'

Cedric and Louella were puzzled to see her so suddenly and unexpectedly even-handed but Edmund looked suspicious.

'Forgive me for asking this, Gussie,' he said. 'But what's the catch?'

'Catch?' she bridled. 'Why should there be a catch? Why shouldn't it be simple family feeling?'

Because it never is with you, Edmund thought, but he only gave her his wry look. And all the others waited to see what would be said next.

'There are one or two conditions,' Augusta told him, 'naturally.'

'Such as?'

'Well, this way you and Louella would get two thirds of the inheritance between you, so I would expect you to get back together again.'

His response was more of a sigh than a word. 'Ah!'

'In case it's escaped your notice,' Louella said, 'I don't want to get back together with Edmund. I'm happy as I am.'

'I'm not asking you to be happy,' Augusta said. 'I'm telling you to do the right thing.'

'And what if I refuse?'

The answer was smug. 'Then you won't get the money.'

Winifred was several paces behind the others in this conversation and missed the last exchange entirely. Annoyance made her more slow-witted than usual. It also made her shout. 'Two portions for her and Edmund and one for us,' she yelled, her face pink. 'Oh that's fair! That's very fair! I don't think!'

'If we get it,' Louella said. 'Anyway, it's a darn sight fairer than four for you and two for us.'

'How d'you make that out?' Cedric bristled. 'You can't count. They're only getting an allowance. If you're going to count that way, it's one for us and two for you.'

They were all shouting now, the noise of their anger increasing by the second. Louella's initial nervousness had pushed her out of control.

'You and your children. Blood suckers the lot of you.'

'Why shouldn't they inherit? They're as much family as you and Edmund.'

'She'll only spend it on that woman,' Winifred shouted.

'My name's Fancy,' that woman shouted from the other end of the room.

'And very fitting!'

'I think,' Edmund said quietly into the uproar, 'none of this is necessary.'

They rounded on him. 'Not necessary! What are you talking about? Not necessary?'

'This is all hypothetical,' he explained. 'Nothing's happened yet. It might not. And anyway we're all forgetting something. Gussie's the youngest in the family, the youngest of the four of us except for Louella. You could outlive us all, Gussie. I hope you do. So all this talk of wills is unnecessary.'

'You'll pardon me for saying so,' Cedric said heavily, 'but I don't think so. We've got to know what's going to happen to the money. And the property.'

Edmund looked down the room hoping to catch Muriel's eye. Having stepped out of line, he needed her encouragement or some sign of support. But since Winifred's outburst, she and Fancy had turned their backs on the argument and seemed to be fully occupied playing with the monkey. 'What happens to the money and the property,' he said, 'can be decided here and now, for good and all.'

'Exactly!' Augusta smiled, glad to see that he was being sensible about it. 'Just what I've been trying to do.'

He turned to look her straight in the face, gathering his courage for a confrontation. 'No, Gussie,' he said gently and sadly. 'It's not. It never is. All you ever do is muddy the waters. And it's all unnecessary. If Ceddie and Lou and I decide what *we*'re going to do, and stick to it, we can avoid all this chopping and changing.'

His gentle sadness alarmed his sister but Cedric was intrigued. 'What do you have in mind?'

No, Augusta thought, we don't need to hear this. Whatever it was she knew she wouldn't like it.

But Edmund was speaking again before she could stop him. 'We make a decision, here and now, that whatever sort of will Augusta makes and whoever she leaves this money to, if she *does* die before the rest of us, we simply ignore the will, and whoever inherits, divides the money equally between the other three, or however many are left. That way we shall all be sure it's going to be fair.'

The shock of hearing him say such a disloyal, impossible thing, caught Augusta in a spasm of emotion that felt uncomfortably like fear. 'You couldn't do it,' she protested. 'It wouldn't be legal.'

Now that he'd begun, Edmund found it easier to proceed. 'It would be fair,' he told her. 'And that's better than legal.'

'It's a brilliant idea,' Cedric approved. It would put paid to all Augusta's nonsense at a stroke. 'Don't you think so, Lou?'

Her husband's long speech had given Louella time to recover. 'Yes,' she said. 'It's excellent. If we all stick to it.'

'And what about us?' Ethel asked.

'You'd inherit in the usual way,' Cedric told her. 'The same as most people, when things are *normal*. Your uncle's right. This way we could see that things are fair. It only needs an agreement. We could do it this afternoon.'

'And no nonsense about Edmund and I getting together again?' Louella asked.

The lure of money was greater than the need for family respectability. 'There's no point telling you two what to do,' Cedric allowed and grinned at them. 'You'll go your own way to the devil. No, this is simply an agreement about tactics.'

'Now look here,' Augusta said, waving her plump hands at them. They were talking to one another as if she wasn't even in the room. And she couldn't believe what Cedric was saying – after all that nagging to get her to do something about Louella and Edmund, and all the effort she'd made to do it. Her heart was beating painfully and she could feel the hot blood rising in her cheeks, the sweat damp under her armpits. They *couldn't* just ignore her wishes like this. They *mustn't*. She couldn't bear it. What was the point of having all the money if you couldn't do what you liked with it? She could feel her power draining away just as the need to fight them was most intense. 'You can't ignore a will. There are rules and regulations, laws . . .'

There was a commotion at the other end of the room. Co-co, having been taken out of his cage by Fancy Pepperell, had suddenly leapt to freedom. Now he was swinging across the curtains, arm over long arm, his amber eyes glinting

The entire company turned in their chairs to watch as he jumped off the curtains, flew through the air, paws outstretched, and landed on the mantelpiece, where he picked his way delicately among the knick-knacks, heading towards the table.

'Oh I say!' Evelyn drawled. 'Hadn't somebody better do something, I mean . . .'

Co-co sat on the edge of the mantelpiece, scratched his belly and gazed at them balefully. Then, as if Evelyn's voice were an invitation, he unleashed the spring of his long legs and jumped down onto the young man's shoulder, crossed his chest like a drawbridge, reached the table and went bounding off towards the sideboard. There was a dish full of fruit in the middle of the table and lying at the very top a small bunch of green grapes. He snatched them up with one swift movement and stuck them in his mouth as he ran, dodging their grabbing hands and scattering their tea and cakes, his long tail swinging over the plates.

'Stop it someone!' Cedric shouted. 'Damn thing! It'll have the teapot over.'

But Co-co was already on the sideboard and the sideboard might have been designed for a monkey. It was a huge piece of Victorian furniture, four feet wide and as tall as the room with a back panel that was a gothic complication of carved galleries, open cupboards and shelves backed by mirrors. He climbed as if he were in a tree, chattering happily.

'Go it Co-co,' Fancy encouraged, following the animal into the dining-room area.

'Get a chair,' Cedric instructed.

Edmund said a ladder would be more to the point.

But nobody got anything and Co-co began to eat the grapes. Being a fastidious creature, like all monkeys, he spat out the pips, which fell straight down onto the table. The first one landed in Edmund's tea, the second and third were embedded in the cake Winifred was just about to eat.

'This is too much, Augusta!' she cried, holding up the spotted cake for everyone to see. 'You'll have to do something.'

Muriel had followed Fancy down to the dining-table and had been watching with alarm. Now she felt she really ought to try to help. 'If someone would send for a broom,' she suggested. 'We might be able to knock him down.'

Fancy was giggling and so were Hereward and Ethel and Ev. 'Well it *is* funny,' Hereward said, when his father glared at him. 'You've got to admit.'

What happened next wasn't funny at all. Having demolished the grapes, the monkey squatted on his haunches and emptied his bladder. The stream of piddle descended in a graceful curve to spatter across the table, bouncing into cups of tea, casting dark droplets on the tablecloth and leaving a long yellow streak across the white icing of Augusta's splendid birthday cake.

There was pandemonium. Winifred and Ethel jumped from their seats screaming, Fancy shrieked, Percy and Hereward guffawed with embarrassment, Louella cried that it was 'too disgusting for words', Evelyn bleated 'Oh I say!' until his wife hit him, Cedric bellowed and stamped about the room and Augusta was so embarrassed she couldn't look at her relations and was reduced to screaming at her pet.

'You bad, wicked creature!' she yelled. 'Look what you've done. You've ruined my party. Come down at once, do you hear me!'

'I don't know why we came here, Ceddie,' Winifred said, pushing away her plate. 'It's always the same. Only this time it's worse.'

432

'I think it's time to go home,' Cedric said, rubbing his trousers with a table napkin. 'We can't stay here in this mess, and we've said all that needs to be said, haven't we Edmund?'

'I think so,' Edmund said, taking Muriel's arm. 'Make a quick exit, eh?'

'Right!' Fancy agreed, taking Louella's arm.

They were all on the move, cleaning themselves or heading out towards the hall. To Augusta's fury and distress, the party was suddenly and dramatically over.

'You can't go,' she cried. 'You're not to. This is my birthday and I'm not well. I told you. What about my new will? We haven't talked about it.'

'There's nothing to talk about,' Cedric said. 'It's out of date. We've said all that needs to be said.'

'I'm sorry we had to do this, Gussie,' Edmund said. 'But we can't go on playing games for ever. We're all getting a bit too long in the tooth.'

They straggled out into the hall, still mopping themselves down. The monkey's appalling behaviour had given them common ground. They exclaimed at the mess he'd made and told one another that monkeys were never good pets, as if they were experts on the subject. Coats and hats were donned as they justified their departure. They said goodbye to one another with laughter if not affection and kissed Augusta – although rather perfunctorily. Then they followed one another out onto the drive, heading for their cars. None of them looked back.

Chapter Thirty-Five

To be summoned to Monk House at nine o'clock on a Monday morning was a new experience for Mr Charles Tilling. Since his unfortunate encounter with the parrot, he'd been careful to send a junior to take Miss Monk's instructions. But this time, alerted by the urgency of the hour and the peculiar tenor of the lady's voice, he decided he ought to go himself.

'A presentiment, eh?' the elder Mr Fordham teased.

'Let's say an assessment,' Mr Tilling replied. 'She's never called us out in the morning before.'

She'd never been so cool about what she wanted either. Nor so quick. The new will was drawn up and ready to be signed by four o'clock that afternoon. Mr Tilling and his junior witnessed it together.

Then, in his customary way, he waited at the door for his final instructions, wiry legs flexed ready to depart, wiry head tilted towards the lady.

'Letters to all interested parties,' Augusta said, 'don't you think?'

'I will bring them up for signature tomorrow afternoon,' Mr Tilling promised.

'A good day's work,' he said to his junior as they walked briskly back to the office. 'I think we can be well pleased with ourselves.'

Left on her own in the drawing room, Augusta relapsed into the depression that had been dragging at her ever since the collapse of that awful tea party. It still made her hot to remember the awful way Co-co had behaved – how could he have been so foul? – but the memory of her brothers' treachery was worse. It would need a sizeable revenge to soothe the humiliation of *that*. Drawing up the new will had pleased her – briefly – but her action wouldn't bring any immediate reward and that was what she craved. Until the letters had been signed and sent, there would be no telephone calls to answer and no reason to be the centre of attention. She'd paid them back. Every single one of them. But she would have to wait for the satisfaction that would come when they all knew it.

She spent the rest of the afternoon making demands on her three unfortunate servants, insisting that her chauffeur-cum-handyman stoked all the fires, polished the car seats and cleaned her boots for the second time that day, sending her maid on innumerable and unnecessary errands, requiring Mrs Henderson to serve tea in the bedroom. But her domineering brought her no relief. It was her family she needed to dominate and they had slipped out of her grasp. Her sense of grievance grew by the hour. How dare they say they were going to ignore her wishes? How dare they be so heartless? Where was their family feeling?

And then, as if all that weren't bad enough, at five o'clock Mrs Henderson came in to put the finishing touch to a miserable afternoon.

'I'm clocking off now,' she announced. 'I've left your supper all ready. You've only to go down to the kitchen and fetch it.'

Augusta was irritated. 'Clocking off?' she said. 'Whatever for? It's not time.'

'I'm going up the 'ospital,' Mrs Henderson said. 'I told you last week. Remember? To see me sister. She's had her leg seen to. I'll be back tomorrow morning. Now was there anything else?'

With all three of her servants gone, the house was far too quiet for Augusta's peace of mind and her supper was a miserable affair, cold meats and pickle and a pile of dry bread and butter. She wouldn't have given it to Chu-Chin. But she ate it to pass the time.

The evening hours stretched before her interminably. She couldn't go to bed until ten and she had no idea how

435

to occupy herself until then. Waiting had never been easy
for her and it was impossible now. She tried reading but
she couldn't keep her eyes on the page. She tried
embroidery but she pricked her finger and stained the
canvas with blood. She ate the remains of a box of
chocolates but they lasted hardly any time at all. She sat
by the window and tried to look out, but the garden was
hidden in darkness except for the Lebanon cedar, which
was a monstrous presence in the middle of a lawn as vast
as a black lake. The moon that had lit her way to the
postbox the other evening had shrunk to a slice of white
melon – and pitted melon at that. If I were ill now, she
thought, no one would know.

Thought was father to symptoms. She felt unwell at
once, her throat constricting as her breathing changed.
This is my dyspnoea coming back again, she thought,
listening to it with satisfaction. I shall have to call the
doctor. And went out into the hall at once to do it.

Dr Felgate had just settled down to an evening with his
wife and his nice new wireless when her call came
through. He recognised the sound of her laboured
breathing at once.

'Ah, Miss Monk,' he said. 'What seems to be the
trouble?'

'I'm ill,' Augusta panted. 'I'm all on my own in this
house, I've got no medicine and my dyspnoea is back. It's
terrible, Doctor. I can barely breathe.'

But you have enough breath to complain, the doctor
thought. 'Do you have any aspirin in the house?'

There was a rasping pause while she considered. 'I
think so.'

'Then my advice to you is to take two tablets and settle
for the night. Breathlessness always passes, you know. It
will all look quite different in the morning. I will write out
a repeat prescription for you and have it sent round first
thing.'

'But what if I collapse in the night? What if I pass out?'

'I don't think there's any danger of your doing that. If I

436

did, I would come out and visit you now. Breathlessness is unpleasant but it will pass. It always does, now doesn't it. Think of how you were last time. Take the aspirin.'

'I feel so ill, Doctor. This is worse than last time.'

Dr Felgate thought about it for a second. There was just a possibility that she could be telling him the exact truth but experience of her behaviour persuaded him otherwise. Nervy women were rarely as ill as they appeared. 'Take the aspirin,' he said firmly. 'Should you get any worse – which I very much doubt – call again. Otherwise I will come round tomorrow.'

Augusta flung the telephone back on the hook in a fury. How dare he fob her off like this? It was insupportable. A doctor should be prepared to attend his patient whenever she wanted him. That's what doctors were for. I shall tell Edmund, she decided. Let him know how ill I am. That's only fair as he was the one who made me ill in the first place. Now he can make amends. He can ring Dr Felgate on my behalf and *make* him come out to me. She took up the receiver again and pressed for the operator. Oh come on, girl, do. What a time you're taking.

Edmund and Muriel were laughing when the telephone rang. Muriel had spent most of the day entertaining her workmates with the story of the monkey and she was still bubbling with the memory of it.

'Nancy Cartwright laughed so much she had tears in her eyes,' she said. 'I know it was awful but it made a wonderful story.'

'And it gets better in the telling,' he understood, smiling at her as he took up the receiver. 'Oh, hello Gussie.'

Muriel made a grimace and then waited as Augusta's voice rattled angrily along the wire. Now and then Edmund held the receiver away from his ear so that she could hear a few words. 'So ill . . . You've no idea how ill I feel . . . It's disgraceful. A doctor has a duty to his patient . . .'

'Well,' he said patiently when the tirade finally came to

an end. 'I don't see how I can help you, Gussie. It's not up to me to tell the doctor his business. If he thought you were seriously ill, I'm sure he'd come out to you.'

'But that's just the point,' Augusta said, hot with exasperation. 'He won't. Somebody's got to make him. Oh, you're all the same, the lot of you. No earthly use to me at all.' And she hung up in fury for the second time that evening.

It's too bad, she thought. Why are they all being so callous? What if I were to collapse? It would be a different story then. It's all very well that stupid doctor saying take two aspirins. What good are aspirins if you can't breathe? He wouldn't say two aspirins if I were choking to death. I've a good mind to take something to make me worse. Just to show him. He'd come out pretty quickly then.

She realised that she was in the kitchen although she had no sense of having walked there. The condiments cupboard was immediately in front of her, ready to be opened and searched for assistance. Salt? Would that do? Vinegar? No, that was for stings. Mustard. Yes. That was the thing. You took mustard to make you sick. She remembered that from her childhood. Mustard in water. That was what she needed.

It took her very little time to mix the required dose. She was careful to put the mustard tin back in the cupboard so as not to leave any incriminating evidence, then she swallowed twice to prepare herself for the sickness that would follow and drank the mustard mixture as quickly as she could.

It tasted horrible and made her heave almost as soon as it was down her throat. She stood beside the sink, feeling sick and wondering whether she could get to the telephone before she started to vomit. But she couldn't. There wasn't time. It all came back, almost at once, bringing part of her supper with it. And then it was over and a total failure.

Damn, she thought, looking at the mess she'd made. Why did it have to go and work so quickly? It's no use going to the phone to tell him I've *been* sick. He won't take any notice of that. I've got to *sound* sick. He's got to *hear* how ill I am. She was panting but nowhere nearly badly enough, even when she concentrated on it. Damn, damn, damn. But she wouldn't be beaten. Not now. She couldn't be beaten. Now that she'd started there was an awful and growing desperation in her. She had to go on, no matter what it cost, on and on until she got her own way. If mustard wouldn't work, she'd have to find something that would. But she wouldn't be beaten. She'd make him pay attention, somehow or other.

She opened the cupboard where all the cleaning materials were kept, knelt down beside it and scrabbled about among the soaps and mop heads. There had to be something here, soda or soap or something. By now she was in such a state that she was knocking things over. Come on, come on, there must be something. There has to be something. What's this?

It was a bottle of domestic bleach. '*Use for cleaning table tops, sinks and drains,*' the label instructed. '*Use in solution for cleaning minor wounds. Not to be taken internally.*' It was just the thing.

Somewhere in the back of her mind she knew that this was poisonous stuff and that she was taking a risk. But her need to be believed and her craving for attention pushed the knowledge aside. Something had to be done. And she was going to do it.

She rinsed her glass and mixed her second potion almost carelessly, watching as the bleach clouded the water. Then she replaced the bottle and walked out into the hall, glass in hand. This time she was going to be right beside the telephone when the sickness struck. She caught sight of her own reflection in the hallstand mirror and for a few seconds stood where she was, the glass raised as though she were about to drink her own health, admiring her image. Then she downed the mixture in quick greedy gulps.

The pain was instant and terrifying, burning her tongue

and the back of her throat, tearing down her neck, filling her nose as if it were going to explode. She grabbed hold of the hallstand for support, gasping for breath, too frightened to think. Oh dear God! What have I done? Get the doctor! Quick! She was fumbling with the telephone, her fingers clumsy. Please, please, somebody help me!

'Get Dr Felgate,' she said to the operator. But it was so difficult to get the words out that the girl didn't understand what she was saying and she had to repeat herself, even more painfully. 'Dr Felgate! Please!' her voice rasping and wheezing with effort and agony. The pain was in her stomach, making her writhe, burning and burning as if she'd swallowed fire.

'Please!' she gasped when she heard the doctor's voice. 'You must – come. I can't . . .' Waves of terrible sickness were making her retch. 'Oh God! Oh God! Please help me.'

This time the doctor had no doubt at all about the state she was in. 'I'll be with you in five minutes,' he said.

He was a little surprised to find the house in darkness. There was only one light on as far as he could see and that was in the hall. But he rang the bell, once, twice in his usual way and waited with some impatience to be admitted. Seconds went by and nobody came. He rang again but there was still no answer and no sign of anyone approaching. Finally he lifted the letterbox and bent down to peer through. And at that moment, another car pulled up in the drive and Edmund and a strange young woman got out.

'Ah!' the doctor said. 'I've rung but there doesn't appear to be anyone to answer. I had an urgent call.'

'She telephoned me too,' Edmund said. 'I thought we'd better call round and see how she is.'

'It's all very quiet,' the doctor said. 'Is she on her own, do you know?'

'She shouldn't be. She's got a housekeeper.'

Muriel was looking up at the dark house. 'But this one doesn't live in,' she said.

'I've got a key somewhere,' Edmund remembered, producing a ring laden with keys. 'Had it as a young man. Is this it? No. That's . . . Of course, it might not work. I haven't used it for years. Here it is. This is the one.'

It was rusty but it opened the door. The three of them stepped into the hall, the doctor at a stride, Edmund gingerly, Muriel following behind.

Augusta was lying on the floor beside the hall stand, horribly still and hideously contorted, her back arched, her plump hands flexed into claws, her mouth wide open and flecked with foam, her eyes staring and glassy. It took only one glance to tell them all that she was dead.

CHAPTER THIRTY-SIX

Rose overslept on that Tuesday morning and, as she was the family alarm clock, so did everyone else. Breakfast was an impossible rush and, although they got Bertie off to school in good time and were only five minutes late to work, the telephone was already ringing as Netta put the key into the lock.

It was Muriel, sounding rather subdued, to say that she wouldn't be in to work for a day or two.

'Why?' Rose asked, cheerfully. 'What's up?' She was still in a hurry and hadn't recognised the anxiety in Muriel's voice. But her expression changed to shocked surprise as she heard what had happened.

'But that's dreadful!' she said. 'Oh Mu! That's dreadful!'

'The doctor said it was a heart attack,' Muriel told her. 'Massive he said. She must have died while he was driving to the house. She sounded perfectly all right when she telephoned us. She was grumbling. You know the way she does. In fact, we only went there on the off-chance. Edmund was a bit worried after she telephoned and he thought we ought to check. We never imagined we'd find her like that.'

'Poor thing!'

'Edmund's in an awful state. What with finding her and then having all the funeral to arrange and the solicitors to see and everything. I can't leave him.'

'No, 'course not,' Rose agreed. 'You stay where you are. We'll manage.'

'I'll come in on Friday and do the accounts.'

'There's no urgency,' Rose told her. 'Leave it if you ain't up to it. And if there's anything we can do, you know where we are.'

'Poor Miss Monk,' Mabel said, when the news had been relayed to everyone else. 'Alive one minute and fallen down dead the next. Ain't it awful! Fallen down dead.' Her eyes were round with delighted horror.

'It's worse that she died all on her own,' Rose said. 'You imagine lying there, dying all on your own, with no one to help you. I think that's the most terrible thing. And she was no age to die, now was she. Poor Miss Monk.'

'Don't waste your sympathy on *her*,' Netta said in her trenchant way. 'She was a nasty cantankerous old thing. Always shouting and carrying on. It's Mu we ought to feel sorry for. Mu and that Edmund of hers. They're the ones. It must've been awful for them.'

'And to think we was all in here only yesterday, laughing and joking about that monkey,' Marigold said. 'It don't bear thinking about.'

But it bore a lot of talking about. It was the main topic of conversation in Ritzy Street for the rest of the week. And on Thursday it was front-page news in the local paper, under the headline *'Death of Kennington Heiress.'* Which set them all talking again.

Late on Friday morning, Muriel came into the workshop as she'd promised, to do the accounts and to tell them that Edmund was recovering – slowly – and that Augusta's funeral had been fixed for the following Wednesday. By then there was a large pile of correspondence that needed attention. She and Rose stayed behind after the others had gone home in order to catch up with it. It gave them the chance to talk the whole thing over at length and for Rose to offer a bit of comfort.

So she was tired when she finally got home. And to her annoyance, she found yet another letter waiting for her. It had come in a large official envelope, addressed to her personally and marked *'Private and Confidential'*.

'I thought I'd finished with business for today,' she said wearily as she opened it.

But it wasn't a business letter. It was from Fordham, Tilling and Fordham, requesting the presence of Mrs

Rose Jeary at the reading of the will of the late Miss Augusta Monk at Monk House at five thirty on Wednesday afternoon, after the funeral.

'Well blow me down!' Netta grinned. 'She must've gone and left you something.'

'Has she Mum?' Bertie asked. 'What d'you think?'

There was some cheerful and ribald speculation as to what it might be – a chamber pot, the medicine cabinet, Miss Monk's old clothes, the parrot – even the monkey.

'You're being dreadful the lot of you,' Rose rebuked them, half laughing and half ashamed to be making fun of the poor woman. 'Still, I don't have to take it if I don't want to, do I?'

'You take it, whatever it is,' Netta advised. 'You can always flog it and make a few bob. You've earned it, all those years putting up with her nonsense.'

That Wednesday afternoon, Ritzy Clothes shut down early as a mark of respect and the inhabitants of Ritzy Street turned out in force for the funeral, packing their first-floor windows to watch the carriages leave Monk House and to comment on the clothes of the mourners. And at twenty-five past five, Rose crossed the street to join them on their return, dressed in suitable black and feeling decidedly out of place.

The feeling increased when she was ushered into the library. It was the worst room in the house, for that or any other occasion because Miss Monk had been no reader so it had rarely been used. Now it struck stale and cold, despite the fire in the grate. The books were dust-stained and unkempt, the carpet faded to the colour of cold porridge, even the mourners looked musty.

Cedric was standing with his back to the fire, coat-tails raised, warming his backside: Winifred was slumped on the sofa next to Louella; and Edmund was in the armchair, withdrawn and miserable, his long pale hands in his lap and his long chin sunk right down onto his black tie. Percy and Hereward were whispering to one another by the drawn curtains of the far window and Ethel was sitting by the table holding her husband's hand, her nose pink and her eyes bloodshot. The sight of her aunt's coffin being lowered into the grave had torn her with an uncontrollable sadness and – to her own surprise as much as everybody else's – she'd wept all the way back to the house. Now she looked round suspiciously to scowl at Rose.

Mr Tilling stepped forward from the bookcases, where he'd been pretending to examine the books. 'Ah!' he said. 'The full complement. If we could gather round the table, ladies and gentlemen. Perhaps you would sit here, Mrs Jeary?'

The three older members of the family left the fire reluctantly to sit at the library table, Winifred and Cedric side by side and Louella making sure she was next to Mr Tilling and as far away from Edmund as she could get.

'As you will have understood from my letter,' Mr Tilling began, 'Miss Monk gave instructions for a new will just before she died. I have it here as you see.'

'You mean she actually made this new will?' Cedric asked. 'I wouldn't have thought there'd have been time. Given when . . . I mean it was only Sunday we were here for her birthday.'

'It was drawn up on the following Monday, signed and witnessed that very afternoon.'

'If that's the case,' Cedric said ponderously, 'there are a few things that need to be cleared up arising out of those letters you sent. We've got a few questions to ask, haven't we?' And he looked round at his wife and sister-in-law for support, which was given at once with nods and stern expressions.

'Ask away,' Mr Tilling said affably. 'I'm here to serve you, in so far as it is within my competence.'

Cedric took a letter from his inside pocket. 'For a start they're not signed,' he said, 'and then, with the exception of our names and addresses, they're all exactly the same.'

'That is correct. They were not signed because, as you know, your sister died before signature was possible.

However they were sent to you according to her instruction.'

'That's all very well,' Cedric said, 'but I think you'll find you've made a mistake. Only a little one. Trivial really. It could happen to anyone. Look here. I'll show you what I mean.' And he read. ' *"I feel you should be informed that I have decided not to make you a* beneficiary *under the terms of my new will."* "*A* beneficiary", you see. That ought to be "*sole* beneficiary", oughtn't it?'

'Perhaps it would be helpful if we were to proceed to the reading of the will,' Mr Tilling said, flexing his fingers. 'That should make Miss Monk's intentions clear.'

But Cedric wasn't agreeable to that. He swung his body first towards Edmund and then towards Louella, asking, 'Did either of you have a different letter?'

Neither had.

'There you are, you see,' Cedric said to Mr Tilling. 'A mistake. She couldn't have cut us *all* out. It's got to go to someone. We all know that. She told us herself, that Sunday. She said she intended to divide it between us.'

'Oh poor Aunty!' Ethel said, her tears flowing again. 'I never thought she'd go and die. I mean, not actually *die*. I never thought we'd actually be reading her will. It was all a sort of game, wasn't it, changing it round every five minutes. Poor Aunty!'

'Well now perhaps we shall see the end of it,' Edmund said quietly. 'If Mr Tilling will kindly read the will.'

So the will was opened and the reading began.

Sitting on her own at the foot of the table, Rose had a good view of the entire family. Ethel's tears surprised her – she'd always seemed the least sympathetic of them all – but Cedric and Louella were running horribly true to form. She was appalled by how little grief they showed and how avidly greedy they were, their faces rapacious as they listened to Mr Tilling's calm voice declaiming the solemn words of the will.

'*I hereby revoke all previous wills . . .*'

Rose let her mind wander. She knew that whatever was

going to be left to her would come right at the end when everything else had been disposed of, so there was no need to pay attention.

'. . . *all goods, monies and properties of which I die possessed . . .*'

They haven't kept this room clean at all, Rose thought. There's even dirt on the lampshades and that pink glass is so pretty when it's clean. I hope whoever inherits will tidy things up a bit.

'. . . *to the one person who has remained faithful to me all these years, to whom I could turn when I was in trouble, who invariably gave me an honest answer – Rose Jeary of 26 Ritzy Street.*'

The sea was roaring in Rose's ears. With the exception of Edmund who was smiling at her, the Monks were all open-mouthed and red-faced and on the move, shouting. 'What?' 'Rubbish!' 'She can't do this.' 'It's not legal.' 'It's one of her tricks.'

Rose had to check what she'd half heard. 'Do you mean she's left this house to me?'

'House, contents and capital,' Mr Tilling smiled at her. His dark eyes were gleaming under that wiry hair of his, as if he were enjoying some private joke. 'You are the sole beneficiary.'

'We shall challenge it,' Cedric said, his face engorged with anger. 'She can't play this sort of trick. Not on her own flesh and blood. It's monstrous!'

'That is your prerogative, of course,' Mr Tilling said.

Louella was lighting a cigarette, her long fingers stiff and awkward. 'Now look here,' she said to Rose, blowing smoke through her nostrils. 'We can't let this stand. You must see that. It's totally unfair.'

To be under attack immediately after such a surprise left Rose without the power of reply, almost without words. She supposed it was. What else could she say? It didn't seem possible that this great house was hers. And capital too. That's what he'd said, wasn't it?

'We're family, when all's said and done,' Louella

continued, driving home her advantage. 'She made enough wills in her lifetime to make it quite clear that one or the other of us would inherit. This is an aberration. We shall have to fight it. You understand, don't you.'

Rose supposed she did. This house, she thought, and that great garden and all her lovely furniture. It would be a beautiful place if it was lived in and cared for. There's masses of room, she thought. Netta could have her own flat here if she wanted to. Just think of the meals we could cook in that great kitchen. And the hot baths. I could have a hot bath every day just the way I've always imagined. What luxury! A hot bath and fires in all the rooms. There's stacks of coal down the cellar. We could be warm and clean and well fed. All the lot of us. All the time. And what a Christmas we could have! We could put a Christmas tree in the hall and decorate all the rooms and throw a party for all our friends. The drawing-room's big enough to dance in. Wouldn't that be a lark.

'So you see,' Louella was saying, 'It won't work, will it? It would be much better to give it all up now, sign it over to us and have done with it. We know how to run it. You wouldn't have the first idea. You see that, don't you?'

'You want me to refuse it?' Rose asked. 'To say I won't accept it?'

'Yes,' Cedric joined in. 'It would be better all round. I'm sure you can see that.' The trouble with this young woman was that her face was so calm. There was no knowing what she was thinking, no knowing whether he ought to bully or persuade. 'You *can* see it, can't you?'

Although there was no outward sign of it, energy and determination were beginning to return to Rose Jeary. 'No,' she said. 'I don't think I can.'

'You're not going to tell me you think you deserve this money?' Louella asked, her voice sharp.

'Yes,' Rose said firmly. 'I think I do. If it goes to you, you'll waste it. I shall make it work.'

'How can you possibly say we'd waste it?' Winifred bristled. 'You don't know what we'd do with it.'

'You'll do the same as you've always done,' Rose told her. 'Go on a spending spree. Your daughter'll spend it on clothes, the way she done last time, your sons'll go abroad, the way they done. You all waste money, all the lot of you. Look how you've spent it over the years. Mr Monk bought shares in a TNT factory that blew up. Remember? My sister Netta worked in your factory, Mr Monk. She was one of the ones injured in your explosion. She ain't been right since. Bronchitis every winter. Always coughing. That's what you done with your money. And you ain't much better neither, Mrs Louella. You had a studio built. Lots of money that cost. And you just run off and left it. That's how important it was to you. You just run off and left it. That's what *you* done with *your* money. You can't deny it.'

'This is different,' Louella said, fighting back furiously. 'This is property and a great deal of money. Our grandfather's money. He worked bloody hard to get it.'

'Then I shall make it work hard too,' Rose said. 'That's what money's for.' Her mind was made up. She was in perfect control. 'Are there papers for me to sign, Mr Tilling?'

'In the drawing-room,' Mr Tilling said. 'If you would kindly follow me.'

The minute the door closed behind them, Louella brayed into action. 'We must stop her,' she said. 'She can't be allowed to get away with this.'

Winifred and Cedric agreed at once and loudly. But Edmund stood up and prepared to leave. 'Count me out of it, Louella,' he said.

'That's typical of you, Edmund Monk,' his wife sneered. 'You can't even stand up for your rights. You really are the most fuddy-duddy old man . . .'

But he'd already left the room.

Rose ran back to Ritzy Street dizzy with excitement and disbelief. Her hands were shaking so much she had a struggle to open the door.

'Whatever is it?' Netta said, flinging an arm round her shoulders as she stumbled into the hall.

'We're rich!' Rose said, her voice showing how stunned she was. 'She's left me all her money. Nearly thirty thousand pounds the solicitor said.'

Netta let out a whoop that could have been heard at the other end of the street and brought Bertie and Mabel running into the hall to find out what was going on. Soon all three of them were shouting and laughing and leaping about in triumph.

'Don't crow too soon,' Rose warned. 'The Monks are going to contest it. The solicitor says we'll have a fight on our hands. He warned me I might not get it. It's just . . .'

' 'Course you'll get it,' Netta said. 'If she's left it to you, why shouldn't you?'

The answer to that came four days later in a letter from Mr Tilling. Mr Cedric and Mrs Edmund had been in communication and had announced their intention of contesting the will, as he feared. They had already set the date of the hearing. It was to be in the Court of Chancery in the Strand on Monday, December 20th, 1926 at ten a.m. before Mr Justice Mercury.

'Perhaps you would be so kind as to call my office, so that we may take instructions,' he concluded.

'What's he mean "take instructions"?' Mabel wanted to know.

'I suppose we've got to work out what we're going to say,' Rose told her.

'Say the old gel left everything to you,' Netta advised. 'That's all there is to it. Show them the will and let them get on with it.'

'If only life were so simple,' Rose said. 'This is going to be very tricky if you ask me.'

That was Mr Tilling's opinion too. 'They intend to try to invalidate the will by endeavouring to prove that Miss Monk was not in her right mind when it was written.'

'Was she?' Rose asked.

'Oh indeed she was, as I can testify. However, I *do*

think you would be wise to hire a good KC. They are bound to take the best advice they can afford and we should be ready to parry any attack.'

His use of the plural was comforting. '. . . *we should be ready.*' But she had a nasty feeling this was going to turn out to be expensive. 'Won't he cost a lot of money?'

'I'm afraid he will,' Mr Tilling admitted. 'Silks command good fees. However, it has to be said that there are times when one has to spend money to earn money. I do believe this is one of them.'

'How much is it likely to be?'

'It depends on the length of time the case takes. You ought to be prepared to pay at least a hundred pounds.'

The figure was so shattering she could feel the colour draining from her face. 'A hundred pounds?'

'There *is* a great deal of money involved.'

'I keep my family on five pounds a week,' Rose told him, 'and we think we're living well.'

Mr Tilling smiled at her. 'The rich live at a very different rate, Mrs Jeary, as you will find when this inheritance is finally and incontrovertibly yours. The question now is whether you wish me to proceed.'

'What will happen if we don't fight them?'

'I'm sorry to say it is likely that the money will become theirs by default.'

'I see.'

'So do you wish me to . . . ?'

'I can't give you an answer yet,' Rose said. 'I shall have to talk it over with my family. And the firm. If I've got to lay out money like that they ought to know. It's their money as much as mine.'

As soon as she got back to Old Farm Street she sent Mr Thomas off to make a pot of tea, told all her workers to stop what they were doing and gathered them round to explain what was going on.

'It will take all our present capital,' she said at the finish, 'and we might lose. If we win it won't matter how much it cost. We'll be able to expand the firm, take on

451

more workers, buy new machinery, pay good bonuses. Sky's the limit. But if we lose we could end up with nothing. And I really mean nothing. We could be back where we began, working at home on the dining-room table. If the case drags on – and I can't say it won't – it might even eat into the reserves and if that happens I shall have to give up the lease on this place and sell off the machines. I thought you ought to know.'

'Neck or nothing,' Netta said. 'That's about the size of it.'

Gert was looking worried. 'You ought to count us out,' she said, glancing at her cousin. 'I mean to say, we ain't been here all that long. It ain't up to us.'

'You're part of the firm ain'tcher?' Netta said. 'Well then. You have your say same as everyone else. So tell us what you think.'

'It's a lot of money to lose,' Pug said. 'Would you still be able to pay us?'

'If it's a hundred pounds I could probably manage it,' Rose said. 'If it's more, I might have to lay you off till Netta and me can earn enough to take you on again. I wish I could tell you different but that's the honest answer.'

'Have a go!' Nancy Cartwright advised. 'That's my opinion. Nothink venture, nothink gain. If it goes wrong, it goes wrong.'

'We've built up from scratch once,' Netta pointed out. 'We could do it again if we had to.'

'You gonna ask our Mu what she thinks?' Mabel wanted to know. Muriel was still spending most of her time at home and was consequently the only one who wasn't at their impromptu meeting.

'No,' Rose told them all. 'It wouldn't be fair. I'll tell her what we've decided but it'ud be embarrassing for her to be in the middle of it all. She's got loyalties both ways poor Mu. It's *your* opinions I want now.'

'If you ask me,' Marigold said, 'I think you ought to fight for it. You can't just hand it over – not when it ought to be yours. That'ud be daft.'

Mr Thomas was gathering up their empty mugs. 'She's right, Mrs Jeary,' he said earnestly. 'It'ud be criminal to pass up a chance like that. I mean to say, anythink worth having you got to fight for. Rule a' life that is. Fighting. What I mean to say is, you wouldn't do us down. We all know that. Have a go. That's my advice.'

'There you are,' Nancy grinned. 'We're all behind you. Hire yourself a lawyer and get on with it, gel.'

Rose looked round the circle at their honest faces – Netta's Amazon-fierce and Mabel's trustingly vacant, an anxious looking Mr Thomas, Nancy and Marigold grinning in exactly the same way, Pug worried, Gert half smiling – and she thought how hard they all worked and what an effort they'd made to get where they were. She was touched with awe at their generosity. They were offering her their livelihood, trusting her with their future. What could show greater trust and generosity than that? Beyond them, worn machines and heaps of pale cloth waited on every table and the long columns of sunlight slanting in through their high windows were full of dancing dust. My firm, she thought, my firm and my friends. And was moved to tears.

'Thanks,' she said, huskily. 'Thanks ever so much. I *do* appreciate it. If we win, I'll turn this place into the most modern factory you've ever seen. I promise.'

'*If!*' Netta blazed, grinning hugely. 'That ain't the sort of word for *us*. You say when.'

The Monk family were hard at work mustering their forces. A formidable KC had been instructed, Cedric had prevailed upon his old friend Dr Vermont to give evidence about Augusta's state of mind at the time of her gallstone operation, Mrs Biggs had been run to ground and required to attend and Louella had taken it upon herself to visit Chelsea and put pressure on her reluctant husband.

'We've got a date for the hearing,' she told him. 'Five days before Christmas. Which hardly gives us any time at all to prepare. So you'll just have to jolly well stop mucking about and join us. It's all hands to the pump.'

Edmund gave her his wry smile. 'Is the ship sinking?' he said.

'Don't start that,' she said severely. 'You know perfectly well what I mean. I haven't come all this way in this weather to make jokes.' It had been an unpleasant day, grey and chill and spitting sleet and she was steaming with damp and bad temper. 'You must make up your mind,' she said. 'After all, you'll expect to join the share-out.'

'Shall I?'

'You know you will. So you're to be there and be prepared to give evidence.'

'I don't see what earthly use my evidence would be.'

'You're doing this to try my patience,' Louella said. 'And don't say "What patience?" because I'm not in the mood for it. I've come here for an answer and I shan't go away until I've got one.'

'Very well,' Edmund said. 'I'll agree to be present in the court.'

'And so I should think.'

'But there's a price.'

'What price? What are you talking about?'

'I want a divorce. That's what I'm talking about.'

Muriel had been sitting in her armchair, listening and saying nothing. Now she put out a hand as if she wanted to deflect him. But he ignored it.

'I will give you grounds,' he said. 'We're quite agreeable to that, aren't we Muriel?'

'I can't think about divorce with this hanging over my head,' Louella said, an edge of hysteria entering her voice.

'I can't appear in Chancery with the thought of no divorce hanging over *my* head.'

'Oh all right then. But I can't talk about it until after we've won this case.'

'You're determined to win, I see.'

'Well of course we shall win,' Louella said fiercely. 'It's

454

the only justice. I must be off. I've got a lot to do. So we can count on your support, can't we?'

'I shall be there. I told you.'

'Oh dear!' Muriel said when their unwanted visitor had stomped out through the front door and disappeared into the murk. 'I don't like this. You're not going to give evidence against Rose are you?'

'No,' he said seriously. 'Don't worry. I'm on *your* side. I don't want this money. Oh, I know I put up a fight for it back at the tea party but now it's been left to your Rose, I think she should have it. It's always seemed tainted to me – all those rows and Gussie's silly tricks – and I've never really expected to get any of it. Not when it came down to it. Not with Cedric and Louella in such hot pursuit. I earn a good salary, we've got this house, we're all right as we are. Don't you think so?'

She smiled at him lovingly. 'More than all right,' she said.

CHAPTER THIRTY-SEVEN

Netta Boniface decided to wear her bright red cloche hat to the hearing. 'Show 'em we're gonna win,' she said, pulling it firmly down over her ears. 'That's what I say. Let 'em see the sort a' mood we're in. Where's me red gloves?'

'Well they'll see you coming, and no mistake,' Nancy Cartwright laughed. 'You *are* a caution, gel.'

Netta had arranged for Bertie to spend the day with his great friend, Sonny Richardson, so that the rest of the family could travel to the court together. To nobody's surprise, Nancy and Marigold and Mr Thomas had joined the expedition too, saying that they couldn't let Rose go and face 'all that' on her own.

Rose was glad of their company, for the nearer she got to judgement, the more alarmed she became at the enormity of what she was doing. As the days passed, she tried hard to convince herself that she stood as good a chance of winning as anyone else but at night she lay awake trembling to think of the price they would all have to pay if she lost.

The weather didn't help much either. December was sleet-stung and colourless with cold and that morning, as they dodged through the traffic on their way across the Strand to the Law Courts, the first snow of the winter began to fall. Fat flakes swirled before their eyes to dapple their winter coats and settle in white clumps on Netta's red hat.

'Come on! Quick!' she yelled, dragging Mabel across the road. 'Let's get inside in the warm.'

But when they walked through the impresssive portals into the Law Courts even she was subdued. It was a daunting place and the gentlemen who were busily occupied about the Court of Chancery were even more discouraging than the building. They were so obviously men from another world, talking through their noses in an awful upper-crust way, '*Nyah, nyah, nyah*', and set apart by their fancy dress, which was, at one and the same time, antiquated and full of unquestionable power. Rose watched as they strode along the corridor – black gowns flapping like wings, heads crowned by white wigs, important papers under their arms, sealed and beribboned – and what little confidence she had began to leech away.

She was introduced to her own KC but his avuncular condescension did little to encourage her. It seemed to her that he spoke too softly and cared too little. Fortunately there wasn't time for conversation. He assured her that she had a very good case and then they all filed into the court. And that made her feel even worse. For there were all the Monks – except for Edmund – sitting side by side on the long benches, wearing their best clothes and hideously determined expressions. She noticed that Louella was sitting beside a woman in a bright red suit, that Winifred had a cold and that Cedric was looking disapproving. But where was Edmund? And had Muriel come with him, the way she'd said she would? There wasn't time to look for them, for they'd hardly settled onto the benches before the clerk to the court was on his feet and intoning, 'Be upstanding for Mr Justice Mercury . . .'

The judge was ill-named, being fat, ponderous and slow-moving. He brooded over the court like an awesome red tent, peering at the benches with an inscrutable expression on his face. And Rose's heart sank even further. This didn't look like the sort of man to agree that a servant should inherit a fortune.

Under his weighty leadership the case got under way. The Monks' KC made a long largely incomprehensible speech, Rose's KC a short one that was equally obscure. Then the expert witnesses were called.

One after the other they testified that a will made by a man – or a woman, yes indeed, m'lud, or a woman – whose health could be called into question was open to dispute – at the very least – and could be discounted altogether. Legal precedents were referred to at length. Various states of incapacity were described. Interminable questions were asked.

Mabel watched it all with her mouth open in amazement but Netta was restive. 'What they on about?' she hissed to Rose.

'They want the judge to think that Miss Monk was out of her mind,' Rose explained. 'I think they're trying to soften him up.'

Netta snorted so loudly that Mr Justice Mercury's eyebrows were raised in admonition.

But at last all the technical questions seemed to have been settled to everybody's satisfaction. And then, just as Rose and her friends were expecting the real business to get under way, the judge announced that the court would adjourn for lunch.

Netta was disappointed and said so, loudly, but Rose took the chance to look round the benches for Edmund and Muriel. And there they were, right at the back, keeping out of sight of their relations but nodding in her direction when the rest of their family had left the courtroom.

Muriel was swathed in a paisley shawl and looked surprisingly warm for such a cold day. And tactful as ever, she didn't say a word about the hearing.

'I'm starving,' she said, slipping her hand through Rose's elbow. 'Let's go to Lyons Corner House. It'll be like the old days, Rose. You don't mind going to the Corner House, do you Edmund?'

Edmund said it would be an adventure, so that was where they all went. By now the snow had set in and was falling heavily. The pavements and roofs were white with it, the street lights had been lit and traffic was reduced to a crawl, through mud-coloured slush as their drivers peered through fan-shaped peepholes in windscreens mounded with snow.

'What a day!' Mr Thomas shivered. 'I'm for a nice hot cup of tea.'

They crowded round three of the Corner House's filigree tables with their sandwiches and salads and five pots of tea, sitting arm to arm and knocking knee against knee. Rose was wedged between Netta's protectiveness and Muriel's concern. Edmund couldn't find anywhere to hang his hat and was reduced to nursing it. And Mr Thomas took up a position at the edge of the group so that he could order more tea if it were needed. Eating in such cramped conditions rapidly turned their gathering into a sort of party. Soon they were laughing and teasing and making fun of the judge and the KCs and criticising the lackadaisical speed of the proceedings.

Rose sipped her tea and tried to eat a sandwich. She was in too much of a state to want to discuss what was going on. The morning had been painful to her and, as far as she could see, entirely useless. Now she was in a limbo of anxiety and guilt. If I lose, she thought, I shall hurt them all and they're being so good to me. And yet, there was still a hope – wasn't there? – small, fluttering, easily quenched but still a hope. If only they'd hurry things up.

'That clerk to the court's a funny-looking feller,' Nancy Cartwright observed as she munched her salad. 'Brown whiskers and grey hair, very peculiar.'

'He's nice though,' her daughter said. 'He keeps looking at Rose and smiling.'

Rose hadn't noticed. 'Does he?'

'You watch when we get back. See if I'm not right.'

'He can smile all he likes just so long as he gets a move on,' Netta said, fiercely. 'There's been a darn sight too much palaver if you ask me. You got any more tea in your pot Marigold?'

'It'll be better this afternoon,' Muriel hoped.

Things certainly got moving that afternoon but whether or not they were better Rose couldn't be sure. The business of the will was discussed at last. New witnesses were called and, as Mr Tilling had warned her, it was plain that they were there to be questioned about Miss Monk's state of mind.

The first to arrive at the stand was Dr Vermont from Bury St Edmunds, suave in a grey suit, a dazzling white shirt and a magnificent bedside manner.

He agreed that Miss Monk had been a patient of his but said he couldn't be entirely sure about her state of mind. 'She *claimed* to have gallstones,' he said. 'However when I came to operate, I discovered that there were in fact no gallstones present, which leads me to believe . . .' he paused, looking round the court to achieve the maximum effect for what he was going to say next.

'Which leads you to believe,' the Monks' KC prompted.

'That the lady suffered from what we know in our profession as "nerves". Which is – ah – shall we say – a tendency to – ah – overdramatise symptoms.'

'Or to put it another way,' the KC prompted again, 'that the lady's judgement was not always to be trusted.'

Dr Vermont nodded his sad agreement. 'Quite.'

Even though she knew that this man's evidence would tell against her, Rose was impressed by how smoothly it was given. Even when her KC pressed him to a further definition of 'nerves' he was quite unrattled and simply repeated his earlier evidence in slightly different words. He ain't telling a lie, Rose thought, but he ain't telling the truth neither. He's putting on an act. And she recognised, with a surge of impotent anger, that the act was artful and manipulative and could easily win the case for Cedric Monk, who was sitting behind his counsel looking hideously smug.

The next person to take the stand was Mrs Biggs, stoutly wrapped in a tweed overcoat and clutching her familiar shopping bag. Well, that's better, Rose thought. At least she'll be honest.

She was, but she didn't help Rose's case much either.

'Yes,' she said. 'I knew her a long time. A lifetime you might say.' And when asked to elaborate on the sort of person her mistress had been, she said she was 'Difficult. Couldn't keep staff for love nor money. I'd hire 'em and two days later she'd up and fire 'em. Never ending that was. Touchy, you see. Bad-tempered. Fly off the handle at the least little thing.'

'Would you have any opinion as to her mental state?' the Monks' KC asked.

'Her mental state?'

'Yes.'

'Was she right in the head, d'you mean?'

'Yes.'

'Well sometimes she was,' Mrs Biggs said, speaking carefully. 'But then again, sometimes she wasn't. She had sort of turns.'

'What sort of turns?'

'Well she'd scoff down a great plate a' steak and chips, for instance, and then she'd say she didn't feel well and you'd have to send for the doctor. Or she'd be in bed groaning one minute and up and dressed and out shopping the next. I couldn't keep pace with her half the time, if you really want to know.'

But is that evidence that she wasn't in her right mind? Rose wondered. The judge was taking notes up on his high bench but his expression was still inscrutable. Cedric and Louella looked like cats that had stolen the cream. Now what? Were they going to call any other witnesses?

The next name to be called was that of Mr Cedric Monk.

He spoke with booming insincerity agreeing that, yes, it was a very difficult time for the family. They had all been so fond of their sister.

'A tragic loss,' his KC commiserated. 'We will endeavour to keep this as short as we can.'

'I would appreciate that,' Cedric said.

He's acting too, Rose thought, watching him as he smoothed his waistcoat over his paunch. Don't they ever téll the truth in a law court? It was all unreal, like watching a play.

Cedric had learnt his lines well. His sister had always been delicate, he said, even when they were children. 'I always felt – perhaps I shouldn't say this – I always felt there was more to her illnesses than met the eye. Or more than we were told when we were children. We had to treat her so carefully, you see, in case she had a tantrum. Mother was very careful to avoid a tantrum. She was afraid my sister would have a brainstorm.'

Glancing round the court, Rose could see that this was the most telling piece of evidence yet. A brother reluctantly revealing the family secrets and looking pained to have to do it. Winifred and Louella were wearing exactly the same false expression, Edmund had covered his mouth with his fingers, the judge was listening intently, leaning forward.

'I'm afraid she was always a little unbalanced,' Cedric confessed, hanging his head. 'We did our best to cover up for her, naturally, but it was always difficult and towards the end – well, I'm sorry to have to say this – towards the end she was definitely unhinged. The day before she made this will, she bought a monkey and let it run about the dining-room during a family tea. She seemed to think that was a normal thing to do.'

'And you did not?'

'We thought it was unhygienic.'

'But not normal?'

'No. Definitely not normal. It did its business all over the table.'

There was a titter round the court and the judge raised his eyebrows. I've lost, Rose thought, shrinking with despondency. He'll decide against me. How could anyone think she was sane when they hear things like that?

Her own KC was on his feet, holding the edges of his gown with both hands. All the money you're costing me! Rose thought, watching him. And the sense of waste made her stomach ache.

But when he called his first witness, the tenor of the case suddenly changed. For the first man into the witness box on her behalf was Dr Felgate – and Dr Felgate was his usual sensible self.

He agreed that Miss Monk could not be said to have enjoyed good health. She had been an invalid for many years, he told the court. And when asked to elaborate, he did. 'She spent several weeks in hospital with kidney disease, for example. She had an operation for the removal of gallstones. She was prone to fainting attacks and periodic bouts of severe pain. At the time of her death she was suffering from dyspnoea or shortness of breath.'

The important question was asked, 'In your opinion, Doctor, would any of these conditions affect her ability to make an informed decision?'

'She was always entirely in her right mind,' the doctor said firmly. 'I spoke to her on the telephone a matter of minutes before she died and even though she was in extreme pain, there was no sign whatever of any mental abnormality or weakening.'

'You had two telephone calls from Miss Monk on that particular evening, I believe.'

'I did. The first was about half an hour earlier. She was suffering from breathlessness. I gave her advice, which she took, and told her to telephone again if her condition worsened, which she did.'

'At what time would this be?'

'Between eight and nine o'clock in the evening.'

'The will in question had been signed at four o'clock that afternoon, as we shall hear. So this would be several hours after Miss Monk gave her signature?'

'I presume so. Yes.'

'Tell me, Doctor, did you have any foreknowledge that your patient would die of a heart attack?'

'Other than her breathlessness, none whatsoever. Her heart had always appeared strong. However, that is the nature of a heart attack. It comes upon the patient suddenly – often without any warning at all.'

The judge was making notes.

'And you had no indication that Miss Monk was suffering from any disease of the mind?'

'None whatsoever. She had a very bad temper, everybody knew that, but she was always in full possession of her faculties. Mental illness is a very different thing from simple bad temper.'

Mr Tilling was the next to take the stand and he was equally firm in his opinions, agreeing that Miss Monk had made several wills, but declaring that each and every one was fully intended and seriously meant at the time of writing.

'She was a lady of strong opinion and strong character,' he said. 'Every will was a serious document.'

'To be taken seriously?'

'Indubitably.'

'Would you say that Miss Monk was in full possession of all her faculties at the time of writing the will in question?'

'In full possession. She knew exactly what she was doing and why she was doing it, as you will see from the manner in which the bequest was expressed. She told me she wanted to leave her entire estate . . .' He read from his notebook, ' " . . . *to the one person who has remained faithful to me all these years, to whom I could turn when I was in trouble, who invariably gave me an honest answer – Rose Jeary of 26 Ritzy Street.*" Those were her own words. I took them down verbatim.'

'Were these instructions to you given calmly?'

'Completely calmly.'

'With no sign of bad temper or mental aberration or hysteria?'

'None whatsoever. She was in full command of herself and the situation and completely calm.'

There was a frisson in the court, a rustle of paper, subdued whispering. The judge was making notes again. Cedric was writing furiously, beckoning to the clerk to have his note passed to his KC; Winifred and her sons were muttering to one another and glaring at Rose across the courtroom; Louella was shaking with anger.

'Now what?' Netta whispered.

'I don't know,' Rose whispered back.

The clerk to the court handed the note to Cedric's KC. It was read. Nods were exchanged between the two men.

'Tell me,' the KC said to Mr Tilling. 'How many times did Miss Monk change her will?'

'Fourteen.'

'Fourteen times,' the K C said, leaning on the words so that nobody could fail to notice them. 'Fourteen times and always – what were your words? – "fully intended and seriously meant".'

'That is so.'

'Would you say that such frequent changes are – shall we say? – normal?'

'In so far as they were consistent with the situation, yes, they were perfectly normal.'

'Let me put it to you another way. Do you consider it normal for a woman to change her will fourteen times?'

Mr Tilling flexed himself like a small sharp bird about to fly away. But he didn't fly. He pecked.

'Miss Monk confided in me upon several occasions,' he said firmly. 'She told me that in her opinion the only thing her relations were interested in was her money. Whenever they became too grasping – as she used to put it – she paid them back by cutting them out of her will. It was an exercise in control.'

The KC allowed himself an expression of scathing disbelief. 'And you would call that normal?'

'In the circumstances. Yes. It was always done calmly and it was always perfectly reasonable. However . . .'

Oh don't spoil it now, Rose thought, as the court waited for what he was going to say next. Please don't spoil it. You were doing so well.

'However?'

'I have to say that the will we are concerned with today was made in a completely different frame of mind. This

465

time there was no talk of punishment. She hardly mentioned her relations. She was adamant that she wanted to leave her money and property to somebody outside the family. It was her view that of her relations none was worthy of the inheritance and that Mrs Jeary was. I have to say I had never seen her in such a determined mood. Nor in such perfect control of herself and her affairs.'

'Now what?' Netta asked as the solicitor went back to his seat.

Mr Justice Mercury was clearing his throat.

'He's going to adjourn for his tea,' Nancy whispered.

But she was wrong. He was announcing that he was going to give judgement. And after the verbosity of their long day, he was surprisingly succinct.

'The facts in this case are simple,' he said. 'Everything depends upon the answer to a single, pertinent question. Whatever her state of mind in the preceding months and years – and it has to be said there is conflicting evidence upon the matter – was Miss Monk in her right mind when she wrote her final will and testament? From the testimony of the doctor who attended her at that time and the solicitor who drew up the will, it is plain to me that she was. I find for the defendant.'

For a little while Rose was too stunned to take it in. She watched as the judge pitched his red tent and left, listened as the order was given for the court to clear. But she couldn't believe what she'd heard. The Monks rushed out together, glaring back at her but she sat where she was. It was as if she'd lost the power to move or think.

'Come on, our Rose!' Netta said. 'We've won!' And at that, and at last, they all jumped to their feet to laugh and cheer, as if she'd released them from a spell.

'Here, does this mean we can live in Monk House?' Mabel wanted to know.

'We can have Christmas in Monk House!' Rose said, as they walked out of the court. 'Think of that!'

'We'll throw a party,' Netta said. 'Invite all the neighbours and everyone at work and all.'

'Just think of the size of the turkey we can cook in that kitchen!' Rose said. 'We'll have a Christmas tree in the hall.'

'And sparklers,' Mabel said, clapping her hands. 'Shall we have sparklers, our Rose?'

'Sparklers and mince pies,' Rose promised, 'and a Christmas bonus for everyone and lots and lots of presents.'

Muriel was running after them to throw her arms round Rose's neck. 'I'm so glad!' she said. 'So glad. Oh dear, dear Rose!' Her brown eyes were full of happy tears.

Rose realised that Edmund was standing behind them and turned to say what she could to make amends. 'I'm sorry I had to take it. I mean it was your money too . . .'

He interrupted her. 'I don't want it,' he said. 'Never have. You ask Muriel. I'm glad you've got it.' And he bent his head to kiss her cheek.

They were all a little tearful.

'I never thought I'd actually win,' Rose said. 'Not really.'

'What are we going to do now, our Rose?' Mabel wanted to know.

'We're going to take a taxi home,' Rose told her.

'We'll never all get in a taxi,' Marigold said, laughing at the idea.

'Well, a fleet of taxis, then. We're swells now. We can afford it.'

Out in the Strand the noise of the traffic was muffled by snow and thick flakes were falling steadily. They hesitated at the entrance, turning up their collars, winding their mufflers more tightly round their necks, pulling their hats down over their ears. And Rose realised that somebody was calling her name.

'Mrs Jeary! Excuse me. Mrs Jeary!'

It was the court clerk, he of the brown whiskers and the grey hair. Oh God! she thought, watching as he ran down the corridor towards her. They've made a mistake. He's going to tell me I haven't won after all.

'I'm so sorry to disturb you,' he said as he reached them. 'But I couldn't let you go without . . . Being the same name and coming from Kennington, you see . . . I've been wondering about it all through the hearing. Of course it *could* be a coincidence but I had to ask. Oh dear, I'm not making myself at all clear, am I?'

They were all looking at him, Marigold, Nancy and Mr Thomas baffled, Netta suspicious, Mabel blank, Muriel and Edmund curious, Rose, calm-faced but with the oddest sensation growing in her chest. Nobody said anything.

'It was the name,' he explained. 'Jeary. I was out in France during the war, you see. I had a private of that name in my company. I wondered whether you were related.'

Rose found that her mouth was suddenly dry. She had to swallow and lick her lips before she could speak. 'Jeary?'

'Jack Jeary,' the clerk said. 'I suppose his name was John, really, but we all called him Jack. Jack Jeary.'

'The Kenningtons,' Rose said, looking at him steadily.

'That's right. Oh I'm so glad I met you, Mrs Jeary. He *was* your husband, wasn't he? He was a fine man. A good soldier. Very brave. You must be very proud of him. He deserved that medal. I wrote the dispatch. It was a dreadful pity it had to be posthumous. A dreadful pity.'

The little group was silent, caught in the shock of what they'd just heard. Muriel reached out for Rose's hand and held it tightly.

'So he's dead,' Rose said and her voice was little more than a whisper.

The clerk's face crumpled with concern. 'Didn't you know?' he asked.

'No.'

'Weren't you notified? I wrote to Mrs Jeary. I'm sure of it.'

'That would have been his mother. She didn't know about me.'

'Oh my dear Mrs Jeary, I'm so sorry. How clumsy of me. Come and sit down. Oh how could I have been so clumsy. I'm so very, very sorry. To give you such a shock.'

She allowed him to lead her to a bench and sat down without noticing where she was. Tears were pricking behind her eyes. 'I've always known it,' she said and tried to reassure him. 'It's not a shock really.' She was struggling to open her bag, her fingers trembling. 'I've got a picture here,' she said, finding the little snapshot. 'This is his son.'

'He's exactly like him,' the clerk said, as she held the little card between them. 'The spit and image.'

Bertie's trusting face gazed up at them both, his dark hair falling thickly over his forehead, his dark eyes smiling at his mother, the way he'd done when the picture was taken, the spit and image of his father. To Rose, with the warmth of her victory so abruptly reversed by the chill of this revelation, the sight of him was suddenly too much. Tears spilled out of her eyes and ran down her cheeks. Oh Jack, she mourned, my own dear, darling Jack.

'He died a hero,' the clerk said, gently. 'If that's any consolation to you.'

'Were you with him when he died?' she asked. 'Do you know how it happened? I should like to know.'

'He took out a machine gun single handed,' the clerk said. 'He saved a lot of lives. We were the second wave to go over the top and Jerry had a machine gun in the worst possible place for us. Your husband's platoon was directly in the line of fire. They were going to be mowed down and they all knew it. There were casualties everywhere from the first wave. Dead and wounded. We were waiting for the whistle which was the signal to go over. And Jack said, "Damn this for a lark. I'm going to deal with that bugger." Or words to that effect. And before we could stop him he was out of the trench and running. It's a wonder he wasn't shot to bits before he got there, but he wasn't. It all happened very quickly, you understand. We couldn't have stopped him. Not once he was running.'

'And what happened then?'

'We saw him run right up to the emplacement. We couldn't believe he'd got so far. Not under that fire. We saw him with a grenade, pulling out the pin with his teeth, and that was the last any of us saw before the explosion. It was a direct hit. He blew the whole thing to smithereens. Then the whistle went and we had to go over and I didn't find out what had happened to him until those of us who were left got back. There were so many casualties that day, it wasn't a surprise. He was dead when the stretcher bearers got to him but they reckoned he'd been dead when he hit the ground. He was a very brave man. I wrote out my dispatches that night.'

'And he won a medal.'

'The Military Medal.'

Rose was weeping freely now, as Muriel held her hands and Netta rubbed her shoulders. But they were tears of pride for the heroism of his death and tears of release, because she knew at last and for certain. 'Where was he buried?' she asked. 'Do you know?'

'Yes. I do. I could send you the details if you'd like me to.'

'Please. I should like to go there. To show Bertie.'

'I'm so sorry to have been the bearer of bad tidings.'

'It's not your fault,' she said. 'It's the war. I knew he was dead. I've known for a very long time. In a way you've put things right by telling me.'

'Will you be all right?' the clerk worried.

' 'Course she'll be all right,' Netta said. 'She's got all of us to look after her.'

'And I've got things to do,' Rose said, smiling at the circle of anxious faces around her. 'You think of all the things I've got to do. There's a taxi to hire, for a start.'

'That's right,' Nancy Cartwright encouraged.

'And there's a house to inherit. A firm to run. Clothes to make. All that money to put to work.'

'And a son to raise,' Muriel said, lovingly. 'Don't forget that.'

'As if I ever could,' Rose said, as she wiped away the last of her tears and put the snapshot back in her handbag. A son to raise.

TWO SILVER CROSSES
Beryl Kingston

A big, poignant and heartwarming story of war, flight, a divided family . . . and the power of love to change lives.

In 1926 the Holborn twins, Ginny and her blind sister Emily, disappear from their comfortable home in Wolverhampton. Why? No one knew. Ten years later, aspiring solicitor Charlie Commoner is dispatched to France to track them down. What he finds instead is a mystery, a tragedy and a love affair. But as the Second World War darkens over Europe, so, too, does the legacy from a terrifying disease that holds the family in its grip . . .

As warmhearted as Maeve Binchy, as compulsive as *The Shell Seekers*, *Two Silver Crosses* is unputdownable.

'Beryl Kingston understands how to weave dialogue, character, theme and a thumping love affair into unity.' SUNDAY TIMES

MAGGIE'S BOY
Beryl Kingston

When Alison married Rigby Toan the sun shone and everybody envied them their happiness. Rigg was the perfect husband – loving, ambitious and attractive; Alison couldn't believe her luck.

But then the recession takes hold and Rigg's facade is stripped away: his flashy car and sharp suits bought by expensive lies. As debts spiral out of control and their home is repossessed, Alison is forced to open her eyes to the world and to the sort of man her husband really is.

From his position as private investigator, Morgan watches as Alison trudges the weary path of poverty and despair. But even he underestimates the inspirational strength of her determination to eventually win through.

'An enthralling story of bad times turned good and the enduring belief that love conquers all' *Company*

OTHER SAGAS AVAILABLE IN ARROW